The Breach
Book One

ALEXANDER GOBLE

Also by Alexander Goble
In Plain Sight

ISBN: 0-9970859-0-8
ISBN-13: 978-0-9970859-0-7

Acknowledgements

To my mother, for taking the time to read all my crazy ideas
and help me form this one into an actual novel.
Thank you from the bottom of my heart

To anyone that decided to give this book a chance,
Thank you

Dedication

To my family, for not rolling their eyes when they hear I'm writing another book. Means the world to me that you are all willing to show your support, even if I've yet to earn it.

The Breach

Book One

Prologue

BBBRRRRRRRRRIIIIIIIIIINNNNGGGGG

Just like that, it was the end of an era.

Aaron's senior year at Crest Hill High School was officially over, the freedom every student had dreamed of since the first grade was only a few steps away out the side door. Though he'd prepared himself for the getaway seemingly every waking moment for the last few years, hearing the bell ringing and planning his quiet escape in his head over and over again, Aaron couldn't help but take a moment and let it all sink in. Students were high-fiving each other in the halls, wearing their well-traveled letterman's jackets in spring to show school pride for the very school they were so happy to finally leave. Couples peppered the hallway; some eager to begin the next chapter of their lives together, while others struggled to hold back the sense of dread for the ensuing split that was to come now that the comfortable confines of a strict school schedule meant they were on their own to make decisions and meet new people other than those unfortunate enough to be stuck in the same class as them.

He'd seen enough, the brief moment of nostalgia passing as quickly as it arrived. Though he was equally as excited as most of his now former classmates, Aaron had little interest in sticking around while everyone said their goodbyes and signed each other's yearbook with the promise to keep in touch that they knew deep down would never be kept. High school was everything people said it was, a social battlefield that he was more than happy to leave behind once and for all.

School was the ultimate test for Aaron, in more ways than one. He was never the most popular or the punching bag for those that enjoyed the occasional roughhousing at the little guy's expense. At just over six foot, Aaron was left alone, for the most part. The best way Aaron could think to describe high school was a necessary boredom. He knew he had to graduate; no one wanted to be the loser that dropped out to do better things with their lives, only to end up working the late shift at the gas station or cleaning puke off the bathroom floor for a living. That being said, school was unbelievably boring. Aaron was no savant, far from it when you saw his math scores, but in general nothing interested him. History was history, better off in the past. Science was for nerds, always would be. He was more than happy to wait till someone else invented the flying car and just buy one like everyone else. Gym was interesting in that it didn't require sitting at a desk for 90 minutes, but it still lacked any real world application. As fun as he thought it was to shoot hoops, there was no athletic scholarship in his future. Aaron spent most of his time at school just trying to stay awake till that bell rang to let them out for the day. He'd hear the jokes about students being nothing but house-trained cattle, moving from spot to spot when they heard the bell, and he couldn't have agreed more. School was pointless if you asked him, which no one ever did.

Then there was Ronnie Holtzman, the defacto drug dealer of Crest Hill. Ronnie made it his personal goal in life to antagonize Aaron as much as possible. They were evenly sized so it never came to blows, but Ronnie never missed out on the opportunity to call him out or insult him whenever there were the most possible people around.

"Hey, Butt-munch. You still into old dudes or what?" he called out in the middle of the cafeteria one day, to a low roar of giggles from around the room.

Aaron never dealt with Ronnie's "business"; he saw no point in buying drugs, especially from a deranged teenager who had it out for him for whatever reason. Ronnie and Aaron had completely different social circles, neither overlapping at any point. He never saw Ronnie at a party and he never even knew about the parties he would hear Ronnie loudly reenacting on Mondays. It was a thorn in his side as to why Ronnie sought him out of all people to pick on. Aaron was more than happy to leave Ronnie in his past forever.

Looking back on the last four years, there wasn't much Aaron saw worthy of holding onto or even remembering. He declined to purchase a yearbook for his senior year, there was nothing in there he wanted to look back on. It was the analogy of a veteran who had no interest in reliving those years at war. He was there, he lived it day after day, and he didn't need a book to remind him of all the times he fell asleep or daydreamed during class.

"Well I'll be damned, Aaron the Great is still in the building. After all that meticulous planning, he was unable to accomplish the simple task of pushing open a door. You DO know these doors are push right?"

Aaron smiled, that was the voice of just about the only thing he gave a damn about in this school, his best friend Jack.

Jack was the resident geek of Crest Hill. He knew more about comic books and algorithms than he did about style or cars, and since he was short, pudgy, and wore glasses he was quickly categorized as a nerd in the social scale of high school. Usually, that would be the death of anyone's social life, but damned if Jack wasn't infectious enough to, eventually, be liked be everyone in school. The girls saw Jack as safe, there was no sense of sexual tension with the guy that could recite Pie to the twenty fifth decimal, so they flocked to him for help on homework and just to talk. Like wise, guy saw all the attention he would get from the girls and invite him into their inner circle in hopes on learning more about the opposite sex. Jack loved every minute of it, soaking it all up. He'd played the part of school punching bag, this was way better.

"Heard Laura gave you a goodbye peck on the cheek, wouldn't have been able to sleep tonight if I didn't check up on you and make sure your heart didn't explode."

"What, you heard about that? It was just aOH HOLY SHIT IT WAS AMAZING! Pretty sure we're in love," Jack bragged.

"Pretty sure her boyfriend, the all-state defensive end, would beg to differ."

"Your just jealous, not like you hooked up with your crush before graduation."

Ashley Meyers.

She was the one that got away, in the sense that Aaron never had the nerve to actually say a complete sentence to her in the six years they had been in school together. He met her in the eighth grade, paired randomly in a science lab, and had been quietly obsessed with her ever sense. She was the literal definition of the girl next door, living only a block from where he lived. Ashley was the kind of girl you wanted to date, even marry, in a sea of girls that were mainly looking to lose their virginity or get back at their parents in one way or another. He got in a few words here and there over the years, but not enough to convey how he really felt. In the height of his prepubescent teenage emotions, he almost wrote a letter to give her at their graduation. The letter would explain how he felt about her and why they were perfect for each other; it would result in her falling in love with him even though she probably didn't even know his last name.

Goddamn Jack and his stupid comic book stories about Peter Parker and Mary Jane. Shit like that didn't actually happen in real life.

"Maybe it already happened, maybe I just didn't tell you about it so you'd feel bad. Maybe I wanted you to have your moment when it finally came."

"Yeah, and maybe Bruce Wayne thought about putting an ad in the paper for a new sidekick after the last one got off'd by the Joker."

"Uhhh... did he? You know I have no idea what you're talking about when you start rambling about comic people."

"Ugh, remind me again why I put up with you?"

"Put up with me? You do know you're the nerd right?"

"Hey, I have more friends on the football team than you do dude," Jack countered proudly.

"If by friends you mean guys that are dumb as shit and need you to explain to them how the alphabet got into their math homework, then yeah."

"Fuck you."

"I love you too buddy, but for the last time I will not be your boyfriend," Aaron joked, poking him in the belly like the Pillsbury Doughboy. "I'm just to superficial for that kind of commitment right now."

"Says the guy who didn't just make out with Laura Edelstein."

"It was a peck Casanova, keep it in your pants."

"Hey," Jack had paused for a moment, regaining his composure and looking Aaron right in the eye, "not for nothing, but he would have been proud of you today."

4

"Thanks."

Jack was referring to Aaron's father. Aaron barley knew him before he passed; a freak accident at the old steel mill took him away when Aaron was only four years old. He could still remember the look on the man's face when he answered the doorbell and saw him standing there with his hardhat in his hands, a look of sorrow on his face. His mother had collapsed on the doorstep when she heard the news, they had to help her into the house and onto the couch she was so inconsolable.

After that things changed for Aaron. His grandpa came to live with them and help out around the house. Aaron's mother was a shell of herself for a long time, walking around like a lost soul most of the day. It was his grandpa, at the age of sixty-three, who picked up the shattered pieces that was their family and put them back together. He'd get up in the morning to pack Aaron his lunch and be there every afternoon when the bus dropped him off. As time went on they grew close, Aaron knowing his grandpa more than he ever did his father.

On his sixteenth birthday, his grandpa took him out to the garage and handed him a pair of keys. Aaron was just excited at the idea of having a car; he lost his breath when his grandpa pulled back the cover on his father's old car. It was a vintage '67 Shelby. His father had been a real car enthusiast to hear his grandpa tell it, was happy to spend the day in the garage tinkering with them any chance he could. In honor of him, Aaron's grandpa said the car was his. The only stipulation was that he had to learn to take care of it and keep it up to snuff. Happy to have such a cool car, Aaron quickly agreed. Every weekend after that, he and his grandpa spent hours in the garage working on that car. It started as a mechanic's lesson, but always ended in him getting real world advice from his grandpa.

"So, can I drive it?" Jack asked, pulling Aaron back to reality.

"Did you jus ask me if you could drive the Shelby? Are you nuts, that's like, …like, …like asking Batman if he hates his parents."

"Batman, a.k.a. Bruce Wayne, lost his parents in a tragic shooting in Crime Alley after a midnight screening of the Mask of Zorro. He never really knew his parents, he became Batman in an effort to honor them and protect his city."

"No, you cannot drive," Aaron said, unable to formulate a response to the level of geekery he just witnessed.

"You just got uninvited to my wedding."

"IT WAS A PECK DUDE, you're not even dating."

"Gentlemen," Mr. Wheeler nodded as he passed. "Hope this little scuffle isn't the band breaking up. You two are so good together."

"He's just JEALOUS Mr. W. I kissed Laura today."

"Well, I guess it's just a matter of time till you tie the knot then. I'll wait for my invitation in the mail."

"THANK YOU, at least someone shows a little appreciation for the moment."

"Dude, he was mocking you. You know that right?"

"Either way, he's happy for us," Jack said, making an effort to storm off towards the Shelby.

Mr. Wheeler was a good guy, one of the few staff members that was liked by everyone. Aaron had a different view of Mr. Wheeler, but that was only because he and his mother had recently become an item. At first he was 100% against it, no one wanted their mom dating a member of the staff. It was downright embarrassing. Not to mention Aaron had no interest in a new father figure in his life, he and grandpa were just fine. If Mr. Wheeler and his mom got serious, he didn't want his grandpa to leave.

Aaron's fears were put to rest when he was called into Mr. Wheeler's office. They sat and talked for a while, Mr. Wheeler was actually pretty cool. He'd served in the military as a mechanic and had some cool war stories that he would tell from time to time about his experiences overseas. They got along better than Aaron anticipated, Mr. Wheeler going out of his way to treat him like every other student when they were in school. Aaron wasn't sure where their relationship was going, but he was ok if Mr. Wheeler eventually asked to marry his mom. They were happy together, and seeing his mom happy was a welcome sight that he didn't want to go away ever again.

When he got to the Shelby, Jack was leaning again the passenger side of the door, doing his best James Dean impression to look cool.

"Say, you wouldn't happen to know where my friend went would you? He was yea high and yea wide, likes math and picture books. I just hope he's ok, not really built for survival if you know what I mean."

"Mock me all you want, I'm a new man after today."

"If you cream on my seats your paying to have this upholstery steamed."

"I promise nothing," Jack said, sliding into his seat in a failed attempt to look as cool as he probably felt.

"So, you coming to Laura's party tonight?"

"Jesus, you don't let up do you?"

"What, she said I should come and I'm not going there alone. Need my wingman Goose."

"What happened to the wedding bells I just heard about, thought you already sealed the deal on your future."

"Oh, it's happening. Just can't rush love man. Gotta let her feel it to."

"Cause that doesn't sound rapey AT ALL," Aaron chided.

"Shut up."

They rode in silence most of the way home, Jack turning up the volume to sing along with the songs he liked. Aaron didn't want to admit it, would die before he did, but Jack had a voice. He was nailing the ballads, was a true romantic it seemed. As he pulled up to Jack's house, Jack sat in his seat for a moment.

"You leaving?"

"What makes you say that?"

"Don't fuck with me. I know you better than you know yourself Aaron. All you ever wanted was to find out what else was out there. You were only tethered to this town for as long as school could hold you."

Jack was right. Aaron had a burning urge to get out town. Maybe it was the thought that there was only so much in this little town, maybe it was from the talks he had with grandpa and Mr. Wheeler. Either way, he was itching to hit the open road and find his own path. It wasn't as if he had to stick around for a job, and college was never really an option. Just the idea of more school made him want to slam on the gas pedal even harder.

There was nothing for him here.

"I may see what the world has to offer, but I've got all the time in the world right?"

"Yeah," Jack nodded, getting out the car and waving as he drove off.

That was the last time Aaron would see Jack for another 10 years.

I
Present Day

The sun pierced through a thin crack in the floral, hand-me-down curtains tacked up over the window in an effort to give the room character as well as block out the sun at all hours of the day. Slowly, minute-by-minute, it crept up Aaron's face towards its ultimate goal of a full on assault on his eyes. He'd been lying there for quite some time, unable to sleep but unwilling to get up either. Instead, he was now in an intense game of chicken with the sun that he was destined to lose, again.

Sounds about right.

Aaron finally kicked the covers off and rolled out of bed, feeling the warmth of the sun on the bridge of his nose and knowing the inevitable was only moments away. He sat up on the side of the bed and scratched the back of his head while unleashing a yawn that would have made his grandpa proud. His grandpa was never a morning person, seems that gene made its way down to Aaron.

Thanks Grandpa.

Stretching his legs out, bracing for the unforgiving chill of hardwood floors against his bare feet, Aaron contemplated falling backwards and retrying the sleep thing again.

BAM BAM BAM.

Aaron sat up at the sound of someone pounding on the apartment door, instantly mad at whomever the asshole was standing out there banging on the door this early in the morning. Aaron looked at his phone, the phone he'd forgotten to plug in last night and was running on 13% battery.

8:03 AM.

BAM BAM BAM.

"Aaron, you in there? I know you're in there, your car's still parked out side. Open up man."

Glen.

Glen was the closest thing to a friend Aaron had these days; they both worked at the same shitty dive bar in the heart of Austin, Texas. The Rusty Knuckle was really a sight for sore eyes, looking more like a building about to be condemned by the city and bulldozed for a new bookstore or juice and yoga studio than an establishment for hard working college students to spend their flush, student loan packed pockets on cheap beer and overpriced liquor. They came in droves during the weekend, eager to engulf as many twenty-five cent beers as it took to become legendary for a weekend or for Aaron and Glen to convince them that the $8 shot of Jack Daniels was a steal. Aaron and Glen had a side bet, whoever got a college student to buy a round of shots for the bar got to keep the tip jar to themselves that night. By the end of most nights they were laughing so hard they usually forgot to keep the bet and ended up splitting the tips 50/50 as always.

Aaron never was one to connect with people, but Glen was just as much of a recluse in his own way that the two just clicked. Neither had the other's phone number and bothered to ask about anything personal. They were just two guys that liked shooting the shit after hours. Glen, of the two of them, had his life in order. He was more than just an employee at the bar, he was the owner.

At least he would be once his dad handed him the keys. Glen would tell Aaron that day could be any day now, but they both knew his dad was a stickler that would make sure Glen was ready before handing over his castle. He'd let Glen run the show, putting him in charge of opening and closing, and recently he'd even let Glen become part of the discussion with liquor vendors.

This was also Glen's apartment.

Aaron had somehow convinced Glen to let him crash here for a few days while he was out of town meeting with new liquor vendors. Glen had been hesitant at first, but Aaron promised to be a good house sitter. In all reality, Aaron was just happy to spend a night in a bed that wasn't in a ratty motel room covered in God only knew what or consisted of the back seat of the Shelby. He didn't like the term homeless, he preferred to think of it as freedom to choose where he laid his hat each night, but Aaron hadn't slept in the same place for seven days in a row in over a decade. It was either the back seat of the Shelby or the cheapest motel he could find that had a decent lock on the door and cable.

"*Com'on man, open the door,*" Glen demanded. "*Man you need to open this door right now, I have company,*" he whispered loudly.

Company. Glen had been out of town for two whole days and managed to meet someone.

Business trip my ass.

Glen was the co-owner of a bar, in Austin of all places; he could basically point at any girl in the bar and have a halfway decent shot of hooking up with her. It was just part of the gig Aaron assumed. Glen told him it was all about confidence, he said they picked up on it like a shark smelling blood in the water, but every time Aaron tried to meet a girl at the bar he'd end up getting puked on or calling a cab for her and the guy she met while he was serving other assholes their drinks.

"*Aaron, don't make me kick down my own door man. If I do this it's coming out of your tips for the rest of the month to pay for the new one. Just open the goddamn door.*"

Fighting the urge to ignore him, falling back in bed and putting a pillow over his head to block the now rhythmic pounding on the door still seemed possible, Aaron conceded it was probably not a great idea to squat in his bosses apartment. As much as he hated working at a bar sometimes, there were only so many nights one could handle shitty loud music and bar fights, he liked Glen and wasn't ready to leave town just yet. The money was decent and he wasn't exactly flush at the moment.

"Alright, alright. Jesus," he said loud enough to be heard through the door, "you castle awaits my lord."

Aaron did a quick glance around the apartment, realizing he'd put off cleaning it thinking he had more time, and cringed.

"Mi casa, su casa," Aaron said as he opened the door to the angry face of Glen staring back at him, not amused.

"Get the fuck out of my way. You almost lost your job you know that," Glen said pushing past him to set a case of bottles on the counter.

Following behind him was a woman, no older than twenty-two, in a skin-tight black dress that had clearly been on and off multiple times recently, judging by the fact that the dress was currently on backwards, with the tag and zipper sticking out at the neck. Aaron thought about mentioning it, but she looked at him with a knowing glance that said she was well aware how she looked and didn't give two shits.

"I'm the best bartender you have," Aaron rebuked, half joking since he was the ONLY bartender Glen had. "The Rusty Knuckle just wouldn't be the same without my handsome charm and you know it."

Glen was in the bedroom; he'd disappeared to change his shirt for reasons Aaron couldn't fathom. This girl clearly didn't care much about anything other than the free booze Glen could provide. She was already hovering around the case he'd set on the counter, taking a personal inventory on her own accord.

"Did you use my tea tree soap?" Glen said, coming out of the bedroom with the same angry face he'd gone in there with.

"Uhhh, noooo," Aaron lied, unaware exactly what tea tree soap was but almost positive he'd used it regardless. Soap was soap; he didn't know it was special soap.

"Get your shit and get out," Glen said, moving back to the counter and his new girlfriend.

"You said I could stay the weekend, it's Sunday. That's still the weekend."

"I lied."

"Well that's not such a great quality to have," Aaron said, looking at the girl the entire time he spoke with a knowing glance. "You should be more honest when you make commitments."

"You know what, you're right," Glen agreed. "Me and my new lady friend were just about to do unspeakable things to each other on this counter, but a promise is a promise so if you want to stick around that's ok with me. What about you Hannah?"

"It's Hillary," she corrected, moving her eyes to focus on Aaron, "and I'm game if he is."

Aaron began packing, fast.

All of his shit fit into the single duffle bag he had. He made the pact to his 18 year old self when he left town after high school that he would never be weighted down with material items or worldly possessions. He bought a duffle bag at an army surplus store right after school and never kept more than what he could fit in that bag.

"A word, please," Aaron requested from Glen as he walked towards the door, they were already starting to undress even as he walked past.

"WHAT?" Glen asked, reluctantly following him to the door.

"Where am I supposed to go? My shift doesn't start till 6 and I have no cash for a motel room. You want me to just sit in my car for the rest of the day?"

"I don't give a shit what you do," Glen said, putting his arm around him and pointing to Hillary as she continued to disrobe on the counter. "You see that girl? That girl is twenty years old, a sorority sister from the University of Texas, and she made a pact with the rest of her sister to remain a virgin till after graduation, you know that?"

"I did not, but that explains the case of liquor you came in with," Aaron offered, trying to leave as Glen's arm wrapped tighter around his shoulders. Aaron was no slouch; he was mildly impressed with Glen's newfound strength.

"That's the best part. That girl, a future leader of the next generation, says she and her friends found a loophole. The Poophole Loophole to be exact. See what she means i-."

"I get it," Aaron said, removing his arm from his shoulder and walking away as quickly as possible. "You two have fun now."

"OH, I will," Glen smiled.

"Ok then."

"Hey," Glen said, forcing Aaron to turn around one last time. "Tell you what, how about you open the bar for me tonight. You can work a few extra hours pro bono for the mess you left me."

Glen handed him the keys to the bar and shut the door in his face.

II

Aaron got in his car and peeled out of the parking lot, leaving the pure evil that was taking place inside apartment 3B as far away as possible. He looked down at the gas gauge on the dashboard and winced, he had just enough to get to the bar, he'd deal with finding gas money later. Austin was a pretty cool town, the police weren't the aggressive type all over the news, it was highly likely he could get away with parking the Shelby in the back of the bar for a few days without so much as a complaint.

I hand you these keys and you are accepting responsibility for her, understood Aaron?

His grandpa's voice rang in his head like a siren; he would have killed him for even thinking about leaving the Shelby parked behind a bar, unattended. This was his family legacy, it was to be protected and maintained as if it were a real human being. Since that day he'd learned how to properly tend to each and every need the Shelby could have. Aaron couldn't name more than 6 presidents, but he knew the phone numbers for all the certified mechanics and spare parts distributors by heart. Some kids got flash cards, he got pop quizzes at dinner from his grandpa, needing to know how many liters of oil the Shelby needed and how often the spark plugs needed to be checked.

Ten years later and she still purrs when I turn the key grandpa, I kept my promise.

Aaron had been thinking a lot about his grandpa recently. He'd never been the nostalgic type, but for some reason he kept hearing his voice in his head and thinking about how his grandpa would react if he could see what he'd become. A part time bartender at the ripe age of twenty-eight. No wife, no kids, no home, no career. Just the same stubborn attitude toward the future he had when he drove out of town ten years ago.

He remembered speeding home to tell his grandpa that he wanted to see the world right after dropping off Jack. The stories that he and Mr. Wheeler told had inspired Aaron to find out what was out there for him. His plan was to say good-bye to Jack at the party later that night and then hit the open road. The expression he got from his grandpa was a unique mixture of excitement and sadness. He was thrilled that Aaron was taking his life into his own hands, willing to pave his own road of adventure just like he'd done all those years ago. On the other hand, he was heartbroken. Aaron's grandpa had showed up at their door to help keep the lights on and Aaron feed while his mother recovered. Aaron's grandmother passed before he was born, his grandpa had been living in Boca Raton, FL with some old war buddies before he moved in with them. After awhile he couldn't image leaving and decided to stay. The idea that Aaron was leaving hit him hard, even though he did his best to hide it from showing on his face. Aaron had become as much his son as his father was; the same man raised them both.

Aaron pulled up to the bar running on fumes and parked in the back, but told himself he would grab gas after his shift and take her somewhere else for the night.

He sat back in the driver's seat and just stared at the steering wheel while he let his thought creep up on him even further. The bar wasn't supposed to open for another four or five hours so he had nothing but time to mull his thoughts a little more. It seemed like a positive move, if anything it would help remove what he saw earlier back at the apartment. Just the thought of it made him shiver in his seat, Aaron realized this was a prime example of why he chose to be a loner most of his life.

Less of these moments.

After he'd left town that night, too excited to get out there than he didn't want to see Jack and get talked out of it, Aaron had little to no contact with anyone back home.

Except his grandpa.

He'd call every week to fill him in on where he was and what he was doing. Those phone calls were as much for his grandpa as they were for him. Looking back on it now, ten years later, the only thing he would have done differently was to ask his grandpa to tag along. Odds are the answer would have been no anyway, his grandpa was no spring chicken and a life on the road was anything but comfortable. Still, the idea of the two of them cutting out across the country made Aaron smile just thinking about it.

As time went by, the calls become less and less frequent. Aaron became too busy trying to find ways to earn cash to keep on going and increasingly embarrassed that he had nothing to show for all his time on the road. Lying was not something he was naturally skilled at so they both knew when he was embellishing his travels to make it sound better than it really was. He still hadn't found himself, or what he loved. He was just in a rut of trying to survive and keep positive, something that grew harder and harder each day when life beat him down with its surprises. A flat tire here, stiffed on a paycheck there, and pretty soon life became one big roller-coaster consisting of nothing but the sudden drops. The few times he did call home, he could hear the worry in his grandpa's voice as he told him everything was fine, just part of life on the road and so on.

To his credit, his grandpa never bought a word of it. He would always say there was a warm bed at home if and when he ever wanted to come back. He knew how important it was for Aaron to be on his own, but he was also worried that his grandson was losing himself in the process.

"Come home, just for a little bit," he would say over and over again. "Let me see how that beautiful car is running these days. Would love to drive her over to Main Street and showoff. Your mother says hi by the way, she misses you."

At one point Aaron was ready to pack it in, to tuck tail and go home to his warm bed. He was going to make the call that night to tell them he was coming home when his phone rang, something it never did since Aaron never gave the number to anyone.

The name on the screen made him sick to his stomach.

"Hello?"

15

"Aaron? Aaron is that you? It's Mr. Wheele-."

"I know," Aaron cut him off, knowing what he was about to say and couldn't wait any longer for him to say it.

"Son, it's your grandfather. He hasn't been doing very well lately so your mother and I took him to the hospital to have them run some test to see what was wrong. He stayed overnight so they could run som-."

"He's gone," Aaron cut him off again, unable to hear anymore of the story.

"He passed in his sleep last night. Doctor's say he didn't suffer, it was peaceful. I'm sorry Aaron, I know you two were close."

Aaron didn't say anything for quite sometime, fighting back the tears he knew would eventually come pouring out, struggling to keep it together while on the phone.

"How's mom?" he finally got out.

"She took it pretty hard. She's doing ok but she feels incredibly alone right now. I do the best I can but she would really like to see you."

There was just no way Aaron thought. He wanted nothing more than to be on the road back home to help his mother grieve, but grandpa's sudden death struck something inside of him like lighting strikes a tree. He had dodged going home all those years and now it was too late. He would never get to say goodbye or take his grandpa for a ride in the Shelby ever again. To go home now would mean all of this, all of his trials and tribulations on the road, would have been for nothing. Just a waste of time that kept him from being with his grandpa in the end.

"I just can't right now, I have some things going on that I can't get out of," he'd lied to Mr. Wheeler, knowing he probably didn't buy a word of it. "I will call mom later and talk to her."

"She'd like that, thank you," Mr. Wheeler said, never passing judgment in his voice.

Aaron hung up the phone that night, barley clicking the END button on his screen before collapsing on the motel floor in tears. His emotions tore at him, he went through the stages of grief right their on the dirty maroon carpet. Aaron told himself it wasn't true, through gasps as the tears continued to roll down his chin, there was no way his grandpa would go so easily. The man was fighter, an Army man all his life, that wouldn't go out like this.

Denial turned to anger when he stood up and punched the TV screen with everything he had in a white-hot rage. The screen cracked on impact, spider webbing to the edges until the entire panel was destroyed. Aaron fell to his knees and begged for it not to be true. He wasn't the religious type, but at the moment he was willing to make an exception. He rocked back and forth on his knees, offering himself or the Shelby for just one more chance to talk to his grandpa.

He fell asleep that night, after empty the mini fridge of all of it contents, in a quite stupor. He was numb, unable to feel anything. He didn't want to move from that spot, there was no point anymore now that the man that he had grown up idolizing and whom had inspired his journey in the first place, was no longer there to share it with.

When he awoke the next morning he expected to feel a wave of acceptance wash over him, but it never came. Even now, sitting in the Shelby, Aaron realized he still hadn't reached that final stage. He wasn't bitter anymore, he knew what happened wasn't anyone's fault and time really did help heal all wounds, but he would never be able to accept that he missed the chance to talk to him one last time because his ego kept him from calling and being exposed.

Enough of this shit.

Aaron got out of the Shelby and walked to the backdoor of the Rusty Knuckle. He remembered he had the keys, a parting gift from Glen to get him to leave this morning, and he could open the bar whenever he damn well please. He'd been sitting in his car stirring up old memories that wouldn't do him any good now. He needed a distraction, something to keep his mind on the upcoming night's activities so he could afford to buy gas for the Shelby.

Walking around the to the front, cause he had the keys and wanted to feel like an adult opening his business instead of a deadbeat weaseling his way in through the back, Aaron couldn't get the thought of his grandpa out of his head. He turned the key and opened the door to a dark and quite bar room. What should have been peaceful and tranquil was actually depressing and offsetting. Aaron realized he'd never set foot in the Rusty Knuckle when there wasn't loud music playing or student's yelling, either to let loose after a test or just to be heard over the loud music. The Rusty Knuckle Aaron knew was loud, full of life and excitement till the early hours of the morning, yet the place he just unlocked the front door to wasn't any of those things. It was cold, dark and uninviting. It practically dared him to enter instead of flee back to the safety of the sunny sidewalk he'd just left.

It was the personification of death.

Grandpa.

He fought the growing urge to leave and come back just as Glen was arriving to open up with him, but for reasons he couldn't explain he kept walking inside until he was fully immersed in the darkness. Aaron quickly found the light switch and flipped it on.

The place came to life. The lights behind the bar beamed a welcoming come hither essence that made him instantly feel better. This was the Rusty Knuckle he knew, Aaron almost felt silly for thinking about running a moment ago. He was a grown man, how was he still offset by the dark like he was still five?

Aaron felt his phone vibrate, an odd sensation that he wasn't used to seeing as how he didn't have many people trying to reach him. He looked down and saw that he missed a call from Glen. He must have dozed of or been daydreaming deeper than he realized to miss his phone ringing. He checked the voicemail and paused, the history on his phone showing the last voicemail he had was from 720-885-6287.

His mom.

The last time she had called was a few days after Mr. Wheeler had called. She still wanted to talk but Aaron wasn't ready. His mother had left a voicemail, the sound of her voice told him she had been crying, asking him to call her as soon as he could. She wanted to hear his voice, even if it was for just a minute.

Aaron finally worked up the courage to call her a few days later, she breaking down only moments before he did. They cried in silence for what seemed like forever, neither one know exactly what to say to the other after so long and due to the circumstances. She finally broke the silence and told him that his grandpa didn't want a funeral, he was cremated and that was that. They'd had a small wake at the house the other day and everyone was asking about him. Aaron dodged the open-ended question and asked how she was doing now. She cried a little more and lied that she was ok.

They spent the next hour or better talking, him telling her about his life on the open road while she told him what was going on in town. It was still the same boring town Aaron remembered, the biggest news his mother had to offer was that they were getting a Wendy's later that year.

The conversation turned back to grandpa, with both of them sharing stories and remembering him in the moment. Even though he'd been avoiding the call for weeks, Aaron didn't want to hang up. Eventually they both had to go, she was getting ready for a movie night, Mr. Wheeler was taking her out to get her mind off of things, and he made up having a job he had to get to. She told him she loved him and missed him, offering the same warm bed his grandpa had, before blowing a kiss and hanging up.

Aaron's phone rang again, pulling him out of memory lane.

"What?" he answered, the caller ID on his phone spoiling the surprise of who was calling him.

"Jesus, is that how you answer your phone? No wonder you have so few friends."

"Yet I can't seem to get rid of you."

" You still bitter about this morning? You got to get over that man; she was HOT and ready to go. You were just killing the vibe as a third-wheel."

"You call me just to reminisce Romeo."

"A gentlemen never tells about the THREE times he made her climax."

"Classy, I'm hanging up now."

"Suit yourself los-," Glen started before being cut off by his phone ringing again.

"Other line is ringing, should probably take this. Do everyone a favor and get yourself checked. You're too young to die and I need the job," Aaron said before killing the line.

His phone continued to ring and vibrate, while the screen read UNKNOWN. Not even knowing why, usually he would just send it to voicemail; Aaron clicked the green phone icon to take the call.

"What?"

"Well I'll be damned, you haven't changed at all," said a familiar voice.

Jack.

Aaron sat on the other end of the phone call listening to him ramble on and on, as if they hadn't spoken in ten years or something. Jack picked up the conversation like they they'd just spoken yesterday. Not sure whether to be surprised that Jack had the ability to skip ten years of their lives like it was nothing or concerned for why he was calling now, after all this time.

"Hey," Aaron cut Jack off during another tangent about a new Batman movie he was rather passionately trashing, "What's up?"

"What? A friend can't call another friend to catch up?" Jack stalled, clearly hiding something. Jack was never great at lying; he'd once told Aaron's grandpa they'd only been drinking soda while a beer can sat empty on the table right next to him. Aaron had to admit he wasn't much better at lying, probably why they got along so well. Neither was good at keeping secrets so they never had any between them.

"Over seven thousand days you could have called, has to be a reason you picked today," Aaron said.

"And they say you can't teach an old dog new tricks, when the hell did you learn math?"

"Comes in handy when you pinching every penny to get by," Aaron sarcastically blurted out without thinking. He'd never let anyone on to his struggles, though he was sure grandpa and his mother already knew enough to connect the pieces to that puzzle. For whatever reason, instead of the default, sheltered answer he usually gave people, clouded in generalities and stretching of the truth, Aaron let Jack in.

Maybe he's right; something's haven't changed since high school.

"No shit? So Aaron the Great, had a plan for everything since the fucking 3rd grade, THE master strategist, has been leading the life of a drifter. That's very Reacher of you buddy."

"Very what?"

"Reacher? As in Jack Reacher, the world's most badass drifter. Dude goes from place to place with the shirt on his back using the skill's he got in the military to bring justice to those that fucking NEED it. He's like Batman without the cape, and killing. Lot's of killing."

Aaron laughed. He had no idea what Jack was talking about but took an odd pleasure in knowing that Jack never grew out of his nerd phase. These days nerds and geeks were the popular ones, accomplishing the task their ancestors dreamed of. Now the super rich and famous, not to mention powerful, were the biggest nerds and geeks around.

"Sorry, never killed anyone. Gonna to have to find a new character to portray me as. More on the side of a beat down James Bond, without the skill or swagger, than anything at the moment."

"That's what you get for bolting and not saying goodbye, Karma is real as herpes, which I can only assume you've caught multiple times by now."

There is was. Aaron was wondering how long it would take before Jack brought up his sudden departure. All those years ago he'd fully planned on going to that stupid party to be his wingman, but after talking with his grandpa and seeing the twinkle of sadness in his eye he couldn't bear to see his best friend look at him the same way. Like a bandage, he figured the best way to handle it was just leave. Nothing drawn out or painstakingly awkward, just him hitting the road and catching up later.

Later never came though. At eighteen, the plan made perfect sense. Hit the road, find yourself and become the man you were supposed to become, and then reconnect a few years later. Sure he'd planned on there being a little animosity between him and Jack, but once he came back and had a beautiful wife and awesome career he'd be able to smooth things over pretty quickly with his best friend. They were never mad at each other for very long; Aaron didn't see how this could be any different once Jack saw his selfish decision was for the best.

Now Aaron sat in an empty bar he worked part time in, at twenty-eight.

Alone.

"I didn't mean anything by it Jack, just got excited about the open road and burned pavement first chance I got," Aaron stretched the truth, something he'd become unnervingly good at over the years.

"It's cool. Wasn't like I needed you to be the wingman anyway. Me and Laura were meant to be anyway, you were just supposed to be there to bask in the moment with me."

"So you two ended up together? I gotta be honest Jack, I didn't think Laura would ever settle down like that, good for you pal."

"Three kids and a puppy."

"Holy shit," Aaron blurted out, honestly shocked that Jack had procreated three times.

"Oh, not with me. We never spoke again after that day. She went on to marry some asshole, Benny I think was his name, and got knocked up right after high school. She works at the grocery store now, assistant manager of the night shift. Smokes a pack a day, sounds like a slowly dying Terminator when you talk to her."

"Sound like you dodged a bullet."

"Oh, I Matrix'd the shit out of that."

"Right," Aaron agreed, having no clue what he was talking about.

"YOU DON'T KNOW ABOUT THE MATRIX?" Jack yelled into the phone.

"Oh the MATRIX, yeah I know about the Matrix, duh. I thought you said MADDOX'D."

"You're lying. I can't even see your face and I know your lying. Jesus Aaron, it was only the most popular movie of a generation. A part of me hates you right now."

"Sorry man, movies are a luxury I don't really have. Last movie I saw from start to finish was at a drive through I snuck into about ten years ago. Was something about teenage witches or something? Hard as shit to follow, think there were more movies before it that explained what was going on."

"Yup, I definitely hate you."

"So," Aaron started to steer the conversation back on track. Just like old times the two of them could go back and forth for hours without even remembering why or where the conversation started in the first place. "You called because…"

"Cause you're not on Facebook and a fella just wanted to reconnect," Jack stalled.

"Now you're lying, don't forget I can tell when your lying just as well as you can tell when I'm lying. What's up Jack?"

Jack offered silence in return, which made Aaron all the more anxious. Last time he got a phone call out of the blue like this his grandpa died. He instantly started worrying something had happened to his mom.

"Jack, stop fucking with me. Is everything ok, is my mother ok?"

"Oh she's fine, she walks around town practically glowing most days. She's in a great place Aaron."

Aaron sighed a deep breath of relief; at least his mom was ok.

So why did you call Jack?

"I mention I am the head librarian now? Yup, I run this library like a tyrant with a heart of gold. Practically created a new Dewey Decimal system I'm so good."

"Jack," Aaron called him out for stalling.

While part of him grew increasingly frustrated with his antics, Aaron was happy Jack got a job at the library. Ever since the 3rd grade, Jack had wanted to be a superhero. Save the world kind of thing. As time went by and Jack understood he wasn't going to be able to fly or stop bullets without drastic advancements in science, he gave up on the superhero dream. Still, he never gave up on saving the world, or at least making it a better place than it currently was. To land a job as head librarian wasn't going to get him on the five o'clock news or anything, but it gave him the ability to spread knowledge to others. Not to mention it allowed him unlimited access to just about any book there ever was. Small town meant small library. If Aaron could guess, he'd guess Jack had read close to every book in that library by now.

"Dammit Jack, what is it? Spit it out."

"Sooooo," Jack drug his feet as long as he could, "Don't shoot the messenger, but I wanted to let you know that our ten year high school reunion is coming up next month…"

Seriously, a fucking reunion?

"I'm busy," Aaron bluntly answered.

"Oh I know right. That's what I told her. I was like, 'Aaron's pretty busy, not sure he's gonna have the spare time to come back for this thing,' and then she was like, 'well you tell Aaron that if Harry Mallavoy can fly in from Haiti for one night then Aaron can get his ass here.'"

"Who said that?" Aaron asked.

"I guess this Harry Mallavoy, whom for the record I don't even remember from high school cause he sounds smart and I knew the smart kids, is some kind of phenom doctor that choose to go the route of Doctor's Without Borders instead of becoming a world renowned surgeon for a big hospital and making all the money."

"Jack, who told you to ask me to come to the reunion?" Aaron asked again.

"You don't have to come, I get it. I'll just tell them you a contractor for NASA and you kinda need to be at your job if we ever want to get to Mars. I got this. That and fuck Harry, show boater."

"JACK," Aaron yelled now. "Who told you to call me?"

Aaron really didn't even need to wait for him to answer; he already knew what Jack was going to say before he said it.

"Ashley," he finally answered, "she asked me man, she's head of the committee in charge of the reunion."

Dammit.

IV

Ashley Meyers.

Aaron had been saying her name in his head for the last hour or better as he slowly prepared the Rusty Knuckle for the night ahead. He took his time, carrying each case one-by-one up from the basement to keep him occupied with busy work in a feeble attempt to keep his racing mind at bay.

Ashley Meyers.

He tried to remember the last time he'd thought about her since leaving town and surprisingly he couldn't think of a single time she'd crossed his mind. She was just a simple high school crush.

Ok, maybe she did ONCE.

That night at the drive-in movie he told Jack about, he'd snuck in to meet a girl that he'd been flirting with on and off at the Renaissance Fair he was working at the time.

She was a fair maiden, in charge of helping people to their seats to watch the jousting competition. Aaron was head weapons manager, which was a trumped up way of saying he handed the "between jobs," actor a sword before each show. They were not allowed to carry real weapons around the fair, so they had to be kept under lock and key specifically for the jousting and sword fighting shows people paid extra for.

Every time she would seat a new family, she would look over at him seductively. Aaron was only twenty-one at the time; he was as experienced with women as he was with the weapons he was tasked with managing. Looking back at it now, he realized she was just toying with him to pass the time. Day in and day out it was the same thing, a mass of over-excited, over-fed people showed up demanding to be entertained with the thought of horrific violence that showed just how far modern society has come. Sure we still beat the hell out of each other for sport, but we now have the decency to do it in hand to hand combat, with a referee.

There may have been a mutual attraction between them, two young, decent looking individuals sweating their asses off in a field four days a week, but it was painfully obvious to Aaron now that she had absolutely no interest in being with a fellow fair worker. This was the type of girl that wanted you to steal a car for her just cause she wanted to see if you'd really do it. She wasn't going to actually fall in love with someone that held a job or gave a shit about her; she was always going to go for the ones that would give life or limb to please her. She just picked him, likely cause he was the young, dumb, new guy that didn't know any better than to ignore her.

One afternoon, after the jousting competition concluded with the same actor taking a dive off the horse as always, she broke routine and walked down the stairs and over toward him. The tension in his legs started to give and he casually leaned against the weapons locker like he was too cool to care about his job just to keep from getting dizzy and passing out right in front of her.

"Andrew, me and a few of these other bitches are going to the drive-in tonight, you should totally come."

"...It's Aaro-" He cut himself off, realizing how stupid he sounded and that she didn't give a hot fart what his name was. His name was on his fucking nametag, clear as day, she was purposely ignoring it. "Ehh, not really into movies. Might check it out later though, if I have some free time."

She didn't hear a word he said, she was too busy seductively applying lip-gloss to her lips like a skilled artist carefully applying paint to their canvas. She just looked up at him, with a look that said he was an utter idiot if he didn't go, and walked away while a thin smile formed on her face.

He was going and she knew it.

That night he was getting ready to head to the drive-in when he realized he had no money to get in. Payday wasn't until the end of the week and it was only Thursday. Aaron had to pay for the motel for the night and that left him with exactly $3 too his name for a delicious dinner from the vending machine at the motel. He wasn't going to show up at the drive-in and embarrass himself by being turned away. Whatever shot he had with this girl would go up in flames if he did that.

He was also twenty-one and he didn't make every decision with his head, leaving other parts of his body to lead the way.

He was going to that fucking movie.

Aaron hatched a plan that he would sneak over the fence in the farthest point of the drive-in; he'd then casually walk toward the convenience stand and act like he was just bumping into her and the night would be off and running. At no point in his planning did he account for the fact that he would have no car to take her back to and that she would be with all the other girls from the fair that would call his bluff immediately, he wasn't the strongest liar after all.

Throwing logic to the wind, no one ever got the girl listening to logic, Aaron followed through on his plan. He hopped the fence and made his way toward the convenience stand. He got halfway there when he realized he'd ripped his pants wide open, his boxers were just hanging out for anyone to see. As fast as he'd gone over the fence to meet the object of his every desire, he went back over again and jogged to his car. He drove the rest of the way back to the motel in shame, he'd blown the best chance yet of having a torrid affair on his road trip.

The only thought that popped into his head on his way back was, oddly enough, of Ashley. He thought about the girl he knew back in high school, the girl next door that would have never put him in his current situation. To be fair, Aaron had managed less than a full sentence between them to know anything about her, but he had an ideal of her in his mind that she would be the kind of girl that would see him, with his boxers lightly blowing in the calm summer breeze, and make the best of it. He quickly got mad at himself for being such a pussy in high school, maybe if he would have said more than a few syllables to her over half a decade he could have been her friend or even dated her. Then he wouldn't have been stuck trying to figure out how to please the exotic creature that was the fair maiden of the Renaissance Fair, the one that haunted his dreams in the best and worst way possible. Aaron was positive the girl at the fair would have crushed him and never let him live it down.

Now, Aaron stood behind the fully stocked bar and wanted to punch himself in the face.

For ten years he'd been resistant to going back home, he'd missed saying goodbye to his grandpa for fuck sake, and now it was all he could think about. Just her name, her goddamn name, had taken him from the hardened asshole that could never go back until he had something to show for it, to the asshole that melted to putty and wanted to get in his car and drive all night to see her again. Life on the road had convinced Aaron of one absolute truth, being alone truly was lonely.

Ashley fucking Meyers.

He continued getting ready for the nights events, though a this point that consisted of making sure all the bottle labels were facing the same direction. Even in his attempt to slow down and drag out the preparation, he'd somehow increased the pace and finished faster than expected. He looked around for something, anything, to do to keep his mind busy and off the ridiculous idea of going back for a girl he didn't even know.

Hell, she probably only knows your name because it's on a sheet of paper, she didn't personally invite you stupid.

As he got ready to mop the floor, again, Glen mercifully walked in the front door.

"Look at this, the Rusty Knuckle isn't on fire," he observed dramatically, "and here I had visions on my way over here of what I could do with the insurance money."

Aaron didn't respond, just went about getting the mop bucket ready. Filling it with warm, soapy water and stringing out the mop so it wasn't too wet when he went to clean the floor in round two.

"Oh I get it, you're doing the silent treatment thing chicks do. You know, I learned a few other things chicks do from Hilary earlier, you wouldn't happen to do any of those things too would you?"

"Fuck you," Aaron responded, nowhere near interested in playing this game with Glen right now.

"Ooh, still sore from this morning, but rein check?"

"Why are you here?" Aaron stopped messing with the mop and looked up at Glen. "Shouldn't you be out somewhere, doing something? Anything?"

"I missed you," Glen joked, sliding behind the counter and hugging Aaron from behind in a bear hug.

"Get off me you lunatic, you know how many different kinds of STD's you probably have right now. Hillary looked liked she blows dudes for grades, drugs, groceri-," Aaron started.

"Don't forget booze, she goes HARD for booze."

"Nice. Nothing more depressing in life that waking up every morning realizing you're my boss and you make more than I do."

"As long as you wake up at someplace other than my apartment, I can live with that."

"Is it wrong I secretly hope your nuts fall off one day, as a symbol that there is still good in this world? The only way you could be more depressing is if you vape"

"Is it wrong I have been paying you below minimum wage for over a year?"

"Is it wron-, wait, what?"

"Nothing."

Aside from the now burning rage in his stomach for being paid no better than an twelve year old making shoes in China, Aaron was glad Glen showed up when he did. He was the perfect distraction from his thoughts, it took a full-frontal assault to put up with and interact with Glen some days.

"So, you gonna tell me why you're acting like the kid at school that just found out his girlfriend's been banging the entire football team while he was at chess club?"

"No," Aaron responded.

∎

It was 2AM and Aaron was lying on one of the tables on the patio of the Rusty Knuckle, looking up at the stars in the sky. No matter how many problems he had, no matter how bad some of his days were, Aaron always found comfort in the stars. It sounded sappy, so he kept it to himself, but lying there looking up at the infinite amount of stars made him feel microscopic in comparison. Surely, by this logic, there was someone else having a rougher go at life than he was. It was probably wrong to find comfort in a hypothetical person's misery, but damned if he didn't spend a few nights creating a backstory on some poor bastard that was making out worse than him at that moment.

The night had gone like every Friday night. The college students made there way down from campus like a herd of brain dead zombies in need of flesh. They started slowly, with just the most aggressive alcoholics showing up early to get as much quality time in the bar as possible before the weekend was over, but quickly filled every bar and most of 6th Street with their masses. The first time Aaron saw that many people converge in one place he thought there it was a special occasion, some sort of Mardi Gras in Austin. When it happened again the next night he realized that was just how this town operated. Student's studied hard, and as a result they partied just as hard if not harder.

Glen was the man of the hour, swooping in and snatching nearly every girl's number that walked in the front door and even got in a few sloppy make out sessions in the back hallway with those he couldn't wait to meet up with later. He was only one man after all, or at least that is what he'd tell Aaron most nights. As much as he wanted to hate the guy, Aaron had to admire the lifestyle Glen led. He was able to live in the moment and forget the what if's and could be's of the world to enjoy the happiness right in front of him. Glen wasn't the type that gave a shit about taxes or parking tickets, just the next sexual conquest and party he could throw.

They always turned the music up loud to start the night, a rhythmic invitation for the ladies to come by and dance to the music always led to a mass of eager guys swarming over like mosquitos to a bright light. Pretty soon every bar on 6th street was playing music, not to mention the live acts that littered the streets and rival bar's patios. At around midnight, the scene got its second wind, with street vendor's showing up in force to feed as many of the drunken college students as possible. They, with new life, then returned to finish of the night by dancing on bars, making wildly inappropriate and inaccurate statements to anyone who would listen, and passing out or puking on the street before a friend helped them into a cab or bus back to campus. The smart ones had an Uber already lined up, they just causally walked/stumbled out of the bar and into a waiting car like they were a celebrity.

Now it was time for 6th Street to recover. Aaron wiped the bar down and mopped the floor, one more time, while Glen checked the register and settled the bar for the night. When he was done, all bar stools and chairs flipped up on to their respective tables as the floor dried, Aaron went outside to lie on the bench and look up at the stars.

"Here's you cut," Glen interrupted his tranquility, throwing a thin stack of bills on Aaron's chest. "Took out your pro bono hours earlier so now were square."

"What a guy," Aaron sarcastically mocked.

"You gonna tell me who she is?" Glen asked, sitting at the bench seat connected to the table Aaron was lying on.

"What?" Aaron deflected.

"Don't bullshit me. Earlier tonight a girl pulled her tits out and hollered from the top of her lungs she was a goddess. You didn't even look up from the bar, you just kept scooping ice like your life depended on it?"

"So I was doing my job, like a good employee you just illegally underpaid, and your giving me shit?"

"Don't change the subject. I may be an asshole, a well liked and sexually advanced asshole, but I can tell when something's not right. You've worked here long enough I got you figured out. You play along and act like your having fun, but in reality you are just going through the motions. You're miserable. Most times a girl takes her shirt off in the bar or a cat fight breaks out, you react like anyone else would in an attempt to blend in with the crowd, you could really care less."

"You've seen one pare of tits, you've seen them all," Aaron offered, still looking up at the stars.

"Yeah, but it's more than that. You drive around in that museum of a car you somehow manage to keep in excellent shape, and play a part. You're not really here. Never are. I LIVE for this; it's everything I wanted in life. I get to work at my dad's bar, have all the authority in the world and none of the responsibility. Every girl that walks in here wants to be with me and every guy that walks out of here wishes he were me. This is the best life I could possible imagine."

"To be a king," Aaron said, still staring up into space.

"That's the thing. This is MY dream. You play the part, you rile up the crowd and do a shot when asked or to get the party rolling, but you don't want to do this forever. Normally you play it off so well I sometimes wonder if maybe you aren't more like me than you're willing to admit, but tonight you were a ghost. I'm not sure you even looked a single person in the eye tonight."

"Just got some shit on my mind right now."

"Shit on your mind is the understatement of the year Aaron. I don' know what planet you're currently on, but it's not Earth man," Glen said, a level of genuine concern in his voice that Aaron had never heard before. "Only time I go full on space cadet is when I'm wrapped up with a girl I can't get my mind off of. So I will ask you again, who is she?"

Aaron sat up and left the stars in the sky behind. He slid down so he was sitting across from Glen as he spoke. He told him everything, or at least the parts that mattered to story. Aaron told him about losing his grandpa in a stubborn reluctance to return home until he crowned himself a champion and now finding out that an old high school crush had mentioned his name for a stupid reunion and now it was all he could thing about but to go home and see her again after all these years.

"Jesus man, you a deep motherfucker you know that," Glen said, running his hands through his hair and coming out with a cigarette in his right hand in a single fluid motion. "I know most people that work at bars have a story of what got them there but damn man."

"Well, this has been helpful," Aaron said, getting up to leave.

"Sit the fuck down," Glen said, lighting up his cigarette and motioning for him to stay put. "I'm not allowed to comment on what you just told me? Some of us aren't designed to bottle our emotions like you."

"I've noticed," Aaron said, sitting back down.

"Look, I'm just a bartender, but if you ask me it sounds like you know exactly what you need to do," Glen said, sending a cloud of smoke out of his mouth and into the early morning air.

"I wish it were that simple, but for me going home means admitting failure and tucking tail between my legs. I promised myself I wouldn't go back till I had something to show for my decision to leave. I go back now, I'm breaking my own promise and going to look like an asshole in the process."

"The fuck crawled up your ass and died to make you so serious?" Glen pondered, already finished with his cigarette but producing another one from his chest pocket. "You left ten years ago, the fuck even remembers you or why you left anyway? Half that old ass town probably thinks you got drafted or went to college or some shit. You sit here and act like you're the former fucking mayor that ducked out in the darkness of night to abandon the town folk for your own selfish reasons. Grow the fuck up and go home, no one give a shit what you did or didn't do. Look around you, life is fucked. Everyone knows this. Failure isn't the exception anymore, it's the standard."

For ten years Aaron had seen his life through a single spectrum, now sitting there with Glen he suddenly realized how ignorant that really was.

Glen was right, no one gave a fuck. Jack didn't care; if he did he wouldn't have called him today. He would have been fine never speaking to him again if he'd been irrevocably hurt by Aaron leaving the way he did. Same with his grandpa and is mother, they obviously wanted him to find what he was looking for, but didn't really care if he came back empty handed as long as he actually came back. The negative aura that surrounded the decision to return had been lifted; he was free to return with a clear conscious.

"Are you telling your only bartender to go home, not knowing if or when I will return?"

"I'm saying you BETTER go back and tap that fine ass you can't get your mind off of. I throw a rock in this fucking town and could hit twelve assholes that will play bartender for me, probably take less money too. The fuck are reunion's for anyway if not to sleep with those that you were too chicken shit to seal the deal with back then?"

"Yeah," Aaron replied, not really sure what to say in response. "I guess I should head back and start packing."

"Shut the fuck up, I know you have one duffle bag you live out of. I saw it on the couch this morning and it's pathetic. Grown man needs to own more that one pare of nasty-ass shoes he wears every fucking day," Glen said, pulling out a much larger wad of cash than what he had laid on Aaron's chest earlier. "Go buy some new clothes so you don't show up looking like a fucking hobo for Christ sake."

"Thanks Glen, I really appreciate this."

"If you ever tell anyone I did this I'll deny every word of it," Glen said, no humor in his voice.

V

Aaron raced back to the motel, or at least he went as quickly as he could. As soon as he hoped back into the Shelby he remembered he'd coasted here on fumes and had to refuel or he wasn't going anywhere. He got out of the car and walked to the closest gas station, four blocks away, to fill his container with gas.

The infinite, dark night sky was usually a depressing backdrop to his silent drive back to the motel or any empty parking lot each night, but tonight it offered a calm and welcoming aura as he walked down the empty streets of Austin. Aaron couldn't explain it but he felt like a weight had been lifted off his back, one he'd been carrying around for years. It had made perfect sense to him that he was only admitting failure by going back, when in reality the only thing he was failing was himself. He'd spent the last few years utterly miserable, sleeping in his car and working odd jobs to afford the bare necessities. Not once had Aaron even remotely thought of the future, of what he could do to make his life better. He was trapped in the grind and it was eat or be eaten 24/7, no time to think about anything else.

As he continued walking towards the gas station, he decided he'd text Jack to tell him he'd be coming back for the reunion, maybe even longer. He was somewhat surprised when his phone dinged in response; it was close to 3AM in the morning right now.

SERIOUSLY?!?!

...

DAMN, YOUR ALREADY WHIPPED AND YOU HAVEN'T EVEN SPOKEN TO HER, IN LIKE...EVER.

Aaron turned his phone off and walked the rest of the way in silence.

■

When he woke up the next morning, Aaron got to do something he hadn't done in years.

He got to go shopping.

With Glen's money burning a hole in his pocket he the road and found the nearest outlet store he could find. Glen didn't give him a fortune and Aaron knew he'd get a lot more for his money buy buying last years clothes for half the price.

Not half and hour later, Aaron walked out of the store with two bags full of new clothes. It was his first day of school again, after his grandpa took him shopping for a few new shirts and shoes to wear for the upcoming year. Aaron hurriedly changed in the driver's seat, wiggling back and forth frantically to get his new pants on, then wrapping his old clothes in a bag and throwing them in the trunk where they belonged.

A new man, or at least a better-dressed one, Aaron hit the road. It was roughly a fifteen-hour drive from Austin to Silverton, CO. If he kept his stops to a minimum, and why wouldn't he, he wasn't on a sightseeing road trip, he would be there by nightfall. Aaron had called Jack earlier this morning, Jack was eager to hear he was really coming home and it wasn't just a drunken text, he then proceed to call out, "Avenger's ASSEMBLE," over the phone loud enough Aaron had to pull the phone away from his ear to avoid going temporarily deaf.

"Jesus Jack, I'm fucking driving," he said, putting the phone back to his ear.

"So?"

"So maybe give me a heads up before you start yelling so I don't take the Shelby off a cliff or into oncoming traffic for fuck sake."

"Wait, doesn't Austin have the Hands-Free law? You know holding your phone is against the law right?"

Aaron did, but he didn't really care. Until the other day his phone was mainly used to connect to the Internet when he was around free Wi-Fi and to log the occasional girls number. He didn't use it in the car and had no interest in hooking up any new technology to the Shelby. The car was a classic, still had the tape deck it came off the assembly line with, and he had no desire to ruin it by putting in some third-party Bluetooth receiver just so he could make and take phone calls that never came.

"What was that? You're breaking up. Did you say turn around and head south towards Mexico?"

"Fine by me, been saying it for years, this country is too crowded as it is. Send a post card, or don't. We don't care"

WE.

Low blow Jack.

They both knew it wasn't Jack that got Aaron to come back; it was the mere mention of Ashley that peaked his interest. No point in trying to hide it from Jack, they never could keep secrets from each other.

They bantered back and forth till Jack had to open up the library and hung up. The plan was all set, Aaron was going to meet Jack at the library later tonight and spend the night at his place.

Tomorrow he would see his mom for the first time in ten years.

Nervous wasn't the right word for how Aaron felt at the moment. He wasn't afraid to see her; he was actually looking forward to it. He just didn't have anything to say when she would, eventually, ask where he'd been all this time. Even after Glen's pep talk last night, he was still anxious about the situation. He might not have anything to be embarrassed about, but that didn't keep him from becoming self-conscious about it anyway. Odds were she would embrace him with open arms, happy just to see her baby boy again, but the dark thought kept creeping back into his head of the chance that she would be bitter and cold towards him for staying away for so long.

Less than an hour ago Aaron had vehemently bashed the thought of upgrading the interior of the Shelby while talking to Jack, now, as he drove in silence because it was 2017 and no one had any fucking cassette tapes anymore, he wished he'd had the money to at least upgrade to listen to his phone or a podcast to fill the suffocating silence that allowed him to keep coming up with worst case scenario's. There was the radio, and beggar's can't be choosers, but fuck the radio.

Just fourteen hours to go pal.

■

At nightfall, Aaron rolled into town.

Silverton was a fairly small town, with a population around six hundred give or take, but driving into town was to take a step back in time. Aaron thought about it a lot while he was driving in and it made sense that time slowed down in a place like this, there wasn't exactly a booming economy to capitalize on and the people that had the most say in the town were of an older generation that liked to keep things as simple as possible.

Aaron hadn't been back in ten years and the place looked the same as it did the day he left. If he didn't know how the town operated, choosing to shoo away most big box stores like the plague, he would have been thoroughly creeped out by what he saw. Driving down Main Street, Silverton appeared able to withstand the forces of time. Every building, most were built in the early nineteenth century, looked as good as new. Aaron had seen buildings that looked to be on their last leg, hell the Rusty Knuckle was the shining example of a building well past its prime, falling apart from the inside out just slow enough to keep the inspectors at bay on occasional pop-ins, but every building on Main Street looked as if it could have been a recently finished construction just celebrating is Grand Opening. Even the damn windows were flawless; there wasn't a broken or cracked one of them on the entire street. The town reminded him of a snow globe, not matter how much you shook it or how much the world moved around it, Silverton stayed the same.

Being on the road, Aaron got used to seeing the staples of commercialism everywhere he went. You couldn't go ten miles without passing a Starbucks, Wal-Mart, or McDonalds. Now, slowly rolling down the street soaking up the nostalgia that was his past, Aaron took in the shops that lined the street. Each one was a family-owned and operated small business. There was no Lowes or Home Depot, just Eddie's Hardware and Appliances that took up a prime real estate spot on the corner. Everywhere he looked, there was the mom and pop alternate in the real world. DK's Grocery and Supply, named after the husband and wife owners Don and Karen, sat across the street from the hardware store. It's lights cutting out against the darkness of the street since they were the only store still open in town at this time of night.

That was, expect for the Wendy's at the end of the street.

Like a sore thumb, the fast-food chain stuck out against the timeless town. Aaron remembered his mother telling him they were getting a Wendy's, the excitement in her voice was undeniable, and there it was. Shoved in back of Main Street like the redheaded stepchild it was. At close to nine o'clock, the fast food joint had a nearly empty parking lot, minus the two cars that likely belonged to employees since the windowpanes were a dead giveaway that no one was inside. It appeared most in the town saw fit to go home for dinner rather than stay out and eat off the value menu. He drove past and looked in the window at the deathly bored teenager leaning against the counter, likely willing time to go faster to make his shift end sooner.

Just around the corner was the library where Jack worked.

Aaron pulled into the library parking lot, which was just as empty as the Wendy's parking lot he noticed.

Looks like books are as popular as square hamburgers on Saturday night in Silverton.

He sat in the Shelby for a moment, realizing this was it. Any chance of skipping out again with cold feet went out the door as soon as he walked inside that library. Jack might zip-tie him to a chair if he got the sense he was feeling flighty. Aaron kept waiting for the urge to slam his foot on the gas and burn out that never came. As hard as it was to come back, now that he was actually here, it was almost harder to leave.

Aaron finally got out of the car and walked up the front steps of the library. The building used to be the town's old church, but was renovated back when he was in high school to become the new library once a bigger church was built on the edge of town. Not everyone was religious in Silverton, but those that were took it very seriously and fought tooth and nail to get a bigger church to accommodate future generations of Silverton. Wendy's notwithstanding, the new church may be the last new piece of architecture built since he left.

Cracking the solid oak doors, expecting a long squeal from the hinges that never came, Aaron slipped inside.

He found Jack in the communal area where students would be tutored after school and on weekends, lording over a stack of oversized manuscripts, each one open to a specific page. The long tables were buried under piles and piles of books that Jack had pulled to read, seemingly all at the same time.

"Well, I guess that squashes any fear I had of you throwing a surprise welcoming party," Aaron said, breaking the silence when Jack didn't look up at him.

"Who would care," Jack responded, never looking up from the book he was intently reading.

"Fair," Aaron nodded; walking down the steps to the desk that Jack was standing over.

Jack looked up and smiled; coming around the desk he was behind to hug him. Aaron wasn't really the hugging type, but let Jack have this moment. It had been ten years after all. Truth be told, he was just as happy to see Jack, it had been too long since he'd been genuinely happy to see someone that wasn't holding his check on payday.

"The hell are you reading?" Aaron asked, walking around the desks to look at all the open books Jack had displayed around the room.

Most of the books were just pages and pages of text, enough to make Aaron go cross-eyed after trying to read the first few he looked at. A few had drawings, and those immediately drew his attention. The gothic drawings were just like the kind he remembered from high school when they'd read Divine Comedy about Dante's trip to Hell. Aaron didn't truly read two pages of that book; he didn't really read any book in school with a friend like Jack around. Jack was a living, breathing stack of note cards. He would just sit there and ask the question he had to answer for the paper and Jack would go on a rant about the subject, with Aaron franticly writing down what he could to answer the question as if he actually read the book.

"Is that the devil?" He pointed to one book with particularly graphic interpretation of what a beastly creature from Hell would/could look like. "Oh shit, are you in a cult?"

"Cults operate under the false ideals of a single entity with selfish intentions in desperate need of attention and loyalty," Jack said without looking up from the book he was still reading since Aaron walked in. "Since it's just me here either that means I am the world's most ineffective cult leader or you're still an idiot."

"Call it like I see it pal," Aaron said, lifting the book with the drawings to illustrate his point. He showcased the drawings like he was a prize girl on a game show, waving his hand down the page, "You a witch?"

"Dude, witches aren't fucking real," Jack said, finally looking up from the text he was reading. "Now you're just being an asshole."

"Ok, so help me out, what the hell is all of this?"

"This," Jack said, grinning from ear to ear, "This is the map to underworld."

"The what now?"

"The Hot Gate's themselves!" Jack clamored.

"Riiiiight," Aaron nodded, not understanding a word Jack was saying.

"Com'on man, Hell. This is the map to Hell."

"Ookay," Aaron said, putting the book down on the table like he found it, "and what pray tell do you want the map to hell for?"

"Dude, think about it," Jack said, talking with his hands intently, "if there is a way IN to Hell, that means there is a way OUT of Hell," he said, nodding excitedly in agreement to his own statement.

Aaron stared back at him, more lost than ever.

"Jesus Aaron," Jack said, throwing his hands up in despair, "If there is a way in and out of hell, that means there is a gate or a door or something that acts like a gateway for both sides. That MEANS, there is a door or gate or something that can be SEALED. You and me buddy, we are gonna close the gates of Hell, once and for all," Jack smiled. "And I've figured out just how were gonna to do it and live to tell the tale."

"We are gonna do what now?" Aaron asked as Jack continued to ramble on with his plan.

VI

The Devil's Backbone.

Jack would say it over and over again, each time with more gusto as if Aaron had even a remote idea of what he was talking about each time he said it. Jack spoke of the Devil's Backbone in such a causal tone it was as if he were talking to a group of parents after a PTA meeting about something as monotonous as the mail schedule or the newspaper headlines.

Except it wasn't mundane, it was the fucking DEVIL.

For the last hour, Aaron had listened to Jack ramble on about this, doing his best to keep up but only getting fractions of what he was saying. Part way through his impromptu lesson, Aaron realized Jack missed his calling by not becoming a teacher. Sure, he was lost trying to follow along, but the fire in Jack's eye as he spoke about something he was clearly passionate about was oddly inspiring. All the time on the road and Aaron had never once gone about something or even remotely felt the way Jack looked at this very moment. He did his best to nod and interact with key phrases such as, "obviously," and, "and why wouldn't you?" to let Jack have his moment. Aaron could tell Jack had been bottling all this up for some time, just happy to have Aaron back so he could talk about it and not be put in a padded room afterward.

"… so that is why you and me need to go down there and finish this off once and for all," Jack concluded, looking at Aaron intently for a reaction.

Shit.

"Well…obviously, I mean, why wouldn't you right?" Aaron said.

"Dammit Aaron, you've been saying the same thing over and over for the last hour like a broken speak-and-spell," Jack yelled, "are you with me on this or not?"

Aaron took a moment to ponder his options.

Option one was simple, tell Jack he was fucking crazy and needed a girlfriend or a dog. Obviously spending this much time around books and not real people had its side effects. It was one thing to be passionate about something, reading anything and everything you could on the subject to better understand it, but Jack was tip-toeing on the line of lunatic that writes on the sidewalk with his own shit to avoid forgetting an idea. Kids believed in this stuff, maybe extremist churchgoers too, but there was a point were you had to grow up and realize monster's weren't the winged creatures that bit your neck, they were the assholes that paid with a check for a pack of cigarettes and copy of USA Today at the grocery store. He didn't want to crush his friends' idea, but maybe coming from him it would be better than some other asshole that wouldn't be so delicate.

Option two was the darker path, it was to nod and go along with it all. Aaron had missed Jack more than he realized until seeing him in person just now. If it meant they got to hang out a little while longer while he went on his harmless quest than so be it. Who was the victim here, besides time, which Aaron had wasted a good portion of in his own life. So they went on some hunt and try to find some gate that opens to Hell or whateverthefuck Jack had been rambling on about for the last hour. As long as it didn't involve a human sacrifice, what was the big deal? All Jack ever wanted to do was save the world, so why not let him live out his fantasy. If he was lucky, maybe they would come across some owl or black cat Aaron could convince him was magical and that would be the end of it.

Option two.

"I'm in, let's go stab a Redback," Aaron said, "wait, can I call them that?"

"Dude, I'm being serious. If you're in, you have to take this seriously."

"Oh! I'm serious," Aaron said, flipping a book closed for effect, "I've about had it with this shit and it's time you and I put an end to the…uhh…door…thing that keeps those assholes from wandering around like perverts with their dick's in their hands, am I right!" he said, going up for a high-five.

"You didn't understand a word I said," Jack said.

"Nope, not a word."

"Ugh, just forget it man, it was dumb anyway."

Aaron could see the rejection on Jack's face and it broke his heart. Jack was always willing to listen to what you had to say and help if you needed it back in high school, it's how he got along with all social groups and didn't end up upside down in a trashcan. Even if he weren't looking at his best friend, he would have felt bad for the kid that everyone could rely on. Jack went out on a limb, even to tell Aaron, and in turn he wasn't responsive to any of it.

"Come on Jack, it's me. The guy that got through probably half of his senior year by sitting next to you and frantically writing what you said. I'm not good with oral lessons, my mind wanders relentlessly when I don't understand what I'm listening to, it's why I didn't even bother with college," Aaron offered, "You know if you want to do this I'm in, but you have a full head of steam on something that I can't even fully wrap my mind around right now. I mean, you want to stab the Devil man."

"I never said anything about stabbing anyone," Jack mumbled, still looking down at his book.

"Really? Cause I'm pretty sure you were motioning it earlier when you were pointing at that demon drawing in the book. Thought that was code for stab."

"You can't kill the Devil dude, you just have to lock him back in his cage so he can't control the gates anymore. All we have to do is lock him up and throw away the key."

"That easy huh?"

"Nothing worthwhile is easy Aaron," Jack said, closing the book he was standing over dramatically. "The only way for evil to succeed is for good to do nothing."

"Whatever happened to fighting fire with fire?"

"WE ARE NOT FIGHTING THE DEVIL! This will not be a battle of strength, but a battle of wits," Jack yelled, breaking his own rule of yelling in a library.

"Ok, ok, calm down buddy. Just tossing out ideas is all. You want to do this, we'll do it, ok?"

"Seriously?"

"Sure," Aaron said, standing up from behind the table he was sitting at, "Fuck it right. Not like I have to be at work on Monday. May as well save the world, would look great on a resume no?"

"So we are really going to do this! BadASS man, we are fucking do this!" Jack said, as excited as the time he got a peck on the cheek from Laura.

"Oh, we will, but first thing's first."

"What's that?" Jack asked, stilled hyped up on adrenaline as he paced back and forth.

"I need a drink."

■

Jasper's Bar & Grill was the only bar in town, so most nights it was the busiest place in town. Silverton didn't have five-star dining or an Applebee's, it had Jasper's. The town's people would all converge in the old school style pub and socialize after work, and then the dinner crowd came through, followed up by the locals that liked to close the place down most nights. Aaron remembered going to Jasper's with his grandpa and Mr. Wheeler on weekends to get a milkshake and listen to their stories. It always started with he or Jack asking a question about their past.

"What was it like before TV?" Jack had asked one night.

After than, they were off to the races. Mr. Wheeler and grandpa would go back and forth; telling stories like it was a competition and the last one to speak or the coolest story one. Back and forth they would go, sometimes for hours, before one of them would have the good sense to bow out and end the night. Grandpa and Mr. Wheeler grew to become pretty good friends over time, grandpa saw the way Mr. Wheeler made Aaron's mother feel and respected him for treating Aaron the way he did. They were close to a dozen years apart in age, but they shared the same interests and social style, never talking over the other, that made them fast friends. It was weird to say, but some of Aaron's best memories as a kid were in a bar.

Aaron had expected a crowd, especially on a Saturday night at 10P.M., but when he and Jack walked up to the front door he almost swallowed his tongue.

Turns out, as Jack had conveniently forgotten to mention on their walk to Jasper's, tonight was a casual cocktail party for all reunion members that came to town early. As he stood outside, looking inside through the window at all the familiar faces just behind the door, Aaron locked eyes on one in particular.

Ashley Meyers.

She was standing at the bar, waiting for her drinks as she interacted with a couple of their former classmates. Even behind a dirty window she was just as beautiful as he remembered. Wearing a navy blue sweater that showed off her still amazing figure, and a black knit scarf, she was better than any poster girl Aaron had ever seen. Talking with their classmates, her amber-red hair draped down the left side of her face as she constantly tucked it back behind her ear. Bar's were not particularly well lit establishments, mainly because people went to bar to have fun and it was easier to do that in public if you were under the guise of being in the shadows. That being said, Ashley's pale white skin seemed to radiate off of here even in low light. Aaron didn't want to use the world angel, not after the pop-up lesson he'd just had with Jack about the supernatural, but it was hard to explain otherwise why she appeared to glow amongst the rest of them.

This fucking town has immaculate window washing EXCEPT at Jasper's. Good to see your luck followed you home pal.

"Dude, you're staring," Jack interrupted.

"I wasn't staring, just haven't seen her in a while," Aaron said patting his coat pocket and glancing around like he was looking for something to look less creepy to anyone on the street now that Jack had called him out.

"You want me to go in there and get her? Or maybe I go in and grab a peanut bucket so we catch your drool out here on this perfectly good sidewalk."

"Shut up."

"Or maybe I call the fire department, report a fire in your loins," Jack continued.

"Just get inside," Aaron pushed him, almost shoving him through the front door by accident.

"Careful man, this coat is MINK."

"No it's not."

"But it could be," Jack shrugged, daydreaming in the front door of Jaspers.

"Just go get us a round will you, I'm not stabbing at demons until you pay the tab at the end of the night."

"Dude, we are not stabbing an-," Jack started as Aaron walked off towards the vicinity of where he saw Ashley through the window outside.

This is it pal, you're balls dropped so time to go talk to her like an adult and not slur your words.

He saw here standing at the bar, still talking to the same people he saw her with a minute ago, and made his way toward her. He didn't sprint; he tried to make it look as casual as possible. Just another guy walking to the bar to order a drink, nothing weird. Aaron ran through about a dozen things he would say when he got to her, deciding to go with the casual hello like any normal person would do after not seeing anyone for ten years.

More like seventeen since she never noticed you in school either.

Aaron realized, too late, that everyone was wearing a nametag. HELLO, MY NAME IS was on everyone's chest to read. He knew some of the people here, but realized that ten years was a long time to expect everyone to remember everyone and as he looked around he noticed that there were more unfamiliar faces than not. Aaron panicked and turned to recoup and grab a nametag before talking to Ashley. Last thing he wanted was to be the guy that walked up to her and she didn't even remotely remember.

Smooth pal.

He didn't make it five steps the other direction when a loud voice cut through the music and crowd noise like a hot knife through butter.

"You have got to be shitting me. Hey everyone, look who finally decided to grace us with his presence," someone shouted as everyone in the room turned to look at Aaron.

VII

Ronnie Holtzman.

Part of Aaron had completely forgotten about the asshole since he left town, happy to drive away and never think twice about the low-level drug dealing scumbag. Jack had mentioned him when they spoke on his drive back when he gave a brief rundown of the current state of affairs in Silverton and Aaron was honestly shocked to hear he was still alive. Someone like Ronnie was operating on borrowed time, having done nothing to change his ways since high school meant it was only a matter of time before he wound up dead or in a federal prison.

Jack explained that Ronnie never got the help he desperately needed after high school despite his attempts to be a friend and go to meetings with him, instead Ronnie went for the glamorous life of a degenerate, unsuccessful drug dealer that stained the town of Silverton with his presence. He would scrape together whatever he could to buy drugs, hop on a bus into town to make his purchase, then come back and try to sell it to the regulars at Jasper's. The vicious cycle always ended the same way, with everyone telling him to piss off, immediately followed by Ronnie doing his own product behind Jasper's in the closest thing to an alley that Silverton had.

He'd been arrested more times than Jack could remember, never posting bail and most of the town convinced he did it just for a warm place to sleep and a square meal. Ronnie wouldn't even put up a fight when the police were inevitably called, Jack mentioning an infamous night the town still talked about when he was caught trying to sell meth to an off-duty officer, he was so content with being caught and arrested he even cuffed himself and got in the back of the police car on his own accord.

Hearing this was no shock to Aaron. Ronnie had been the bane of his existence back in high school, picking on him for no good reason. They were never friends; most people at school didn't consider themselves friends with Ronnie since he was held back a few times. He was old enough to legally drink his senior year so he became popular enough that people invited him to parties for the booze. Aaron had never crossed paths with Ronnie, they'd been in the same class since 8th grade when he was put in Aaron's class after being held back yet again, and so he was always miffed at why Ronnie has chosen him to be his punching bag. He would rant to Jack some nights, pissed and confused to what he had done or said that made Ronnie put a bull's eye on his back.

Now, in front of everyone at Jasper's, Ronnie was picking up right where he left off. Standing no more than ten feet across from him, Ronnie smelled as bad as he looked. His clothes were littered with holes and tears, his pants no better. He was almost rail thin; Aaron attributed this to the stories he'd heard about Ronnie eventually doing all the drugs he'd purchase in hopes to resale for profit after he struck out with everyone in town. Ronnie had a full, un-kept beard that was besieged with grey hair from a hard life. In a different scenario, he could see himself taking pity on someone like Ronnie, but he knew all too well that Ronnie brought this on himself and deserved every moment of hell on earth he experienced.

"Do tell, did you fly here on your private jet or did you ride a limo from that mountain of cash you must have being a man of the world and all," Ronnie taunted him.

"From what I hear, I could have rode in on a dying horse and it would have been an upgrade to anything you ever did your life," Aaron shot back, no longer the timid eighteen year old he was in high school.

If this low life piece of shit wanted a fight, he's going to get one.

"Easy now Mr. Big Shot. I didn't mean nothing by it, honest. Just wanted to bask in your glory for a moment is all. Not all of us got the opportunity to leave this piss bucket of a town and make it big ya know," Ronnie said, holding his hands up in surrender, a beer bottle in each hand. "You DID make it big didn't ya Mr. Big Shot?"

"Hard to answer your question honestly, what with shoveling manure up at Campbell's ranch likely being your definition of a making it big it Ron," Aaron mocked him, "By that logic, then yes, yes I did make it big."

"Oooh," Ronnie responded, waving his beer clad hands in false fear. "Well then let me be the first to bow in your presence your Majesty," as he began to kneel.

"Tell you what Ron, to show everyone here that this is all water under the bridge, I'll buy your next round," Aaron offered, even going for a wallet he knew was practically empty. "Way I figure, you look like you only have about one round left in you before you piss yourself and black out in front of all these people. From what I hear, that's should be a wrap on a pretty casual Saturday night for you right?"

"I'm gonna skin you al-," Ronnie started before another loud voice cut him off.

"OK, that's enough. No one is skinning anyone in my bar. You two can either calm the fuck down or get the fuck out," Jasper said from behind the bar, pointing to the door for their reference.

"You dickbags don't even know how to throw a real party anyway, this place is lame as shit," Ronnie said as he smashed both bottles on the floor and turned to leave. He pushed and shoved his way to the front door and threw open the door.

"Hey Mr. Big Shot, hope you plan on sticking around so we can finish our little discussion. Wouldn't want you to run away again before we got to settle this like real mean," he yelled as the door closed behind him.

■

The bar went back to normal as soon as Ronnie left, most in the bar having seen Ronnie's antics enough to ignore it the moment it was done. No one there wanted Ronnie to ruin the reunion, everyone laughing and continuing his or her banter so quickly it was hard to image a confrontation had just happened in the middle of the bar.

"Did that just happen!" Jack said, sliding over to Aaron excitedly, holding two bottles of Miller Lite.

"Yeah, yeah I guess it did," Aaron responded after taking one of the bottles, slightly embarrassed.

"I was totally going to back you up, just crowded ya know. Took a minute to get over here and then I was IN."

"I know pal," Aaron said, patting him on the shoulder like a noble knight.

"You talk to her yet?"

"No. Was on my way over when I noticed everyone had these nametags on and came over to grab one so she knew who I was, then Ronnie happened."

"Man, fuck that guy. He's probably outside right now trying to steal a car or selling, he's not worth the time of day. Just forget about him. Look around, everyone else already has," Jack said, waving his arm toward a crowd of former classmates that carried on like nothing had happened.

"Should we call the police?"

"Why? So he can get another warm bed and dinner paid for by the people of Silverton? Screw that, let him freeze his nuts off like the animal he is."

"I hope a dog shit's on his face and bites his nuts," Aaron lashed out, louder than expected to alarm some of the closer patrons at the bar who overheard him.

"Yeah. I mean, little dark and specific, but ok," Jack tried his best to be a friend, "Let's just forget about it and have some fun yeah?"

Fun.

As Aaron stood there, sill reeling internally from his confrontation with Ronnie, he found it hard to focus on anything other than finding Ronnie and beating him to a pulp. Guy's like that shouldn't be allowed to wander the street, hell they should be put down. Society found it acceptable to euthanize animals that no one cared for or could take care of, Ronnie was a perfect example of why that rule should work both ways. The scourge of Silverton was allowed to wander the streets and be a total dickbag to anyone he wanted and the best punishment he would get is a few nights in a jail where he would be feed and clothed, with a bed and toilet to boot. They should just taser him in the balls and push him in a river to wash down stream for someone else to deal with.

Fuck Ronnie Holtzman.

Aaron stood there; nursing the beer Jack gave him and let every dark thought about Ronnie creep into his head. Dozens of ideas flashed by him before he realized Jack was talking and he didn't hear a word he said.

"What?" Aaron asked, frustrated from being interrupted from daydreaming of ways to hurt Ronnie.

"I said, you should actually go talk to her instead of standing here looking like a mime that hasn't taken a shit in weeks."

Ashley. He'd been so mad after dealing with Ronnie that Aaron had almost completely forgotten why he was walking over there in the first place. His head popped up and he started looking for where she was now.

"Oh, oh, look at this," Jack narrated, "He's out of his moping shell ladies and gentlemen, he has a scent and he's looking for his prey."

"Shut up," Aaron said, still trying to find her in the crowd of people inside Jasper's.

"Hey, Colombo,' Jack nudged him, "She standing by the front door saying her goodbyes."

Shit.

Jack was right; she was standing at the front door, pulling her dark navy pea coat on over her shoulders and buttoning up. After she finished buttoning her coat she started to wind her scarf around her neck like it was earlier at the bar. Aaron pushed through the crowd, imitating a fierce running back that would not be denied the end zone, and nearly bumped into her once he got to the front door.

"Hey Ashley," Aaron started, already farther along in conversation than he'd ever been before. "Not sure you remember me, I'm A-"

"Mr. Big Shot right?" She smiled.

"Yeah, sorry about that," Aaron said, shoving his hands into his pockets like a teenager getting yelled at by his parents. "Ronnie and I never got along, seems he still has it out for my after all these years."

"Relax," she said, patting him on the shoulder. "Ronnie's an asshole, ask most people here they'd agree you let him off easy by not punching him in the face."

"And what you would say?"

Ashley paused at the question, caught off guard from a boy she probably didn't even remember from high school. For the few moments she thought about her answer, Aaron felt his heart beating faster. Her soft lips, the lips he would daydream in class about one day kissing, curled up in a smile as she spoke.

"Aaron right?" she said, sidestepping his question altogether.

"Yeah, that's right! I'm Aaron," he said, sticking his hand out to shake hers like an eager car salesman. "I didn't think you would remember me to be honest, we didn't really talk much in high school."

"Well, your name IS written on your nametag," she smiled; nodding at the tag he'd hurriedly applied after his incident with Ronnie. His penmanship looked worse than a distracted toddler writing with his left foot. "But I remember you. You're Jack's friend right? He talks about you non-stop you know, he's practically a walking billboard for how awesome you are. You pay him to do that?"

"He works mainly on commission, but the benefits are not bad I hear. Get's to be ring side at all my bar fights."

Ashley laughed.

If Aaron made a list of all the things he wanted in his return to Silverton, seeing her smiling and laughing would have been damn close to the top of the list. He'd had imaginary conversations in his head back in high school that ended with her laughing and telling him he was so funny, but they were just that, imaginary. To actually see her smile and giggle, her nose twitching slightly as she laughed, was everything he hoped and imagined in would be.

"Hey, so me and Jack were just headed out, can I give you a lift?"

"Jack and I," she corrected.

"Right, Jack and I were just heading out, you wanna ride?"

"You still drive the '67 Shelby?" she asked, quicker than he expected since he didn't think she once noticed or looked his way in high school when he was in that car.

"I do actually, she's parked just outside the library if you don't mind a little walk."

"She huh?"

"Yeah, my grandpa used to call the car a she. Guess I just picked it up and kept it going without even really thinking about it. A generational thing for sure right?"

Ashley smiled again, likely enjoying every moment of his awkwardness as he kept talking just to avoid dead air and awkward silence.

"Suppose a little walk wouldn't kill me, give me time to hear about some of your famous worldly adventures."

"Uh, yeah. Cool," Jack said, unsure exactly what Jack had been saying about him and worried he was walking into a trap of some sort. "Let me just go grab Jack and we'll head out."

Ashley nodded and Aaron disappeared into the crowd to collect Jack. If he thought he'd moved with purpose walking toward her, he was now practically bulldozing people to clear a path back to Jack. When he got back to the bar Jack was chatting with another couple, deep in conversation that the three of them found particularly funny.

"Time to go," Aaron said, grabbing the beer out of Jack's hand and putting it on the bar.

"What? Seriously? Dude, you shart or something, cause I may know how to clean that up so no one knows what happened. Just something I read ya know," Jack said with an uncomfortable silence afterward.

"I just offered Ashley a ride home and she said yes, so we are leaving. Now."

"Seriously?" Jack said, not convinced.

"Seriously," Aaron said, waving over to Ashley to confirm his story. She waved back and Jack almost fell off his stool in shock.

"Damn dude, who the fuck are you? You've been back in town for a few hours and you've managed to tell off the town drunk and get the girl. Can I have your autograph?"

"Just shut up and move," Aaron said, pushing him forward into the crowd towards the front door and Ashley.

They all met at the front door and headed out, Jack grabbing a handful of candies from the basket by the door.

"These little things taste JUST LIKE root beer you guys, I'm not even joking. You want some," he offered, as he shoved a few in his mouth.

"Jesus Jack, those candies are for ki-."

Aaron didn't have a chance to finish the sentence before Ronnie jumped him and sucker punched him in the face.

VIII

The pain didn't hit right away, the shock of it all was too sudden for anything other than his animalistic reaction to take place. Aaron rolled off the ground and was quickly back on his feet. He went straight at Ronnie, hitting him with his shoulder right in the stomach as he picked his malnourished frame up off the ground easily before slamming his down on his back.

"THE FUCK IS YOUR DEAL RONNIE!" Aaron yelled, already pulling back with his hand balled into a fist to repay him for the punch in the face.

Aaron connected with Ronnie's face, his hand colliding into Ronnie's jaw with everything he had. He could hear and pop, but judging by the immense amount of pain that shot through his wrist and up his arm he wasn't sure if it came from him or Ronnie. Ronnie's head jerked to the right, blood and possibly a tooth ejecting out of his mouth on impact from Aaron's fist. Aaron settled over Ronnie's chest, breathing harder than he'd ever remembered breathing before, but ready to continue the fight if necessary. The thing about most fights, that movies and TV always got wrong, was that they usually ended as quickly as they began. The idea of two men battling it out between devastating blows over and over again was impractical. They would be severely injured after just a single hard shot to the head, much less half a dozen or more.

Ronnie lay on the ground, making no attempt to fight back after having his jaw broken. Aaron had assessed it was Ronnie's jaw that popped since the shot of pain that he had experienced in his hand had gone away, though it was still possible that was due to the amount of adrenaline coursing through his body at this very moment. He waited in attack mode for any reason to continue, but Ronnie's body language made it clear he was not interested in trading more blows.

"I...I ot ou ood," he mumbled through bloodied mouth and broken jaw, grinning from ear to ear.

He's fucking smiling.

He just jumped me outside Jasper's were the entire town was around to see him get his ass handed to him and he was smiling.

"You're sick Ronnie, you need help," Aaron said, any anger he just had for Ronnie washing away only to be replaced by sadness for how far Ronnie had fallen. He didn't have far to fall after all, but this was a horrible state to be in. Jumping a guy you hadn't seen in ten years cause he got to leave town and you didn't? Everyone in town knew Ronnie was only a few footsteps away from the inevitable, but it made it easier to actually see it in person. Aaron understood now why everyone just chose to ignore him. Ronnie wouldn't accept anyone's help and it was just too hard to watch him fall, so turning your back was the best scenario. Children would hide under their sheets, feeling safe as long as they were unable to see the monsters, the monsters would be unable to see them. The town of Silverton used a similar logic with Ronnie, out of sight, out of mind.

"Are you ok?" Ashley asked as Aaron walked back towards then, leaving Ronnie lying on the ground behind him.

Aaron felt his left eye and flinched as his fingers found purchase on the tender part around his eyebrow. Ronnie was a similar height as him, so when he swung and connected with Aaron's face, his fist had hit right on his left eye and eyebrow line. Aaron knew he was going to have one hell of a shiner later, he chuckled to himself that it would only serve him right for their to be a class reunion photo tomorrow night for everyone to remember this occasion.

"I'll live," he said, giving her a small smile to say thanks for asking and in attempt to show her it didn't hurt as bad as it actually did.

"What should we do about him?" she asked, looking over at Ronnie, still lying on the sidewalk where Aaron had left him. Ronnie was still laughing to himself, though no one knew what for.

"He's just lying there, laughing. Guy is crazy, like a real life Joker right here in Silverton." Jack chimed in, his mouth still full of root beer candies. "Guess that make's you Batman dude."

"Pretty sure Batman wouldn't have been jumped walking out of bar," Aaron countered.

"Fair point. Batman would have anticipated this," Jack agreed; fist bumping Aaron as they both grinned like children.

"Guys," Ashley scolded them with a glare. "This isn't funny, Ronnie's a mess and needs help."

"Of course he does, but who in this town hasn't offered it to him one way or another?" Jack said. "He doesn't want our help? So be it. Let him lay in the street until he comes to his senses and crawls back to whatever hole he lives in. My conscious is clear."

"Still, we can't just leave him out here like this. I think Aaron might have really done some damage. What if he's not getting up because he can't?"

"He jumped me," Aaron defended.

"And I'm not saying any one of us would have reacted differently, most of us would have punched him back in the bar earlier, but that doesn't mean we just leave him here. We are better than that aren't we?"

She was right. As much as he hated that she was and wanted to leave Ronnie to rot on the sidewalk outside Jasper's, Ashley was right.

"Leave him, I already called the police," a voice said from behind them.

The three of them turned to see whom the Good Samaritan was and Aaron had to blink to make sure he wasn't hallucinating.

"Mr. Wheeler?"

∎

Mr. Wheeler stood in front of Aaron and embraced him with a hug. Aaron was not the hugging type but had already shared a hug with both Jack and Mr. Wheeler in the few hours since his return. He was surprised to see Mr. Wheeler at Jasper's for a number of reasons, mainly because he'd been gone for ten years and Mr. Wheeler was sixty-seven. Not many sixty-seven year olds hanging out at bars around midnight from what he could recall from the Rusty Knuckle, figured it was even fewer at Jasper's. Age aside, Mr. Wheeler was never the bar patron type, much more suited for a night at home than being out and about with the younger crowd.

"Good you see you," Aaron said, the hug lasting longer than he expected but not complaining either. "What are you doing at Jasper's?"

"Always did love a midnight cocktail," he joked.

"Seriously?" Jack asked.

"Only joking. I had to come by, this is a reunion after all and I did watch all of you come through Crest Hill. Never had kids of my own, always had my hands full with you guys. Thought I'd drop in and see how you all turned out."

"How'd we do?" Jack asked as if he was unaware of the satirical tone Mr. Wheeler took.

"You all turned out to be wonderful adults, couldn't have asked for a better group of kids."

"What about him?" Aaron said, turning to look at Ronnie, still lying on the sidewalk.

"Ronnie has had a tough life. Not what you'd want for anyone, but we can only do so much before the burden falls on him to get help. I myself have offered numerous times to counsel him and help him apply for jobs, but he seems content on living this life he's made for himself," Mr. Wheeler said, sadness in his voice.

"You tried W, we all did," Ashley said, putting her arm on his shoulder for support.

"Well it was nice to see you Mr. Wheeler," Aaron started, trying to break the sad aura that had fallen on them. "We were on our way to drop Ashley off so we should be heading off now."

"You're not going anywhere young man, you're coming with me to get that eye looked at." He said, trying to get a better look at it in the dark with the low light Jasper's sign gave off above the front door.

"It's fine really, probably looks worse than it is," Aaron lied as the pain reasserted itself in his left eye, having left for a moment from the shock of seeing Mr. Wheeler. His eye now throbbed, he could feel his rhythmic heartbeat pulsating in his left eye.

"Still can't lie very well I see," Mr. Wheeler smiled, grabbing Aaron's arm so he couldn't walk away. At sixty-seven Aaron was surprised at the strength of his grip.

"Dude it does look pretty bad," Jack agreed.

Not helping.

"Come on, let's go get you fixed up. Your mother will be thrilled to see you, though we should probably patch you up as best we can before that so she doesn't worry."

"MOM?" Aaron yelped.

"Dude, I forgot to tell you," Jack said, slapping himself on the side of the head. "Mr. Wheeler and your mom got hitched a couple years back. W is your step-dad!"

The revelation should have surprised him, but it was more of a confirmation than anything. Even before he'd left town he could see that his mom and Mr. Wheeler had a connection. He and grandpa were happy to see her smile again and Mr. Wheeler was just about the best guy they could imagine would come along. They all got along well and Mr. Wheeler never tried to play the dad role. He understood that Aaron's grandpa was the man of the house and abided by his rules, eventually becoming very close with Aaron's grandpa.

Mr. Wheeler marrying his mom was just the next logical step. Under different circumstance Aaron would have congratulated his step-dad and been happy to come over for a toast and see his mom. Now though, he stood on the sidewalk outside of Jasper's with a cut up let eye after getting his bell rung by Ronnie's sneak attack. He hadn't had a chance to look at himself in a mirror, but he could only imagine what he looked like. The last thing he wanted to do was see his mom after all this time looking like he'd just had the crap kicked out of him, even if he had won the fight.

"That's awesome Mr. Wheeler," Aaron offered his hand to shake, with Mr. Wheeler gladly accepting. "I'm glad you two are happy, mom always lit up when you were around."

"It means the world to hear you say that Aaron," Mr. Wheeler said, still holding his hand after shaking it. "We are incredibly happy and would love to have you over for...what time is it? One? How about breakfast?"

"I would love to, but like I said, we are giving Ashley a ride home and can't just leave her stranded out here," Aaron politely countered, unsuccessfully pulling away from Mr. Wheeler's grip on his arm, only making it tighter.

Damn Mr. Wheeler, you work out?

"Nonsense. They are both invited as well. Your mother loves Jack like her own child, you two were nearly inseparable back when."

"It's true, your mom does love me."

"Shut up," Aaron said.

"Just saying," Jack said, shrugging.

"What about Ashley?" Aaron asked, she was standing right next to him through all of this. He'd spent all this effort into just talking to her and now he was having a small family reunion of his own while she stood there awkwardly trying to be cool during the whole thing. After all those years he'd finally been able to have a conversation with Ashley, followed immediately by a fight with Ronnie and now an invitation for a sleepover and breakfast with his parents.

Smooth pal.

"Thing's have changed since you went away Aaron," Mr. Wheeler said, "Ashley and your mother run the Silverton book club. Your mother probably likes Ashley more than she does Jack."

"Hey!" Jack objected.

"Seriously?" Aaron asked, looking over at Ashley, who was smiling the same way she had earlier as he fumbled though his words trying to talk to her.

"Yeah, were pretty tight. Don't worry, she hasn't shown me your baby pictures or anything," Ashley admitted, still smiling. "We are working our way back, I've only seen you up to the third grade. You were adorable back then, what happened?"

"You saw his baby photos? No fair, I wanna see them too!" Jack faked being upset, now smiling just like Ashley.

"I think I'm going to go lie down next to Ronnie," Aaron said, looking over at Ronnie still lying on the sidewalk. "Doesn't seem so bad now."

"Oh quite your whining," Mr. Wheeler ordered. "It's settled, were having breakfast at our house no let's get going so we can fix you up before your mother see's you."

"I'm not going anywhere without my car," Aaron protested.

"You still have her?"

"Yeah, I still have her. Good as new too."

"You guys and that car," Ashley cut in, shaking her head.

"Memory serves me, you mentioned her before I did last we spoke," Aaron argued as Ashley rolled her eyes.

"We gonna stand here with our dicks in our hand talking about cars or are we going to go get some shut eye and pancakes." Jack demanded.

"Jesus Jack," Aaron started, Ashley putting her hand on his other arm to interrupt him.

"It's fine, he's like this most of the time. He's harmless, though I'm not sure how he has had a longer relationship than I have."

"OH SHIT, that's right man. I'm seeing someone! Shit completely slipped my mind," Jack said, punching him in his arm.

"I think I need to lie down now," Aaron said, actually starting to feel lightheaded.

"Give me the key's before you pass out so I can drive us home," Mr. Wheeler said, taking the keys from Aaron and securing them in his pocket.

"Can I drive?!" Jack asked excitedly.

"NO," the three of them said in unison.

"Jeez, I get it," Jack said.

"I would like to get behind the wheel myself if you don't mind," Ashley asked between the three of them while Jack pouted walking away from them.

"Age before beauty my dear," Mr. Wheeler said before Aaron could say yes.

They started walking towards the library to recover the Shelby from the parking lot just as the flashing police lights began to light up the area behind them, a squad car finally arriving to take care of Ronnie as he lie on the sidewalk, still laughing.

VIX

Mr. Wheeler pulled the Shelby into the parking lot of DK's Grocery and Supply just as Aaron was starting to wrap his head around the events of the night. Ashley had called shotgun on the walk there, something Aaron didn't even think to do since he'd never had anyone but him in the car since he dropped Jack off at his house ten years ago. She and Mr. Wheeler chatted the whole way there, even thought the drive took them all of ten minutes.

To keep all his ducks in a row, he made a mental checklist, though the more he ran through it the more he couldn't be sure he hadn't suffered a concussion by what the checklist contained.

Jack, his one and only best friend, had concocted a plan that he wasn't even remotely comfortable with, or aware of, to go to the gates of Hell and close them once and for all to stop evil in dead it's tracks. Aaron had no idea what that entailed or why he needed to be involved, but he'd blindly agreed to participate because Jack was his best friend and he would be damned if he let him go at this nonsense alone. At the very least he would be there to make sure things didn't get out of hand and Jack didn't get himself hurt.

On top of all of that, Jack had failed to mention that he was in a relationship. It only came up once Ashley spilled the beans and Jack copped to it and acted like he'd forgotten to mention in conversation. Judging by the overly thorough rundown of what was going on in Silverton since he'd left, Aaron was fairly confident that Jack hadn't forgotten to mention anything. He was keeping it a secret for a reason and he fully planned to figure out just what he was hiding as soon as possible. He didn't like the fact that Jack had been able to lie to him so easily; they had never been able to withhold information from each other back in high school. The inability to lie to each other had made them close; knowing they would always be truthful to each other had its comforts in the battlefield of high school.

I guess nothing stays the same forever.

Mr. Wheeler had appeared out of thin air after his scuffle with Ronnie. Looking back Aaron realized it was highly likely Mr. Wheeler was in the bar the whole time, even witnessing the initial confrontation with Ronnie, Aaron had just been too focused on Ashley to notice much of what was going on around him. While he was the same old friendly Mr. Wheeler Aaron remembered from high school, a lot had changed since those days. The main difference being Mr. Wheeler had married his mother. This wasn't really a surprise, they had been together since he was a sophomore, making high school even more interesting than it already was for a sixteen-year-old boy just trying to survive the day and manage the raging hormones that came with puberty. He was happy for them, he'd seen his mother go through some dark times after his father's death, just the thought that she'd found a piece of happiness in Mr. Wheeler was enough for Aaron. He wondered if they had an actual wedding, which he was not invited to, or if they just when down to the courthouse and filed the paperwork nonchalantly. Knowing how Mr. Wheeler liked to keep things low key, he assumed the later. That and it was less hurtful to think he wasn't invited to his own mothers wedding even though he'd been gone for so long and it made perfect sense as to why his invitation would get lost in the mail, hell, he didn't even really have a mailing address to send one to now that he thought about it. Mr. Wheeler had aged well, he still had stark white hair and dressed the part of a sixty-seven year old, but Mr. Wheeler was spry as ever. He was at Jasper's at close to midnight for crying out loud. Aaron had worked at the Rusty Knuckle for close to a year and not once did he recall a single person over the age of fifty coming into the bar. It had been Mr. Wheeler than notified authorities on Ronnie's condition, thankfully leaving out the part where Aaron cold-cocked him in the face to put him in that condition. The police had arrived right as they were leaving, picking up Ronnie and putting him in the back of the squad car to take him to the station. Aaron wondered in that was his plan all along, that he really had nothing against Aaron other than he saw him as his meal ticket to a warm bed and at least one square meal.

Last, but certainly not least, was Ashley.

Ashley Meyers, currently riding shotgun in his car, just like all the daydreams he'd had back in high school.

Aaron had worked up the courage, or was still running on the adrenaline from the confrontation with Ronnie in Jasper's, to actually talk to her. He'd almost missed his chance, she left soon after Ronnie did and he had to run over a few people in the bar over just to get to her before she left, but he'd managed to get to her and start up and actual conversation that would have made eighteen year old Aaron proud. He even offered her a ride home and was about to be the gentleman that dropped her off at her doorstep when Ronnie jumped him at the door and screwed everything up.

After the fight, Aaron had come to learn that Ashley was co-chairman of the Silverton Book Club with his mother and that they were actually very close. Close enough that his own mother had thought it ok to show her some of his pictures from her photo album. Mortified wasn't even good enough to describe how he felt at the moment. All the idea's he'd worked up in his head blew out the window the moment he realized Ashley knew too much about him. Acting suave or playing it cool wasn't going to work with the woman that had seen him in his whitey-tighties posing as Spider-Man for an impromptu photo shoot back when he was seven.

That about sums it up for you pal, you're screwed.

To add that last pinch of salt in the wound, Aaron's face currently hurt more than he could have imagined after just one punch.

Working at the Rusty Knuckle, he'd been part of a few scuffles here and there that ended with the Austin police coming by and cuffing the asshole that just couldn't keep his partying at a respectable level. Once he'd been the recipient of an errant fist to the face, leaving him with a sore jaw for days. That was child's play to the hit Ronnie had landed on him earlier. Having no notion of what was to come, Aaron had taken the full brunt of Ronnie's fist. Right now, his left eye was throbbing bad enough that swallowing a whole bottle of Advil seemed like a logical first step to tackling the pain.

Aaron and Mr. Wheeler walked in the sliding doors of DK's Grocery and Supply and headed directly for the frozen foods section. Mr. Wheeler grabbed a bad of frozen peas from behind the sealed door in the freezer isle and slapped it on his face, only the second time tonight Aaron had been hit in the face unexpectedly.

"This will help reduce the swelling," he'd said, walking off to another isle Aaron couldn't see with a bag of peas in his face.

"Where are you going? Why can't we just get an ice pack instead of me holding a bag of frozen produce on my face?"

"Peas are small, the form to your face better than an ice pack would," Ashley said, somehow standing right next to him.

"Jesus Christ, you scared the shit out of me. I thought you stayed in the car."

"I was going to, but then Jack wanted to talk about the 'current' Civil War and why Captain America had to be evil so I decided I'd come in here and read a magazine instead."

"You left Jack alone in the Shelby!"

"Relax," she said, "W has the keys, he can't do anything but adjust his seat."

"W?"

"Yeah, that's what I call him. No one call's him Mr. Wheeler but his students. He's W to everyone else. Even you're mom calls him W."

"Huh, makes sense," Aaron nodded, holding the bag of frozen peas tightly to his face. He could acknowledge that he probably looked ridiculous, in front of Ashley of all people, but the cold against his throbbing eye felt too good to remove it.

"Breaking News. This just in from our sources at DK's Grocery and Supply, it appears a local, they are calling him Aaron, has pee all over his face. More on this story as it develops."

"Dammit," Aaron said, hearing Jack's voice and Ashley giggling, "Can't anyone stay in the goddamn car?"

"Dude, you're not suppose to leave people in cars. That's fucking illegal ya know," Jack argued.

"That's for babies and your pets asshole. Shouldn't you be on the candy aisle or something?"

"What is everyone yelling about?" Mr. Wheeler asked, returning from wherever he'd wandered off to.

"These two couldn't stay in the car," Aaron said, pointing to them like a toddler.

"Free country," Jack fired back.

"Where did you go?" Aaron asked Mr. Wheeler, who was holding a handcart full of random items.

"Your mother would kill me if she found out I was at the store and didn't get the stuff on her list," he answered defensively.

"Ohhh, Mr. W is whipped..." Jack teased.

"Shut up Jack, try acting like your not twelve years old anymore will you," Mr. Wheeler, or Mr. W, or W said.

"I'll grow up when I wanna," Jack said, turning and walking toward the register where they kept the king size candy bars.

"So, Mr. Wheeler, Ashley says you go by W. That true?" Aaron asked.

"Wondered when she'd call you on that," he smiled. "Mr. Wheeler is what my student's call me. Most everyone else in this town calls me W, but you're welcome to call me Mr. Wheeler if that's what works best for you."

"W is fine, sounds better. Like I'm not talking to my counselor."

"W it is then. Shall we pay and get going?"

They paid for their items, W graciously buying the peas that Aaron held to his face as they checked out. The employee working the register took one look at his face when he pulled the bag down to let him scan the barcode and told him he could keep it there while punching in the code for the item. Inside his handcart, W had picked up some ointments and bandages that Ashley applied as they drove to the house. It wasn't how he'd drawn it up in his mind, but Aaron was enjoying the personal attention he was getting from Ashley in the back seat of the Shelby. As she rubbed the ointment over and around his eye, they only thing Aaron could think about was how his breath smelled. It had been at least twenty-four hours since he last brushed his teeth and he was terrified he smelled like a wet fart as she tried to apply his bandages. Aaron lost track of where they were and how long they'd been on the road, it seemed like only minutes when he'd hope it would take hours for them to reach the house. As he contemplated how long till they got there, he felt the bump as W pulled into their driveway and parked the Shelby.

He was home.

∎

They walked into a dark, empty house. It was now close to three in the morning and his mom was likely fast asleep upstairs. Aaron caught himself tiptoeing through his living room like a cat burglar in the cartoons he'd grown up on.

The living room was just like he remembered it, with the TV in the corner and the two couches formed in a makeshift L to allow prime viewing from any spot. Aaron's grandpa had designed the layout just like he'd had in his Boca Raton place before coming to stay with them, saying it made perfect sense, the most practical living room layout. Neither he nor his mother had argued and the furniture never moved again. The hardwood floors, spotless as always since his mother found out about the swifter mop that picked up dust flawlessly. She would make one run around the house every day, judging by the clean floors obvious even in the dark, Aaron assumed that ritual hadn't changed.

On the wall just above the TV was the family portrait. He stood at the feet of his mom and dad, no older than three or four when the photo was taken. Aaron remembered the photographer's assistant making funny faces just off camera to make him laugh in an attempt to get a smile on his face. It had worked; he was smiling from ear to ear like a child that just won the candy lottery. His mom and dad towered over him, both with a hand on his shoulder as they held each other's free hand just behind him. They all looked so happy in that picture, a new family just hitting the ground running. The picture was a fond memory of a better time, as well as a cruel reminder of what Aaron had lost at the same time.

Next to it was another family photo. This one was of him, mom, and grandpa. It had been taken on a fishing trip they'd taken when he was ten. His grandpa was standing on the dock of Lake Millawaya, just outside of Silverton where the best fishing in the state was, holding a cooler that was likely full of equal parts fishing bait and cold beer. He was smiling from ear to ear, just like Aaron was in the other photograph. Aaron was standing next to him, wearing an oversized inflatable vest incase he fell of the boat while fishing. He remembered asking why he needed a life vest if they were just going to be sitting and he knew how to swim, his grandpa responded by saying bluntly, "because I said so, that's why."

Aaron's mother was in the back of the picture, wearing an oversized sun hat and large sunglasses. She was sitting on the dock, reading a book and unaware a picture was being taken at the time. Aaron's mother hated boats, never trusted them and didn't like the idea of wearing a constricting life vest to save her. She'd grown up never learning how to swim, perfectly happy with leading a full life on solid, dry land. The water never called to her, she hated the idea of pools. Called them filth buckets every summer when he and Jack would run off to find relief at the community pool on the hottest days. Looking at the photo, Aaron realized now that his mom wasn't happy then, she was still trying to figure life out without his father. Seeing her smile when she was around W was in stark contrast to the woman in this photograph.

"Welcome home," W said, walking up next to him without Aaron realizing. "Your mother kept everything the same so you wouldn't feel weird when you came home."

"Yeah, it's kinda weird to walk into the past though. I guess I just assumed she would move on with her life while I was gone. I didn't expect her to keep everything the same just for me."

"You don't have kids Aaron so it's hard to imagine, but if and when you ever do you will understand that they always come first and are the first thing you think about when you wake up and the last thing you think about each night. Your mother never stopped caring about you, she spent forever hoping you'd walk through that front door and surprise her. After awhile she made peace with the idea that you were off on your own adventure, but she never gave up hope that you would return eventually."

Tears began to well up in Aaron's eyes. He never knew that was how she felt. He loved his mother, despite the hardships she'd faced with his father's untimely death; she'd always been there for him. Even on days when he'd come home from school and could tell right away that she'd been crying, she'd fixed him dinner and asked him how school was. Grandpa had helped with the day-to-day stuff, taking him to school and baseball practice, but his mother never missed a game. She was just trying to make it all work and it took longer than she'd expected it to, even for her.

Aaron felt an immediate sense of anger for dodging his return for so long. Being out on the road and fighting to make it by day after day had left him cold and narrow-minded. He couldn't see the forest for the trees and understand that all his mother wanted was for him to come back, even if it was just temporarily, to make sure he was ok and see her son.

"Don't bury yourself with it son," W said, seeing Aaron wrestling with emotions. "She doesn't hold it against and never will, she'll just be thrilled to see your home."

"Yeah," was all Aaron could muster, sniffing hard to quell his emotions.

Jack and Ashley had made a beeline for the guest bedroom, racing to see who got the bed and who had to sleep on the floor. Jack stumbled on the way and Ashley won the race, claiming the bed as victor. Jack threw down his jacket in disgust. Aaron smiled from afar, happy to see Ashley win and get the bed, even if it was against his best friend.

Bros before, oh screw it. Way to go Ashley.

All the commotion of the impromptu race had caused enough of stir that the lights upstairs came to life.

Mom.

■

Aaron's mom made it down the flight of stairs from the landing she was standing on when she saw him in a blur.

Words were not spoken; there was no time to lose. She crossed the living room and embraced him a hug that threatened to extinguish his very life force if it went on much longer. She squeezed tighter and tighter, equal parts overcome with joy to see her son standing in her living room after all these years and terrified he was a mirage or figment of her imagination that would disappear as quickly as it arrived. The tighter she squeezed, the more real the moment became.

For both of them.

All the nerves and anxiety Aaron had felt seeing Ashley through the grimy window at Jasper's paled in comparison to what he felt in this moment. He'd been trying to talk to her for as long as he could remember, that struggle seemed beyond childish as he stood in an embrace with his mother in their living room. There were nearly a billion things he wanted to say and she likely had a similar count on her end. Instead of blurting them out in a flood of noise between the both of them, the mutually agreed to keep this moment simple. Just a mother and son, together again after so long. Too long.

"When W texted me that you were really here, that you'd actually come home, I couldn't sleep a wink," she finally said, breaking the silence between them.

"You text?"

"I'm old Aaron, I'm not dead," she said, nudging him in the ribs.

"Fair enough, just don't recall you being much of a technology person. Memory serves me, you gave up on the TV for good, I believe the exact quote was, 'If it wants me to watch it wouldn't be so darned complicated to use,' before you threw the remote down and walked away."

"People change Aaron, we all have to accept things change eventually. Even if we don't agree with it," she said, finally pulling away from their embrace and giving him a knowing look that only a mother could give.

W had been standing just outside the kitchen, allowing them this moment, but had walked back into the living room to stand beside his mother. The two of them were a good match; even standing in a dimly lite house at three in the morning they looked good together. The type of couple you would see on a brochure selling you life insurance or a dental plan.

Aaron glanced over at the guest bedroom and noticed that the door was shut. He was glad that both Ashley and Jack had the consideration to give him this moment alone with his mom, but quickly worried what was going on behind that door. Aaron knew Jack would never try anything with Ashley, she was too smart for his tricks and to hear him tell it he was spoken for, but Ashley had mentioned earlier that Jack had talked him up quite a bit and now he was nervous as to what else Jack was over sharing at this very moment. Jack would never have done it maliciously, but he had a way of shooting himself in the foot like a child contestant on Kids Say the Darndest Things. He cut himself off from coming up with any worse case scenario's and let himself get back to what was happening right in front of him.

"Alright son, lets take a look at that eye in the kitchen," W said; receiving a worried glance from his mom that went from W, to Aaron, then back to W.

"What happened to his eye? Aaron, are you alright?"

"I'm fine mom, just a little misunderstanding at Jasper's earlier."

"Ronnie jumped him outside the bar and got a good lick on him," W elaborated.

"You were in a fight?"

"You should see the other guy," Aaron joked, misjudging the situation completely. Humor wasn't going to get him anywhere.

"Young man, if you think you are going to be fighting while staying under my roo-," his mother lamented him, even throwing his a finger waging while putting the other hand on her hip.

Classic angry mother pose.

"Relax mom, it wasn't a fight. Ronnie had too much to drink and took a swing at me. I handled it and W called the police to deal with Ronnie. I'm fine, he just caught me off guard is all," Aaron told her, feeling like he was pleading his case in front of a grand jury.

"I still don't like that you are already fighting with him, you've only been back for a few hours," his mother said, folding her arms and wearing a look of concern and anger.

"Honey, it's fine. I saw the whole thing and Aaron is telling the truth. Ronnie got out of hand, as he usually does, and lashed out at Aaron. Aaron subdued him and I called the police to take it from there," W chimed in, finally.

"What do you mean subdued?" she looked at the both of them suspiciously.

"He means Aaron said HELLO with his fist," Jack said, leaning out of the guest bedroom just long enough to get a word in before Ashley pulled him back in and slammed the door.

Aaron's mother stood in silence, looking at both he and W like they just got caught red handed trying to steal from the cookie jar. Aaron began to mentally prepare his defense when W just shrugged and grabbed the hydrogen peroxide from under the kitchen sink.

"No fight huh," his mother said, looking back and forth at them both accusingly.

"Way I remember it, Aaron made sure it wasn't a fight. He took care to make sure Ronnie wouldn't be any harm to himself or anyone else. Boy's got a hell of a right hook by the way," W said as he shot Aaron a smiling nod.

Not helping.

"Well that better be the last of it with Ronnie," his mother relented, plopping down on a stool in the kitchen island as W worked on Aaron's eye.

The peas to the face had helped keep the swelling down, but it wasn't going to stop it. Already, the area around his eye was puffing up and turning a yellowish purple as it started to bruise. The pain had subsided thanks to the Advil W had picked up at the store, Aaron quickly dry swallowing four the minute they were back in the car. Aaron watched out of his right eye as his mother tried to keep a straight face as she watched W work his magic. Not quite sure where he learned to dress a wound so efficiently, Aaron was thankful W was there to work on him if only to break the tension he could feel emanating off his mother right now.

"So, you find what you were looking for out there?" she finally asked, the question sitting on her lips for the last twenty minutes judging by the look on her face.

"Honey," W tried to interject on Aaron's behalf. "He just got home, we can wait to put the full court press till later can't we?"

"It's fine W, thanks though." Aaron waved him off.

He'd been running through the answer to this question for the last forty-eight hours since he realized he was going to return to Silverton. Every answer he came up with in his head seemed both horrendously dishonest and obviously fabricated to pathetic and sheepish. There was no good way to tell someone, your mother of all people, that you'd effectively wasted two decades of your life chasing a dream you didn't even really want anymore. The excitement of being alone and on your own quickly evaporates when you realize how hard life is and that everyone needs help. After thinking it through for the entire drive from Austin to Silverton, Aaron came to the only conclusion he could think of.

Tell the truth.

"I've been asking myself that question for so long, I've forgotten what I was looking for in the first place," Aaron admitted for the first time to anyone but himself.

The response he received was not the one he'd been expecting. Aaron had been prepared for anger, sadness, even resentment and lashing out, but what he got was a smile from both his mother and W. They looked at each other for a moment before his mother leaned across the kitchen island and took his hand in hers, smiling back at him.

"Life is not easy Aaron, no one can prepare you for how hard it really is once you try to go at it alone," W started.

"We are not meant to do it alone sweetie. When you father died, I lost myself. I realized for the first time in my life I had no one else to help me through it all. Your grandpa came down and saved us both. It took me quite awhile to open back up, to accept that I needed help and than someone could be there for me. W was the first one I opened up to, he understood exactly what I was going through, losing his first wife to cancer when she was only thirty. We connected on a level I'd only had with your father, I knew then that I'd been going about it all wrong. I was shutting people out, determined to find a way to do it alone. W made it clear I needed help, together we figured out who we were after our losses."

"Mom, I had no idea," Aaron started, trying to wrap his head around what she must have been going through, all while keeping a smile on her face for him.

"The hardest part of life is discovering who we are," she said, still holding his hand. "The second hardest part is coming to terms and finding happiness it what we discover."

The moment was cut short when the doorbell rang, startling all three of them as it cut through the calmness of the early morning. Aaron could hear Jack yelp from the guest room.

Aaron offered to answer it and started walking towards the door, with W a step behind him. Jack and Ashley had come out of the guest bedroom. Aaron almost tripped over the lounge chair in the living room when he saw Ashley in her pajamas. No one he knew wore pajamas, it was 2017 after all, but Ashley stood there in her pink and white pajamas, somehow looking even more beautiful than she did back at the bar. He quickly looked away when she looked over at him, easily catching him staring.

Smooth pal.

He reached the door as they all converged. Aaron wasn't sure why everyone was so interested in who was behind the door until he realized the two window panels that ran next to the door were glowing red and blue.

The police were outside.

Aaron reached for the door just as the officer on the other side rang the bell again, pulling off of the button when he realized the door was opening.

"Hello officer," Aaron said, the officer responding by ignoring him completely and looking over at W.

"Mr. Wheeler, you asked to keep any updates on Ronnie's condition when you called about him earlier," the officer stated like an autonomous robot.

"That is correct officer, I asked to be updated if Ronnie's condition changed or he needed anything," W said, stepping forward.

"I regret to inform you that Ronnie escaped the patrol officer's car on the way back to the precinct. He fled on foot and was followed, but we lost him."

"My god," W said, showing true concern for Ronnie even after what he'd done earlier to Aaron. "Is there anything I can do?"

"Mr. Wheeler, Ronnie was found dead a few hours ago. The coroner will have to do a full autopsy to confirm the cause of death, but it appears there was no foul play."

"OHMYGOD," Aaron heard Ashley say behind them, walking away back towards the guest room. He wanted to run after her but thought better of it, allowing her her space.

"What happened?" Aaron asked the officer.

"Initial reports is that it was an overdose," the officer coolly replied before handing W his card and walking back to his car parked in the street.

"Ronnie's dead?' Jack asked, confirming what he heard while not believing the inevitable had actually happened.

X

     The three of them sat in the living room while they digested the news.

     Ronnie was dead.

     Both Jack and W had a hard and sad look on their faces. Having dealt with Ronnie on a regular basis for most of their lives, he always found a way to bounce back and cause trouble once again. Everyone in the town had offered to help him in one way or another, but he just wouldn't have anything to do with it. Ronnie thought the only way for him was alone. It had to have been a slap in the face to realize that even with the best intentions, they lost him. Knowing you did your best only went so far and with a sudden death, they had just seen Ronnie no less than two hours ago, hurt. Aaron could tell they were both processing the situation in their own way; he wasn't going to start asking questions until they were ready to talk.

     Aaron began to think; maybe he and Ronnie weren't so different after all.

They both went about their lives thinking they, and only they, could do what needed to be done. Neither was overly interested in taking handouts or help, though Aaron had settled for working to make his way instead of the life of a vagrant that Ronnie had decidedly landed upon. The utter stubbornness that came from going about each day thinking that he was doing the best he could with the hand he'd been dealt had been slowly killing Aaron. He didn't see a way out other than winning the lottery or finding peace in living out the rest of his life alone as a bartender in Austin watching people have the time of their lives as he wasted his behind the counter. Coming back to Silverton, even for the few hours he'd been here had shown Aaron that he wasn't meant to waste away by himself, he had a great friend and family that was better than anything he had on the road. Freedom be damned, it was overrated the more he thought about it. Ronnie and Aaron had both found solace in their own personal abyss, thinking it was them against the world for way too long

It ended up costing Ronnie his life.

Sitting there battling his on mortality and decisions he'd made, Aaron realized that even though Ronnie was a real low life that practically sought out trouble, he had an impact on all of them in one way or another. Ronnie was the town mascot for disappointment, likely finding a way to let each and every person in Silverton down in one way or another. Even then, these people tried there best to help him. Aaron had been to a lot of places in his travels, seen drastically different towns and cities along the way. To see an entire town band together to help one person was beyond rare, it was basically unheard of.

W sat on the end of the couch, his mind lost in thought. Aaron had no doubt he was running through all that had happened to Ronnie in his life and what he could have done differently to avoid this outcome. W had more information on Ronnie than any of them since he was his counselor at Crest Hill. To most people, Ronnie was a problem child that grew into a troubled adult. There was more to the story than just a kid that was mad at the world, there always was. Ronnie never let anyone in, so that story remained a well kept secret that W likely knew enough of to never give up on him. They had to have had conversations that shed a new light on Ronnie's life, otherwise Aaron found it hard to believe W would have made it his mission to help him any way he could.

Jack sat next to Aaron on the other couch. He was less lost in thought and more overcome with shock than grief like W was. Everyone in Silverton knew that if Ronnie didn't change or seek help he would end up this way, but for it to actually happen, the same night as his scuffle with Aaron no less, was hard to wrap your head around. Jack had a pretty open mind, he wanted to concur Hell for crying out loud, but the real life gut punch of having a police officer tell you that someone you know just died was more than he was ready for right now.

No one is ready for that visit Aaron thought. After he'd closed the door and they went to sit in the living room to absorb what they'd just been told, Ashley escaping to the guest room with his mother in tow, Aaron couldn't help but connect this moment to the one he'd had all those years ago when the police rang the same doorbell to tell his mother that his father had been in an accident. Standing there and listening to the news again, almost eerily similar in the way the police address a death with a strict dialogue that felt rehearsed to the bone; it was no easier to hear. Ronnie and he had their issues, of that there was no doubt, but that didn't mean he wanted him dead. Aaron had some dark thoughts in the heat of the moment back at Jasper's, enough to even catch Jack off guard, but they were nothing more. Just a mental lashing out for being embarrassed in front of everyone.

In front of Ashley.

"Are the police even supposed to give us that information?" Jack finally said, breaking the silence since the officer left the front porch. "Isn't that supposed to be kept under wraps, what if they come back and find out there was foul play? They can't just knock on a citizens door and drop that bomb can they?"

"Charles was an old student of mine," W explained. "He was the one I called at Jasper's about Ronnie. I didn't want the police coming down and arresting him, so I called Charles to come get him and drive him around for a bit to sober him up. He was going to drop him off at the shelter afterward."

"He did punch Aaron in the face, maybe he should have been arrested," Jack said.

"And how well has that worked out in the past? Ronnie has been arrested more than anyone in this town and he never learns. I hoped a friendly hand tonight was what he needed, more than a cot and toilet behind bars. He's spent enough time in jail that if the system was going to change him it would have by now. Charles was the closest thing to a friend Ronnie ever had. They both came from a rough past that shaped who they were. Charles decided to listen to me, apply himself in school. He graduated and went straight to the police academy, where he excelled. He chose to come back to Silverton when he could have been stationed anywhere he wanted. Charles told me he came back to see if he could help someone like I helped him. He was convinced that he could get through to Ronnie when everyone else failed."

"I get it," Aaron nodded. "Can't keep banging your head against the wall hoping for a different reaction. You did what you thought was best W."

"Now I'm not so sure. Maybe if I'd had him arrested he'd still be alive. He would wake up in the morning, angry as hell at the world, but he'd still be alive."

"Don't beat yourself up over it. Ronnie made his choice. It's hard to live with, I get that, but you did the best you could with the situation."

W just quietly shook his head at Aaron's words; unsure he'd done the right thing and likely never would be. When someone dies as a result of a decision you made, there was no end to the second-guessing if it turned out to be the wrong decision.

"Was that why Charles was so robotic at the door?" Jack asked, noticing the same body language and demeanor that Aaron had.

"Charles had to have taken the news harder than anyone. He tried everything he could to get Ronnie on a better path. It's seems overly cruel that Charles had to be the one to find Ronnie like that," W trailed off.

"Speaking of taking it hard," Aaron whispered to Jack sitting next to him. "What's the deal with Ashley? She didn't seem all the broken up earlier about Ronnie after our fight, I didn't think she would have reacted that way to the news."

"I wondered the same thing, she's never been overly emotional ya know," Jack nodded in agreement. "She's more like you ya know, she keeps shit close to her."

"What's that supposed to mean?"

"I'm just saying, she doesn't wear her heart on her sleeve. She didn't even break down when Devin cheated on her and split town. Just rolled off of her like nothing."

"The fuck man," Aaron whispered in a yell, punching him in the arm. "You didn't tell me she and Devin were still a thing?"

Devin Porter.

Fuck that guy.

Devin was the high school prom king three of the four years they went to Crest Hill, thought only twice with Ashley. He'd been seeing another girl their junior year and no one knew about it till she was crowned queen instead of Ashley. Born with a silver spoon in his mouth, Devin was the golden boy the minute he hit puberty. He was taller, stronger, and, of course, better looking than anyone in school. It wasn't even fair when he was around, the girls all flocked to his side and the guys followed suit to be his friend and wingman. Devin was also athletic, lettering in football and baseball all four years. Of all the people Aaron loathed in high school, Ronnie didn't even compare to Devin Porter. He had it all, the grades, the talent, and the girl.

He had Ashley.

They started dating sophomore year and were together till the day Aaron split town after graduation. If he wasn't bad enough to be around, cocky as anyone Aaron had ever known, he also was dating the girl of Aaron's dreams. Devin knew he was the king of school and took every liberty to enjoy it. Just the thought of the arrogance he had back then made Aaron mad sitting on the couch. The only thing that kept him from punching a pillow as hard as he could was realizing that Ashley had dumped that sack of shit once and for all. Devin was the asshole that peaked in high school; he was probably working at a frozen yogurt stand trying to make enough just to pay alimony for the eight or nine illegitimate kids he'd fathered along the way.

Yeah, fuck that guy.

"Dude, you ok," Jack said, Aaron realizing he'd been watching him the whole time. "It happened almost eight years ago, I just forgot."

"Like you forgot about your girlfriend?"

"Can we not do this now?" Jack pleaded, nervous. "Why don't you go check on her huh?" he said, nudging Aaron off the couch.

"And the fuck am I supposed to say? 'Hey, I know we didn't really know each other and this night has been a real dick punch, but you wanna talk about your feelings?'"

"Sure, go with that."

"Would you just go talk to her for Christ sake," W interrupted, looking at them like he was trying to watch Leave it to Beaver and they were being too loud. "She's upset, but maybe it's not what you think Aaron. Maybe you should grow a pair and just go talk to her."

"Yeah!" Jack agreed, motioning a fist bump for W who ignored it completely.

"And you," W pointed at Jack. "Shut up or be useful and start some damn coffee."

Aaron tapped on the door lightly to see if they were still awake. On the brief walk from the living room to the guest room he'd come up with a scenario where Ashley and his mother had just fallen asleep on the guest bed, emotion getting the best of them and wiping them out.

"What?" Ashley responded, killing all hope of him dodging this entirely.

"Just wanted to make sure you guys were ok," he said, whispering through the door even though everyone was still awake after the news. "Saw you run off when the officer told us what happened, just wanted to see if you needed anything…or wanted to talk…"

Just hearing the words come out of his mouth made him feel stupid.

You want to put on a RomCom and talk about boys while we paint each other's toenails and gossip too? Jesus Aaron, really?

He stood at the door, the deafening silence enough of an answer for him. He couldn't believe that was his move, asking the girl that Jack had JUST told him wasn't really a talker or overly emotional if she wanted to talk. Aaron thought about tapping on the door again, but couldn't see any possible outcome where this didn't just make it worse for himself. He turned to walk back to the living room when the doorknob began to turn. Aaron spun around, expecting to see Ashley face appear in the crack between the door and the frame, and put on the most welcoming, supportive face he could.

Instead, his mother greeted him. She smiled at him, a smile that lacked any innocence. Of course she had to know Aaron liked Ashley. She was his mother and he was a notorious liar. If it wasn't tattooed across his forehead, his body language gave it away. She slipped out the door and gently closed it behind her, Aaron hearing the click as the door settled into its frame.

"What?" Aaron said at the look his mother was giving him. She just smiled at him like she knew a secret that he didn't and was thrilled to lord it over him.

"You should go in," she said, still smiling. "She could use a friend right now."

Aaron nodded, mentally preparing himself, and grabbed the doorknob to go inside.

■

Ashley was sitting on the floor at the foot of the bed. She'd been crying, obvious from the wads of tissue laying around her and the sniffing as he walked into the room. She looked up to see it was him and gave a faint smile before going back to the tissue to wipe her face. Aaron wanted to tell her than she could have looked like the devil girl from the Exorcist and he wouldn't have minded. He was just happy to be alone in the same room as her and not pass out.

Yet.

He walked over to the window and sat on the padded ledge. His mother had converted grandpa's old room into the guest bedroom they were in now. One of his grandpa's favorite parts of this room was his ability to sit on the wide window ledge and just look out the window. Rain, snow, day, or night, he would sit there and look out the window, all while seemingly happy as could be. It was his happy place he'd told Aaron when he was younger, a window into the world that allowed him to see everything he wanted. Aaron didn't realize till later that it had a perfect view of the backyard, where he and Jack would play day and night for years. His grandpa just loved to sit and watch them play, finding joy in seeing Aaron having fun and enjoying life after losing his father so young. Every laugh and every smile Aaron produced was a signal that his grandpa had done what he came to do, to keep things as close to normal as they could be so Aaron could grow up in a loving home.

Now he was siting in grandpa's happy place, trying to figure out what to say to the sad woman sitting on the floor at the foot of the bed. She didn't make any attempt to start the conversation so Aaron knew, against everything he believed in, he would have to be the one that started the conversation. To say he was less than conversational would be understating it, most of his interactions consisted of a head nod or eyebrow shrug to let the person know how he felt without succumbing to a dreaded conversation.

"Rough night huh?"

"Yeah, you could say that," Ashley mumbled.

"Were you and Ronnie close? He didn't seem to bother you back at the bar but you took it pretty hard when you found out about him."

"No. Ronnie and I weren't close. I did my part to help him, but he ignored my attempts completely. We all knew this day was coming, wasn't necessarily a shock to anyone."

"W seems to be taking it pretty hard," Aaron noted

"Yeah, he was probably the only one, aside from Charles, that hadn't given up on Ronnie."

"You knew about Charles?"

"Yeah. Your mom had him over for a book club meeting to get to know the town when he came back from the academy. We talked a bit, he was a freshman the year we graduated and knew some of the same people I did, and he told me why he came back to Silverton. I told him if anyone needed help it was Ronnie, was like a light bulb just clicked in his head. From there on he was determined to get to Ronnie before it was too late," she said. "I can't even imagine what it must have been like for him to see Ronnie like that. Ronnie was a real asshole all the way to the end, finding a way to hurt one of the only people in town that still cared one last time before he checked out."

Ashley didn't come off as the sad girl that was badly shaken by the news of Ronnie's death. If anything, she appeared to be more agitated than sad. Aaron couldn't understand what had her so upset if it wasn't the news of Ronnie's apparent overdose.

"So what's up then?" Aaron prodded, carefully.

"It's nothing," she tried to deflect, sniffing as she spoke.

"I may not be a great communicator, less so when it's with a pretty girl from high school on my mom's guest room floor, but I can tell when something's not right Ashley. What's going on?"

"Pretty huh," she said, looking up at him and meeting his eyes. She wasn't mad, so Aaron took it as a win and kept going.

"I've seen worse," Aaron joked, instantly regretting it and wishing he could take it back until she laughed.

"Real ladies man," she smiled. "Must put the moves on all the crying girls you come across."

"First off, that sounds bad when you say it like that, second, my mom says I'm a real catch so that's something right?"

"Sure it does," she said, patting him on the leg in sarcastic support.

"So, you going to tell me what's going on?"

"It's not a big deal," Ashley said, pulling herself off the hardwood floor and onto the edge of the bed so she wasn't looking up at him and could hold an actual conversation. "I just kinda snapped. It's been a rough couple of weeks planning for this reunion. Nothing has gone right and now Ronnie's death is like some sort of omen that I should just give up on the whole thing, send everyone home."

"What are you talking about? Jack has been talking up your reunion for the last twenty-four hours like it was the Mardi Gras of Silverton. He's pumped and so is everyone else by the atmosphere I saw at Jasper's earlier. At this point I'm pretty sure you could hold a burger party at Wendy's and people would have a good time."

"Jack doesn't know the half of it, only what I tell him and what he wants to hear," she sighed. "Truth is, there really is no reunion. I wasn't able to book the conference hall at the Silverton Inn, couldn't come up with the deposit needed to reserve the room. By the time I had amassed the money needed the room has been booked. I've been scrambling around town trying to put SOMETHING together but it seems the harder I push the worst things go. Isn't there a scientific theory for that?"

"Don't ask me, I spent most of my days in class daydreaming abou-," Aaron cut himself off, embarrassed.

"Daydreaming about what?" Ashley asked, a small smile forming on her lips.

"CARS," Aaron blurted out

"Huh."

"It can't be that bad right? There has to be somewhere we can do it right? Everyone in this town knows about this reunion, has to be someone that can help out." Aaron said, trying to refocus the conversation as it spiraled out of control.

"That's just it. I've been trying and failing for weeks now. I tried the rec center, town hall, even tried to do it in the city park. Would have frozen our asses off but it would have been something, but nothing worked. I showed up earlier to Jasper's tonight to plead my case to have the reunion there, tried to tell Jasper that the tips and food purchases alone would make it worth his while to close the bar down for one night. He wouldn't budge, said it was too little notice to bring all his employees in and that many people would break the fire code for number of people in a building at once."

"Jesus. I worked at a bar and remember it being shoulder-to-shoulder most nights. I don't think anyone ever thought about the fire code," Aaron mentioned, offering no solution to the problem.

"So now I have no venue, no food, no alcohol, and now Ronnie's death. I can't win. I don't know what I'm going to tell all those people that flew into town for this. Harry flew all the way in from Haiti! I can't even imagine how pissed they are going to be at me," she said, throwing her head in her hands.

"Has to be something we can do," Aaron said, thinking out loud. "What about the school?"

Aaron looked up, as Ashley jumped in place, at Jack standing in the doorway. Neither knew how long he'd been standing there or how much he'd heard, but judging by the look on his face he knew enough. He had that look that said he had the answer but wanted them to figure it out on their own. Assuming they had failed the test, Jack got impatient and blurted out the answer like a game show contestant on TV.

"What?" They both said in unison.

"The school. Why not use the school to do the reunion? Isn't that were most people do reunion's anyway?"

"Great," Ashley mocked, clapping her hands together. "I'll just call the Superintendent right now and ask if I can have the keys to the school to throw an impromptu reunion tonight. You think she's awake right now? Let's all get on the call, the more the merrier."

"I can help with that," W said, walking up behind Jack.

"Dammit, doesn't anyone respect a closed door? Were the two of you listening in the whole time?"

"Not our fault you didn't close the door while you talked to the 'pretty girl'," Jack mocked, with W smiling behind him.

Ashley blushed and Aaron clinched his fist hard enough to crack a few knuckles to avoid tackling Jack right there in the doorway.

"Anyway," W said, getting back on track. "Jack may have failed to mention, but I was promoted to vice principle last year."

"Oh wow, that's amazing W, congratulations," Aaron offered, while Jack rolled his eyes.

"He doesn't get it, gonna have to spell it out for him," Jack said, looking over his shoulder at W.

"I have my own set of keys to the school. I suppose I could allow for the reunion to take place there, only if I were allowed to chaperone of course."

"OHMYGOD," Ashley jumped up and hugged W. "That's amazing W. I can't believe you would do that for us!"

"Would be nice to see you all again one more time, maybe we could even hold a moment of silence for Ronnie with his other classmates if that's not too much?" W asked.

"Not at all W, it's the right thing to do," Aaron said, walking towards the rest of them standing in the doorway, but stopping short of the group hug that had developed in front of him.

"I'm glad I could help then, I'll grab my keys and you can start setting up after breakfast."

"I don't know if we have time for breakfast W," Aaron started before getting a stern look that he'd never seen from W.

"You're not going anywhere until you have breakfast, would break your mother's heart."

"Yeah!" Jack agreed.

"Oh shut up, you just want pancakes."

"Damn right I do, who doesn't? You some sort of comfort food Nazi?" Jack eyed him up and down.

"It's fine," Ashley said, putting her hand on his shoulder. "We can discuss how we are gonna pull this off while we eat. W helped by letting us use the school, but we still have no food or beverage for a reunion that happens in less than eighteen hours."

"I might now someone that can help with that," Jack offered

"Who?" Aaron asked.

"Did I mention I was seeing someone?" Jack smiled.

XI

Breakfast turned out to be as nurturing as it was therapeutic. The three of them crowded around the kitchen table as Aaron's mother and W whipped up a meal fit for a King. The smell of breakfast in the air acting as the signal of a new day, a new beginning, and they all made an effort to try and move on from what happened to Ronnie last night. Stewing around wasn't going to bring him back, the best they could do was plan a nice memorial for tonight to say their good-byes. Jack popped in and out of the kitchen to offer his unwanted assistance and steal bites of food as it was being prepared. Half a dozen times Aaron's mother yelled at Jack to leave if he wanted to keep all his fingers intact, though the threat didn't seem to hold much weight since Jack was sneaking back into the kitchen only moments later for a new score. W played along; sliding Jack samples while his mom wasn't paying attention, until she caught on to his antics and sent him out to the kitchen table along with Jack as punishment. If Aaron had to guess, W had helped Jack on purpose, having no interest in cooking after his task of frying bacon was completed, and was looking for a reason to be sent away so he could wait and read the paper with his coffee.

Ashley sat next to Aaron at the table, she'd sat next to him not even thinking about it, but the situation was not lost on him, having dreamed of sharing a meal with her other than being in the same cafeteria in school. She grabbed a notebook off a shelf in the living room to write in while they waited for breakfast to be prepared. Aaron did a double take when he realized that Ashley didn't just grab something to write on, this was her notebook that she'd left at his mother's house from a previous visit.

She keeps personal stuff over here too? This is like the goddamn Twilight Zone.

As Aaron watched Jack's failed extraction missions in the kitchen with awe, he had forgotten how resilient Jack was when he wanted something within reach, as Ashley furiously wrote in her notebook. He looked down and what she'd been writing and let out an audible laugh that drew her ire in the form of a deathly cold stare.

"What?" Aaron asked.

"You tell me, what pray tell do you find so funny?" Ashley fired back, still staring at him like a wolf about to demolish its prey.

"Nothing, it's nothing," he insisted.

"Aaron," she said, slightly tilting her head in examination as she eyed him. "Less than ten hours ago you were standing outside of Jasper's bar staring at me through a grimy window like a homeless person stares at donuts through a bakery window. Now you're sitting next to me openly laughing. Either you just grew and lost your balls simultaneously or your think something is funny. Which is it?"

"That's not...I wasn't...you sat next to ME!" Aaron said, tapping his index finger on the table defiantly.

"Spit it out, what's so funny," she said, that small smile forming on her lips at his sudden awkwardness.

"I wasn't staring." Aaron demanded.

"Look, it's fine. I get it. I was your high school crush, everyone had one," Ashley said, patting him on the arm. "You don't have to be embarrassed."

"JACK!" Aaron yelled, turning his head toward Jack.

"I didn't do it."

"Ashley says I had a crush on her in high school, care to share how that idea got in her head?"

"Seriously?" Jack said, relief washing over him. "Dude that's old news. I told her than a couple years after you'd left town. Didn't think you were coming back, didn't think you'd care to be honest."

"So you wouldn't mind if I called Sarah and told her you had pictures of her from each yearbook taped inside your binder since the eighth grade?"

"Uh, her vagina turned out to be busier than highway I-70 on Memorial Day dude. Doubt she'd even remember who I was since I didn't leave her with a baby."

"Eww Jack, that's disgusting," Ashley said, shriveling her nose at him.

"Just saying," Jack shrugged.

"How about you keep your thoughts to your self until called up from now on," Aaron said, glaring at him for telling Ashley about his crush.

"Your loss," Jack said over his shoulder, on his way back to the kitchen for more food.

As shitty of a thing as it was for him to do, Jack had a point. Aaron had cut town as soon as he could, leaving loose ends all over. It wasn't Jack's fault for assuming he wasn't coming back and sharing a harmless secret of a high school crush that meant nothing after the final bell.

All that being said, now he was back in town and sitting next to Ashley. Any chance of him playing it cool had been wiped away now that she knew he had feelings for her back then. It was hard to act disinterested when she already knew that he would be hanging on her every word even if he didn't want to. After all these years, time had done little to quell his interest in Ashley. A part of him felt like it was just yesterday that he'd left Crest Hill for the last time, still lovesick for the girl that he could never have.

That girl that was currently sitting less than a foot away from him, in his house.

"So," Ashley said, reattaching her evil glare on him after Jack walked away. "What is so funny?"

"It's not that big a deal alright. I just saw your map of the town and it looks like a toddlers plan to rob the city."

"It does not." Ashley defended, now upset.

"Come on," Aaron said, snatching the notebook from under her arm and holding it up on display. "You even have dashed lines for a trail and a big X on top of the school. Wait a second, is this a treasure map!" Aaron gasped, eyes widening in sarcastic excitement.

"Shut up," Ashley said, poking him in the rib to make him flinch enough to grab the notebook back. "We only have a few hours to put this all together, excuse me for not creating a realistic rendition of the town to your liking."

Aaron grabbed the pencil from behind her ear, a small spark of static shock from his hand touching her ear feeling like a thousands volts, and quickly drew a crude stick figure along the dashes.

"That's me, I'm on the trail boss," Aaron said, proudly pointing to the stick figure as she grew more impatient.

"You think you're funny huh?" Ashley said, leaning in toward him. Her lips coming within centimeters of his right ear, the small hairs around his ear tingling and sending goose bumps all over his body as she whispered to him. "I used to think you were kind of cute back in high school, shame you never said hi."

A horse tranquilizer would have been less effective. Aaron froze in place; the words ringing in his head made him unable to do anything but continue breathing. He couldn't move, blink, or think. She had effectively found his main power switch and fried his brain. He sat in stunned silence as she smiled at him, at least that's what it looked like out the corner of his eye, and went back to planning as if nothing had happened. Aaron sat motionless for what seemed like hours, unable to do anything but hear those eighteen words replay in his head again and again.

"Whoa," Jack said, coming around the corner from the kitchen and seeing him frozen in place. "You just see a ghost or something? You look like shit dude."

"I'm...good," Aaron said, finally finding the power to speak after swallowing his bone-dry throat. "I'm good."

Ashley smiled to his left.

"Breakfast is ready!" Aaron mother announced, bringing out plates of bacon, eggs, pancakes and hash browns to fill the center of the dining room table. "Eat!"

Aaron absentmindedly fumbled around the table with his plate, filling it up with food he wasn't entirely sure he would be able to stomach at the moment, as everyone else dug in around him. Pouring syrup on his pancakes and reaching for his cup of coffee, Aaron noticed Ashley out of the corner of his eye. Her evil smile was gone, replaced with a seductive look of interest at him, quickly looking away when her eyes meet his.

■

After they finished breakfast, Aaron hugged and kissed his mother good-bye, only being freed from her bear hug after promising it wouldn't be another ten years between visits, and they left. He shook W's hand and thanked him for the patch-up job on his eye, of which the swelling had greatly reduced in the last few hours. It was still tender to the touch, would be for a while, but it could have been much worse had W not been there to treat it for him. Aaron's medical experience had been to ride it out, not having insurance or the money to pay a doctor out of pocket. Any bruises or cuts that were not life threating got wrapped and iced, the rest was up to his body to handle, or at least that was the deal Aaron had made with himself.

The three of them got into the Shelby and he slowly backed out of the driveway, waving and smiling to his mother the whole time, while trying not to get sideswiped by oncoming traffic. Aaron spun the wheel and hit the gas, jolting the three of them forward and out of sight from his mother and W, still waving as they disappeared behind the neighboring tree line.

"Where to first?" Aaron asked Ashley, riding shotgun. Jack had called it, but Aaron overruled it as the driver and owner of the car, to a displeased Jack

"Bet if I had boobs you'd let me sit up front," he'd mumbled as he climbed into the back seat.

"You do have boobs" Aaron shot back, Jack blushing and sliding into his seat.

"I figure we head over to DK's and grab supplies first since it's the biggest task."

"Uh, who pays for all this," Aaron asked, as casual as possible to hide that he had less than twenty-five dollars to his name. "Did you get a stipend or funding from the school or something?"

"God bless plastic," Ashley said, tapping her purse sitting next to her feet.

"Wait, you pay for all of this?" Aaron said, surprised.

"We did receive a SMALL budget from the city, I'm talking less than four hundred dollars small, to put towards a reunion, the rest is supposed to be handled by fundraising or donations. I didn't bother with either seeing has how before thing morning I didn't think there was actually going to be a reunion. Would have been hard enough telling everyone there was no reunion, even worse if I would have taken money from them on top of it."

"Anyone going to ask Jack what he thinks?" Jack said from the back seat.

"Hadn't crossed my mind," Aaron joked, seeing Jack stir in the rearview mirror.

"What is it Jack, what's your grand scheme," Ashley asked as she read over her own notes, not even bothering to look up and listen to his reply.

"How about we go see my lady friend and have her help us out."

"Hahahahaha, your lady friend!" Aaron started laughing, "Cool your jet's Hef, this have an-."

"That might actually work," Ashley nodded, looking up from her notes and cutting him off mid sentence. "You really think she would be willing to help?"

"Why not?" Jack shrugged. "She went to school with us and she actually like's you, shouldn't be a problem to reel her in on the plan."

"Wait, who are we talking about now?" Aaron asked, looking between them both and the road, completely confused. "Is Jack really dating someone from high school?"

"Dating is such an old-fashioned phrase isn't it," Jack openly pondered in the back seat while Ashley rolled her eyes up front. "What IS dating really?"

"They are sleeping together," Ashley informed Aaron, to a loud clap from Jack in the back. "They are friend's with benefits."

"UP TOP!" Jack said, leaning in to offer Aaron a high-five in celebration.

"I'm driving you idiot," Aaron said, not even turning to acknowledge him. Jack leaned over towards Ashley and offered the now stale high-five.

"For the assist!" he said, waiting for Ashley to respond.

90

"He's not going to stop till you do it," Aaron said, as Ashley rolled her eyes and gave a faint effort of a high-five in response.

"COUNTS!" Jack cheered, falling back in his seat and shaking the Shelby slightly.

"Ok, so the new plan is go pick up Jack's 'business partner' and then what?"

"Let's see how this goes first," Ashley sighed. "She doesn't like most people, hopefully you're not on her shit list."

"What's she going to do, shoot me?" Aaron joked.

"Dude, if she doesn't like you, the best case scenario would be a bullet wound. She's scorch the earth type of vindictive to those she doesn't like."

"Seriously?" Aaron asked Ashley, getting a small smile in response to confirm Jack's statement.

"No pressure, just about to meet my best friend's lover and she may or may not shoot me in the face on sight," Aaron mumbled to himself.

"She won't shoot you in the face," Ashley reassured him. "She'll go for a leg to make it last longer."

"Ok then," Aaron said, not sure if she was joking or not. "So where does Medusa live?"

"Just keep driving north till you get to her house," Jack offered from the back seat, already having pulled his phone out to play games on.

"Quick reminder," Aaron pointed out. "I have no idea who we are talking about, how the hell will I know when we get to her house?"

"Trust me, you'll know it when you see it," Ashley said.

XII

The house that stared back at him, filling his entire windshield as he pulled into the driveway, shouldn't have been possible. It's shouldn't have even existed.

It couldn't.

Aaron spent his entire childhood in Silverton, seeing every square inch of this Podunk town in all it's glory. Silverton was practically hidden from the rest of the world, set inside a small valley within the Rocky Mountains that acted as guardians over the town. From one end of the town to the other was maybe seven hundred acres, give or take. Silverton was home to around six hundred fifty plus citizens, most having been born and raised in the same town. Everyone knew everyone, was hard not to become familiar with people that you saw every single day, like it or not. Not much changed in Silverton, plain and simple. Businesses that ventured in were quickly shown the exit by the city council, the rest not even bothering to break into the town since there was little to no growth opportunity to be had with such a small town.

These basic facts about Silverton made the house that Aaron was drooling over impossible. It sat just on the edge of town, just off interstate 550 and Mineral Creek, taking up more land that any single family member owned in Silverton. It easily took up over seven or eight acres of land, amounting to a small mansion in comparison to anything within an eighty-mile radius. Silverton Town Hall paled in comparison to this thing. It was a three-story villa; with at least four full-sized garages that Aaron could see as he pulled up. Two of the four garages were open, revealing luxury cars that were expertly washed and detailed. Aaron saw a cherry red Tesla Model S parked in the middle of the first one; the car had an entire garage all to itself and it's futuristic power center glowing red as it charged the electric beauty. In the adjoining garage was an alpine white BMW X6 M series, a stock model of this sedan started at around $102K. Sitting next to it was a metallic grey Mercedes G-Class SUV, easily a $120K vehicle from what Aaron had heard. The rest of the garage doors were closed, Aaron could only imagine what was behind door number three and four, but it was safe to say whatever it was, it was extravagant and expensive.

The driveway he slowly drove up was brick, something Aaron had only seen in magazines and movies. The brick set driveway created a path towards the mountain villa that Jack's lady friend called home. It was outlined in stone, with each outer wall consisting of hundreds of unique stones, no two even remotely the same. Dozens of full-length windows caught the glare of the sun as it continued its rise to the middle of the sky by noon, each windowpane outlined by wooden beams that helped to offset the stone walls for a distinctively modern mountain villa architectural design. There was a fountain just outside the front door, which Aaron chose as a good a spot as any to park since there were no assigned spots to park. Ashley and Jack popped out of the car and made their way towards the front door, Aaron climbing out of the driver's seat and leaning against the roof of the Shelby to take it all in.

"Someone we know lives here?"

"Yep, crazy huh?" Ashley said, Jack not bothering to answer as he turned and continued towards the front door to ring the bell.

"No shit," Aaron said to himself, stepping back to close the door of the Shelby as the front door opened and Jack's lady friend was finally revealed.

Debbie Thompson stood at the doorway, smiling at Jack and Ashley.

Aaron had to think deep to remember Debbie. The first thing that popped into his mind was that she was always called "Deb," and she HATED it. Drove her nuts that people shortened her name when she made it clear she went by Debbie. As far as he could recall, Debbie was your average high school student. She wasn't the most popular, but wasn't an outcast either. She stayed with her clique of friends and didn't make waves, choosing the path of least resistance to survive high school. Aaron had a couple of classes with her, she was always good in school from what he remembered, but not enough to be a valedictorian or Rhodes Scholar. She was just your average, everyday high school student.

And now she was the owner of easily the largest house Aaron had ever seen in his life.

"Who's that? Who's out by the car?" He heard her asking Ashley and Jack, covering her eyes in an attempt to block out the sun and make out his face from so far away.

"That's Aaron, he's back in town for the reunion and helping us out," Ashley pleaded his case.

"Jack's Aaron?" Debbie said loudly, Aaron unable to decipher whether it was excitement or rage in her voice.

"The one and only babe," Jack said, sweeping his hand towards Aaron like he was showcasing a prize on a TV game show. "I told you he wasn't dead."

"You told her I was dead?" Aaron called out, slowly making his way towards the door since he didn't see a weapon in Debbie's hand and deemed it safe enough to proceed, with caution.

"No, she told me you were dead. Said I was just making up stories about you to make up for losing my best friend."

"Awww," Aaron mocked, clutching his heart in a show of emotion.

"Still debating how I feel about you not being dead," Jacked eyed him, his arm wrapped around Debbie. "We'll see how the next few hours plays out, worse case I know were Debs keeps the guns."

Debbie elbowed him in the ribs, causing him to lose his grip around her and stumbled back a few steps in shock.

"My name is Debbie! Call me Debs again and I'll tattoo Jackass on your forehead as a permanent nametag and see how you like someone messing with your name," she glared at him before looking back at Aaron. "Anyway, nice to see you again Aaron. Would you like to come in for some coffee or breakfast?"

"That's really nice of you Debbie, and any other day I'd jump and the offer for breakfast and maybe a tour of your house. I have to say, your garage is a grown man's dream from just what I could see."

"Thank you!" Debbie beamed, Aaron noticing Ashley showing a hint of disdain at her attention towards him out of the corner of his eye. "I would love to show you around sometime. Maybe take a spin in that beauty you have parked by the fountain," she said, motioning towards the Shelby in all its glory underneath the mid-morning sun.

"That would be ama-."

"We really are on a bit of a time crunch Debbie," Ashley cut him off, now clearly agitated by their conversation.

Well I'll be damned, Ashley Meyers jealous.

Over me?

"Of course, maybe some other time," she smiled at Aaron, now somewhat uncomfortable himself with her gaze at him. Aaron noticed Jack glaring at him from behind Debbie, giving him the slice across the neck signal to back off.

"We just wanted to know if you wouldn't mind helping out with the reunion. Things got a little off track and now we are up against the clock for tonight. Jack mentioned you were great at planning big parties and we could really use the help."

Debbie's eyes glowed, whatever Ashley had said it involved the right words because the three of them knew her answer before she could even mouth the words.

"I'd love to! I love planning parties!" she said, throwing her hands up in excitement as she bounced from foot to foot in what Aaron assumed was some form of her happiness dance she did when she got excited about something. "Let me just grab the keys to the Ranger Rover and we can get to it!"

Ashley turned towards Aaron, smiling like she'd just won the lottery, which judging by the house he was standing at was hard to argue.

"Ashley rides with me," she called from inside the house. "We have girl stuff to discuss. You two can follow behind."

The three of them glanced at each other, none of them overly thrilled with how that sounded.

Debbie and Ashley were speeding back towards Main Street as Aaron tried to keep pace. He could have easily outpaced her in the Shelby, but was surprised nonetheless at how fast Debbie drove the Range Rover even if the streets were virtually empty on Sunday morning with most of the town choosing to go to church or an early brunch at Jasper's.

It was not lost on Aaron for second that the Ranger Rover she had casually grabbed the keys for, as if she was a mom grabbing the keys to her mini-van, was in fact a Supercharged Ranger Rover Autobiography. The midnight black SUV that was barreling down the road in front of them was yet another car in Debbie's garage worth close to $200K.

Jack sat completely still and quiet in the passenger seat, choosing to subject Aaron to the silent treatment for what happened back at Debbie's house. He had no intention of hitting on Debbie, hell he didn't think he was from the few sentences he'd actually spoken, but Jack clearly had a different theory. He would glance over at him with a death stare from time to time, just to remind him he was still pissed.

"Ok, enough man," Aaron finally snapped after Jack glared at him again. "I wasn't hitting on her. I didn't even know who she was until twenty minutes ago since neither of you would tell me who she was."

"Not what it looked like to me," Jack mumbled under his breath, just barely audible to Aaron.

"Seriously? Jack, Ashley was standing RIGHT THERE. You honestly think I would be trying to hit on Debs with her standing next to me?"

"Don't call her that! Her name is Debbie!" Jack perked up in the passenger seat and punched Aaron in his right arm.

"What? You called her Debs earlier," Aaron argued, ignoring Jack's weak effort at a punch. For a brief moment he felt bad for Jack, a grown man should hit harder than that.

"I'm her boyfriend, I get a pass."

"Not what it looked like to me," Aaron mumbled under his breath, just barley audible to Jack.

"I heard that."

96

"And?"

"And…Shut up," Jack said

They sat in silence for a couple more minutes when Aaron had to ask the question that had been sitting on the tip of his tongue since he pulled into the mountain villa Debbie called home. It was the elephant in the room that couldn't be ignored any longer.

"So…Debbie seems…well off," Aaron prodded Jack.

"What, now you want her money too?" Jack sneered back, leaning against the passenger window as he continued to sulk.

Aaron jerked the wheel of the Shelby to the left, just enough to get Jack's head off the window it was leaning against, and than jerked the wheel back to the right, sending Jack's head back to the window with a thud.

"Ugh, what the fuck dude?" Jack said, now holding his head.

"Enough man," Aaron stared at him, taking his eyes of the road for longer than he should have but taking the risk since the roads were barren on the outskirts of town. "I'm not trying to steal Debbie from you, end of discussion."

"Ugh, FINE," Jack said, still rubbing his forehead. "You could have given me brain damage doing that ya know."

"Worth it," Aaron smiled, the both eventually laughing about it moments later.

"So, what's the deal? How the hell did Debbie from high school become Debbie the billionaire?"

"Kind of a long story," Jack sighed. "Debbie left town a few years after graduation, she was/is some sort of savant with computers. She moved out to California to take a stab at the thriving technology scene, eventually landing with a small group of code writing wunderkinds that had lead the way during the whole Dot Com era. She ended up being a main code writer on some software that was eventually purchased by Microsoft, she was a millionaire overnight."

"Your telling me Debbie moved to California, became a tech savant, made millions, then came back to live in Silverton by herself on the outskirts of town?"

"Like I said dude, it's a long story."

"Keep talking, were not at D&K's yet," Aaron prodded for more information, now fascinated by this girl he barely remembered from high school.

"So it turns out, she fell in love with this big wig CEO of this other tech company that had been trying to steal her away for a few years. After she sold her software to Microsoft, she officially retired and started dating the guy. Things were great; parties in the Hamptons and money coming in by the fucking dump truck. They were unstoppable together. He would take her ideas to his company and bring them into reality, selling them off to the highest bidder for millions upon millions."

"But…" Aaron said, waiting for the other shoe to drop.

"But…Money was nothing to them so naturally they started looking for other things to bring them happiness and keep the spark alive. Debbie's idea of happiness was starting a family, she spent most of her days looking at real estate and baby books, they were financially secure enough that neither had to work another day of their lives. Hell, their kid's grandkids wouldn't have had to work at the rate money was coming in."

"But…"

"But her husband had a different idea of how to find happiness. His was through coke and strippers, and more coke."

"Ahh, the booger sugar," Aaron said, Jack nodding in agreement.

"Debbie found out about it when one of his most frequented female clients called her one night to inform her she was HIV positive and wanted her to know since they'd both been with the same guy recently. Turns out she knew all about Debbie, her piece of shit husband made no effort to hide that he was married. The money was just good enough that they didn't really care. Hard to say no when some flaccid dipshit comes to you with an offer for $5k for a BJ that will never happen before he passes out from his drug binge and forgets the transaction entirely."

"Jesus."

"Yep. Debbie got tested and when her results came back clean, they hadn't been sleeping together for some time so she knew he was up to something all those late nights, she immediately filed for divorce. And in California…" Jack smiled.

"The spouse gets half," Aaron finished the sentence, now understanding how she could afford all those cars and that house.

"Bingo. She took the sonofabitch for close to three billion dollars, made him pay for her lawyers and court fees too. Turns out, quite little Debbie is a fierce lion when you cross her. She sent out a mass email to all their friends exposing him, ending with him losing his company and fleeing to Mexico to avoid tax fraud charges. Imagine that, rich billionaire asshat wasn't even paying his taxes. Now he's a fugitive of the state and can't come back without paying all his debts and spending a few dozen years in federal prison for tax fraud."

"Holy shit."

"Right? So she took all her money and moved back to Silverton. She refused to live in town, something about having a Scarlett letter now and being too ashamed to live amongst us. I keep telling her that half the people in Silverton fart dust, they wouldn't care what she did."

"How did you two meet?"

"What? I can't meet a nice billionaire and woo her?"

"Um…" Aaron paused, too long for Jack's liking.

"Fuck you," he responded, with a visual to send his point home incase Aaron hadn't heard him. "She comes into the library every couple of weeks, has for the last two or three years. We hit it off, we share common literary interest, and one thing lead to another."

"All the way to pound town," Aaron concluded.

"SHE'S A LADY DUDE! Would you want me talking about Ashley like that?"

"Pretty sure you do don't you?"

"…Shut up…"

∎

Aaron pulled the Shelby into the empty parking spot closest to Debbie's Range Rover. He always left an empty space between his car and another, a barrier for the Shelby to lessen the risk of parking lot accidents from distracted drivers. He and Jack got out of the Shelby right as Ashley and Debbie exited the Ranger Rover. The somewhat frazzled look on Ashley face, along with the anything but innocent smile from Debbie immediately worried Aaron.

What were you too talking about?

"You too have a nice chat?" Aaron asked.

"We did actually," Debbie said, putting her arm around Ashley's waist as Ashley's usual pale skin tone turned a shade pinker in a blush.

Shit.

"So, we were thinking," Ashley started, choosing to look at Jack to begin with before meeting Aaron's eyes. "We should split up. We'll take the supply store, you two can grab the liquor and we can meet at Crest Hill in a few hours?"

"Wait, why are you dividing us up?" Jack piecing together what was going on. "How about me and Debbie go to liquor store and you and Aaron grab supplies?"

"No one asked you Jack, shut up and go get alcohol before I change my mind about letting you see me naked," Debbie shot back.

"Liquor store it is, let's go dude," Jack said, tapping Aaron on the chest as he walked back towards the Shelby.

"Uh," Aaron started, unsure how to bring up the fact that he had no money to buy the amount of alcohol this reunion was going to require. "So do I get just whatever or…" he trailed off.

"Relax sexy," Debbie assured him, pulling out her purse as Ashley's skin turned a shade pinker. "Take this and buy whatever you want, it's on me."

She handed him a solid black credit card. Aaron had heard about these, but they were more a myth than anything. When you were getting by from paycheck to paycheck and living out of vending machines and dollar menus, the idea that there was a card that had no limit seemed about as realistic as Santa Claus.

"Oh, cool. Thank you," Aaron said, graciously accepting the card as his worry about paying for the liquor melted away.

"For you, anything," Debbie whispered, Ashley shooting her a look of disapproval. "When you two are done buying the grown up drinks, swing by Mitchells and have him fit you two for suits. Tonight is going to be special and you two should be dressed the part."

"What's going to be so special about it?" Aaron asked, unsure he wanted to know the answer.

"It's Ronnie's memorial," Ashley jumped in, Debbie's smile all but confirming that was not what was going to be special about tonight.

"Oh, ok," he nodded, turning to walk back towards the Shelby and seeing Jack sitting in the passenger seat like a puppy he'd forgotten in the car. He was looking at him with anxiousness for what was going on outside his window. Aaron wondered if Jack was in on this, prepared to grill him later for answers.

"See you at the reunion," Debbie smiled and waved seductively, as Ashley turned yet another shade of pink. "Tell Jack he's invited too, I guess."

XIII

The mission had been set, both Aaron and Jack choosing to accept as Jack kept uttering in his best Mission Impossible voiceover in the short car ride from DK's to the liquor store. They were to acquire any and all forms of alcohol they deemed necessary for the reunion to be a success. Just because everyone was there to catch up and reminisce did not mean for a second that they were not all going to be relying heavily on a little liquid courage to get through it. As Glen had so eloquently pointed out, what were reunions for if not well organized Meet Cutes for young adults to quell untapped fantasies? Sure there were a few people that may have been genuinely excited just to see their old classmates, but they were few and far between those that had ulterior motives. Harry Mallavoy did not fly all the way in from Haiti just to bump elbows with old classmates, not since the invention of Facebook and Twitter allowed anyone to stay in contact if they truly wanted. Aaron had to guess that Harry had someone on his mind that he couldn't quiet shake and the reunion provided the perfect opportunity to lay his mind to rest once and for all.

Aaron just hoped that certain someone wasn't Ashley.

He also hoped Debbie wasn't going to make things more awkward than they already were between he and Ashley. For a while there they were getting along pretty well, Aaron had managed to have even a few conversations with her without passing out or vomiting. Ashley was just the girl he'd always suspected she was, funny and down to earth. Considering the circumstances in which they met, having his eye caved in by Ronnie only a matter of minutes after getting out his first few full sentences with her, she hasn't come up with a reason to bail or runaway so that had to count for something. Aaron had spent the last year or better in the Austin bar scene, where the women were all treated like royalty. Bars simply wouldn't run without them, they were the ones that brought the guys in from all around the nation to actually pay for the drinks. They knew it and acted accordingly, expecting the world on a platter and usually getting it. To see Ashley, still as drop-dead gorgeous as any of the girls in Austin, but human enough to blush when Debbie called him sexy, told Aaron he'd made the right choice to come back and he'd been beating himself up for not coming back sooner.

It was all playing out nicely, until Debbie entered into the equation and things got messy. She was Jack's girl, plain and simple. Aaron could never and would never do anything to mess with that, regardless of what Jack thought at the moment. If he'd arrived in town to find Jack had married Ashley he would have supported it. It might have taken him biting his lip hard enough to bleed, but he would have swallowed his pride and been happy for them. Just like he was happy for Jack and Debbie now.

The only caveat to this was Debbie didn't seem to have the same mentality when it came to loyalty. It was understandable that she wouldn't be so keen on settling down with any one person after what happened to her back in California with her billionaire douche ex, but Jack was a good a guy as she was ever going to find and it made it uncomfortable for all of them when she made advances on him, however playful and harmless they really were. Somewhere in Aaron's mind he'd have found a way to turn this into a positive, that it was nice to see two girls battle for him, but this wasn't late night cable. Jack was his best friend and Debbie's arrival had made him anxious for what was going to happen tonight.

"It's going to be a special occasion," Aaron repeated Debbie's promise, or threat, in his head as he parked the car next to the liquor store. They could have easily walked from DK's, but they both knew they were not going to carry what they bought all the way back so they drove a few blocks and took the lazy way out.

What are you up to Debbie?

"You think they are wine or champagne coinsures?" Jack asked as they walked into Stuckey's Liquor.

Stuckey's was a small venue, just off Main Street to keep the so called vagrants from the heart of the town when they got the urge for a drink in a paper bag vs. the one's served at Jasper's. Silverton wasn't an overly proud town, but the people here that wanted a drink usually chose to get it at Jasper's in the presence of friends or family. That being said, there were still those that chose to drink alone or have a party at their house instead of bear the crowd that inevitably formed at Jasper's around six most nights since it was the main restaurant and bar in town. For that there was Stuckey's Liquor, the small building holding just enough to be considered a liquor store but not much more than what you could find in a grocery store these days. The neon orange sign glowing even in the mid-day let Aaron and Jack know they were open for business. Odds are, they would find a handful of domestic beers and a few imports, mixed in with an eclectic array of wines and hard liquors that fluctuated depending on the season in Silverton.

"What?" Aaron asked, opening the door to an audible ding that let the store attendant know they had customers.

"The girls. Debbie and Ashley, you remember them? I just asked which do you think they drink, wine or champagne?"

"The fuck would I know? Both? Debbie strikes me as a tequila kinda girl more than anything."

"Debbie loves champagne I'll have you know," Jack defended.

"Then why the hell are you asking me if you already know what she likes?"

"Just trying to make this a team effort is all, you are in this just as much as me dude."

"In what? What do you know about tonight that you're not telling me?" Aaron cornered him, alarming the lady behind the counter that a fight was going to break out on Sunday morning.

"I don't know anything, I'm just as lost as you hombre," Jack said, pushing his way around Aaron to go down the first aisle, grabbing a shopping cart to start loading up. "Debbie is a bit of a wild child as you can tell, but this is a new level dude. She's never been like THIS before. Usually she just says what she wants, having billions gives you that luxury ya know. Now she's acting all coy, playing mind games with you and I. I'll be honest; I don't think I've ever seen Ashley blush before today. Even when she dumped Devin and was mad as hell, she was still Ashley ya know? This is different. Whatever Debbie has planned it's got his off her game too."

Well shit.

The first aisle, there were only three in the whole store, was lined with the suitcases and six-packs of beer. Shocking no one, Stuckey's had the biggest supply of Coors on hand. It was easier to get a locally brewed beer than it was to get a Blue Moon craft beer or Guinness; eighty percent of the aisle was of Coors products. Aaron and Jack grabbed four 20-pack suitcases of Coors Original cans, along with a few six-packs of Heinekens cause Debbie was buying so Jack said to grab and he'd take those home for later. They turned the corner and went down the second aisle, the aisle assigned to bourbon, whiskey, rum, tequila, and more.

The good stuff.

"So what do you think Debbie has planned for tonight? What kind of thing does she seem likely to pull on such short notice?" Aaron asked Jack, already hallway down the aisle looking at all the choices like a fat kid at a donut shop.

"It's Debbie dude," was all Jack offered in return.

"The hell does that mean?"

"It means…" Jack said, walking back to the cart with three 75ml bottles of Maker's Mark. "It means she could be planning a spur of the moment act of kindness like paying for a new wing of the school and naming it after Ronnie, or it could mean she's planning an Eye's Wide Shut style orgy for the after party and want's us dressed nice for pictures. Who the fuck knows with her right?"

"I'm sorry, did you just say orgy?"

"Yep. She picked up some weird shit in California. She's seen things they won't even film porno's about."

"And this is supposed to make me feel better how?"

"Who said anything about making you feel better? I'm just telling you how she is the coolest girl I've ever met, but she has a wild card essence to her than means she could be planning just about anything at this point. We could get to Mitchell's and be fitted for suits that make us looks like chess pieces, all part of a bigger plan for a massive live version of chess with the class of '07."

"What?"

"Never mind, just pick a bottle and make it expensive, you have Debbie's card in your pocket, let's make it count."

"Are you stealing from your girlfriend?"

"Stealing? You told me she said to get whatever we wanted, so I am doing just that," Jack said, putting two bottles of Captain Morgan Spiced Rum in the cart. "Plus, look at this place. We could buy every single can and bottle in this place and it wouldn't even make a dent in her bill. Probably pays more for cable."

Aaron found it hard to argue. After what he saw back at her mountain villa, the inventory of Stuckey's was nothing. He decided he would play along and get something nice while the opportunity presented itself. Aaron saw the bottle and walked right too it, the bottles being something of a legend for him back in Austin with the Rusty Knuckle. Pappy Van Winkle's Family Reserve sat on the shelf all by itself, a thin layer of dust having collected on the rim of the bottle telling Aaron it had been there for some time, untouched. When he noticed the price tag, hanging on the back to avoid scaring people away until after they picked it up and formed a sensory bond with it was one of the older tricks in liquor retail, he almost dropped it.

$1500.

The bottle in his hands was worth more than just about everything he owned combined, minus the Shelby. Aaron almost put it back when he remembered he had Debbie's card and she did tell him to get whatever he wanted.

Maybe Ashley and me can share this together later.

"Maybe Ashley and I," Jack grinned, standing right next to him. Aaron didn't even realize he was actually whispering what he was thinking, now nervous if he'd been so obvious when Ashley was around.

"Do it," Jack urged. "If you don't, I will."

Aaron nodded and put the bottle, gently, in the cart in the little bin next to the handle that was designed for delicate items.

They rounded the corner to the third and final aisle and grabbed a dozen or so bottles of wine, mixing a white and red variety to cover their bases, before heading to the register. When Jack pulled the cart up the register, the lady behind the counter looked at the cart and then the two of them a couple times to make sure she was seeing this right. Was likely they were Stuckey's biggest sale of the year, or at least right up there at the top judging by the haul they had in the cart.

"You two throwing some kind of party or should I call the police and give them a heads up?" she asked, not joking.

"Just ring us up Nicole," Jack said, clearly frustrated with her though Aaron had no idea why. Past history had to be the answer, though he could not place Nicole for the life of him so he doubted she was from their school. Nicole was in her later fifties, Aaron trying to remember if she was possibly a mother or aunt of one of his classmates that he just forgot about.

"Were stocking up for the reunion tonight," Aaron offered, for some reason feeling bad the way Jack sniped at her for no good reason.

"I don't care if you take it home and pour it all in a fucking hole you two idiots dug, not as long as you can actually pay for all of this," she barked back.

Fuck you too then.

"You'll have to ignore Nicole," Jack said to Aaron, noticeably loud enough for her to hear him. "She has this thing where she cannot, for the life of her, be polite to any other human being."

"If by thing you mean a desire for you to get hit by a bus, I DEFINITLEY have a thing, still do to this day as a matter of fact."

"Pleasant as always," Jack whispered back under his breath.

"I have a shotgun under the counter and I can justify shooting you surprisingly easily Jack, speak again and you lose a leg," she glared at him.

"Annnd we're at physical violence, a new speed record Nicole," Jack sarcastically said, wandering off to look at the makeshift cigar shelf next to the door.

"So, what's that all about?" Aaron asked, stepping up the register to pay.

"Do I look like a fucking diary to you? Either pay for this shit or put it back and go the fuck away."

"Jesus, you could use a trip to church lady," Aaron said, handing Nicole Debbie's Black Card. The total came out to just over $3,000, making him sweat even though he wasn't actually paying for any of it.

"I could use a vacation and a nice plowing, but instead I gotta get up early and open this shithole so you derelicts can get your freak on at all hours of the day," she complained, handing him back Debbie's card and receipt.

"You need me to sign anything?"

"Oh, you want to forge Deb's signature so I think your not using her card? Maybe I get a frame for it to put behind the register? Debbie called and told me you were coming dipshit, you think I would have just run a Black Card you handed me without blinking an eye? Would be a pretty shitty manager doing business like that wouldn't I? You callin' me a shitty manager?" she growled.

"And here I thought Ronnie was the town's black eye," Aaron said, immediately feeling crappy for speaking ill of the dead.

"The fuck did you just say?" Nicole asked, her arm sliding towards the shotgun under the counter as she eyed him. "You talking shit about my son you like prick?"

Aaron froze.

The moment presented many obstacles. First off, Nicole was currently fondling a loaded shotgun under the counter with the look in her eye that she was more than ready to pull it out and make ground beef out of him. Add that to the startling discovery that Ronnie's parents, or at least his mother, were still alive and one lived in Silverton all this time. Cap it all off with the glaring issue that Nicole obviously hadn't heard the news about Ronnie's death yet, though it made sense being that they only found out a few hours ago themselves.

Well shit.

"Nicole, holy shit, I had no idea," Aaron offered. "Ronnie never spoke about you so I figured you'd passed or moved away."

"I can't tell, are you trying to get shot or just stupid?"

"Nicole, ma'am, I am sorry to be the one to tell you this but Ron-"

Jack walked up behind him and grabbed his arm. Aaron spun and saw the look on Jack's face.

Not now, not like this.

Aaron nodded in agreement. He grabbed the front of the cart and began walking towards the front door with Jack in tow.

"The fuck are you doing, don't just walk away from me. Get back and say what you have to say like a real man you pussy," Nicole called out after him.

Jack and Aaron walked quietly out of Stuckey's, neither one of them saying a word all the way back to the Shelby.

■

They sat in the Shelby for what seemed like forever, neither one knowing what to say or wanting to say anything. Aaron had no idea about Nicole still being around, but drawing instant conclusions as to why Ronnie had turned out the way he did. Nicole was a real piece of work, growing up with her must have done a number on Ronnie. He was always an asshole, but now that Aaron had met his mother he didn't seem so bad. A product of his own terrible environment had caused Ronnie to be at a disadvantage at such a young age. Aaron wondered if anyone else in town knew that Nicole was his mother or if everyone knew and realized there was nothing they could do to really help Ronnie as long as she was still around to harp on him every single day.

"Did you know?" Aaron finally asked Jack.

"Yeah, I knew," he muttered, head down as he spoke as if he were in trouble. "She was always harping on Ronnie, W and I tried our best to keep a distance between the two of them, they always came back to each other. Would have been kinda nice if not for the fact the Nicole was the fuel for Ronnie's fire, literally handing him the bottle each time."

"How long did you know?"

"I found out a few years ago, by accident when I made the same slip and mentioned Ronnie around her. She blew up and I quickly made the connection. No one got THAT mad when you talked about Ronnie, not unless they were related. I told W about it and turns out he new about her since Ronnie walked into his office back in high school."

"And he did nothing? That doesn't sound like W Jack."

"Oh he tried. He notified the authorities, tried to get child services involved too. Problem is, in a small town like Silverton, there are only so many officers that are already over worked by the six hundred of so other townspeople that are always up to something. Vandalism, robbery, you name it. Silverton may be small, but there a shitload of people that act like assholes more often than you'd think. Mix that in with the fact that Nicole had never been abusive with Ronnie, at least not physically, so it was hard for W or the police to prove anything. No one could ever build a strong enough case for mental abuse, just wasn't enough cooperation from Ronnie to tell the authorities what was really going on at home."

"Jesus. All four years I wished Ronnie would get arrested or move so I wouldn't have to deal with him. Turns out he was fighting more demons than anyone could have imagined."

"Don't beat yourself up over it, none of us knew. W couldn't exactly tell any of the other students why Ronnie was the way he was. The cherry on top of it all was that Ronnie had been held back enough times that by the time he was a senior he was legally an adult so W couldn't even try to get him emancipated. Ronnie was too far gone, not willing to listen to anyone by then, especially not another adult, that trust was gone forever."

Aaron started the Shelby and let the engine idle for a minute while he thought about what Jack said. Ronnie had been through hell and had made it out the other end, but with too many scares, too much baggage, to become a normal citizen. It made sense now why Ronnie never ran away from Silverton the first chance he got, or why he never tried to apply himself in any way. Ronnie was lost, through no fault of his own or of others. His mother, Nicole, had effectively ruined his life, still around everyday to bury him deeper and deeper in his own hell. Aaron realized that the last interaction Ronnie had ever had with anyone was their fight last night.

Ronnie when out fighting, somewhere in there was darkened irony that Aaron didn't care to dwell on. They were late for their meeting with Mitchell so he put the Shelby in reverse and peeled out of the parking lot of Stuckey's, heading north to Mitchell's for their fittings.

■

The fitting at Mitchell's was uneventful; Aaron hardly even paid attention while Mitchell brought out option after option that he could tailor for them in an hour or better Aaron always thought tailoring took some time, a craft that couldn't be done in the blink of any eye, but apparently Debbie's money cast a wide shadow as the moment he and Jack walked in Mitchell all but pushed his other patrons out the front door and put the CLOSED sign in the window. For the foreseeable future, Jack and Aaron were his first and only priority.

"What is your favorite color Aaron, let's start there," Mitchell sigh, frustrated that nothing he brought out caught Aaron's eye.

It wasn't his fault, they were all nice suits, the hair on the back of his neck stood up when he thought what the price tags said on most of them. The issue came from Aaron being utterly clueless as to what to look for or expect in a suit. Living on the road, and in your car on lean days, didn't provide the luxury of becoming familiar with the fashion world. A clean, or remotely clean, shirt was good enough. Jeans had the same criteria, though looser on the clean portion once it became cool to wear well-worn jeans just about anywhere.

"Uhh, red," Aaron answered, to Mitchell rolling his eyes.

"Black?"

"Better, not a color, but better. Now, what is your favorite fabric?"

Aaron stared back at Mitchell, a blank look on his face.

"Never mind, just put this on and let me get your measurements," Mitchell said, handing him the suit in his hand and walking away in a huff.

"Yeah, Yeah ok," Aaron said, popping up to try it on, just happy to being doing anything other than sitting and being yelled at like a child. "Oh wow Mitch, this is pretty nice. What is this? Silk?"

"It's a Brioni and my name is Mitchell," he called back, working on Jack in the other room.

"Brioni," Aaron said out loud, still holding the suit in his hands. "Sounds classy."

"Debbie got me a Brioni last Christmas," Jack said from the other room. "She said it's the suit Bond wears and I told her I wanted to be buried in it."

"Wait a second, how much is this suit? There's no tag on it."

"That's cause my man Mitchell here doesn't bother with tags on the good suits. Only a few people in town can afford them and they don't ask about pricing?"

"I am not your bloody man Jack and if you don't hold still I assure you the next pin will go somewhere very unpleasant. Now hold still and pipe down," Mitchell chided him. "As for you Aaron, just put on the bloody suit so I may reopen my store."

XIV

The two of them drove down Main Street on their way to the high school; luxury suits bagged and hanging from the windows in the back. Aaron had tried to shake Mitchell's hand after he'd swiftly tailored their suits, but all he received was a simple nodding gesture as they were hurried out the door. Mitchell flipped the CLOSED sign on the door to OPEN in a single fluid motion as he closed the door behind them.

"He didn't like me did he?" Aaron asked Jack as they walked back to the Shelby, suits hanging behind them like makeshift capes as they both held the wire hanger in their curled fingers over their shoulders.

"Nah, he loves closing his shop to fit hillbillies with suits they could never afford if not for a beneficiary looking out for them. Probably why he got in the business in the first place."

"How much does this suit actually cost?" Aaron asked, hanging his over the back window behind the driver seat, Jack doing the same with his on the opposite side.

"You really want to know?"

"Yeah, your right. Best not to know," he nodded, sliding into the driver seat.

"$20K," Jack said as he slid into the passenger seat smiling.

"WHAT?"

"You asked."

"I just said I didn't want to know. SERIOUSLY? Now I'm gonna be nervous the whole goddamn night wearing this thing."

"Relax, I'm just messing with you dude."

"Jesus Christ, that is NOT funny Jack."

"It's actually $40k."

"I will punch you in the face," Aaron vowed. "Just Shut. UP."

Jack laughed, not stopping for a few blocks.

∎

They pulled up to Crest Hill High School and parked the Shelby.

Aaron wasn't sure if they were late, Ashley had only said to meet them here in a few hours, never providing a solid time they were expected. Since they only other car in the parking lot was Debbie's Ranger Rover, he had it on good authority that they were probably late.

Shit.

Jack must not have cared, as he slowly sauntered through the parking lot towards the main doors. He pulled them open, the click of the thick metal doors unlatching a sound Aaron had not heard in forever. Instantly, he was right back in school.

Literally.

The hallway still smelled like over mixed cleaning solvent, the janitor appeared to pass his recipe down to the next generation, as the tile floors shined in the setting sunlight that broke through the glass panels on the doors. Each wall was lined to the end of the hallway with lockers, only breaks coming for doorways and the occasional water fountain. He laughed to himself, thinking that even with all the new forms of technology, you couldn't find a payphone or VCR anymore; there were still water fountains. The top minds in science and engineering still unable to improve on the water fountain design.

At the end of the hallway was the trophy display case. As Aaron and Jack made their way down the hallway, or memory lane as Jack called it, the contents of the display case came into focus. Silverton was a small town, with only a couple of other local schools to call rivals. As such, the display case at Crest Hill High School was less than impressive, used more for pictures than actual trophies. There was the loan shining trophy in the middle of the display case, awarded to the class of '06 for the schools only championship. Crest Hill was the 3A State Champs in football; the team photo proudly displayed next to the trophy showed team captain Devin Porter standing smack dab in the middle of the photo, smiling from ear to ear.

Bet you're not smiling anymore are you, asshole.

The rest of the display case was littered with ribbons from spelling bee top five finishes, as well as a few chess match ribbons for the school's near first place finishes. Crest Hill seemed to pride itself on participation more than anything, the numerous *We Tried* ribbons that filled the display case proof enough of their appreciation in effort alone. Aside from the football trophy in the middle, Crest Hill's display case read like a sad story of what if's and could have been's.

"Where do you think the girls are at?" Jack asked standing behind him.

Aaron looked down both hallways branching off to the right and left of the display case. Not much had changed from when they had gone to school here. Sure, there was a new coat of paint and other minor tweaks that came with upkeep over time, but for the most part the school remained untouched. The sole new addition that they noticed was new layout of the front office. Some of the walls had been removed to make the principles office a little bigger and turned the vice principle's office into a large conference room. The vice principle's office was now across the hall next to the teacher's lounge and nurse's office.

"Probably in the gym getting stuff set up."

Jack agreed and they both headed down the right hallway towards the gymnasium.

■

"You're not dressed?" Debbie said the moment they walked into the gymnasium.

Aaron and Jack stopped dead in their tracks, mesmerized by the women that stood before them. Debbie and Ashley both resembled princesses from a movie, both appeared to glow in the bright lights of the gymnasium as light reflected of the polished hardwood floor back up at them. Debbie wore a midnight blue gown that fell softly to the floor and glided along with her every move. The gown had a plunging neck line and a high slit up the middle of the dress that came to a stop about four or five inches from her waste, exposing her well defined legs with every step she took. Jack may have been having a heart attack from the look on his face.

Aaron would have laughed if he weren't experiencing the same exact thing looking at Ashley. She wore a very similar form-hugging gown that split up the middle to show off her legs, only hers was hot-rod red. Unlike Debbie's gown, Ashley's gown wrapped around the top of her chest, with straps wrapping around both arms just off shoulder. Her amber-red hair fell over her shoulders and just on top of the dress. She caught him looking at her and blushed, but Aaron didn't care. He could only image the color of red he was just looking at her. When they had mentioned they were going to get dressed up for the reunion he didn't know what he was expecting, but now staring at Ashley he was lost for words. He smiled at her, receiving a smile in return, before forcing himself to break away from his gaze and look around at the rest of the gymnasium. He couldn't care less about what was going on around him, just didn't want to stand there drooling over Ashley and make the moment uncomfortable for the both of them.

Judging by the look of it, Ashley and Debbie had been here for at least a few hours getting things ready. There were banners hung all around the gymnasium doors welcoming the class of '06 to their ten-year reunion. Inside the gymnasium were all the makings of a party. There were long, folding tables put up everywhere, each one covered with a white tablecloth and a sign hanging on the front to explain its purpose. There was a table labeled DRINKS that was waiting for them to fill, right next to a table labeled NAMETAGS, that was just in front of a table in the back corner labeled COATS. The whole place was an OCD person's fantasy. There wasn't a place to sit that wasn't properly identifiable the moment you walked into the gymnasium.

Debbie and Ashley had done a marvelous job getting things ready, but they hadn't done it alone. Peppered throughout the gymnasium were a handful of former classmates helping get things set up for tonight. Aaron noticed a few of them, others he had no idea who they were and wasn't inclined to walk up and ask them either. He concluded that Debbie and Ashley likely bumped into them at DK's earlier this morning and told them what was going on, the ones that were here now having volunteered to come early and help set things up. Most of them were now working on building a temporary stage that would take up a third of the gymnasium. Aaron had no idea what it was for, the best guess was a band, but it seemed impossible that Debbie and Ashley had found someone to play on such short notice.

Just as impossible as the $3k in liquor and a suit worth possibly five-figures that was sitting in the Shelby outside.

"Why aren't you two dressed?" Debbie repeated, upset.

Jack stood there, mouth still agape at the sight of Debbie, unable to form a response.

"We figured you'd need help setting up, didn't want to get our suits dirty is all, we can change in the locker room if you don't need us for anything, looks like you have pretty much everything under control in here though."

"Oh, I can't stay mad at you," she smiled, putting her index finger on his chest.

That got Jack out of his spell.

"Just go get your suits and get dressed. The reunion starts in about an hour and I want to get a couple of pictures of the four of us before this thing gets started. Maybe a few singles as well, for later," she smiled, finger still on his chest.

"ALRIGHT," Jack stepped in, removing her finger from his chest. "Pump the brakes Debbie, he's Ashley's and you know it."

"Doesn't mean a girl can't dream," she muttered as she walked away to continue whatever she'd been working on earlier.

"Thanks for the assist."

"Just try not to steal my girlfriend dude, I really like her."

"I promise nothing," he smiled, Jack punching him in the shoulder as they walked out of the gym to grab their suits and liquor from the Shelby.

They went back the same way they came, passing by the display case as they moved towards the front doors. Aaron noticed that some of the pictures and ribbons that had been there a few moments ago were missing; empty spots now peppered the display case. He wondered why Debbie or Ashley had gone to the trouble to remove anything past their graduation year from the display case. It was unlikely anyone would notice such attention to detail and they were rushing just to get the gymnasium set up before 6 when the reunion officially started. As dusk fell on Silverton, the sun setting over the Rocky Mountains, Crest Hill seemed different. The shiny floor and freshly painted walls of the hallway now appeared grim and dirty. The glare of the sun off the polished floors gone, replaced with only spots of dull, well-worn tiles that were highlighted by the sinking sun as it made it's last gasp through the glass panels on the doors. Crest Hill took on a whole different ambiance at night, something that he never noticed since he never spent a night in the school before now. Aaron had never been to a dance or Prom, always finding it easier to stay away than go and feel the humiliation that came with not being able to ask Ashley to one and standing alone or next to Jack as they watched everyone else have fun.

Aaron could see a few cars filling up the parking lot as he got to the front door. He wasn't entirely sure how Debbie and Ashley had managed to get the word out to everyone on such short notice, but as people began to make their way towards the school it was hard to argue with whatever their methods were.

He pushed on door, the PUSH bar sinking with his weight against it, but the door didn't budge.

The door was locked.

"Who locked the doors?" Jack asked, seeing him unable to open the door as he pushed again.

"They aren't locked, at least not from the inside. You can't look this door from the inside; the keyhole is on the other side of the door. It must be jammed or something."

Aaron let go of the door and tried the one next to it.

Nothing.

"The fuck?"

Around released the PUSH bar and tried again, this time putting all his weight into the door, but it didn't budge.

"I don't get it, how is this even possible?"

Aaron was lost. It simply wasn't possible to lock yourself INSIDE a public building. The doors should always open from the inside; it would be a fire hazard if they didn't. Not to mention that it was physically impossible to lock it from the side that had no keyhole.

"Jack you think ma-."

Aaron looked over to see Jack, white as a ghost, standing next to one of the doors. His mouth was fully agape and he was sweating bullets. He couldn't image what had him so terrified, he could see out the windowpanes and there was nothing but an orange sky and a quickly filling parking lot, nothing that would have caused Jack to go white as a ghost.

"Jack, what is it? What's wrong?"

Aaron immediately thought it might be a medical emergency, that Jack was having a heart attack or stroke. He push back from the door and slid over to him, grabbing him by the shoulders, turning him away from the doors and towards him. Jack was still white as a ghost, his skin cold and clammy to the touch, and he had a look in his eyes of pure terror.

"What is it Jack, what's the matter?"

"ohfuck," Jack barley whispered.

"What?"

"ohfuckohfuckohfuck," Jack kept whispering.

"JACK," Aaron yelled, trying to get him to snap out of whatever was happening. "What the hell is going on?"

"ohfuckohfuckit'shappeningohfuckitsreallyhappening."

"What? What is happening? Jack!"

"ohfuckohfuckit'sreal."

XV

Aaron stood in the hallway holding Jack. If he let go, Jack would collapse to the ground, his legs visibly shaking under his pants.

"What is it Jack? You gotta help me out here pal, are you sick? You need me to call 911?"

Jack didn't respond, just stared blankly back at him, face still white as a ghost.

Aaron looked out the windowpane on the closet door, double checking that there wasn't a grisly murder or accident happening in the parking lot that he'd missed the first time he glanced out.

The parking lot was calm; nothing out of the ordinary was going on, just fellow classmates meeting one another and slowly making their way towards the front door. Aaron tried banging his fist against the door to alert someone, anyone, outside that Jack was in trouble and he needed some help, but either they were still too far away from the door or the door itself was thick enough that the loud banging he could hear each time his fist hit the door was silent on the other side. He tried yelling too, but nothing. He may as well have been invisible for his efforts.

I really am back in high school.

Jack had stopped sweating a little and some of the color was coming back to his face. He was still badly shaken and unable to speak, but it looked like whatever had happened was over. Aaron tried talking to him, looking for anything that could be of help to figure out what the hell happened, but it was no use. Jack just stood there, eyes bulging out of his head as he continued to whisper, "ohfuck," over and over again.

"I'm calling 911 Jack, hang in their pal."

He reached into his pocket to grab his phone, still using his left arm to temporarily pin Jack to the lockers to keep him from collapsing.

It wasn't there.

The only thing in his pocket was the key to the Shelby. Aaron switched arms holding Jack up and checked his other pocket, but came up empty. He didn't remember leaving it in the car, but it wasn't out of the question. Aaron didn't use his phone much, it was incredibly easy to misplace when he forgot he had it in the first place. It was probably sitting on the driver seat, having fallen out of his pocket when he got out of the car to come inside.

Fuck me.

He looked around, his head racing for ideas, and his eyes landed on the front office. There was a land line in that office he could use and it was closer so it beat dragging Jack back to the gym to use Debbie or Ashley's phone to call for help. Aaron didn't want to alarm them anyway, it was probably nothing, but seeing him bursting into the gymnasium holding a motionless Jack on his shoulder would have been a lot to process. He wanted to handle this himself, leave them out of it if at all possible.

"Ok pal, we are going to walk over to the front office so I can use the phone in there. You up for it?"

Jack's eyes darted back and forth, he had stopped whispering and taken to rapidly shifting his eyes in his head. Either way, he was still unresponsive. He tried to start walking towards the front office, Jack draped over his shoulder like a wounded solider, but Jack was heavier than he'd expected and he quickly realized it would be an effort to get them both to the front office any time soon.

He had to leave him.

Aaron slid out from underneath his arm, back to propping him up against the lockers, as he slowly helped Jack to the ground. Once he was sitting, Aaron stood up and sprinted towards the front office.

When he got there, the front officer door was thankfully unlocked and he burst through the door towards the phone sitting on the desk closest to the door. Aaron grabbed the phone and started dialing 911.

There was no dial tone.

He put the phone back in its receiver and picked it up again, hoping it was just a poorly timed glitch and it would work, but nothing. The line was dead. Aaron pressed all the buttons to see if anything would work, but still nothing. He double checked to make sure the phone was plugged in, not ruling anything out at this point as circumstances continued to pile up against him, and found that the phone was indeed plugged into the wall for power and connected to the wall jack for service.

The phone should be working.

The fuck is going on?

Aaron threw the phone down and tried the one on the next desk, but still nothing. He quickly tried every phone in the office to find that all lines were down.

What are the fucking odds?

Does this have something to do with what spooked Jack?

An old computer monitor was sitting on the desk he'd last checked, giving Aaron and idea. He could use the computer to dial 911. He remembered reading about the new wave of technology that allowed people to dial 911 from their computer if a cell tower ever went down and they lose reception. Google had rolled out E911, part of their Project Fi that allowed civilians to use an app on their computer to call 911. Aaron just hoped schools were one of the first to adopt this tech. It didn't even don on him that Silverton was unlikely to have Google Fiber all the way out here as he pushed the power on the monitor to boot it up.

Nothing.

The light on the monitor didn't blink at all when he pressed it again and a third time. Aaron suddenly realized he was standing in the dark, bursting through the door and charging to the closest phone, he'd forgotten to flip the light switch next to the door. He walked over to it now and took a deep breath as he flipped the switch up, hoping he was wrong.

Nothing.

Crest Hill had no power.

Well fuck me twice.

Landlines should have still worked even in a power outage, but they were clearly down too. What were the odds that the power AND the phone lines were both out at the exact same time? When he'd looked out the windowpane of the door nothing looked out of the ordinary, there was no massive storm brewing or collapsed power lines. It was just a normal, brisk day in the fall, nothing remotely out of the ordinary that would have caused this.

Aaron looked through the window in the office to check on Jack, make sure he was still sitting up right and breathing.

Jack wasn't there.

He rushed out of the front office to find Jack and almost collided with Jack as he turned the corner.

Jack had regained the color in his face. He was also standing on his own and moving so Aaron took it as a good sign that he was going to be ok.

"Jesus Jack, you scared the shit out of me."

Jack still had a look of abject terror on his face and was slow to form words as he tried to speak.

"Were fucked."

"It's just a power outage pal. Phones are down too, but it's nothing. We'll be fine," Aaron offered, lightly patting him on the shoulder for support and testing how stable Jack really was. He looked like he could go at any minute.

"You don't get it man, we are FUCKED," Jack yelled, punching the wall closest to him and putting a small dent in the locker his fist connected with.

"Calm down Jack, what is going on? Why are we fucked? Help me out here?"

"It's just like I talked about, JUST like I thought it would happen. I just lost track of everything, missed it by a mile when it was right in front of my face the whole time. Now we are FUCKED."

"Slow down, what did you miss? What is just like you thought it would be? What is going on Jack?"

"We have to get to the girls!" Jack said, a look of concern replacing the terror on his face. "We have to protect them!"

"Protect them from what?" Aaron asked, as Jack took off running back towards the gym where Debbie and Ashley were.

■

Aaron caught up to Jack easily, outpacing him by the end of the hallway. He took lead and headed towards the gymnasium. Aaron was still clueless as to what was going on, but if Jack thought Debbie and Ashley were in any kind of danger he wasn't going to just ignore him and do nothing. At the very least he hoped once Jack saw Debbie and Ashley were perfectly fine he'd calm down and explain what was going on.

They got to the gym and both burst through the doors, creating a loud enough noise to scare everyone inside the gymnasium. Debbie and Ashley both dropped what they were doing, Debbie letting out a shriek that echoed through the entire room, and looked over at the both of them in confusion and anger.

"The hell are you two doing? I thought I told you to go get dressed?" Debbie yelled, stepping over the punch bowl she'd dropped, it shattered to pieces at her feet.

Aaron didn't respond, he was too focused on the elephant in the room that started o give life to Jack's worry.

The lights were on.

On the off chance that someone put Crest Hill's gymnasium on its own, separate backup power source, likely a gas fueled generator that would have been hard to miss if not for size than the sound it would have made running right now, it was impossible that there was power in the gymnasium when the rest of the school was dark.

"Ashley, let me see your phone," Aaron said, walking towards her.

Ashley's gown did not have pockets, but she did have a small hand purse that she carried with her. Debbie had a similar bag herself. She nodded, understanding something was wrong by the tone of his words and body language alone, and popped open her purse to hand him her phone.

It wasn't there.

She gave a look of bewilderment as she thumbed through the small bag's contents to make sure it wasn't hiding under anything, then looked up at Aaron with a look of concern.

"It's not in my purse?" she admitted.

"Debbie, check you purse," Aaron demanded, pleasantries not worth the time if something really was wrong.

Debbie did the same song and dance as Ashley, from the initial opening and not seeing it to the frantic rummaging around the small purse to make sure it wasn't hiding under something. She looked up, equally confused, but a look irritation on her face.

"Alright, who took my phone? One of you better fess up, that case had real diamonds in it and I'm gonna be pissed if I found out one of you stole it."

"I don't think anyone took it Debbie, at least not anyone in this room," Aaron said, eyeing everyone to see if someone looked overly nervous or panicked. "Mine's missing too, was in my pocket less than ten minutes ago and now it's gone."

"What are you saying Aaron?" Ashley asked, now anxious.

"I have no idea what I'm saying, none of this makes sense," he said, shaking his head. "Jack and I went to grab the liquor and out suits but the doors were locked an-."

"Wait, how are they locked?" Ashley cut him off

"That's why I said, these doors don't lock from the inside. They CAN'T lock from the inside."

"Maybe you just weren't pushing hard enough sweetie," Debbie chimed in, annoyed and eyeing everyone herself to find the thief.

"I tried all the doors," he said, ignoring her. "They are all locked, or at least jammed enough that I couldn't open them putting all my weight into it."

"That doesn't make any sense." Ashley said.

"Get's worse," Aaron said, looking over at Jack as he stood there still in a state of shock. "Jack had a panic attack, turned white as a ghost and almost collapsed. I ran to the front office to call 911 but all the landlines were down, no dial tone on any of them. Tried turning on a computer until I realized the power was out too."

"But..." Ashley said, looking up at the lights in the gymnasium.

"I know."

"So what the hell is going on then?" Debbie asked, concern creeping into her body language as she shifted back and forth in her stance.

"I have no idea. Jack keeps saying something about how he knew this would happened, that he missed something, but I can't get more than a few words out of him. Whatever happened shook him pretty bad, he's still a shell of himself right now."

Aaron kept the part about him saying they were fucked out of it for now. They both seemed rattled enough as it was, there was no reason to pile on at this point when he still had no idea what was happening. There was no going back from telling them they were actually fucked; even the most rational person would react poorly to that kind of news. Aaron thought of himself as that rational person, but he was becoming more agitated by the minute without answers.

"Well snap out of it, we need to know what's going on!" Debbie said, slapping Jack in the face.

"We are all fucked," Jack muttered.

Well, cat's out of the bag now.

"What did he just say," Ashley asked, look of hope that she misheard him.

"It's nothing, he's just rambling. Don't pay attention to him."

"WE. ARE. FUCKED," Jack yelled.

"Jack, calm down. You're scaring everyone," Aaron whispered to him. "We are fine, you're just shaken up."

"We are fucked and they need to know it!" Jack continued to yell. "You guys have NO idea what we just walked into. We are fucked."

"If you don't calm down, I am going to put you down. Understand?" Aaron told him, grabbing his arms and shoving him onto the first row of the bleachers to sit and get himself together. "We are not going to scare everyone cause you lost your shit back there."

"You still don't get it do you?"

"Get what?" Aaron asked, looking back at Ashley with a reassuring smile that he hoped worked. "What don't I get?"

"If you would have paid attention earlier, you'd know exactly what I'm talking about."

"Earlier when? What the hell are you talking about Jack? The only things you've talked about since I got back are Debbie an-"

Aaron stopped himself, finally realizing what Jack was referring to. There was no way Jack honestly thought that all this really was what he thought it was. It would explain why he was so shaken up and disoriented, but all of this could probably be explained if they just kept their cool and thought it through.

"Jack, we are not in-"

A loud screech filled the gymnasium, most of the occupants in the room, including Jack, grabbed for their ears at the high-pitched sound. Aaron didn't have the same reaction, he had likely lost some of his hearing working at the Rusty Knuckle five nights a week, he immediately recognized the screeching sound to be coming from the speakers as the intercom system came to life.

That's not possible.

Aaron knew there was no power in the building to use the intercom system. On top of that, he'd just been in the front office only moments ago. The intercom speaker was in the main office, but it had been unplugged in and there was no one else in that office but him. The entire school was empty beside the few people that currently filled the gymnasium.

"GOOOOOOOOOOOOOOOOOD MORNING," a sinister voice reverberated over the gymnasium, causing everyone to instinctively duck for cover. ***"WELCOME TO MY HUMBLE ABODE. GET COMFY, YOU'RE GONNA BE HERE FOR AWHILE."***

XVI

"The hell with this."

Aaron didn't need to hear another word. Whatever Jack thought was going on was wrong, the asshole on the intercom all but confirming it for him. This wasn't a supernatural event, this was some asshole trying to play a prank on them and crossing the line. As he looked around the gymnasium, Aaron could feel the tension and fear in the air, it was palpable. Whoever this asshole was that thought this would be funny, Aaron had no idea who would or even could pull something like this off, had another thing coming. It was one thing to spike the punch, it was another to jam the doors and steal their phones just to scare them.

He took off straight for the gym doors, he was suddenly hell bent on finding this sonofabitch and making him regret his every decision leading up to this moment. This douchebag had scared Jack half to death, enough that he'd tried to call 911 for fear it might be something serious like a heart attack or stroke, and now he'd ruined the reunion before it even started. Ashley was crushed, she was scared too, but he could see the look on her face. Even with the Hail Mary that W had thrown her with opening up the school for the reunion, someone still found a way to derail the whole thing even when she'd been so close to pulling it all off. She was dressed up to the nines and looking forward to this more than anyone else if not for the effort she alone had put into it.

Not to mention this was his big chance to have that date with her he'd never had the courage to ask for back when.

And this jackass went and ruined everything. Even after he'd dealt with this prick, the night was all but ruined. No way they were going to go on like this didn't happen.

Wrong move asshole. Now I'm going to find you and physically make you understand all the reasons you fucked up.

By the time he made it to the doors, there were more people in the gymnasium then he thought and they were all crowding around the doors in a sense of panic. Made sense the group would congregate around the exit incase whoever this asshole was decided to take things farther than he'd already taken them, presenting a need to run away as quickly as possible. The sky outside the gymnasium had turned black, a quick turnaround from the dusk he'd seen out the front doors only a few minutes ago. It had been awhile since he had been in Silverton, but he didn't remember dusk turning to pitch-black night so suddenly. The hallways outside the gymnasium doors were also pitch black, a sign that the power was still out everywhere but the gymnasium they were standing in. The unwelcoming darkness of the windowpanes on the doors should have been unnerving, lord knew most of the other people in the gym had the same look of trepidation on each of their faces, but all it did was piss him off.

Aaron began running through a small list of names in his head that were capable, and big enough assholes, to pull something like this off.

Please let it be you Devin, PLEASE. I would enjoy punching you in the face more than anyone.

Finally, after politely moving people to the side and out of his way, Aaron made it to the gymnasium doors and put his had on the PUSH bar to head out into the darkness and personally introduce himself to the asshole behind the microphone in the front office.

"Where the hell are you going?" Debbie called from behind before he could open the door.

"Out."

"Like hell you are," Debbie shot back. "There is some lunatic out there in the pitch-black and you want to go out there and hunt him down by yourself? Are you crazy?"

"You know, you're right Debbie," Aaron said, annoyed, as he turned to face her. "Why don't we take a volunteer to go take care of that asshole that locked us inside the school and stole our phones. Anyone?" he asked, looking around the group for a reaction with his hands in the air.

The gymnasium was silent, quiet enough to hear a mouse fart.

"Exactly," Aaron said, turning back towards the door.

"She's right," Ashley chimed in, stopping him once again from trying the door. "We have no idea who is up there, but we do know they went to the trouble to steal our phones and cut power to the school so maybe we just sit tight and see what they want?"

"Because the last thing these pricks are expecting is an attack. They thinks they have right where they wants us. I say we let them know this isn't going to go according to plan tonight and see how they like being on the other end of things."

"At least take Jack with you, strength in numbers," Ashley pleaded.

Aaron looked over at Jack, still sitting on the front row of the bleachers right where he'd left him. Jack made no effort to move, even when they knew he could hear what they were saying and his name being called into action. He just sat there, dulled-eyed and upset, lost in his own thoughts and completely oblivious to anything going on around him.

"The fewer people the less noise and better chance I have of catching them off-guard, startle them before they can doing anything else stupid."

"When the hell did you turn into Jack Bauer?" Debbie asked him, a mixture of judgment and excitement in her tone.

"I literally have no idea who that is," Aaron said.

"Kiefer Sutherland. 24. Old network TV series" Jack said, causing everyone to turn and look at him.

"Jack, just sit down buddy. Were going to get this all cleared up so I you can get to a doctor," Aaron said, motioning him back to the bleachers.

"I don't need to sit down Aaron, I'm fine. Just caught off guard is all. I think I figured it out though. We are still utterly fucked, but I think I've wrapped my head around it."

"You have to stop saying that Jack, we are not fucked. It's just some asshole playing a prank and took it a little too far is all. I was just about to go introduce myself and see if I couldn't persuade them to change their mind."

"Or die trying," Debbie chimed in.

"Don't listen to her, it's fine. Just sit tight and I'll be right back."

"She's not wrong, you will die trying to stop this," Jack said as the group began talking amongst themselves in whispers. "We can't stop what's happening, only hope to survive."

Aaron saw the look on Ashley's face, of great concern, and wanted to deck Jack for saying that in front of her. He wasn't sure what had scrambled Jack's eggs so badly, but it didn't keep him from being pissed that he was only making it worse. There was no point in trying to argue with him, Jack was as stubborn as they came, so Aaron gave Ashley a reassuring smile, in hopes that it seemed genuine enough to pass as honest, and pushed against the door to settle this once and for all.

The doors didn't budge.

Not again.

He pushed again and again, putting more effort into the door each time, but received the same result. The door wouldn't budge. Aaron quickly tried the door next to it, hoping against hope it would be different this time, but alas, it too was sealed shut. The same doors he and Jack had burst through only moments ago were sealed shut, may as well had been set in concrete.

"It's no use," Jack said. "We aren't going anywhere he doesn't want us to go."

"What is he talking about Aaron?" Ashley asked, now legitimately scared. Debbie too.

Well fuck me.

"I don't know," was all he could think to say, being the truth made it no more reassuring to either of them by the look on each of their faces. "Jack, do you know who is doing this? You gotta tell me pal. If you know who is behind this you need to tell me so we can work on getting everyone out of here."

"He is," Jack said, pointing up towards the speakers in the gymnasium as they started to screech and pop for another incoming message from their imprisoner.

"LOOK," the voice reverberated around them from above the gymnasium, the sound echoing off the hardwood floors worse than a thousands basketball being slammed to the floor repeatedly. *"I'M NOT GREAT WITH INTRODUCTIONS, FACT IS I HATE MEETING NEW PEOPLE. YOU GUYS ARE ALL ASSHOLES FAR AS I CAN TELL, NEVER MET A DECENT ONE OF YOU IN THE ENTIRE BUNCH. PERSONALLY, I THINK THAT PROBABLY HAS SOMETHING TO DO WITH THE FACT THAT YOU ARE HERE, WHICH TELLS ME ASSHOLES ARE ABOUND IN THIS GROUP. WHAT SAY WE JU-"*

"WHO ARE YOU?" Ashley yelled out, cutting off the sinter voice mid-sentence.

Aaron just hoped that wouldn't come back to bit them in the ass later. Clearly this guy liked the idea of being in control and hearing the sound of his own voice, having locked them inside the gym after locking them inside the school. He'd never been in a hostage situation, but he was pretty sure someone interrupting an opening monologue wasn't a great idea. To say the guy, or guys since Aaron wasn't entirely convinced any one person could do everything that had happened alone, was likely operating on a hair-trigger seemed like a safe bet at this point.

"WELL THAT WAS FUCKING RUDE," the voice came back, audibly upset with her interruption, just like Aaron had hoped he wouldn't. *"MY NAME IS NONE OF YOUR FUCKING BUSINESS SUGAR-TITS. I ANSWER TO SIR, KNEELING, AND OBEDIENT SILENCE. ARE YOU HAPPY NOW? WAY TO CRACK THAT MYSTERY AND ASK THE TOUGH QUESTIONS. YA KNOW, I DON'T SAY THIS OFTEN BUT I REALLY THINK YOU ARE GOING PLACES."*

Just like that a burst of smoke filled the center of the gymnasium right where Ashley had been standing. It spread quickly and within seconds half or more of the gymnasium was lost in a wall of smoke that continued to engulf the entire room. The smoke gave off a red hue,

Aaron assumed it was a trick on the eye from the overhead lights, something he'd never seen before. The instant reaction was to assume it could be toxic, but there was no time to worry about later when Ashley was standing at the center of the blast.

"Ashley!" Aaron yelled, rushing towards the center of the red smoke to rescue her as everyone else near the smoke ran for cover screaming and coughing. It was impossibly thick smoke, dense enough to cut with his arms as he pushed towards where he'd last seen Ashley standing. The clouds that should have continued to disperse and fad with every passing second seemed to linger in the air, cutting his vision down to just in front of his nose as he continued to cut his way through the smoke to Ashley.

She was gone.

Ashley was no longer standing where she'd been only seconds ago. There one moment, gone the next, Ashley had disappeared in what would have been an excellent magic trick if not for the circumstances. There was no sign of a struggle; everything was exactly where it had been before the smoke bomb went off. Every single thing was exactly the way it had been moments ago, except the fact a living, breathing human being was no longer standing there.

Aaron stood in the middle of the impenetrable smoke cloud hugging air where she should have been. He was playing a crude version of Marco Polo, calling out her name and swiping his arms back and forth in hopes of making contact with her even though he couldn't see her. It wasn't possible; people didn't just vanish into thin air. The doors to the gymnasium were sealed and the doors to the outside were also sealed, there was nowhere for her to go, forget the fact that she had seemingly disappeared in the blink of any eye.

"Where is she?" Aaron called out, doing his best to keep his cool. Lashing out right now wasn't going to help find Ashley. Whatever had just happened had undoubtedly been a result of her pissing off the voice on the intercom. It was too much of a coincidence that the smoke bomb went off right where Ashley had been standing, only seconds after she'd lashed out. As much as he really wanted to lash out himself, he had to keep his wits about him, try to figure out what was going on and where Ashley was so he could get her and get the fuck out of this place.

"UHHH, I JUST FUCKING TOLD YOU SHE WAS GOING PLACES. ARE YOU DEAF, CAUSE IF YOU ARE, FUCK THAT. I NEVER LEARNED SIGN LANGUAGE AND I'M SURE AS SHIT NOT GONNA START NOW JUST TO

COMMUNICATE WITH YOUR WORTHLESS ASS." The voice shook the room as it roared over the intercom system. **"HOW ABOUT YOU JUST LET ME FINISH AND THEN WE CAN GET TO THE ONE-ON-ONE STUFF HUH? YOU FUCKING PEOPLE ARE ALL SO EAGER TO POP OFF WHENEVER YOU FEEL LIKE IT, JUST A BUNCH OF PREMATURE SHARTSNACKS WORTH LESS THAT THE BUNIONS ON MY FEET. YOU KNOW WHAT? FUCK THAT. YOU THINK YOU ARE SO SMART AND CAN'T TAKE A SECOND TO HEAR WHAT I HAD TO SAY, FINE. FUCK YOU GUYS, GOOD LUCK FIGURING THIS SHIT OUT ON YOUR OWN, DICKS."**

"If you hurt her," Aaron started as Jack grabbed his shoulder. He spun and saw the same look on his face he'd seen back at Stuckey's Liquor moments before he was about to tell Nicole about Ronnie's death.

Not here, not now.

"TAKE A QUE FROM FUGLY, NOWS THE TIME FOR YOU TO LISTEN AND NOT SPEAK UNLESS SPOKEN TO."

Jack had never actually spoken when he looked at Aaron, only showing the same look that he quickly understood.

You can read minds too?

"AS A MATTER OF FACT I CAN, AND I SEE SOME MESSED UP SHIT GOING ON IN YOUR TASTELESS MINDS RIGHT NOW." He responded, to Aaron's internal dialogue.

Well shit.

"HEY! QUICK QUESTION. CAN ANYONE GUESS WHO IS TOTALLY WET RIGHT NOW? ANYONE?? AWW, YOU GUYS ARE NO FUN. IT'S TOTALLY BECKY, SHE'S DTF AND THIS IS JUST MAKING HER HOTTER. I MEAN, WTF RIGHT? THAT GROSS BECKY."

The gymnasium went dark, screams coming from all corners of the room at the sudden loss of sight as they fell into darkness. A few overhead lights clicked back on a moment later, leaving the gym in a warm glow that was more apt to be found in a fancy restaurant than a school gymnasium. The lighting reminded Aaron of which you would find in a theater before the play started. It was almost identical to the lighting in the main tent during his time at the Renaissance Fair years ago.

Suddenly, a spotlight clicked on and glimmered down directly over Becky. She was standing all by herself, terrified and already sweating from the nights events matched with the intense heat that thundered down against her from the spotlight. Becky looked around the gym to realize everyone was staring at her and she immediately turned a bright red from the unwanted attention of her classmates.

"It's…it's not true, he's…he's lying," she shouted, shaking her head hard enough to knock her glasses off trying to defend herself from the voice's lurid accusations. "I'm not…I'm not enjoying this, he's…he's sick."

"TAKE IT OFF. TAKE IT OFF. TAKE IT OFF," the voice echoed around the gymnasium. ***"SHOW US YOUR TITS!"***

"What do you want from us?" Aaron questioned, taking the attention and spotlight away from Becky. Instantly he was washed over with the intense heat that came with the spotlight being cast upon him. "You really didn't seal us in here to get your rocks off on sick jokes did you? Cause that's pretty lame pal."

"HEY EVERYONE, CHECK IT OUT! THIS TANGY BLOODFART IS TRYING TO BE ALL BRAVE AND SHIT. LADIES, YOU SHOULD TOTALLY GET HIS NUMBER. BECKY, DON'T BE SHY NOW."

In the darkness, Becky started to cry.

Aaron wanted answers. Everyone in the gymnasium did, but they were either too scared or smart enough to know now wasn't the time to speak up. The more he thought about it, the less Aaron recognized himself at the moment. Living on the road, by yourself, taught you to watch more and act less. It was far easier to jump into something and regret it than it was to watch and gather information before making your move, especially in foreign situations. Usually Aaron found himself sitting back, waiting for the best moment to act. Instead, he was now yelling out at a faceless intercom system in a shouting match with their imprisoner. If it wasn't for the fact that Ashley had literally gone up in smoke, and he was terrified as to what actually happened to her, Aaron would have been content to blend into the crowd and gather as much information about the situation before making a decision on whether to act or not.

Fuck that, this asshole knows where Ashley is.

"I DO KNOW WHERE SHE IS," the voice responded, reading his thoughts again. ***"AND I WOULD TELL YOU BUT IT'S WAY MORE FUN TO WATCH YOU SQUIRM AROUND***

INSTEAD. THAT AND I DON'T HAVE TO DO SHIT I DON'T WANNA CAUSE I'M ALL GROWN UP AND YOU'RE NOT MY MOM."

"TELL ME WHERE SHE IS," Aaron demanded, hands balling into fists as he spoke.

"ALL RIGHT FUGLY, I'M GETTING NOWHERE WITH THIS ONE, CARE TO STEP IN AND EXPLAIN THE SITUATION OR SHOULD I JUST TOAST THIS MOTHERFUCKER RIGHT NOW AND MOVE ON WITH MY SPEECH?"

Jack stepped forward and put his hand back on Aaron's shoulder, pulling him around so they could talk face-to-face.

"He knows where Ashley is, but he won't tell you. Ever. He doesn't have to. He controls whether we all live or die, he controls whether we come back so he can do it again if he wants. He is in charge now, not us dude."

"What are you talking about Jack, who the hell is this guy?"

"He's the fallen angel, the cast out that makes things go bump in the night," Jack offered, hoping Aaron would understand and not have to actually say his name out loud.

Aaron knew what he was hinting at, it was obvious, but the look on his face must have been one of disbelief or confusion because Jack sighed and spoke the words he had been trying to avoid this entire time.

"He's Satan."

"DING.DING.DING," a bell chimed over the intercom, an exact audio replica of a boxing bell right before and after each round. **"FIVE POINTS FOR FUGLY! SIDE NOTE, POINTS DON'T REALLY MATTER DOWN HERE, UNLESS THEY DO, I HAVEN'T DECIDED YET. LET'S SEE HOW LONG YOU LAST FIRST. PROBABLY NOT A BAD IDEA TO TRY TO EARN SOME POINTS YOU GUYS. BECKY, I'M LOOKNG AT YOU."**

Becky's sobs intensified somewhere in the background.

"All the books, all the research I've been doing for most of the last decade were right. Hell is real dude. I know it's a lot to wrap your head around, it took the wind right out of me earlier, knocked me right on my ass. It's all real. The myths, the legends, the stories, the whole goddamn thing. Hell is real."

"HE'S ON FIIIIIIIIIIIIRRRRRREEE," the intercom rang out.

XVII

"The Devil?"

"Yup," Jack nodded his head in reply.

It still didn't make any sense, but Aaron couldn't argue what was going on was not ordinary. He'd tried as hard as possible to rationalize the night's events since he'd realized the front doors had been sealed shut, telling himself that there was a perfectly good explanation for what was going on. The leader it the clubhouse was that is was a group of deranged lunatics that got word the school would be open and they made their move to cause chaos while they could. Aaron told himself it was probably Ronnie's old gang, having by now heard the news of Ronnie's death, setting out to make everyone he grew up with suffer one last gut punch in honor of Ronnie. It was a stupid, childish thing to do, but Aaron told himself that Ronnie probably didn't keep the best circle of friends, most of them likely to pull a stunt like this.

It's what he would have wanted, they would be telling themselves, making everyone miserable one final time before scurrying off into the dark hole they came from to regroup now that their leader was gone.

It was just easier to put a face to this madness than rely on the possibility that Jack was right, that they had somehow slipped into the bowels of Hell and were stuck here for the foreseeable future.

That was until Ashley disappeared in a poof of smoke right in front of his eyes.

All the ideas he'd had in his head about what was or could be going on went out the door when Aaron saw another human, Ashley of all people, vanish in the blink of an eye. No matter how much he wanted to tell himself this was all still logically possible for a person or persons to accomplish, Ashley's disappearance was the kink in the hose to that theory.

It just wasn't possible.

Unless we are in Hell

Shit.

"I'm not sure I fully by into what is going on here Jack, that we are in the center of Hell and trapped by Satan himself.

"I PREFER LUCIFER, SOUNDS BETTER ON A RESUME DON'T YOU THINK? MOM SAID IT ALWAYS SOUNDED PRESDENTIAL, THAT LYING WHORE, BUT TO HER CREDIT I DID END UP RUNNING THINGS DOWN HERE SO I GUESS SHE WASN'T TOO FAR OFF. BUT STILL, FUCK HER AMIRIGHT? ONE TOO MANY LOOKS IN THE MIRROR AND SHE JUST THREW MY OUT OF THE HOUSE."

"Let's say for the sake of argument I believe you. How in the fuck did this happen?" Aaron asked Jack, choosing to ignore the voice booming down from the intercom.

"FUNNY STORY, I WAS JU-"

"I was talking to Jack," Aaron said, louder that usual to make sure the voice heard him loud and clear. "Not you."

"KEEP IT UP TOUGH GUY, I'LL SMOKE YOUR ASS OUT OF HERE JUST LIKE I DID LITTLE MISS FIRE-CROCTCH EARLIER."

"I would like nothing more," Aaron turned his attention to the speaker on the wall next to the mounted scoreboard as he spoke back to the intercom. "Send me to her RIGHT NOW."

"OH I WI- HEY WAIT A SECOND. ARE YOU TRYING TO TRICK ME INTO PUTTING YOU TWO TOGETHER? THAT PRETTY SLICK, I'LL GIVE YOU THAT, NARDS OF STEEL ON THIS SUMBITCH."

"Are you going just keep hitting on me or are you going to take me too her?"

"Aaron, don't!" Jack pleaded, the effort falling on deaf ears as Aaron continued to stare a hole in the speaker the voice was coming out of. "You're just going to make it worse dude."

He was fighting with an invisible opponent. Intimidation wasn't a valid option as he stood there glaring up at the speaker; he didn't even know what viewpoint this asshole had on them. It was completely possible the Aaron was staring at absolutely nothing right now, looking more like a jackass than a badass to their imprisoner.

"I'LL TELL YOU WHAT. I USUALLY WOULD JUST SNAP MY FINGERS AND HAVE YOU BURST INTO FLAMES LIKE AN OVERCOOKED TURDMELLOW, GET IT? IT'S A BLEND OF POOP AND A MARSHMELLOW, TURDMELLOW! WHATEVER, FUCK YOU GUYS," the intercom rattled. *"LUCKY FOR YOU, YOU JUST BECAME MY NEW FAVORITE FOR THE MOMENT SO I'M GONNA THROW YOU A BONE. I'LL SHOW YOU JUST WHERE YOUR WET DREAM IS, BUT I CAN TELL YOU YOU'RE NOT GOING TO LIKE IT. THIS IS HELL AFTERALL, I MEAN, WHO AM I TO SPARE SOMEONE A LITTLE EXTRA MISERY RIGHT?"*

In a flash of light a large circle appeared over the far gymnasium wall, covering the scoreboard and empty spots where banners were supposed to hang. The circle acted as a portal, the outline of its very existence blurred between the wall and the portal to another place or time.

Smack dab in the middle of the circle stood Ashley, her faced streaked with black lines where her mascara had run from crying. She was standing in the middle of a darkened room, not unlike the one they stood in now, and hand both arms wrapped around her as she continued to sob. There were no more tears, just dry heaves and shaking that made Aaron's blood boil.

"Ashley! Ashley, can you hear me?" Aaron called out, not entirely sure how the portal he was looking into worked. Was it like the two-way mirrors at a police station for interrogations or was it simply a hole in the wall to another place or time that he could yell through to speak to the other side? He had no idea, but wasn't going to miss the chance to speak to her if, by some miracle, she could hear and/or see him.

138

To his surprise and relief, Ashley perked up at the sound of his voice. She looked around the room, searching desperately to find the source of the sound.

"Aaron?" she called out weakly, slowly standing on shaking legs as she spun around the room eyeing every nook and cranny to find him. "Aaron is that you?"

"It's me Ashley, I'm here," he answered, not really sure how to explain where *here* was at the moment in relation to where she was. "Are you alright? Are you hurt?"

Aaron watched as Ashley did a physical inventory of herself, patting herself up and down looking for cuts or bleeding. She was unaware that she was being watched and Aaron felt sick to his stomach as he voyeuristically watched her. After she didn't find anything wrong, she responded that she was ok.

"I'm scared Aaron, what happened? Where am I?"

"I don't know Ashley, you just vanished from the gym in a cloud of smoke. I need you to look around the room and tell me what you see. Is there anything that looks familiar that can help us figure out where you are so I can come get you?"

"I'll…I'll look, give me a second," Ashley said, stabilizing herself and making a move towards the nearest wall to look for clues.

Ashley made it two steps before a large red bar appeared directly in front of her and zapped her; she fell back and landed hard on her side, the tears finding new life as they streamed down her face.

"ASHLEY!" Aaron yelled, utterly helpless.

"Aaron," she cried. "Aaron I'm scared. Please find me, please. I'm scared," she squealed between short breaths, her heart racing just by the look on her face.

"I'm coming Ashley, just stay there. I'll be there as soon as I can," Aaron yelled into the portal opening. "I'm coming."

With that, the portal began to close in on itself. The circle on the wall turned into a whirlpool, swirling around counter clockwise until it was a small speck on the wall. In a few seconds the speck was gone completely, no evidence there had been a window to another place just up on the wall.

"YOU LIKE THE PART WHERE SHE RAN INTO THE ELECTRIC FENCING? WOAH, WHAT. A. RUSH. RIGHT? I HAVE BEEN PLAYING WITH THE IDEA OF A CAGE WITHIN A CAGE, BUT I HAD NO IDEA IT WOULD BE THAT COOL

OR I'D HAVE DONE IN CENTURIES AGO. I AM A FUCKING GENIUS."

"If you hurt her," Aaron started.

"WHAT? WHAT EXACTLY TO DO YOU THINK YOU'RE GOING TO BE ABLE TO DO ABOUT IT? YOU JUST DON'T GET IT DO YOU? YOU ARE MY PLAY TOY NOW FUCKTARD, YOU ALL ARE. I GET A FANCY TO SEE ONE OF YOU BREAKDANCE NAKED OVER HOT COALS; ONE OF YOU IS GOING TO FUCKING BREAKDANCE NAKED OVER HOT COALS. THAT'S HOW THIS WORKS, FOR THE REST OF TIME. YOU SHOWED UP ON MY LAWN AND NOW IT'S MY JOB TO MAKE SURE YOU NEVER LEAVE AND ENJOY EXACTLY 0% OF YOUR TIME HERE. GET OVER IT."

Aaron marched over to the stage that the others had been preparing before everything when to shit and grabbed a miniature speaker that was going to be used for the band that was never going to show up now. He stepped back and hurled the mini-speaker as hard as he could towards the speaker bolted to the wall right next to the scoreboard. Aaron would have missed the speaker by a mile on any other day, but right now he was hyper focused and had more rage coursing through him than the Hulk in a NYC subway at rush hour.

The mini-speaker sailed through the air, finding its target with a direct hit. Both speakers smashed into dozens of pieces and fell back down to hardwood floor, making a mess just below the scoreboard.

Aaron walked back toward the bleacher where Jack was sitting, happy for the momentary respite from his voice, as everyone else in the gymnasium stared at him with wide eyes and mouths agape.

■

Aaron and Jack sat next to each other in silence for what seemed like forever, both trying to process what was going on in their own way. Jack seemed to have fully recovered from his frantic episode earlier in the hallway, all the color had returned to his face. Whatever he'd realized, he was at peace with it and hard at work trying to solve the puzzle of getting them out of this jam.

At least that's what Aaron hoped he was doing, if not they were probably fucked. He had to admit to himself the he had a very different set of priorities at the moment, those in which no one currently stuck in the gymnasium factored in to. Aaron wasn't trying to be an asshole, he cared what happened to them and would like to help them all get out of this if he could, but the cold hard fact of it all was that none of these people in the gymnasium were being held in an electrically-charged, double caged room with their life on the line. If he was being completely honest with himself right now, not a single one of them, himself included, meant a damn thing in comparison to Ashley.

It was juvenile to think they were in love, but he couldn't ignore the connection they had been developing in the last twenty-four hours, a deeper connection than he'd ever had with anyone else before, and he was not going to give up on that just because the odds were currently stacked against him. Shit happened, it was something you learned to deal with relatively quickly when living on your own with no money. The answer was never to fold, to tuck tail and run, it was to just keep fighting. Forge ahead no matter what. Aaron learned from his grandpa showing up at his house after his father died that there were two options in the face of adversity, give up or show up. His grandpa could have easily wiped his hands of the situation, choosing to live out his life with his old war buddies in a tropical climate, he'd earned that right serving his country the way he had. Instead, he'd chosen to pack up his whole life on a dime and move across the country to take on the burden of raising him and keeping his daughter-in-law's family together.

Sitting on the bleachers, Aaron knew there was no other option. He had to get Ashley back or die trying. He was not prepared to lose his life, the mere idea of it made the hair on the back of his neck stand up, but the only other play was to consider her lost and worry about himself and those still in the gymnasium. He was anything but a hero, nothing he'd ever done it his life would be considered even remotely heroic, unless he counted finding a way to survive numerous days on vending machine food a heroic task. This wasn't a move to win her heart, this was just the right thing to do and he was the only one here that was able to do it at the moment.

"Talk to me Jack, how do we get out of this? Whatever THIS is?" Aaron whispered, breaking the silence between them. He'd whispered to keep the conversation between just them until realizing a foe that could potentially read minds would not be caught off-guard with a whispered conversation.

"I don't know man, I just don't know," Jack said, shaking his head in defeat. "I've been running it through my head over and over and the one thing I didn't plan for was how to get out once we got here."

"You what?" Aaron raised his voice slightly, drawing the attention of some of the people in the gymnasium. "Your whole goddamn plan was to close the gates of Hell and you're telling me you didn't bother to maybe think of a plan for what to do once you got there? Seriously Jack?"

"I fucked up, is that what you want me to say?" Jack said, looking at him. "I got caught up in the moment and didn't have all my ducks in a row. I fucked up. I just wanted to do something that would change the world for the better, didn't think it would ever actually happen ya know? Part of me thought the stuff I was reading would always just be a legend, no matter how real it started to feel the more I read."

Aaron's anger faded quickly, realizing that Jack had just gotten carried away on a wild goose hunt and never meant any harm to come to anyone. Part of him knew this when they were standing in the library earlier, when he'd agreed to go along with his plan. Jack had always wanted to change the world, using the hero's in the comic book's he'd grown up on as his main source of inspiration. He was never going to invent something or build anything, that was for people much smarter than either of them combined and he admitted such on numerous occasions. Jack always knew if he changed the world it would be by discovery. Anyone could discover something; all you needed was patience and knowledge to know where to look. Jack had both of those qualities in spades as far as Aaron was concerned.

"Ok, so now that we ARE here, whatever HERE really is, how do we get out? Let's think this through," Aaron said, still holding out hope this was all just a bad dream as a result from a concussion he'd received from Ronnie's blow to the head, that he would wake up any moment back at his mom's house. "If anyone is going to get us out of this it's going to have to be you. You were always the thinker between the two of us. You can do this Jack. You have to."

Jack gave a brief smile, but it faded quickly and he went back to a somber look of residing to a fate he knew was inescapable.

"Let's start with the basics, how did we get here?" Aaron asked.

"I'm not 100% on that part either, but I think I know the fundamentals, " Jack nodded, playing along with talking out the problem. "When Ronnie died, Death came to collect his soul."

"Excuse me, WHAT?" Aaron said. "Death? As in the hooded guy with the axe?"

"It's a scythe, but yeah, that guy."

"Well this just keeps getting better and better," Aaron shook his head.

"So Death came to Silverton to collect, but when he did he opened a portal or something that allowed him to take the soul to its final resting place. Odds are, Ronnie wasn't going up the ladder if you know what I mean, so the portal that opened had to have been to Hell."

Aaron gave the gymnasium a quick perimeter scan just in case. He didn't know what he expected to find, just happy there wasn't a winged-demon sitting up in the rafters looking down on them. "So Death brought us all here instead of just Ronnie?"

"That's the part that doesn't make sense. It should have been just a standard transaction of a soul, but somehow all of us got stuck in the middle."

"That doesn't make any sense Jack."

NONE of this made any sense.

"How the hell do a group of people accidentally mosey into He-, the Abyss, and not even notice?"

"We shouldn't, at least not from what I've read. The portal should only be were the body is anyw-. Oh FUCK ME," Jack said, loud enough to draw more looks at the two of them from the others in the gymnasium. "Ronnie's here."

"Like, HERE here you mean?" Aaron said, looking around the gymnasium for Ronnie, ready to beat the living shit out of his soulless corpse. "He did this to us?"

"No. No, it's not like that," Jack said, standing to pace as he spoke. "Ronnie's body, it's in the school, he's here for the makeshift memorial Ashley was going to hold for him at W's request remember?"

"Sonofa…" Aaron muttered.

"Since he's here, that means the portal is here too. We all walked into this without even knowing it."

Fuck me.

"So how do we get out of here?" Aaron asked.

"That's the million dollar question isn't it?" Jack said, still pacing back and forth. "I don't remember ever reading about an escape from…here."

"Wasn't there a book about this we were supposed to read in high school? David's quest or something?" Aaron asked.

"You mean the Divine Comedy?"

"No, the one where the guy goes through all the layers of Hell," Aaron shook his head.

"That's the Divine Comedy dude. Dante's Inferno is just a part of it," Jack said, shaking his head and cracking a smile for the first time since this started.

"Oh," Aaron nodded, feeling more like an idiot than he should.

Who remembers all the shit you read in high school?

"So, how does Dante get out?" He asked.

"He climbs through Satan's waist and pops out on the other side of the world. Dante explains that Santa is the cork to the center of the earth."

"Sooooo…" Aaron started to ask as Jack rolled his eyes at him.

"No we can't just pop out the other side of the world dude," Jack said, shaking his head.

"Why not? We just saw a fucking portal open over the scoreboard for Christ sake, you can't tell me that popping out in China is that far fetched."

"China?"

"Yeah, isn't China on the other side of the world?"

"I mean, I guess," Jack started, but shook his head. "No. No, that's crazy. We don't even know where he is. He could be ANYWHERE, it would take an eternity to find him and that's not even factoring in saving all these people. Saving Debbie. Saving Ashley."

Ashley.

"So what are our options?" Aaron asked.

"Well, I can think of one, but it's not much better than your climb through Satan's bellybutton to China theory," Jack admitted.

"Lay it on me, I'm all ears."

"We kill him," Jack offered, a smile growing across Aaron's face.

XVIII

Kill the Devil.
Recuse Ashley.
Escape Hell.

Aaron couldn't help but shake his head just reading the to-do list back to himself. It was bad enough that even the idea of this all being real, or as real as it could be, began to sink in, now he had to figure out how to do the impossible.

Jack had continued to think of ways to defeat their captor, doing it as an improvised song in his head using general terms instead of actual people or places in attempt to throw of their mind-reading imprisoner from finding out what was really going on. The Devil was Ducky; the gymnasium they were all trapped inside was Bathtub. He paced back and forth in front of the bleacher, having the mannerisms of a lunatic that was just reciting the lyrics to a song stuck in his head over and over.

"Sooooo, when the Bathtub overflows, and the Ducky washes away," Jack sang to himself, trying to spark an idea that just wasn't there. "The toys in the Bathtub all drowned."

Jack hauled off and kicked the bleachers, sending a cracking noise echoing through the gymnasium and causing everyone to glance over at him. Aaron saw his frustration, but was happy that it just looked like he was losing his mind to the rest of them, and hopefully their captor as well.

Aaron began taking inventory of all the supplies and tools he had to work with. If the idea of being trapped in his old high school gym by a supernatural entity wasn't bad enough, the gymnasium offered little to nothing in terms of weapons or useful supplies. There were several folding tables, each covered with the same tablecloth, and that was about it. Most of the tables were bare, waiting for the reunion to start to become useful. The table for the coats and name cards would offer nothing unless he suddenly gained the strength of four men in order to weld an eight-foot table as a weapon. There was some useless audio equipment piled up near the equally useless stage, just an assortment of cables and now a single mini-speaker after Aaron had borrowed one to smash the speaker on the wall earlier. The sole useful item in the gymnasium was the microphone stand. If he had to, he could use the stand as a crude, improvised weapon.

He would've been more than happy to find he'd overlooked a machete or sawed-off shotgun someone had just left lying around. Messed up as it was to think it, schools had to worry about these things nowadays, the idea of finding a weapon on school property no longer unthinkable.

Unfortunately for Aaron, but good for the current Crest Hill students at least, there was nothing. It was as hopeless. Aaron did notice Debbie sitting on one of the folding tables and went up to join her, check on how she was holding up.

"You ok?"

"Well that's probably the dumbest question anyone could ask right now don't you think?"

"Fair enough, sorry I bothered you," Aaron nodded as he walked off, he didn't have time or any desire to get berated right now for something that wasn't even his fault.

"I'm sorry sexy, come back," Debbie said behind him.

Aaron paused, momentarily contemplating whether he should just keep on walking or go back and offer his support. He didn't really have time to play whatever this cat and mouse game they had going on, but he also wasn't going anywhere at the moment and decided talking to Debbie wouldn't hurt if it kept the both of them sane for when they needed to make a run for it.

Could we really just make a run for it?

"I'm just worried about Ashley."

"I'm going to get her back, I promise," Aaron said, wondering if he'd sold it enough for her to actually believe it.

"What is going on, who would do such a thing? Do they want money, cause I can pay them if they will let us go."

"I don't think it's about money Debbie," Aaron admitted. "He seems to be content with just holding us far as I can tell."

"WHY?"

"I'm still working on that part, or at least Jack is," Aaron offered as they both looked across the gym at Jack as he continued to pacing back and forth, ranting the entire time. "He's the smartest person I've ever met. If anyone is going to MacGyver us out of this it's him."

"Are you sure, he looks like he's still short a few marbles Aaron. I adore him, but if he's rattled to the point of snapping on us we need to think of a better plan. A backup just in case."

Well…you happen to know how to kill the D-

Aaron took notice that this was the first time Debbie had used his name instead of a childish nickname. She was obviously shaken more than she was willing to let on and he wished he could tell her it would be ok. He did notice that the stripped down, less superficial billionaire that was sitting on the table next to him was a pretty cool person, he hoped that when this was all over she showed more of this side of herself than the billionaire that bought and said whatever she wanted cause she knew she could.

IF we get out of this.

"Jack's fine, that's just how he thinks. Looks weird I know, but now you know why he never got laid in high school," Aaron joked.

Debbie snorted and quickly put a hand over her mouth to hide her laugh.

Aaron nodded in self-approval for making her laugh when he noticed the pile of smashed glass from the punch bowl Debbie had knocked over earlier. With everything going on no one had bothered to clean in up, it just sat there right where the bowl had met the unforgiving hardwood floor. He wouldn't have thought twice about the mess until he realized that because it was Debbie that was financing this whole thing, the bowl was not a cheap piece of plastic that they could have purchased at DK's for less than five dollars, it was a solid glass bowl that was worth more than necessary for a pop-up reunion in the small town like Silverton. Aaron wondered where she'd even found that bowl, figuring she'd likely brought it from home since no one in town sold such extravagant items that no one but Debbie would purchase.

In the pile of glass was a perfectly sharp edged and fine pointed piece of glass. Aaron quickly bent down to further exam them and was pleased to find that they were not a mirage, but actual, useable weapon if necessary. He grabbed it to give it a closer run through when the mini-speaker sitting next to the stage, and the gymnasium's only other makeshift weapon in the microphone stand, began to crackle. The power to it suddenly turned on even though the speaker was not plugged in and the volume knob spun all the way around to the maximum setting. The noise caused Aaron to involuntarily release his grip on the shard of glass in this hand, watching it helplessly fall to the ground and shatter into a dozen of more pieces against the hardwood floor that rendered the best option he'd found as a weapon completely useless.

"HAD TO STEP OUT FOR A MOMENT EVERYONE, TURNS OUT YOU AREN'T THE ONLY NEW GROUP OF DICKHOLES ON MY PLATE AND I JUST CAN'T PLAY FAVORITES NO MATTER HOW MUCH I WANT TO. YOU ARE ALL EQUALLY FUCKED AND THAT IS YOUR GOD GIVEN RIGHT. GET IT!! SHOUT OUT TO POPS FOR THAT ONE! NOW, WHERE WERE WE? WAIT, WHY DO I SOUND DIFFERENT, DID MY NUTS SUDDENLY UNDROP OR DO I SOUND DIFFERENT TO YOU GUYS TOO?"

Everyone in the gymnasium fell silent, half of them looking over at where the speaker on the wall next to the scoreboard used to be, now reduced to a pile of plastic and exposed cables in the wall after Aaron had destroyed it.

The other half of the room looked directly at him as if they were telling on him with their eyes since they were all too afraid to speak up after seeing what happened to Ashley.

"OH REAL MATURE," the voice roared out of the mini-speaker. *"WHICH ONE OF YOU SHIT-STAINS DID THIS?"*

Now everyone turned to look at Aaron.

"OF COURSE IT WAS YOU, WHO ELSE COULD IT HAVE BEEN RIGHT?"

"You come back just to bicker or you have a point to this visit?"

He was taking a risk; he knew that much the moment the words left his mouth. If this was the Devil he was dealing with, he would be

148

able to kill him with the snap of his finger or blink of his eye. Pushing back wasn't the smartest move in the playbook. Aaron was gambling on the hope that he was more interested in torturing than he was in just killing them. If killing them had been his primary goal, he wouldn't have sent Ashley to a different location and locked her up, he would have simply killed her and moved on. Aaron hoped this was the case, mentally preparing to burst into flames at any moment. He never did though, all that greeted him after his retort was dead silence, which bowed well for his assumption that it was more about his pain than it was a sudden death.

"I AM GOING TO ENJOY SLOWLY RIPPING YOU APART PIECE BY PIECE YOU KNOW THAT RIGHT? YOU HAVE TO, EVEN IF YOU'RE TOO COOL TO ADMIT IT, I CAN SENSE YOU FEAR. YOU KNOW YOU'RE FUCKED. HAVE YOUR FUN, YUK IT THE FUCK UP CHUCKLES, CAUSE WHEN THE BELL TOLLS FOR THEE AND I NEED A FRESH SKULL TO FUCK, YOU'RE THE FIRST NAME ON MY LIST."

Aaron hadn't noticed until now that Debbie was grabbing his arm, only realizing it as the promise to have his skull molested by Satan sunk in at the same rate her nails did into his forearm. He winced and looked back at her, Debbie's face begging him to keep quite and stop antagonizing him. The smart play was to do just that, he'd pushed far enough, there would be plenty of time later to get his shots in. Part of him, deep down, wanted these verbal spats to somehow throw him off his game and make a mistake, just enough that he could capitalize on it and get everyone out.

Get Ashley out.

Hopefully.

"LISTEN UP BUTTHOLES," the voice came back. *"I HAVE A SMALL FUCKTON OF TORTOURING AND MAIMING TO GET TO THAT I JUST CAN'T KEEP PUTTING OFF, WHAT'S SAY WE GET THIS SHITSHOW ON THE ROAD HUH?"*

There was dead silence in the gymnasium, he had everyone's FULL attention now.

"ALRIGHT, SO HERE'S TH-"

"WHAT DO YOU WANT FROM US?" Debbie yelled out, unable to hold it in any longer as her nails continued to dig into Aaron's forearm, blood slowly trickling down his arm as a result.

"DID SHE RAISE HER HAND? GUYS BE HONEST, DID SHE RAISE HER HAND TO ASK THAT QUESTION? NOT COOL BARBIE, NOT COOL." The voice shouted through the mini-speaker sitting next to the stage. *"ANYWAY, BEFORE 'OLE SAGGY SILICONE TITS INTERRUPTED ME, I WAS ABOUT TO LAY IT ALL OUT FOR YOU*

*SHARTMUFFINS LIKE BECKY LAID OUT ON PROM NIGHT...AND HOMECOMING... AND PRETTY MUCH EVERY WEEEKEND SINCE SOPHMORE YEAR. DAMN BECKY YOU WHERE A **REAL** WHORE YOU KNOW THAT. GOOD FOR YOU, GIRL POWER."*

In the crowd, Becky's sobs began again.

"YOU WET-FARTS STUMBLED INTO THE WRONG AREA AT THE WRONG TIME. SUCKS TO BE YOU, BUT TOUGH SHIT AND GET OVER IT. LIFE'S NOT FAIR SO WHY SHOULD THIS BE ANY DIFFERENT AMIRIGHT?"

No one uttered a word.

*"OOF, TOUGH CROWD TONIGHT. MAYBE THIS WILL WET YOUR WHISTLES. BECAUSE I'M A SPORTS ENTHUSIAST, WHAT'S SAY WE MAKE THIS INTO A GAME SHALL WE? YOU DILDOS WIN AND I LET YOU GO, JUST WALK OUT THAT FRONT DOOR LIKE THIS NEVER HAPPENED. I WIN AND YOU ARE ALL GOING TO BE MY PERSONAL ADULT DIAPERS FOR THE REST OF ETERNITY. I AM GOING TO PUT YOU FIFTEEN ASSHOLES THROUGH THE **RINGER**, AND I AM NOT GOING TO HOLD BACK SO PREPARE TO SHIT YOURSELVES LIKE SCARY JERRY DID WHEN I SHOWED UP EARLIER. ISN'T THAT RIGHT COLONEL BROWNPANTS? YOU'RE NOT FOOLING ANYONE STANDING OVER THERE, WE ALL KNOW YOU SHIT YOURSELF, I CAN SMELL YOU ALL THE WAY FROM **HERE**."*

Aaron turned to look at Jerry, standing in the corner of the gymnasium all by himself. Judging by the look on Jerry's face and the sweat pouring down all over him as it bled into is unfortunately light colored shirt to produce large pit stains, it was safe to say he'd done the deed he was accused of doing. Aaron found it hard to blame him, anyone would have soiled themselves from the events that had occurred, but it wasn't helping that everyone else in the gymnasium began to whisper and point at Jerry.

"Uh, there are actually sixteen of us, seventeen with Ashley," Jack said, the first time he'd spoken to the voice he'd defined as the Devil.

In the blink of an eye Jerry burst in to flames, so fast he didn't even get a chance to scream before he turned to ash and softly fell to the hardwood floor in a light colored pile of ash. The entire gymnasium erupted in panic, most choosing to go with a primal scream and yelling at the top of their lungs at what just happened while a few rushed to the gymnasium doors and began pounding on them to open, pleading to be let out between sobs.

Aaron stood, stunned, looking at the pile of ashes that used to be Jerry only seconds ago. As everyone else in the gymnasium lost their minds, Debbie screaming and yelling as she ran into Jack's arms and burst into tears, he took note of what just happened as a clear sign that this was not a single or group effort by former classmates to scare them liked he'd hoped against hope was the case.

They were in Hell.

We sure as shit aren't in Silverton anymore.

"AND NOW IT'S BACK TO FIFTEEN, NERD," the voice corrected Jack.

"How does this game work?" Aaron asked, his words getting lost in the crowd noise. "HOW DOES THIS GAME WORK?" he yelled to be heard over the hysterical crowd.

"I WOULD SUGGEST YOU ASK YOUR TEACHER FOR A CLASS SYLLABUS, DADDY'S FAVORITE DINGLEBERRY. NOW GET YOUR CLASSMATES IN ORDER CAUSE SCHOOL STARTS IN TWENTY MINUTES. ROOM 201A. HAVE A WONDERFUL DAY AT SCHOOL, OR DON'T, I COULD GIVE A SHIT REALLY."

With that, the voice left the mini-speaker. The volume knob twisting all the way back to the left as the power light on the unplugged speaker slowly faded.

Aaron looked across the gymnasium at Jack, hoping he'd heard it too and breathing a sigh of relief when Jack nodded back at him to confirm he had. Neither knew how they were going to corral this crowd to follow suit, but they had twenty minutes to do it or suffer the consequences that came with failing on the first part of the game.

Suddenly, the school bell rang, just like it had before and after every period in the past, alerting students that class was about to start or had just, mercifully, finished. The frantic crowd in the gymnasium all paused, looking up at the bell and fell silent. Aaron took the opportunity of a break in the chaos, jumping on top of the folding table he was still standing next to, the table creaking under his weight but not breaking, and addressed the crowd.

XIX

"Look, I don't wanna be here any more than you do, but this is happening and the sooner we realize it and get our shit together, the sooner we have a chance of getting out of here," Aaron called out over the crowd that had gathered around the table he was using as his soap box.

"Where's he hiding that he can see us but we can't see him?"

"Is Jerry REALLY dead?"

"We are going to die in here aren't we?"

The crowd reacted almost exactly the way he thought they would. They were not privy to the information Jack had shared with him back at the library, all they knew was the voice coming out of the speakers claimed to be the Devil and that Ashley and Jerry were now gone.

Jerry permanently, Ashley possibly not far behind.

Ashley.

It was everything he could do to hold back his temper, to unleash a barrage of filthy words and violent threats at the voice he knew was listening and watching their every move.

On the outside Aaron did his best to remain calm and collected to everyone else, judging by how everyone else had reacted to the situation it because alarmingly clear that he was going to have to lead the group if they were ever going to have a chance of surviving this. Aaron didn't see himself as a natural leader, he'd been hiding in the shadows and taking orders most of his life even before he hit the open road, but he emerged the only one that hadn't resulted to screaming at the top of their lungs or suffered a mental collapse that had effectively shut down his central nervous system to make him little more than a zombie.

"I understand you're scared, hell I am too. I get it, this is fucked up in more ways than one, but we have to remain clam and play along for the time being. Losing our minds and screaming at each other isn't going to bring back Jerry or stop this nightmare. We work together, watch each other's backs and put our heads together, we have a fighting chance," Aaron preached, pointing to the mini-speaker next to the makeshift stage where they'd last heard the voice. "He is just trying to mess with us, win the psychological war. We lose our shit, he wins. We break the rules, he wins. He is playing with house money and knows it, so he's not too worried about what we do cause in the end he thinks we are going to fail either way. Let's beat him at his own game, let's be smart and take our wins were we can get them."

The crowd, shockingly, seemed to take heart to his words, now whispering to themselves as the gymnasium filled with the soft chatter of the crowd. They nodded their heads and patted each other on the shoulders, signs that Aaron took as positives considering only moments ago everyone had scattered in a panic once Jerry burst into flame.

Truth be told, every part of Aaron wanted to react the same way they all did, to lose his shit and succumb to the madness that was happening around him. He didn't know what was making him stay sensible during all of this, whatever the reason, it was the only thing keeping him from being just another terrified classmate that shit his pants.

"So what do we do now, what was that bell for?" someone in the crowd asked, Aaron unable to place a name to the face without the nametags that never got made.

"Jack and I heard him say that we had to report to room 201A for further instruction, told us we had twenty minutes to do so or suffer the consequences."

The second he finished speaking he wished he could take it back. Aaron had successfully calmed the crowd and put everyone on the same page, only to induce frenzy when using the phrase 'suffer the consequences,' without even thinking about what it would sound like to a crowd of people sitting on the verge of chaos. The only thing that kept them together, that held the crowd intact and on task, was the light pile of ash behind him that used to be Jerry. Turns out, seeing someone get turned into a well-done Pop-Tart had that effect. They didn't want to hear it, but they all knew he was right. They had to get to room 201A or be just as well off as Jerry was, and Jerry hadn't done anything but be scared enough to lose control of his bowels. They could only imagine what breaking the rules of his sick game would bring upon them.

"That's all great and all, but last time I checked you already tried the doors and they were sealed shut. Just how the hell are we supposed to make it to room 201A in twenty minutes if we can't even get out of the goddamn gymnasium?" another classmate Aaron couldn't place asked.

Shit.

Whoever this guy was, he was right. The doors were sealed shut, there was no way out. Aaron immediately began wondering if this wasn't the plan all along, to trick them into believing they had even a sliver of hope of getting out if they miraculously beat the odds and won the game or defeated him. It would be just the kind of sick joke the Devil would play to crush their spirits and reaffirm that he was in charge and always would be for the rest of eternity.

As if on queue to quell his fears, all the doors in the gymnasium made a loud popping sound as the PUSH bars disengaged from the door and they all gently swung open, providing them with the escape they had only dreamed of earlier. The crowd whispered amongst each other, Aaron noticing a few forced smiles and looks of hope at the open doors. Jack and Debbie walked over to him as he jumped off the folding table, it gratefully returned to it's rigid form with his weight no longer standing in the middle of it, and gave him a smile and nod.

"Who knew you had inspirational speaking in you? Aaron I remember used to produce his weight in sweat during public speaking class. Look at you all grown up," Jack said, patting him on the back.

"For a second there I ALMOST believed we weren't as royally fucked as we really are."

"Not helping," Aaron shot back. "Don't think for a moment you're not leading this charge Jack. Just because I got up and spoke doesn't mean I'm leading anyone. You are the best equipped to figure all this shit out, I'm just going to try and keep everyone else alive long enough for you to figure it out so we can save Ashley and get the hell out of here."

"I don't know, you look like a leader to me," Debbie smiled, looking him up and down enough to make Jack uncomfortable by the look on his face.

"Calm down. He's not the brains of the operation, you just heard him say I was," Jack argued.

"I know baby and I'm super proud of you, but brains don't kill demons, muscles do."

"We'll cross that bridge when we get to it," Aaron said.

"I trust you," Debbie responded, a little too quickly for Jack's liking.

"So what's the plan?" Jack asked. "Are we really going to play along with all this?"

"I don't think we have much of a choice. Beats ending up like Jerry I guess," Aaron said, walking toward the gymnasium doors. The crowd split down the middle like the Red Sea to let him go first, Aaron doubted it was a sign of respect as much as it was a willingness to let him go first and take whatever was out there first just in case.

■

Room 201A.

Aaron hit the door first, with Jack and Debbie a few steps behind him, the rest of the group even further behind them. Everyone walked tentatively, taking extra precaution to give everything in the hallway a solid lookover before feeling comfortable to take another step. Aaron had a similar feeling when he walked out the gymnasium doors, everything that was so intimately familiar from the four years he'd spent walking these very halls felt vastly different, he couldn't put his finger on what exactly was different other than the entire aura that fell over the school that hadn't been there earlier. The dark hallways helped instill fear that shouldn't have existed in such a familiar place, these hallways were as familiar to him and the rest of the group as the back of his hand. Most of his classmates mastered walking the hallways with their heads buried in their phones, most never even bothering to glance up to avoid running into each other.

The tension in the hallway was palpable, everyone waiting for the jump-scare or worse after what happened to Jerry. It was quiet enough Aaron could hear Debbie's deep breathing and swore he could feel everyone's frantic heart beat to match his own. His heart was racing, but not out of fear as much as adrenaline looking for an opening to where Ashley was being held to make a run for it. It would have been a real dick move to give a speech about sticking together and then bolt at the first chance he got, but he was more than willing to be the hypocrite if it meant saving Ashley. Deep down he prayed that would be the case, knowing full well that he could easily be tricked into making a dumb decision in the heat of the moment, he just wanted to be able to do SOMETHING. It was eating him apart not knowing where she was or being able to do jack shit about it.

Aaron stood at the door of 201A, which was closed. He didn't try the door handle until the rest of the group was close enough incase it was another trick and only stayed open for a certain amount of time, leaving those that didn't make it to suffer a horrific fate in the dark hallway once the door closed. Aaron could just imagine having to watch as he was stuck on the other side of a locked door, forced to watch everyone else meet a grisly end right in front of him and do nothing about it.

"Everybody here, we lose anyone?" Aaron asked once they had all gathered around the door. Jack did a quick head count and have him the thumbs up that everyone was accounted for.

Well that wasn't so bad.

He leaned into the handle, with more force than he should have after the last few doors he'd tried were sealed shut, but the handle provided no resistance and twisted all the way down, the door opening easily. They all expected it to be locked; a few gasps escaping the group as the door came open made Aaron shake his head.

Walking into the room, Aaron got all of four steps into the room before he froze in place. He could not believe his own eyes, what he was looking at wasn't possible.

Mrs. Livingston stood at the front of the classroom, providing her stern glare that she'd become infamous for over the years. It wasn't intentionally nasty, just a result of a hard life lived by an old woman that took her job VERY seriously. From what Aaron could recall, Mrs. Livingston was never outwardly hostile to her students, she chose to be strict and professional at all times and that carried a persona with it that automatically deemed her dislikeable to every teenager in the building in their prime rebellion years.

Conservatively dressed as always, Mrs. Livingston wore her white hair in a tight bun that didn't leave a single strand of hair free. Her thick-rimmed glasses sat perched on her wrinkled nose, enlarging her judgmental eyes for even the students in the back of the room to see. Mrs. Livingston wore her signature dark navy dress that looked like the uniform of a colonial cult member. She stood rigidly next to her desk, one hand on the desk with the other placed disapprovingly on her hip as she eyed each one of them as they came through the door. Aaron wasn't the only one that was caught off guard, he peeked over his shoulder to see the surprised and shocked looks on everyone's faces as they were all just as thrown off by Mrs. Livingston's presence as he was.

See, there was one GLARING problem with Mrs. Livingston standing at the front of the room; her stern and disapproving glare falling on each one of them equally without prejudice.

Mrs. Livingston has passed away in the first few weeks of their senior year.

Crest Hill had closed for the rest of that week as the town mourned her sudden death. She'd taken a brief leave of absence to deal with some medical issues, but no one in Crest Hill, or Silverton for that matter, thought anything could stop Mrs. Livingston from doing what she loved. Mrs. Livingston lost her husband in WWII, Aaron's grandpa having crossed paths with him briefly in Berlin before shipping off to a different out post. She never remarried, choosing to throw her life into her work instead of re-opening the wound that losing her true love had caused. She became bitter and cold towards most people, never fully able to come to terms with losing everything in the blink of an eye for a war she grew to despise. Those in her intimate inner-circle spoke of a different woman at her funeral, one that never came out in the public eye. She would laugh and smile all the time, always enthusiastic to teach a new batch of youngsters each year and prepare them for the world ahead.

Now she was standing right in front of them.

Alive.

"Mrs. Livingston?" Jack asked, the first one to break the silence as everyone tried to wrap their heads around seeing her alive again. After what happened to Jerry it should have come as no surprise that anything was possible, but no one expected to see a figure from their past raised from the dead.

"Mr. Harwell, so happy you could join us. On time today, a welcome surprise from your usual tardiness," she looked him up and down disapprovingly.

Aaron had forgotten that Mrs. Livingston had been the strictest kind of professional, choosing to interact with her student's on a last name basis only, using student's first names far to informal for her liking.

"Please take your seats so we can begin class, we have a lot to cover before our test today."

"Test?" Jack blurted out.

"That's right Mr. Harwell, we are going to see how much of the information you have been provided actually sticks and how much we need to reexamine again to make sure it does next time."

Aaron and the rest of the group fell into the room, each finding a seat at one of the multiple double's tables in the room. Jack and Debbie sat together, each member of the group finding a partner to sit with, using the good old-fashioned buddy system to watch each other's backs. Since there were only fifteen of them, Aaron became the odd man out, until he got Ashley back, leaving him to sit at a table all by himself at the front of the class. The worst seat in any classroom unless you were a teacher's pet, which Mrs. Livingston never had.

Yep, this is definitely Hell.

Before Mrs. Livingston could begin her lesson, the speaker in the ceiling chirped to life, always leading with a screeching noise that Aaron had come to believe was just for effect more than anything. The noise was unsettling and annoying, only a few seconds was enough to make anyone cringe and start covering their ears. It made sense that since this was Hell it would be used each time to make them as miserable as physically possible.

"MORNING FUCKTARDS," the intercom thundered down on them. *"TIME FOR YOUR DAILY ANNOUNCEMENTS...BUUUUUUUUUUURRRRRRPPP..."*

Everyone in room 201A was immediately greeted with a gut-wrenching stench as an impossibly terrible odor seeped out of the vents overhead and into the room as the walls rattled from the vibration. Just like in a cartoon, the horrific odor came out of the vents in a green hue that allowed everyone to see the slowly approaching gas as it crept closer and closer toward them. Panic broke out in the room, almost everyone believing they were being poisoned. Screams broke out as multiple people made a mad dash for the exit, only to find the door had been sealed just like the ones in the gymnasium. Unable to escape, they started covering their faces with their arms or choosing to bury their heads in the clothes for protection. Aaron's mind raced trying to come up with an idea when the green gas hit him and he had to fight back the urge to vomit. He was successful, but others were not, several people lurching for trashcans around the room just in the nick of time. When no one passed out or collapsed and died, Aaron understood the gas was not deadly, just another form of torture unleashed upon them.

"AHHH, MUCH BETTER. NOW, LET ME TELL YOU, CAUSE WE ARE TOTALLY BEST FRIENDS NOW, DO NOT GO FOR THE CAFETERIA BREAKFAST NO MATTER HOW TEMPING IT MAY BE FOR ONLY A $1.50. IN TODAY'S ECONOMY? C'MON. THAT'S A FUCKING STEAL. YOU SHOULD HAVE SEEN THE LOOKS ON YOUR FACES WHEN YOU THOUGHT IT WAS POSION THOUGH, THAT WAS PRICELESS. I AM TOALLY PUTTING THAT PIC IN OUR SCRAPBOOK YOU GUYS, WE ARE ALL GONNA LOOK BACK ON THIS LATER AND LAUGH."

Aaron chose to hold his tongue. Half the room was still hurling into quickly filling trashcans, Jack holding Debbie's hair as she continued to dry heave when the gagging wouldn't leave her empty stomach to rest. He would take any opportunity to pester their captor for more information on Ashley, he had no idea when and where he would get the chance again since the voice came and went at will, but held off since the group wasn't going to be able to take another round of torture at the moment and getting everyone killed was not going to help him rescue Ashley any faster.

"NOW ON TO THE BUSINESS PORTION OF THIS ANNOUCEMENT. THE RULES ARE SIMPLE, THER ARE NO RULES. I CAN DO WHATEVER I WANT, WHENEVER I WANT. AS OF RIGHT NOW, I FIND IT MORE INTERESTING TO WATCH MY NEW HOUSE CATS CHASE THEIR TAILS THAN JUST COOKING YOUR ASSES LIKE 'OLE FECAL TROUSERS BACK IN THE GYM. I'M JUST GOING TO SIT BACK AND WATCH HOW THIS ALL PLAYS OUT, SEE IF YOU DISSAPOINTING SKINBAGS CAN BE THE FIRST TO EVER EARN THEIR WAY OUT. EXCITING RIGHT!"

It was obvious that they were not getting out of here, Aaron knew he was just toying with them and would eventually get bored and start picking them off one at time or wipe them all out at once. He had no illusions there was ever a game or that there was ever a chance of winning. Back at the gymnasium he'd jumped up on the table and given a speech about them working together and trying to beat the odds knowing it was all total bullshit just to get them to not screw things up worse than they already were. The ultimate goal was to stay alive long enough to get Ashley back, so if playing his little game meant staying alive just a little bit longer, it was worth it.

As the intercom fell silent, Mrs. Livingston began to start her lecture when the door to the classroom opened and an elderly gentleman walked in.

The man was at least sixty years old, possibly older, but he looked like he kept himself in shape to keep the aging process at bay for as long as possible. He wore a light-grey tailored three-piece suit, complete with a matching fedora. His suit was neatly pressed, his dress shoes well polished and shining in the low light that the overhead bulbs offered. Although he appeared to be in good shape, the man walked with a cane firmly held in this left hand, it's metal tip clacking against the tile floor with every other step he took. He made no eye contact with anyone in the room, he just gently tipped his cap towards Mrs. Livingston, receiving the same critical glare they all had, and walked to the back to the room, sitting at an empty table. The man had a pocket watch, the chain connecting it to the inside vest only visible to Aaron when he unbuttoned his jacket to sit. He continued to have no interaction with anyone, just sat there like a passenger on a bus waiting for his stop.

"THAT WELL-DRESSED SHRIVELED NUTSACK IS HANK. HANK IS HERE TO AUDIT THIS CLASS AND YOU

ASSHOLES. HE IS MY EYES AND EARS, WHAT HE SEES AND HEARS, I SEE AND HEAR. AVOID GIVING HIM A REASON TO REPORT BACK TO ME AND YOU WILL ALL BE OUT OF HERE IN NO TIME, ENJOYING LIFE TOPSIDE AS I LIKE TO SAY. IF YOU FAIL, AND HANK HAS TO GET ME INVOLVED, YOU ARE ALL PERMANTELY GOING TO BE ON ASS-HAIR BRAIDING DUTY TILL YOUR FINGERS BLEED. YOU EVEN SO MUCH AS LOOK AT HANK THE WRONG WAY, GARY, AND YOU'RE FUCKED."

"I wasn't loo-" Gary started to say before he burst into flames standing next to the trashcan he'd been hurling his guts into moments before.

No one in the room made a sound. The panic and fear everyone expressed back at the gymnasium was gone, replaced with an unforgiving reality that they could be next for even the slightest reason.

Better to be quite and blend in that make a peep and be the next one to show up on his radar.

"YOU SEE THAT HANK! HE WAS TOTALLY LOOKING AT ME!" the voice on the intercom yelled down to Hank.

Hank sat motionless, not offering a word in response.

"OH WHATEVER, I KNOW YOUR IMPRESSED. I CAN HEAR YOUR HEART BEATING ALL THE WAY OVER HERE, WAIT, IS THAT YOU BECKY?"

Becky began crying again.

"ANYWAY, ENJOY YOUR DAY BUTT-MUFFINS. I WENT AHEAD AND TOOK THE LIBERTY OF SCHEDULING EVERYONE'S FAVORITE SUBJECT FIRST SO ENJOY THE SHIT OUT OF MATH CLASS, BWAHAHAHAHA," the intercom laughed as his voice faded out into silence.

"Alright class, let's begin," Mrs. Livingston started as if nothing had happened, moving back towards the dry-erase board to write out her first equation.

XX

Fuck math.

Aaron sat at the front of the class trying to stay awake as his eye's gradually glazed over and the irresistible temptation to fall sleep crept up on him. Of all the goddam subjects to be saddled with, math was without a doubt the worst possible one in a landslide. Just listening to Mrs. Livingston prattle ad nauseam about some equation and how to solve it, using the alphabet because of course, made it exceedingly difficult for him to stay focused on the task at hand.

Get out of this classroom and find Ashley.

Does ANYONE like math?

The question circled his mind over and over; if only in hopes of understanding how their captor's decision-making process worked. Aaron told himself that even if Lucifer himself was holding them captive, he HAD to have a method for his decisions. As nonchalant and cavalier as he came across, they were not playing this sick game of his for no good reason. Even a madman sees logic in his own plan, as twisted as it might be to everyone else. If he could figure out how or why he chose his torture's the way he did, the reason they had been chosen to play a game instead of quickly dealt with, maybe he could figure out where Ashley was or at the very least get a step ahead of him and keep himself and everyone else alive a little longer.

Did he choose math because he knew Aaron hated it and he'd been the one to push back the most of anyone in the group, aside from Ashley?

Was math so disliked as a whole that it was easily the most common denominator to choose for the most possible torture for a large group of people?

The questions rattled around in his head as Mrs. Livingston's voice continued on in the background, offering nothing more than the effect white noise gave people trying to fall asleep. She was lost in her own lecture, never once turning to address the class since she began, Aaron was fairly confident that she was not going to call on him to solve a problem, though nothing was impossible anymore. He had to keep in mind that this could all be a trap, luring them to sleep before springing something horrible on them to watch how they reacted. It was this reality that kept him awake when the lure of sleep was so strongly calling out to him.

As if on queue, Mrs. Livingston slowly turned to address the class, the dry-erase board behind her filled from side to side with impossibly difficult equations they could never be expected to solve if they'd had months and a few mathematicians peppered amongst them. She gave a unnerving smile, one that sent goose bumps shooting across Aaron's entire body, and gently capped the dry-erase pen before setting in back in the track at the bottom of the wall-mounted dry-erase board. She dusted her hands, seemingly for dramatic effect since there was no chalklike residue that came with using a dry-erase marker, and looked around the room. Aaron followed her gaze and realized he wasn't the only one struggling to keep his eyes open. Half the room was out cold, sleeping on the desks peacefully with their arms acting as pillows for their heavy heads, the other half supported their heads in the palms of their hands to brace for their increasing weigh as they gradually approached the first level of REM sleep.

Hank was the sole exception; he sat detached at the back of the room. If someone told Aaron he was a robot he wouldn't have argued. Hank sat, eyes fixed forward with laser focus, and never blinked. His eyes didn't shift towards the people looking at him and he made no effort to interact in any way. Aaron wondered in he turned to stone until he was called upon or needed, just a presence in the room to remind everyone that Big Brother was watching at all times.

Mrs. Livingston ignored Hank entirely, aware of his presence but disinterested in it all the same. Aaron found this somewhat curious, since the voice on the intercom made it clear that Hank was his right-hand man and should be treated as such. IF they were both on the same side, presuming that Mrs. Livingston was in fact still dead and this was all just a sick joke to weaken their resolve, it would stand to reason that they would be working in unison. Instead, both treated the other like an insufferable relative they were forced to sit with during a holiday meal. The Hatfield and McCoy aura these two gave off didn't correlate, there was bad blood there and neither made any effort to hide it from anyone who bothered to look. Aaron wondered if that was an opportunity to exploit when the time came.

Disconcertingly pacing towards the door, never letting the group out of her sight even though there was virtually nowhere for them to go aside from crawling up through the ventilation shaft Die Hard style, she flipped a second light switch up. Instantaneously, room 201A become unbearably bright. Aaron hadn't realized it until now, but only a portion of the lights had been on the entire time. The room had been darker that usual, but he didn't give it a second thought after walking down a similarly darkened hallway from the also darkened gymnasium. Aaron had presumed this was just how it would always be, dark enough to be unsettling but not pitch black to cause chaos and confusion that wasn't pre-planned by their captor.

Aaron froze, realizing his paranoia had been correct. Mrs. Livingston WAS using the lights to lure them asleep!

Everyone in the room reacted by shielding their eyes as they adjusted to the bright overhead lights. Anyone that was on the verge of falling asleep was now fully awake and alert, looking back and forth to get their bearings after letting their guard down in the low-lit room. It was now all to obvious the lights had been dimmed to lure them to drop their guard all along. The members of the group that were still awake started shaking those that had fallen asleep to alert them something was wrong.

"My, my, my," Mrs. Livingston started, producing a yardstick from behind her desk and now holding it as a crude weapon. "You little SHITS are about as RUDE as they come you know that?"

Whomever, or whatever, was standing on the other side of Aaron's table was absolutely NOT Mrs. Livingston. In all her years at Crest Hill, no one had heard her utter anything even remotely close to profanity. The consummate professional, Mrs. Livingston rarely ever raised her voice, she always choose the quiet and composed approach that gave her the upper hand in any altercation. Students and parents would loose their shit, resulting to screaming and hollering at her in a packed gymnasium during parent teacher conferences, but Mrs. Livingston always keeping the same tone no matter who was talking to her or what was being said.

"What do you say he have some REAL fun, huh?" she smiled, stepping back to create space between her and Aaron's table.

The aura of the room changed, something bad was about to happen.

It started with her eyes, turning blood red as she stood before them with her eyes wide open so they could see everything. The sclera, iris, and pupil that were present just a second ago were washed away, replaced with a hollow red bulb that filled each eye socket. Her stark white hair fell off her head, fluttering to the ground in multiple piles around her feet, as a dark and thick new mane quickly grew in its place, encircling her entire head. The skin on her face, along with her thick, prescription glasses, cracked and turned to dust, revealing a dark and leathery skin underneath, similar to that of a gorilla. Thick, razor-sharp teeth began to protrude from it's mouth until the tips of the lower set overlapped the upper set in a sickening array that dripped with the saliva of a hungry animal starving for it's next meal.

Mrs. Livingston's cult-like dress was torn to shreds by the enormous bat-like wings that popped out from behind her; each wing had a set of finger-length sharp spikes outlining it that shifted back and forth as if calibrating for optimal effectiveness before battle. Her temporary human form began cracking into dust and blowing away just like her face to reveal a similar, beast-like form underneath. To make matters worse, the brief moment between the fake skin and new skin had revealed to Aaron and the rest of the group exactly what Mrs. Livingston looked like nearly nude, as apparently she chose to wear very little under that floor length dress all those years.

The small and frail figure of Mrs. Livingston had short, flabby arms that offered very little in wingspan or support for heavy objects, not uncommon for an eighty something year old woman. The monster than stood before them now unfolded large, multi-jointed, arms that closely match the length of the wings on its back. Each hand, or claw, have several sharp fingers that swiped back and forth at them harmlessly, though still getting a terrified reaction from everyone each time they moved towards them. The muscles on each arm were defined, even under enough hair to classify it as a werewolf, showcasing the amount of pure strength and power this beast had at its disposal should it feel the need to use it on them.

The final part of the transformation was Mrs. Livingston's petite, basic black shoes. Most of the time they were hidden under her dress, only visible when she walked back and forth. Now they struggled to hold on with every fiber of their being as the gargantuan feet, that they were now unfairly being tasked to contain, continued to push against the seems of the shoes like a water balloon about to explode. The monster looked down, Aaron thought he saw surprise on its face that the shoes had not been torn to pieces like all the other pieces of clothing it was using as a disguise, and used a single finger from its massive claw to shred the shoes into pieces.

Standing in front of them now, in a pile of what used to be Mrs. Livingston, was a full-fledged monster.

100% pure nightmare fuel.

A demon.

As quickly as the lights had brightened, they cast the group into semi-darkness as the demon stood at the front of the class and cackled contentedly to itself.

Yep, we are fucked.

■

Steadily, the group re-adjusted to the low-light atmosphere. The demon's eyes smoldered with an intense red light, acting as an improvised lighthouse to draw their attention back to it.

It seemed to stand in front of them, tranquil and breathing heavily, forever. Aaron got the sense it was enjoying the look of sheer terror on their faces, soaking it up like sun at the beach. The demon made not effort to move towards them, it was either content with being a beacon of terror or it had been giving strict rules from their captor not to harm any of them without permission. Aaron wondered if Hank's presence was all that was keeping it from launching into a full-scale attack against them. It just glanced back and forth, back and forth, as they all waited for what was next.

166

"Ahh, NOW I have your attention. Was wondering what it was going to take to get you goddam ungrateful little shits to pay attention," it hissed. The sound of its voice no longer that of Mrs. Livingston, instead it was replaced with a slightly softer version of the voice that came out over the intercom.

"Now, who's ready to have some REAL fun? How about you learn something you can actually use other than this nonsense bullshit that old hag taught you. What's say we apply some real world scenarios to this crap, huh?"

Par for the course, the room was dead silent. No one wanted to bring attention to themselves with a full-sized demon standing only a few feet away. Aaron caught a glance back at Hank, curious to see if the switch from Mrs. Livingston to demon had elicited some kind of response, but saw the same Hank just sitting there like nothing ever happened.

"Alright. Let's start by asking the obvious question. Who here like's money? Anyone?" the demon asked, glancing back and forth as everyone quickly glanced at the ground to avoid being called on just like they were back in school. *"Ahh, COME ON. You little shits better start playing along and interacting in this class our I am going to just start eating people."*

That worked.

Rapidly, everyone started to raise his or her hand like popcorn going off in the microwave. Anyone that claimed they didn't like money, especially in their generation, was outright lying. Sure there were those that truly believed money was the root of all evil, but dollars to donuts, most would take the money if no one was watching them. Money may not buy happiness, but it bought security and peace of mind. To most, that was a large part of being happy. To have no worries about upcoming bills or what something might cost, only living by what made you happy and always being able to say yes was the dream everyone had at some point or another in their life. Aaron wasn't sure whether or not the demon could read minds like their captor, or if it could tell when they were lying, but he decided the only way to figure out what he was up against was to leave his hand down and find out. As the rest of the class had their hands raised, only he and Hank kept their hands down. The demon glanced him over for a second, but either it couldn't read his mind or simply didn't give two shits about a single human, before moving on with its spontaneous lesson.

"THAT'S more like it," it hissed, pleased with the response it got from the class. *"Now, how many of you wish you had more. That you were not always scraping together every last penny you had to get by and would KILL to be set for LIFE?"*

It hit Aaron at the exact moment it hit Jack, something he would have been proud of if not for the circumstances.

They both knew exactly where this was headed.

Debbie.

"How much money would it take to get you to shut the fuck up and bring back Mrs. Livingston? I liked her lectures better." Aaron abruptly blurted out, trying to distract the demon from its intended goal, using himself as bait to keep it away from Debbie.

Not the sharpest crayon in the box, are you pal?

In a flash, the demon fluttered its wings and was on top of Aaron's table. It grabbed him with one hand and picked him up out of his seat and threw him down violently against the tabletop. All it took was one of it's massive feet to hold him down, the weight of it's leg, along with having the wind knocked out of him from the impact, pinned him to the table with no chance of getting out from underneath it's foot. Aaron tried to wiggle and twist but the weight was too much, it was all he could do to withstand the pressure against his ribcage. It felt like his chest would collapse at any moment from the weight.

"What if I told you I could make all your feeble problems go away, make it so you never had to worry about money ever again. Wouldn't you like that?" it preached, Aaron swore he saw it smile at him, helpless to stop what came next.

To his horror, Aaron saw out of his limited vision being pinned to the table, that some of his classmates were actually perking up as the demon spoke. They were genuinely interested in what it had to say; even if deep down they knew it was a trick. The call of money was an alluring one. If they could secure the money, even at the cost of their own lives, they could release the burden it held on their families or loved ones as their final act.

The demon looked up at the table in the back, where Jack and Debbie were sitting side by side. The color in Jack's face disappeared again; he knew exactly what was about to happen as well as Aaron did and had no idea how he was going to stop it.

Or if he even could.

"Deb's here has BILLIONS," the demon barked, Debbie fainting as soon as she made eye contact with the demon's hollow eyes.

Her still body draped over the top of the table like she was sleeping through a boring lecture.

"First one to bring me her head gets EVERYTHING."

XXI

It was all out war.

For a fleeting moment after the offer left the demon's lips, there was a calm that washed over the classroom. Each one of them took in the offer that had been presented to them and each had their own struggle on whether to accept it or not.

Aaron prayed they would see through the whole charade, that they would choose to protect one of their own given the circumstances and the one making the offer in the first place.

He prayed they were incapable of murder.

He was wrong.

Still pinned under the crushing weight of the demon perched on top of him, Aaron watched as his former classmates shared glances amongst themselves. They were all thinking the same thing; the look in each of their eyes was a clear indicator of what was about to happen before they ever moved a muscle. One table shared a knowing glance with the next and so on, until the entire room was just waiting for someone to make the first move. No one wanted to be the first one to attack; they were all likely still trying to hold on to their own sliver of humanity, telling themselves that what happened in a struggle wasn't entirely their fault as long as they were not the ones to actually start it.

Everyone in the room knew they would have to go through Jack to get to Debbie. Jack was far from what anyone would consider a fighter, he had the body composition of a stand-up comedian if anything, but they all knew how he felt about Debbie and that if necessary he would put his own life on the line to protect her. By now, most of the classroom had figured out a way to rationalize to themselves the act killing one person for such a large sum of money, but adding Jack into the mix muddied the waters. He would not let them harm her, so long as he could help it. He had to be dealt with, something no one really had the stomach to do since his death would be for nothing.

Then again, accidents happen.

The tension in the air became palpable, any hope of holding onto their humanity absconded, along with any chance of Debbie making it out of this alive.

Two tables in front of Jack and Debbie is where it started, the occupants shared one final glance before deciding to make the first move.

"Fuck this, I WANT that money," the first guy proclaimed, bolting out of his chair and jumping on top of his table. He spun around and pointed at the unconscious body of Debbie, she was completely unaware of what was happening and Aaron was glad for it, before issuing a warning to Jack. "Stay out of this, no reason you have to die to. Mark my words though, you try and interfere and you're as good as dead."

The man let out a primal roar; Aaron watching as all humanity drained out of him and by the time the cry was over he was no longer human. It possessed the same blood red eyes the demon had, its face badly disfigured as it attempted to make the same transformation the other demon had made seamlessly. It stood hunchbacked; the weight of its newly sprouted wings just too much to bear initially, causing it to lean forward before it could fully adjust to its new form. It looked back at the demon standing over Aaron, like a child looking for his father's approval, before leaping into the air towards Jack and Debbie.

"NOOO!" Aaron yelled, still helpless to do anything but watch pinned under the demon.

Jack may not have had a warrior's physique; but he made up for it with a brilliant mind. With the semi-demon in midair, Jack waited till the last possible second to pull his table back before it could land. The semi-demon, unable to account for the table no longer being where it needed it to be, caught the back end of the table with the tips of its still transforming feet before slipping down and cracking its skull against the edge of the solid tabletop, effectively killing it on impact. It lay in a crumpled pile while the rest of the group looked on in shock. A few moments later, the body of the semi-demon burst into flame and disappeared into a pile of ash. It never made a sound, never even had the chance.

The sudden movement of the table being pulled back had jarred Debbie back up against her chair, waking her up from the impact, and now she sat shaking in her chair as Jack attempted to calm her. Having just arisen from fainting, it took her a moment to get her bearings straight. The pile of smoldering ash at her feet was all she needed to remind her why she'd passed out in the first place. The look on her face told Aaron she knew she was about to die and fought back the immediate urge to pass out from shock again.

"Everything is ok, you're ok," Jack told her as he gently brushed the hair out of her face and behind her ears, Debbie's bulging eyes focused on the pile of ash where her would be killer had landed after its attempt on her life. She didn't say a word, just shook uncontrollably as she eyed everyone else in the room accusingly. "I won't let anything happen to you."

Lying on his back, Aaron hoped that would be the end of it. That it would be enough to scare the rest of those that had been contemplating making an attempt themselves from trying anything, seeing how quickly their classmate had lost himself and become that monster, only to lose his life in a matter of minutes. That should have been all they needed to know the malicious offer wasn't worth it.

He was wrong, again.

The death of one of their own from succumbing to his greedy desires had done just the opposite; it had stirred the rest of them into action. They now had the knowledge that by succumbing to their desire they would be granted the same powers as the demon that enslaved them. It seemed like everyone in the room felt it was a sure thing that ONE of them would get to Debbie, each one of them telling themselves they would be the one.

Aaron was still helpless to do anything but watch it all unfold.

Slowly, as more former classmates made the decision to attack, the room began to fill with red-eyed semi-demons all waiting for their transformations to be complete. They had figured out that the first one had acted too swiftly; he would have been successful if he'd given his new body a chance to fully transform before jumping into action. It would have been unstoppable by then.

Aaron had only been in a few serious fights his entire life, most taking place back at the Rusty Knuckle in Austin, but he knew there was a point in any fight where you had to decide whether you had a shot at winning or if you were better of tapping out to live another day. No one wants to tap out; it was embarrassing as shit and automatically made you the loser in an argument you were passionate enough to fight over in the first place. Sure, it was better than an expensive trip to the E.R., but only at the cost of your pride.

The other option was to keep fighting, no matter what. Win, lose, it didn't matter what happened, you're not stopping till you're unconscious or victorious. Tapping out may no longer be an option when your opponent is intent on killing you no matter what. You then become forced to fight for your life.

Or someone else's.

Aaron knew Jack wouldn't be able to hold them all off for long, he had practically zero chance of actually defeating them unless he had shit-ton more of those surprises up his sleeve.

He had to get free.

He had to help Jack save Debbie.

Aaron struggled against the crushing weight of the demon's foot, still unable to gain any ground against it. He watched in horror as the newly formed demon crew proceeded towards Jack and Debbie. Just like in a movie they seemed to walk slower than necessary, building up tension and suspense for reasons unknown. Jack stood up and grabbed his chair, swinging it back and forth as an improvised weapon; nothing else around was even remotely serviceable to defend Debbie with. Of all the classes to have a fight break out, math class had to be one the worst. Aside from throwing a calculator at one of them, there was nothing to fight with. Aaron's mind slipped to if this would have happened in science class, with glass beakers and Bunsen burners galore to work with, and found a new level of anger he didn't know he had.

Fuck this.

Stretching out, his limbs felt like they were moments away from tearing apart as he pushed through the growing discomfort, Aaron was able to grab the top of his own chair. Squeezing with everything he had to form a grip while sill being crushed by the demon, he managed to get a hold of it and put all his strength into throwing the chair up at the demon to escape it's clutches. The attempt was ill thought out and dismantled quickly, the demon looking down at him pathetically before using its left wing to turn the chair into rubble with the razor sharp tentacles sticking out along its wing. The only thing left was a small piece of plastic still in the palm of his hand from his vice-like gripe.

Well fuck me.

Aaron looked over at how Jack was fairing, but it wasn't much better. The demon's had grabbed ahold of the other end of Jack's chair and were now engaged in an almost comical tug-of-war for sole possession of the chair. Jack was running out of time, he would only last a few more minutes, if that.

Frantic for ideas, Aaron strained his neck, moving his head back and forth looking for anything he could use to get the demon off of him. There was absolutely nothing, the classroom was barren, something no doubt planned before they ever walked in the room. Would make no sense to allow them to arm themselves, no matter how little that would help them in the long run.

Out of ideas, but not willing to give up, Aaron's eye's landed on Hank. He was still sitting in his seat motionless, unaware or completely disinterested in what was going on around him. He sat in his seat like a robot that had been shut off.

Oh fuck me, that's IT!

Aaron realized that Hank had never interacted with any of them because no one had bothered to interact with him. They had all stared at him, but no one had actually spoken to him.

"HANK!" Aaron yelled, hoping he was right and Hank would respond.

Hank's head came up and looked over at him, making eye contact for the first time and sending a chill down Aaron's spine. Even crushed under the weight of the demon, he still felt goose bumps cover his entire body. For a brief moment Aaron was happy that he could still feel all his extremities, that nothing had been severely damaged due to the colossal weight on top of him. Hank looked over at him, but made no attempt to speak. He just sat there like a puppy waiting for a command.

Here goes nothing.

"Hank, you worthless piece of shit. You really going to let this asshole kill someone without doing a goddamn thing? What kind of asshole just lets an innocent girl get murdered in front of him an doesn't bother lifting a finger to stop it?"

The reaction Aaron received was not what he was expecting. He'd expected total disinterest, for Hank to look over at where Jack and Debbie would die and go back to sitting in silence. There was no proof that Hank would act at all, after all, he was just auditing them on behalf of their captor. He wasn't on their side, but he was the only piece left on the board to play at the moment. Aaron half expected Hank to even join in on the whole thing, only making matters worse but rolling the dice that Hank was the key to getting out of this alive.

What he got was a genuine look of disgust once Hank looked over at Jack and Debbie, followed by sheer anger for being called out. For a brief moment, Aaron hoped Hank would jump out of his chair, or as fast as someone his age could move, and come to their defense. Instead, he got a confused look as Hank's eyes batted back forth, contemplating what action to take next. The only positive to all the commotion was that the demons had paused for a moment to see how Hank would react; Aaron wondered if they knew something he didn't know.

Who are you Hank?

Hank's eye's settled down and refocused on Aaron. He furrowed his brow and began to rise from his seat. Hank carefully placed the fedora sitting on the table back on his head, but left his cane leaning against the table as he carefully walked up to the front of the room till he was standing over Aaron. The demon standing over him seemed to sense what was coming and smiled, lifting its foot off Aaron's chest to allow Hank full access to him.

Their eyes met as Aaron painfully pulled the upper half of his body off the tabletop and into sitting position, struggling the entire time to breath. Once he was in sitting position, Hank tipped his cap at him like a gentleman, then proceed to hit with a hard left hook in the face. The already severely bruised eye that Ronnie had given him earlier screamed out in pain as the entire room went blurry.

174

The last thing Aaron remembered was being picked up by his shirt collar and thrown across the room.

He blacked out on impact with the cold tile floor and what felt like other bodies.

■

When he awoke, Aaron was sitting on the floor in between Jack and Debbie.

They're alive!

I'm alive!

Or are we all dead?

His vision slowly started to come back, the room coming into focus from a blur of soft colors around him. His head still ached, a ringing roared on in his ear from the hit he took from Hank. For an older guy, that man packed a SERIOUS punch. Aaron couldn't rule out that he was supernatural himself. If not, Hank's hand had better be in pieces for his head to feel as badly as it did.

"He's awake," Aaron heard Debbie say, delight in her voice.

"Thank god, I thought you were dead for sure dude. You took a VICIOUS hit to the dome and them took an express trip across the room. Was actually kinda badass, ya know, minus you almost dying and all." Jack said, tapping him on the shoulder a little harder than he expected, causing Aaron to flinch from the pain. "Oh right, sorry."

"Did we win, are they all gone?" Aaron asked, still trying to refocus on the room.

"Well, yes and no. We are still alive so that's a win," Jack started before Debbie cut in.

"But they are holding us hostage. Said they wanted you awake for what happens next."

"What happens next?" Aaron asked.

Neither one of them said a word; they couldn't bring themselves to say what Aaron already knew but needed a minute to put the puzzle together himself.

Debbie.

They were still going to kill her; these sick fucks just wanted him awake to see he'd done nothing to actually stop it from happening. He nearly died for nothing.

"We have to fight them. We can't let them take Debbie," Aaron said, feeling her squeeze his arm at the sound of her own name. "How many of them are there left?"

"Well, we came here with fifteen. Minus the three of us that makes twelve. Now subtract Jerry and Peter and that leaves ten remaining, not counting mama bear leading the pack."

"Who the hell is Peter?" Aaron asked.

"He's the shitbag that tried something first, got a cracked skull and a first class ticket to Fucksville for his trouble."

"So he's really dead?"

"Yep. You die down here, you die for good. Not take backs."

Good to know.

"There has to be something, a way to kill them or make a break for it." Aaron said, hoping Jack would say he had an idea no matter how crazy it was. "What about a way to reverse the transformation, turn them all back to human's again?"

Anything beat Debbie dying in front on them.

"Make a break for it where?" Jack asked. "Even if we managed to get to the front door, we know it's locked or will be by the time we get there. No way we're getting out of here that way."

"JACK, there has to been something. Debbie is NOT going to die!" Aaron demanded.

"You think I like this? You think I haven't run through every possible fucking scenario three times over? There just isn't any move for us to make unless you are invincible and can kick down magically sealed doors and are just holding out on us. We're fucked. Debbie. You. Me. We are up shit creek without a goddamn boat dude."

Aaron refused to think that way, he couldn't. As long has he was still breathing he had a chance to rescue Ashley. Him dying here was not an option, and neither was Jack or Debbie for that matter. He just needed to think of something to get them free long enough to at least try the front door. The only way they were going to do that was to kill as many of those demons as possible to make a break for it.

"Jack, how do you kill a demon?" Aaron asked.

He saw how Peter had died, but Peter wasn't a full-fledged demon yet so mortal injuries could still affect him. When his skull cracked it was game over for him.

"The fuck would I know? My whole plan wasn't to kill ANYHTING. It was to trap...something... and get out while the getting was still good," Jack said, pausing before he laid out his whole plan when he remembered their thoughts were no longer their own.

"Well, how do you kill a monster then? You read all those books, had your nose in every comic back then too, has to be SOMETHING in there about killing monsters."

"Great, which monster you wanna kill? I can tell you how to ice a werewolf no problem. If we run in to 'ole neck bolts I can start a fire that will finish him off quick. Nothing in any book about killing a fucking demon dude. They are hell spawn, you can't just kill what's already dead."

Aaron had an idea.

It was a long shot, but it was the best thing they had and worth a shot. Anything beat sitting there waiting to watch Debbie die before they were killed themselves.

"Ok, I have an idea. It's fucking nuts, but I need you to trust me on this." Aaron started, his vision finally returning and seeing the demons all around him with their backs to them as they sat in some form of hibernation, just waiting to be roused for what was to come.

"I need you two to make a run for the front door," Aaron whispered, now aware he was so close to the demons.

"I already told you, we won't make it out that door," Jack protested.

"All I need is a distraction, just enough to get these guys away from me and a clean shot at the big one."

"Jesus, you can barely stand dude, you can't take on the leader like this." Jack continued to argue.

"I'm fine," Aaron lied.

Jack seemed to contemplate this for a minute before nodding his head and agreeing to make a run for it with Debbie. Aaron could tell he hated the idea implicitly, but didn't have anything to counter with and knew they had to do something or they would be dead.

"May as well die trying right," Jack finally agreed, with Debbie smacking him on the shoulder for being so negative.

"It'll work...it has to," Aaron encouraged them. "On the count of three ok?"

They both nodded.

"One…. Two…THREE," Aaron yelled.

Jack and Debbie locked hands and took off like a bat out of hell towards the front door. The once dormant demons that surrounded them burst to life and chased after them, leaving Aaron all by himself. Debbie was the main target; Aaron was wounded, he had little reason to be kept under guard anyway.

He took the opportunity to find the demon that had pinned him to the table, it was standing right were it was the last time he'd seen it. Right smack dab in the front of the dry-erase board.

Aaron didn't waste time, with every ounce of strength he could muster; he flipped the nearest table, a loud crash as it landed on its side with the legs sticking out in the air. He swung his leg with everything he had and kicked one of the legs off the table. The sharp crack of wood splintering as it broke off from the table, along with the table being flipped on it's side, caused the demon to turn its head towards him and raise both its wings in preparation to kill him once and for all.

By then, it was already too late.

Aaron picked up the table leg, now a crude wooden stake, and hurled it as hard as he could at the demon standing no more than four feet away from him.

The stake pierced the demon's leathery skin, something Aaron wasn't sure was possible when he'd had the idea but had to try, it even drove the demon back against the wall, pinning it as the stake stuck in the wall behind it. The demon let out a horrific howl as black ooze poured out around the wound from the table leg. As soon as the howl started, it ended, with an awesome burst of white light as the demon exploded into flames and turned to ash.

All ten of the demon's newly acquired talent, surrounding Jack and Debbie near the front door as they hadn't made it all the way before being trapped, shook violently before each one collapsed on the ground and burst into flames before disappearing into ash. The whole process lasted less than a minute, when it was over it was just Aaron, Jack and Debbie standing alone in the room as ash swirled around their feet like a dense morning fog.

Hank was there too; he just sat quietly in his seat.

Aaron could have sworn he saw a smile form across his lips.

XXII

"THE HELL WAS THAT?" Jack cried out, his eyes bulging out of his head at Aaron. Debbie stood next to him, equally shocked but thrilled to no longer be hunted by demons wanting her head for a cash prize.

Aaron himself wasn't entirely sure what just happened, unable to form a response as he stood in silence, gazing at the charred section of drywall where the demon had been pinned before it burst into flames. The table leg turned crude stake had gone up in flames with the demon, the murder weapon gone forever.

The perfect crime.

It wasn't supposed to work, at least not that well.

Jack's incoherent rambling as he went through how to kill the classic monsters from movies and TV flipped a switch in Aaron's head, he realized that aside from the fact that it hadn't tried to suck their blood or worn a fancy cape, the demon had all the traits of a vampire. It was tall, hairy and had a massive set of wings to go along with those hideous fangs that stuck out of its mouth. Its goddamn eyes were even red for Christ sake; as far as Aaron was concerned it was as good as a vampire.

So that meant, in his hastily pulled together logic, it could be killed like one too.

Room 201A, and the entire premises of Crest Hill itself for that matter, didn't have any pure silver just lying around, so that was off the table first. As he'd run through the gamut of what he knew would kill a vampire, Aaron could only think of a wooden stake through the heart. He knew garlic hurt them, but this wasn't Home Ec. and there wasn't any food lying around so that was also off the table as quickly as it had popped into his head. Realizing a stake through the heart was the best, and only, option, Aaron tried to remember if it was any kind of stake or if it had to be wooden. His first idea had been to charge the demon, a chair in front of him with the steel legs sticking out as a battering ram, and pierce its heart that way. He wasn't sure if steel would work and didn't want to risk it and find out he was wrong when it was too late.

That and in his condition running even a few feet at full speed wasn't an option. His head was still spinning from the hit by Hank, not to mention the never-ending ringing that fought to drive him mentally insane if it's didn't stop soon. Aaron's equilibrium was off, he wasn't running anywhere in a straight line no matter how hard he tried.

That left throwing a stake at it, still a long shot since he'd landed on his right shoulder and it hurt to move it much less throw a fastball at a supernatural being and hope to hit it dead on target before it moved out of the way. There was no reason to think it wasn't faster than a human, it had wings for crying out loud, and would be able to just step out of the way or fly around it before the stake smashed harmlessly against the wall after missing entirely. The amount of things that would have to go perfectly for it to work seemed impossible, there was just no way it would actually work to impale a demon with a table leg on the first try with a bum shoulder.

On the other hand, they could always just sit there and wait to be executed one-by-one.

Aaron noticed the table legs as they were huddled on the floor and figured it was the best option since it was wood, or at least a version of wood, so it should break if hit hard enough. The flight across the room had resulted in his shoulder, and head, taking the brunt of the impact, his lower body was relatively well off considering. If he could just focus his vision well enough to kick the leg once he'd managed to flip the table on it's side, he was sure he could break it off and use it as a stake.

Once he yelled, "THREE," and Debbie and Jack took off; he sprang into action, flipping the table and breaking off a leg exactly how he'd planned it in his head. The easy part out of the way, he lined up his shot and threw the leg as hard as he could at the demon. Aaron never played football, he knew he'd never make the cut so didn't bother trying, but he'd seen enough games on TV with his grandpa to know that you didn't throw to where the person was, rather where the person would be. When he let go of the makeshift spear, he'd lead the demon in anticipation that it would make a move once it figured out what was happening. His shoulder cried out in agony as he let go, sending a jolt of pain through his entire body in disapproval. Somehow the leg found purchase, right over the where the demon's heart would have been, and the rest was history.

"Dude, the FUCK was that? You just harpooned a demon with a goddamn table leg!" Jack said, his hands still on his head like he'd just witnessed a successful Hail Mary to win a football game he'd bet his life savings on.

"I can't believe that worked," Aaron muttered to himself, still playing the whole thing over and over in his head.

"Uh…it did!" Jack said, crossing the room to embrace him. Debbie followed suit, turning it into a group hug.

"Deb's gonna have to get in line, cause now I wanna have sex with you too," Jack joked as Debbie smacked him in the head.

"What did I say about calling me Deb's!" she shouted, Jack fighting to hold back a smile.

"We just defeated a demon and saved your life, I don't get a pass even once?"

"AARON killed a demon. He can call me whatever he wants, you on the other hand, you better watch your mouth," Debbie pointed at him.

"Ease up on him Debbie," Aaron said. "Jack saved your life by killing Peter when he tried to attack you, he was the only one between you and the rest of the demons while I was pinned down. Wasn't for him, you probably wouldn't be standing here right now."

Debbie looked over at Jack, tears welling up in her eyes. She knew what Jack had done for her, but she wasn't the best at showing genuine gratitude Aaron had noticed. He assumed it was from wearing her heart on her sleeve in her last relationship, only to see it crash and burn and promising never to let that happen again. Aaron could tell she wanted to say thank you to Jack, to hug and kiss him for putting his life on the line for hers, but even after everything that just happened she was reluctant to let her guard down. Debbie started crying and fell into Jack's arms, apologizing for smacking him was all she could muster. It was enough for Jack, he was beaming at the fact that he'd saved a girl's life; just liked he'd seen his superhero idols do in the comic books and movies he loved so much.

Jack was a real life hero.

Aaron turned to survey the room, giving them their moment, and looked over at Hank. He was still sitting at his table; he hadn't moved an inch since sitting back down after punching Aaron in the face and throwing him across the room like a rag doll. Even with everything that had just happened, seeing his classmates turn into demons before killing one with a table leg, Hank was still the hardest to wrap his head around. It made no sense to have a person follow them around if their captor could see and hear everything they said or thought already.

It was overkill.

Why are you really here?

Hank hadn't stopped him from killing the demon, which he should have if he were actually put here to monitor them. The whole point, according to the voice on the intercom, was for him to capture everything and report back if and when there was a problem. Aaron had to wonder how a dead demon, a charred wall all that remained of it now, hadn't been enough to contact their captor. At the very least, he should have burst into flames like Jerry had earlier, undoubtedly breaking the rules by killing one of theirs.

Yet nothing had happened.

A movement out of the corner of his eye caught his attention and he immediately went into a battle stance. His sudden movement startled Jack and Debbie, both of them jumping in response.

"What is it?" Debbie asked, terror creeping back into her voice as she slid behind Jack for safety.

Aaron didn't respond, instead he slowly walked over to where he'd seen the movement. Carefully, he still didn't have a goddam weapon; he made his way towards the far back corner of the room.

Something was huddled underneath one of the tables, now visibly shaking, as he got closer. It's back was turned to him so either it didn't know he was approaching or didn't care, either way it made him nervous that the figure didn't react at all. Aaron grabbed a chair; aware it would be of little use if this were a left over demon that had managed to survive the death of its creator unlike the rest of them when they burst into flame after it died. He gripped the chair even tighter as he came up right behind it, ready to swing the chair with all he had and hope for the best.

He stopped mid swing when he heard the sobs.

It wasn't a demon hiding under the table; it was Becky, along with another member of the group. He was about the same build as Becky, a small and thin man that was shaking just as badly as she was, tears running down both their faces.

"Becky?" Aaron asked, the sound of his voice causing her to jump in fright as she covered her head on instinct to protect herself.

"Becky, it's me Aaron. I'm not going to hurt you," Aaron offered in a gentle tone as she looked over her shoulder at him. As soon as they met eyes she burst into tears again. "It's ok, we won Becky. He's dead. You can come out now, you're safe."

Aaron knew it wasn't true; he just hoped he'd sold it well enough to get her and the other guy out from underneath the table. There was no way to say if they were safe or not, not anymore. Sure, they weren't currently surrounded by red-eyed demons, but that meant very little at this point.

Becky and the other guy must have believed him because they both slowly slid out from under then table and stood to look around the room. The other guy, whom Aaron could not put a name to, saw the five of them were all that was left and went a shade paler than he'd been underneath the table. It settled in that a handful of people he'd known, maybe even been friends with, were now dead.

"We thought you all transformed," Jack said, walking up beside Aaron slowly to avoid spooking them. "Can't tell you how happy we are to see at least someone didn't want to kill Debbie."

Becky, after she'd calmed down enough to speak, told them that she and Tony had slipped under their table when Mrs. Livingston had begun to turn. Aaron kicked himself for not remembering Tony until Becky said his name; he was their class president for senior year after all. His face had been on posters all around the school and he hadn't changed much in ten years.

The two of them stayed under the table the entire time, hands over their ears to block out any noise. Aaron and Jack appreciated that Becky and Tony had reverted to children, choosing to enact the well known if you can't see or hear the bad guys, they can't see or hear you strategy every kid adopted at one point or another. They couldn't blame them for being scared, they all were.

"So what happens now?" Debbie asked.

"I don't know," Aaron offered, looking at Jack to provide insight since it was his area of expertise.

"This is uncharted waters guys, your guesses are as good as mine at this point," was all he could offer.

"In that case, I guess we try the door and get the hell out of here," Aaron said, walking back towards the door.

In his mind he knew there was little chance the door would actually open, so he was stunned when he tried the handle and it opened without a hitch. The five of them stood, with the door wide open, looking into the hallway as they planned their next move. It made sense that they would try and make a run for it, Aaron advising against it knowing it would be a trap that would end poorly for them. They all agreed, but no one wanted to go out into the hallway and see what happened next.

It was Hank that made the fist move, rising from his seat and putting on his fedora while grabbing his cane. He walked to the front of the class, passing by them without so much as a glance, and out into the hallway. He stopped in the middle of the hall as if awaiting further instruction.

Aaron shrugged his shoulders and followed him out into the dark hallway, the rest of them right behind him.

■

The hallway was still and dark, just like it had been on their trip from the gymnasium to room 201A.

Aaron had hoped something would light up or act as a guide for where they were supposed to go next. He didn't like that the hallway remained dark and unsettlingly quiet as the group, and Hank, stood there waiting.

Maybe we SHOULD make a run for it.

184

Before he could begin to think about escaping, the intercom in the hallway shrieked to life, the now familiar screech filling the hallway and causing everyone but Hank to cringe at the noise.

"CLAP. CLAP. CLAP. CLAP. CLAP," reverberated down the hall.

"I GOTTA ADMIT, THAT WAS FUCKING IMPRESSIVE!" The maniacal voice returned as the clapping ceased. *"IT'S NOT EVERYDAY YOU WITNESS SOMEONE GET SPIKED TO THE FUCKING WALL AMIRIGHT? THAT WAS SOME SHIT!"*

Aaron was surprised at the voice's reaction. He was sure it would be one of fury after he'd just killed one his, but instead a chilling voice of enthusiasm rang across the hallway. It was unnerving more so than if he'd been royally pissed and gone about threatening him and the others for what he'd done.

"You seem pretty nonchalant for having just lost one of your own," Aaron said.

" OH DON'T FLATTER YOURSELF, I HAVE MILLIONS OF THOSE GUYS AT MY BECK AND CALL, YOU DIDN'T EVEN PUT A DENT IN MY NUMBERS BY KILLING ONE. SHIT, WAY IT SEE IT, I WON THAT ROUND IN A LANDSLIDE. YOU MAY HAVE OFFED MY GUY, BUT I GOT ABOUT HALF A DOZEN OF YOURS SO THAT'S A WIN IN MY COLMUN WOULDN'T YOU SAY?"

He was right. Aaron didn't want to admit it but a one for eight ratio wasn't in their favor even if he had managed to kill a demon against all odds.

"NOW, THAT BEING SAID I AM STILL HARD AS A ROCK RIGHT NOW. NO ONE EVER MAKES IT MORE THAN A FEW HOURS TOPS AROUND HERE, YET SOMEHOW YOU FIVE ARE STILL FUCKING BREATHING. THAT GETS ME ALL KINDS OF HOT AND BOTHERED. I HAD NO IDEA THIS GAME WOULD BE SO MUCH FUN, WOULD HAVE STARTED PLAYING THIS YEARS AGO. HANKY PANKY, YOU EVER THINK THIS WOULD BE SO MUCH FUN?"

Hank didn't answer, didn't even budge. Just stood there without a care in the world.

185

"TELL YOU WHAT, FOR MAKING IT OUT OF THAT ROOM I'M GONNA THROW YOU A BONE. I'M IN A GOOD MOOD SO WHY THE FUCK NOT RIGHT? I'M GONNA TELL YOU WHERE YOUR GIRLFRIEND IS, UNLESS YOU DON'T CARE ANYMORE. YOU DO STILL WANNA KNOW THAT RIGHT?"

Aaron's heart skipped a beat, maybe more, at the offer.

With everything that had happened in room 201A, Ashley had slipped his mind. He'd been focused on saving Debbie and staying alive in the process, Ashley was on the backburner until they were out of the woods. Standing in the hallway they were nowhere close to being out of the woods, but the immediate threat was taken care of and he was able to refocus on the main goal.

Save Ashley.

"Tell me where she is!" Aaron yelled.

"CALM DOWN SKIDROW, DON'T GET YOUR SHITCAKED PANTIES IN A BUNCH. I SAID I'D TELL YOU, NO NEED TO TAKE THAT TONE WITH ME," the voice chided him.

"Tell me where she is you sonofabitch!"

"ALL THAT PISS AND VINEGAR, YOU REMIND ME OF MYSELF AT YOUR AGE. YA KNOW, IF I WAS MORE OF A LOSER AND BUTT-FUCKING UGLY. STILL, THERE ARE BITS AND PIECES THERE."

"Tell. Me. Where. She. Is." Aaron demanded.

"OK, YOU'RE GONNA LOVE THIS. YOU READY? HANK, GIVE ME A DRUMROLL!"

Hank didn't move a muscle.

"YA KNOW WHAT HANK, FUCK YOU MAN. SERIOUSLY. FUCK. YOU."

"Stop stalling and tell me where she is!" Aaron yelled, Jack putting and arm on his shoulder in an unsuccessful attempt to calm him down.

"WHATEVER, THE PAGENTRY IS RUINED ANYWAY THANKS TO HANK BEING A TOTAL DICK. SHE'S IN THE GYM. THAT'S RIGHT, 'OLE FIRE CROTCH HAS BEEN THERE THE ENTIRE TIME. GENIUS RIGHT? YOU WERE SO EAGER TO GET OUT OF THE GYM WHEN I

UNLOCKED THE DOORS YOU VIRTUALLY RAN AWAY FROM HER."

"You're lying," Aaron countered.

"I THREW HER UNDER THE BLEACHERS BEFORE THE SMOKE CLEARED, THEN WATCHED YOU PLAY COLOMBO AND WALK BACK AND FORTH HOPING SHE'D MAGICALLY REAPPEAR IF YOUR WITTLLE BITTY HEART HOPED AND WISHED HARD ENOUGH. HAHAHAHAHA, YOU DUMBASS. SHE WAS RIGHT THERE THE ENTIRE TIME AND YOU MISSED IT."

Aaron didn't respond, he just started walking back towards the gymnasium. He was sure this was just another trick to mess with him, but he hadn't checked under the bleachers so it was worth a shot no matter how small it was.

"AND WHERE DO YOU THINK YOU'RE GOING?" the voice called out to him, Aaron ignored and kept walking.

He got another three feet before a burst of fire shot out from the lockers lining the walls on both sides of him, coming together in the middle to form a barrier that he couldn't get through.

"I SAID I'D TELL YOU WHERE SHE WAS, DON'T REMEMBER SAYING ANYTHING ABOUT LETTING YOU GO THERE."

The intercom overheard shrieked again before going radio silent, they were once again alone in the hallway.

"So now what?" Jack asked as the familiar bell for class rang throughout the hallway. "Where the hell are we supposed to go if that wall of fire won't let us pass?"

"FIRE DRILL!!!"

Suddenly, a wall of fire shot out from the tiled floor, extending all the way up to the ceiling. The fire alarms sounded in unison with the flashing lights that were equipped to each alarm on the wall. In a darkened hallway, it was all Aaron could do to see what was happening right in front of him with the strobe lights and smoke from the wall of fire. His eyes burned from the heat and constant flickering.

"NO!" Aaron yelled when he realized the wall of fire had cut he and Hank off from Jack and the rest of the group.

As quickly as the wall of fire appeared, it extinguished, the sirens right along with it.

Nothing but a wall of smoke remained in its place.

Jack and the group were nowhere to be found.

XXIII

"What the fuck just happened?" Aaron shouted over at Hank.

Hank didn't respond right away, he seemed to be forming his thoughts before sharing them with Aaron.

Aaron wanted answers, even if he had to beat it out of Hank.

Hank saw the fury in his eyes and began to open his mouth, to finally speak and provide answers.

He never got the chance, before he could form a word, the overhead speaker system cackled and screeched.

Their captor had the floor.

"IT'S CALLED AN AUDIBLE. COACH SAYS YOU JUST GOTTA SWITCH THAT SHIT UP SOMETIMES. COACH SAYS, WHEN THE OPPOSITION GETS A LITTLE TOO COMFORTABLE, YOU CHANGE THE PLAYS YOUR RUNNING AGAINST THEM."

"I am going to kill you if you hurt them," Aaron threatened.

"YA KNOW, ANYONE ELSE AND I WOULD HAVE LAUGHED ONE OF MY THIRTEEN ASSES RIGHT OFF, BUTTHOLE AND ALL. BUT WHEN THE THREAT COMES FROM YOU, IT MAKES ME ALL KINDS OF HOT AND BOTHERED. TO THINK, YOU AND ME GOING MONO-E-MONO IN AN EPIC BATTLE! IT'S FUCKING EXCITING RIGHT?"

"Keep talking asshole," Aaron responded. "You are going to get exactly what you deserve, so just keep talking."

"OH, I PLAN ON IT. LAST I CHECKED YOUR STILL IN MY BACKYARD TURD MUFFIN, WHICH MEANS YOU GET TO DEAL WITH WHATEVER MY CRUSTY BLACK HEART DESIRES, AND LET ME TELL YOU, IT DESIRES SOME KINKY SHIT. LIKE, BUTT STUFF KINDA KINKY."

Aaron didn't bother responding, he just smiled.

"AND JUST WHAT THE FUCK PRAYTELL DO YOU FIND SO FUNNY? A QUICK REPLAY ON THE DAY INCASE YOU FORGOT, I NOW HAVE YOUR GIRLFRIEND AND YOUR NON-SEX FRIENDS."

"I'm smiling cause you're nervous," Aaron said, still smiling. Hank stood perfectly still.

"OH AM I? PLEASE, ENLIGHTMENT ME OH WISE ONE. WHAT IN ALL OF MOTHERFUCKING CREATION WOULD I HAVE TO BE WORRIED ABOUT WITH YOU?"

"You tell me," Aaron shot back without hesitation. "We just killed one of your subordinates and you swoop in to kidnap everyone as soon as we hit the hallway. You ask me, you only try to even the score if you're worried about we might actually beat your stupid little game."

"YOU'RE STUPID," it mocked like a child playing *'I know you are but what am I'*.

"You're scared."

Like before, a single line of fire shot out of the wall of lockers to Aaron's left, stretching across the room until it landed on the opposite locker across from it.

Unlike last time, Aaron wasn't so lucky to avoid making contact. The bolt of fire grazed his left arm, instantly burning his forearm in the process. He grabbed his arm and fought with everything he had not to cry out in pain.

Don't let him see you hurt.

190

Instead, he ground his teeth together and bent forward in agony. He did not make a sound. Hank rushed over to him and grabbed his arm. Aaron wanted nothing to do with him and tried to pull away from him, but the pain was too intense to fight back. Hank held Aaron's left arm as he looked over the damage. The look on his face says it was bad; it was the first time Aaron had seen Hank do anything other than play possum.

"*THAT*, WAS A LITTLE REMINDER OF WHO IS IN CHARGE HERE. YOU WOULD BE WISE TO REMEMBER THAT, THE PAIN YOU ARE FEELING NOW IS NOTHING COMPARED TO WHAT I AM *REALLY* CAPABLE OF."

The tone in his voice changed, he was no longer playing around with him like he had been up to this point. He appeared to take nothing seriously, finding it more fun to mess around with them than scare them.

I was right.

He's scared.

On queue, Aaron remembering he could read his thoughts, another line of fire shot out at them.

This time, Hank was ready.

He clutched his cane and unsheathed a hidden blade from within, using it to deflect the line of fire away from them. The heat from the fire was bad enough though, causing his arm to ache as the heat radiated around his forearm.

"WELL, WELL, WELL," it boomed over the intercom. **"LOOK WHO *FINALLY* GREW A PAIR AND DECIDED TO FIGHT BACK. I HAVE BEEN WAITING FOR LIKE, *EVER*, TO SEE WHEN YOU'D NUT UP AND DO SOMETHING OTHER THAN PLAY A SAD SACK OF A BYSTANDER EACH TIME."**

The lighthearted tone had returned.

"SINCE CRISPY MCFRIED ARM HERE IS ALL, 'WOUAA WOUAA WU WU WOUAAAAAAA,' ABOUT LOSING ALL HIS FRIENDS, I'VE DECIDED TO CHANGE YOUR SCHEDULE FOR THE REST OF THE DAY, CLASS IS DE-FUCK-SMISSED. THIS JUST TURNED INTO A CHOOSE YOUR OWN DEMISE KINDA PARTY, MOTHERFUCKAS."

"What are your terms," Hank responded, Aaron unable to do much but fight the agonizing pain spreading from his severely burnt forearm. He was in shock, thought he couldn't figure out if it was the pain or the fact Hank was fighting for him with a sword he had been hiding the entire time.

"WELL LOOK AT YOU! ACTING ALL IN CHARGE AND WHATNOT. IF I DIDN'T HATE YOU TO THE CORE OF YOUR BEING, I WOULD BE PROUD. IF YOU THINK ABOUT IT, I'M KINDA LIKE YOUR DADDY, AND THIS PAPA IS JUST HAPPY TO SEE HIS LEAST LIKED SON FINALLY DO SOMETHING OTHER THAN SHIT HIS TROUSERS IN PUBLIC."

"Wh....whataretheterms," Aaron barely got out through gritted teeth.

"OH, SPOKE TO SOON DIDN'T I 'OLE BRITTLE BONES. LOOKS LIKE A REAL MAN IS BACK IN THE SADDLE AND READY TO TALK BUSINESS."

Aaron didn't have it in him to respond, instead carefully eyeing Hank's blade. If the burn was as bad as he thought it was, he was mentally preparing himself to self-amputate in order to keep going. He wasn't even sure he could do it, take his own arm, but if it was the only viable option he would convince Hank to do what needed to be done.

Save Ashley.

Goddamnit, save EVERYONE.

"OHMYGOD, IT'S JUST A FLESH WOUND. GET OVER YOURSELF ALREADY," he mocked. *"YOU'RE WAY MORE FUN WHEN YOU'RE NOT CRYING ALL OVER YOURSELF LIKE A BABLING BABY WHO DIDN'T GET HIS MILK FROM MOMMY'S TIT."*

I'm not crying.

"OH BUT ON THE INSIDE YOU ARE, I CAN HEAR YOU WAILING AWAY LIKE A GODDAMN CREED SONG IN THERE."

Aaron couldn't oppose.

"OK, SO LIKE, HERE'S WHAT I WAS THINKING," he started. *"OPTION ONE, YOU GO STRAIGHT TO THE PRINCIPLES OFFICE. IF YOU MAKE IT THERE, ALIVE, YOU WILL FIND YOUR GROUP SAFE AND SOUND...ISH. THEY WERE BEING NAUGHTY SO I SENT THEM TO THE PRINCIPLES OFFICE, NOT RESPONSIBLE FOR WHAT*

HAPPENED TO ANY OF THEM ALONG THE WAY, SCOUTS HONOR."

They were alive, or at least that is what it wanted him to think. Fighting the surge of pain in his forearm, Aaron had no other leads on where they'd be.

"BUT WAIT, WHAT'S IN DOOR NUMBER TWO? SO GLAD YOU ASKED, LET'S SEE WHAT'S IN DOOR NUMBER TWO!"

Behind them, all the way at the end of the hall, the doors to Crest Hill swung open. Aaron could feel a cool breeze as it made its way down the hall toward him, the fresh air an elixir for only a moment before the pain in his forearm came rushing back. He could see out the doors, all the way out to the parking lot. Aaron could see his Shelby sitting there, just where he'd left it, and the group of people gathering outside the doors.

"WERE IN HERE!" Aaron attempted to yell, only coming out as a weak squeak in his condition.

"SERIOUSLY? YOU HONESTLY THOUGHT I WAS JUST GONNA OPEN THE FRONT DOORS AND ALLOW A RESUCE ATTEMPT? DAMN, YOU REALLY ARE DUMB AS YOU LOOK. IT'S JUST A VISUAL AID JACKASS, TO SHOW YOU WHAT COULD BE YOURS IF YOU CHOOSE DOOR NUMBER TWO. THEY CAN'T ACTUALLY SEE YOU. MORON."

"I...idon'tunderstand?"

"SIMPLE REALLY. YOU EITHER GO DEEPER INTO THE SHIT IN HOPES YOU CAN GET TO YOUR FRIENDS AND DIE TOGTHER, OR YOU TAKE THE GET OUT OF JAIL FREE CARD IF JUST PUT ON THE TABLE."

"Wh...why?"

"WHY? CAUSE I'M SUPER NICE DUDE AND YOU ARE BEING A TOTAL DICK BY QUESTIONING MY ACT OF KINDNESS."

"He's lying," Hank urged Aaron.

"HE'S LYING," he mocked, word for word. *"DON'T LISTEN TO DINNER AT FIVE OTHER THERE, HE'S JUST JEALOUS CAUSE HE NEVER GOT AN OFFER LIKE THIS IN ALL THE TIME HE'S BEEN MY GUEST. IT'S NOT THAT*

HARD TO PROCESS, I GIVE YOU A GET OUT OF JAIL FREE CARD AND YOU WALK OUT THAT FUCKING DOOR LIKE THIS NEVER HAPPENED. I KEEP YOUR FRIENDS AND YOU PROBABLY GET CHARGED AS A SERIAL KILLER WHEN THE WHOLE TOWN REALIZES YOU WERE THE LAST PERSON TO SEE EVERYONE ALIVE AND HAVE NO ALIBI. **BUT,** YOU GET TO LEAVE THIS PLACE. NO MORE DEMONS OR FIRE, JUST SHOWER RAPES AND PRISON TATTOS."*

There it was, the catch.

Aaron knew it was too good to be true, you didn't just get to leave a place like this without a Twilight Zone result that made leaving just as bad a decision as staying.

"Aaron, sir. You must listen to me. It's not what it seems; he will never let you leave this place. The moment you walk through those doors you will just be in a different version of this place, all by yourself with no hope of ever seeing your friends again. Do not trust him, do not allow yourself to become weakened by his alluring offer. The result will be worse that the reality you currently reside in."

"I...imgonn-" Aaron started to speak, his eyes getting heavier by the second as his body urged him to sleep. "I..."

"Do not do this Aaron, you are too strong to fall for his traps. I have witnessed your strength with my own two eyes. Do not do it sir."

*"OH WOULD YOU **QUIT** TUGGING ON HIS BALL BAG OLD MAN. HOW ABOUT YOU LET THE MAN MAKE HIS OWN DECISION. HE'S A BIG BOY, LET HIM SPEAK FOR HIMSELF. TOO AFRAID YOUR GOLDEN BOY IS WEAKER THAN YOU HOPED? THAT YOUR GOLDEN TICKET IS ACTUALLY A BIG FAT PHONY LIKE ALL THE OTHERS? I CAN SMELL HIS INDECISION FROM HERE, HE **WANTS** TO TAKE THE DEAL. HE WANTS OUT OF HERE AS BAD AS EVER. WHAT'S IT GONNA BE? TICK, FUCKING, TOCK."*

Aaron tried to answer his ultimatum, but was unable to get the words out before he blacked out from the pain and hit the cold tile floor.

XXIV

Aaron awoke from a nightmare.

He couldn't remember the specifics of the terrifying dream, but the framework was simple enough that even in his cloudy state he could recall most of it.

Aaron had been stuck, a prisoner in an escapable fortress. He'd lost all contact with those he knew. He didn't know what it was, but something had set him back and made it impossible for him to make another move. No matter how fast he wanted to run or loudly he needed to yell, he was stuck in the same place, unable to budge from his horrified stance.

He was immobile.

There were so many opportunities to escape, to flee from his nightmare, but he just couldn't manage to do it. Aaron's body did not respond to anything he told it to do, choosing to stand frozen in place the entire time instead of reacting to the situations as they passed him by.

He'd willed himself to do something, anything, but couldn't manage even the simple task of walking. He was lucky he was able to breath, but even that felt labored beyond reason.

Awake now, Aaron felt an all too familiar pain in his forearm and began to recollect what had happened.

Shit, that wasn't just a nightmare.

Aaron and Hank had been separated from the rest of the group in a blaze of fire, only to discover it was yet another trick by their captor. Aaron didn't remember everything that happened, he must have passed out from the pain if the rapidly increasing discomfort in his forearm told him anything, but he remembered a door opening and feeling a cool breeze before he lost consciousness. He seemed to recall banter, the usual between he and their captor at this point, but what it was about and the outcome was all a blur. Considering he wasn't standing next to Ashley at the reunion, Aaron conceded that he'd lost the argument.

How he was lying on a table, where Hank was, and why he was still alive even though his arm hurt like a sonofabitch, were all mysteries.

Hank spoke, wielded a sword from his cane, and defended him when he was as good as dead as the fire approached.

He wasn't in the unlit hallway anymore, somehow he'd been transported to the Crest Hill cafeteria and placed on top of one of the dozens of rolling benches that were lined up to accommodate the maximum amount of students possible during the lunch hour rush and students on off periods that hung around killing time if they didn't have a car.

The cafeteria smelled just like he remembered, of stale bread and soon to be expired milk, mixed with the always intoxicating aroma of over mixed cleaning solution used on the tile floors. The smell alone should have been enough to put every single student at Crest Hill on a permanent fasting diet, but Aaron couldn't think of a time this place wasn't buzzing with people gorging themselves with food at all hours of the day. To be sitting in a dead silent cafeteria, alone, may have been to most unsettling thing to happen to him yet.

The easternmost wall was lined with vending machines, shelling out candy, chips, soda, and pastries to anyone willing to shove their cash into the money slot that glowed to lure unsuspecting teenagers toward it like moths to a flame. Seeing those ever-enticing vending machines made Aaron's mouth water, reminding him how long it had been since he'd last eaten. Breakfast back at his mother's house seemed like a lifetime ago, all he wanted was a sweet treat and a fizzy drink to wash it down with. Aaron wasn't proud of his diet, only his fortunate genes and empty wallet had kept him from becoming morbidly obese from eating vending machine cuisine more times than not when he was on the road.

Aaron's arm sent a jolt of pain through his body and he instinctively reached his other arm across his body to cradle it. It was only then that he realized his damaged arm had been treated, wrapped in gauze. He didn't remember anything after the tremendous pain of the fire burning his arm, he was barley able to speak much less tend to his wounds efficiently. The one thing he did know was there were no medical provisions in the dark hallway where he'd been burned, and there were no medical provisions in the cafeteria either. Somewhere between here and there he'd been treated, with supplies that were only available in one place that he knew of.

The nurse's office.

The same nurse's office that was right next-door to the Principle's office where Jack and the group were being held, allegedly.

So close yet so far.

A loud crack filled the cafeteria and snapped Aaron out of it, unconsciously putting him in survival mode as he popped up on the balls of his feet in a crouch, scanning the cafeteria for threats.

All he saw was Hank, utter delight displayed across his face as he made his way towards him. Hank was cradling a handful of snacks and sodas; he's bounty from a successful heist. Aaron swiveled around to look over at the vending machines that lined the wall; seeing one of them no longer had a plastic window panel protecting it's contents. Instead, there was a pile of broken plastic pieces and a freshly raided vending machine with little to nothing left in any of its slots.

"Hank, what's going on? Why are we in the cafeteria? Why did you defend me back there? When did you get a weapon?"

"Marvelous isn't it!" Hank responded, a stupid grin still plastered on his face. "Those boxes contain sufficient rations to get us through numerous days, each one of the rations carefully packaged as a single serving to boot! What a time you live in sir!"

Aaron wanted to be furious, to leap off the table and strangle Hank for getting excited about food when they were in the fight of their lives. Who gave a rat's fat ass about Doritos or Mountain Dew when his friends were probably being tortured to death at this very moment while he did absolutely nothing about it?

What about Ashley? She'd been alone since the beginning; she was probably scared out of her mind at this point. Aaron's rage started to come back when he thought about Ashley sitting alone, possibly under the goddamn gymnasium bleachers he'd been next to the entire time, thinking she'd been abandoned.

Aaron's stomach grumbled as he looked over the pile of snacks on the tabletop.

"Sir, I must insist you eat something. You need your strength, you have suffered a mighty blow," Hank said, eying his forearm as he offered up a Twix bar from the pile he'd unloaded on the table between them. "Here, eat this golden offering to build your strength."

"This is a candy bar Hank, it's not going to do a goddamn thing for my strength," Aaron chided, while reaching for the bar and eating it anyway. He was starving and wasn't about to let a perfectly good Twix bar go to waste no matter how mad he was.

"Excellent!" Hank cheerfully smiled as Aaron crushed into the candy bar. "Would you like an elixir to go with it?"

Aaron choose against the neon Mountain Dew Hank was offering, reaching for the bottle of water instead to quench his thirst. In-between each bite and gulp, Aaron wondered if this was all just a dream too. This was Hell after all; they weren't supposed to get the luxury of having candy and soda were they? If he thought it was a trap, or a cruel trick, it didn't stop him from tearing into a poorly packaged bear claw next to quell his hunger.

"Hank," Aaron asked between bites, his mother would have been furious with him for talking with a full mouth. "Did you treat my arm?"

"I did sir," Hank acknowledged with a tip of his fedora brim. "You were indisposed and unable to tend to your injury, so I took the liberty of doing it myself. I hope you approve, I must admit I am not a skilled healer so I did only the best I could sir."

"Where did you get the gauze?"

Hank looked at him confused.

"The stuff you wrapped my arm in," Aaron said, tapping his forearm where the white gauze was.

"Ahh, yes. Gaze was it?"

"Gauze," Aaron corrected, losing his patience.

"Gauze, very well sir. I found a small room with a plethora of healing goods. The container this gauze was entombed in contained an artful display of it being wrapped around an injury. I took the liberty of making a judgment call in your state and wrapped you up after washing the wound quite thoroughly. I hope this was not the incorrect call sir, I again must admit my healing knowledge is not quite as robust as others."

"Hank, do realize we were RIGHT NEXT DOOR to the rest of the group when we were in that room?" Aaron yelled, startling Hank. "You could have done something! You could have saved them dammit!"

Hank lowered his head in shame, unable to make eye contact with Aaron. Aaron didn't care, Hank had been so close to the rest of the group and done nothing, reverting back to his old habit of being a bystander while chaos happened all around him.

"Sir, please... forgive me," Hank started, his voice weak and trembling. "This world...this scenery...it's all quite unrecognizable to me. I have seen so many places, so many horrific scenarios, that I cannot imagine there is nothing I haven't seen before. Still, each time, each new placement, I find myself lost once again. I never seem to find my footing, the world around me always changing, thrust into unrecognizable situations one after another."

The guilt hit Aaron like a freight train, immediately mad at himself for not seeing it before.

Hank was just as fucked as he was.

Perhaps even worse.

"Hank," Aaron started, as Hank cut him off.

"You MUST believe me sir, I had not inclination of where we were at the time. I would have done more if I had known, that I swear to you. I have spent an eternity down here, watching some of the bravest men and women fight against all hope and lose swiftly to the hand they were dealt. Watching such despair can take a toll on one's soul, though that was the point I was brought here I must assume. You are the first one, the only one, that has fought back and succeeded, it was the reason I choose to snap out of my pitiful state of constant self-sorrow and lend a hand toward you noble cause."

"Hank," Aaron said, this time Hank raising his head to look at him face-to-face. "Who are you?"

"That is a story for another time sir, for now we must remain focused on retrieving your friends and getting you out of here."

"Hank, I'm not going anywhere until you tell me who you are and what your story is," Aaron demanded, Hank reverting back to his shell at the stern demand. "Please."

Hank sighed, thought Aaron was unsure if it was because he didn't want to tell his story or because he knew they weren't going anywhere until he did.

"Many believe there is only one way to get here, to be imprisoned in this place after death," Hank started, sifting aimlessly through the remains of his bounty on the table. "Those who believe such a thing would be wrong or at the very lest uneducated to the extent of such banishment."

"When you die, you either go up or you go down," Aaron offered bluntly, using his good arm to point.

"Death is not the only path, you of all people should know that by now."

Hank was right; Aaron and the rest of the group had been very much alive before they had been thrust into this nightmare. Jack's explanation of exactly what had happened was still foggy at best to Aaron, but the gist was they were caught in Death's portal for Ronnie.

Wrong place, wrong time.

"So is that how you got here? Sucked into this mess by circumstance?" Aaron asked.

"My situation was much more...involved...shall I say."

"What the hell does that mean? You do something horrible and wind up here as a result?" Aaron asked, suddenly realizing he didn't know anything about Hank and may be sitting with a crazed mass murderer for all he knew.

"I suppose you could say that."

"What did you do Hank?" Aaron asked, balling his good hand into a fist incase he had to fight his way out of this.

"Take ease sir, I wish you no harm. I am not the villain to assume me to be," Hank offered, noticing his newly formed fist. "I was cast out."

"Cast out of where?"

Hank did not answer right away, only offering a knowing glance back at him. It took a moment for Aaron to piece the puzzle together.

Who just get's cast out of their own life like that?
Don't you have to die before you face ultimate judgment?
Isn't casting out only fo-... OH SHIT!
"YOU'RE AN ANGEL?" Aaron shouted.

"WAS an angel to be exact," Hank offered solemnly.

XXV

"Wait...WHAT?"

As many times as Hank told his story, it made Aaron's mind spin. Listening and retaining information was never his strong suit, that was Jack's foray, so he had Hank run through it all one more time just to get it all down.

"Sir, I must insist that we move on from this. We are losing time and ground the longer we sit here. I am fully aware of the unspeakable things that could be happening to your friends this very moment and implore you to take action."

"I plan to Hank, but right now I need to understand exactly what you are telling me."

Hank sighed, relenting as he began his story yet again.

Hank's real name is/was Hadriel.

He was the real deal, a full-blown angel, wings and all. Hadriel spent his time overlooking those around the world, watching as they made their way through life. He saw the struggles of everyday human life, the accomplishments, and the failures. Hadriel witnessed it all. Time went by, at a pace that was tough for Aaron to fully comprehend as Hadriel described it, with each human's entire existence only amounting to a few days in Hadriel's time. He had seen an unimaginable number of human timelines from start to finish, witnessing entire generations form and fall in a matter of weeks.

To Hadriel, humans were nothing more than a subject to be constantly observed. There were few rules where he resided; there was no need to establish such boundaries when everyone that existed in that plain consisted of such purity. No one ever thought about harming another, never thought about violence or selfishness to jeopardize everything.

"Jeopardize what?"

"In Arcadia, there is no singular place. It is amassed of numerous locations and divisions that all combine to create a singular entity that we could all connect to and interact inside of," Hank explained. "Arcadia was only as strong as it's weakest link. If something were to compromise its integrity, its purity, it would be dealt with swiftly to ensure Arcadia was to remain pure for all eternity."

"And Arcadia is…Heaven?" Aaron asked, again.

"What is Heaven?" Hank responded, curious.

"Bright, happy place up in the clouds you go when you die if you were a good person. All white, everyone's nice, and everything's great."

"Incredible, you know of Arcadia? How can…YOU…know of such a place's existence? Arcadia is only for those that are worthy. Do all human's know of Arcadia like you do?"

"In theory, yeah," Aaron nodded, still cradling his burned forearm with his good arm. "Heaven, or Arcadia, is more of a myth to most people. There are the real nut cases that swear they have been there, that they saw it when they were on the brink of death, but other than that it's really just a goal that helps keep some people on the right track and away from bad decisions."

"What about you sir? Do you believe in Arcadia?"

"Sure. It helps to think there is a happy place those you love go to when they die. That they aren't just rotting in the ground. Life's tough Hank, you probably know that better than anyone after watching so much of it, it's just nice to think there is a reason for the struggle. That there is a prize waiting for us at the end if we do things the right way."

Aaron hopped Hank couldn't read his mind like their captor, if he could he'd see right through his bullshit and that, honestly, Aaron never bought into the idea of an afterlife. Having his father taken from him at such a young age, Aaron found it hard to believe there was a higher power watching over them, making the decisions on who lived and died at any given moment. It was far easier to believe that shit just happened, that there was no bigger picture and they were getting face value on this life.

It was easier to direct his anger as circumstance, rather that direct it at an all-mighty Entity.

Aaron had to come to realize there was a bigger picture, that there WAS someone overlooking their every move.

That someone was Hank and he was sitting right in front of him.

Aaron did everything he could to hide his rage, to keep from lashing out at Hank for why they would take his father from him. To hide his desire to beat it out of Hank as to what the purpose was for him to lose his father, what the bigger picture was for it.

"Are you ok sir?" Hank asked.

"I'm fine," Aaron shot back, looking over at the vending machines to conceal his rage from Hank.

"Is it Marcus?" Hank asked

Aaron's head snapped back toward Hank.

"What did you just say?"

"Marcus. Are you thinking about Marcus sir? Is that why you have become upset?" Hank offered again.

"Where did you get that name?" Aaron demanded, looking Hank square in the eye, unblinking.

"It's your father's is it not?" Hank asked, confusion spread across his face at Aaron's sudden hostility.

"What do YOU know about my father?" Aaron said through gritted teeth.

"Sir, I just advised you on my assignment in Arcadia. I was tasked with watching over all humanity. I saw his life just as I saw yours and everyone else's."

"You let him die!" Aaron shouted, causing Hank to lean back at the outburst. "You sat and watched my father be taken from me and did NOTHING you sonofabitch! You had the power to do something, to make sure a boy didn't have to grow up without his father, yet you turned your back on him and let it happen. You turned your back on me. You are a coward Hank, you didn't deserve to be in the Ark or whatever the fuck you call it. You DESERVE to be down here, to rot for doing nothing!"

Aaron was ready to a fight, to let out every ounce of hate and sadness from over the years. Somehow, he was staring at the one responsible for taking his father away from him.

Hank was going to pay for what he'd done.

"If you think for one moment that I had anything to do with your father's demise, you are SORELY mistaken sir! I have witnessed more death, more despair, than you could EVER imagine. Imagine bearing witness to every death, every war sir. I had no power whatsoever to stop what happened, only to watch it unfold in front of me like a play I could not rewrite no matter how much I may have wanted to. You must tame you hatred towards me, it is ill conceived and inappropriate. We are NOT enemies sir, I had no hand it what happened to your father."

"Say whatever you want old man, whether it was you or God himself that decided to take him from me, your taking the beating for it."

"God?" Hank questioned.

"That's right, we know all about him too. Surprise asshole. Most people look up to him; to the one they think created all of us. You can count me out of that group; I only look up to flip him off for what he took from me for no goddamn reason. IF you see him after you die, let him know it was me that sent you back to him," Aaron growled, raising his fists to fight.

"Fascinating. Absolutely fascinating," Hank said, losing all interest in the impending battle between them. "You believe there is but one that rules over all, that this individual would be capable of making such decisions."

"Stop stalling grandpa and take your beating, let it be the ONE honorable thing you did in your miserable existence."

Hank, still in deep though, pointed his arm hand toward Aaron and flicked his wrist downward. Instantly, Aaron's legs lost all feeling and he collapsed into a pile on the tabletop. He couldn't move his legs, unable to feel anything from the waist down.

Aaron was paralyzed.

"WHAT DID YOU JUST DO TO ME?"

"I kept you from making a mistake you would come to regret," Hank offered.

"YOU PARALYZED ME!"

"On the contrary, I only subdued your central nervous system to allow me a moment to explain myself. You will regain full bodily function in a few minutes. If you still wish to come to blows after what I have to say, that is your decision to make. I have no ability to affect freewill. I only thought it wise that you acquire all the facts before jumping to a conclusion that requires my death as repayment for your fathers."

"I'm going to destroy you," Aaron promised.

"Maybe so, but for now you will have to make do with listening."

"What make's you think I want to hear a word you have to say?"

"What made you put your life on the line for Debbie back in room 201A?" Hank responded. "You are not a brute, far from it in my humble opinion. Someone willing to risk their life for another they hardly know is not someone willing to blindly kill without crippling regret afterward. You must think about what you are conspiring to do, it is not what you want."

"Guess we'll find out in a few minutes won't we," Aaron threatened.

"There is no God," Hank started.

"Bullshit."

"Pardon?"

"Bull-shit," Aaron reiterated. "You are going to stand there and try to tell me there is no God after what has happened? Look around you Hank, this is HELL. If there is a Hell, there is a Heaven. If those exist, that means there is someone running both. Ergo, God is real."

"Incredible," was all Hank was able to offer in rebuttal.

"My legs are tingling, which means you better hurry and conjure up a better lie than that if you think you're going to convince me not to kill you."

"Sir, I assure you, there is no God," Hank said again. "At least no how you describe him."

"Seriously, you're just going to hang you hat on this? Oh well, your funeral."

"I don't think you properly understand what I am saying sir," Hank began, showing no concern or hiding it better than Aaron thought he would. "Arcadia is not governed by any single entity. There is no singular power that is greater than the other. All oversee Arcadia together. Each entity shares a singular conscious, which is why there are no rules in Arcadia. They are unnecessary when we all share the same consciousness; no entity is able to act out without all knowing it is about to happen and preventing it. It is impossible for one to act, say to save a life, without others putting a stop to it before it could happen."

Aaron wasn't drinking the Kool-Aid just yet, but his anger had recessed enough with his curiosity now peaked.

"What about Jesus?" Aaron asked, now more curious than angry as his legs continued to tingle back to life.

"I am unfamiliar with the name?" Hank questioned.

"God's son, Jesus," Aaron offered.

"Sir, I just told you that there is no God," Hank responded, frustrated with repeating himself again. "Whomever this individual is, I have no doubt he is part of the collective conscious in Arcadia if you speak so highly of him, but to say he is special from any one of the others would be improper. There is no hierarchy in Arcadia."

"Huh," Aaron muttered, nodding his head as he tried to wrap his head around this.

"So IF there is no God, that means there is no Lucifer either right? So who is holding us down here? He said his name was Lucifer, why would he say that if Lucifer doesn't exist?"

"Down here is a different situation, in fact, it is a polar opposite of Arcadia. Down here, they still share a collective conscious among themselves, but there is no effort made to stop a singular entity from acting out on their own accord. Unlike in Arcadia, where even the thought of rebellion will cast you out, down here it is encouraged. Each action is treated as a building block, each decision a reaction instead of an action. He will say and do anything to fool you. The one that enslaves you and your friends is named Zadkiel."

"You said that even the thought of rebellion get's you cast out, is that why you're down here now?"

"The circumstances of my withdrawal from Arcadia are difficult to relive sir, forgive me," Hank said, taking another deep breath to calm himself. "I was cast out of Arcadia in an act of betrayal."

"Who betrayed you?"

"Back in Arcadia, Zadkiel and I shared more than just a collective conscious, we were brothers. We were both tasked with overlooking the Earth below and came to grow a tight bond between one another. Zadkiel found love with Haziel, there love was one that would stand the test of time, or so I'd hoped."

"Wait, you can fall in love in Arcadia? If everyone shares a collected conscious doesn't that make it…awkward? Knowing everything the other person is thinking and whatnot had to create obstacles right?"

"If course there is love in Arcadia, what would be the point of such bliss if unable to share with another? A collective conscious only allows for no secrets, it is not a tell-all book on each person. Think of it like…radio…you are aware of radio no?"

"Yeah, I've heard of it," Aaron smirked.

"A collective conscious is like radio, a constant stream in the background. You can chose to listen in intently if desired, or you can turn in down and tune it out if you wish. It is always there, always available, but it doesn't make us machines. Most entities exist as they did before, just with a constant connection to the collective. Someone is always listening, always aware, that is how each entity is governed."

"Sounds…different."

"Zadkiel and Haziel became one."

"Woah, TMI Hank."

"TMI?"

"Too much in information."

"Apologies sir, to become one in Arcadia is to form an everlasting bond with another. I believe you refer to it as marriage."

"Oh."

"As I was saying, their union affected our bond as Zadkiel focused on his life with Haziel and not on our assignment. I would cover for him as best I could, but it was only a matter of time before the rest of the collective conscious became aware of his deficiencies and reacted. When the time came for Zadkiel to be held accountable for his actions, he accused me of being the cause for his absence at his post."

"Sounds like a real dick."

"Zadkiel claimed that my subconscious, a current only he was capable of hearing due to our bond, spoke of desire to enforce my will upon the humans. To change the course of nature and make decisions as I saw necessary. Zadkiel claimed he created distance between us to avoid being a part of it."

"But it wasn't true?"

"To an extent, it was I'm afraid. Over time it became more and more difficult to watch the wars and violence happening below. I took my strained connection with Zadkiel to be the source for my discomfort, but looking back on it I cannot say it wasn't my subconscious begging me to act. To do something, even though I am not entirely sure what I could have possibly done had I chosen to act."

Aaron fell silent, thinking of his father again as Hank acknowledge the elephant in the room.

"I saw what happened to Marcus, your father. It would be untrue to say I wanted to intervene, I simply played my part. The longer I sit down here, rotting away, I can only wonder what would have happened if I'd have opened Pandora's Box and intervened at some point."

Aaron didn't respond, leaving the silence hanging in the room between them.

"So how did Zadkiel get down here too if you were the one caught of treason?"

"Treason sir?" Hank asked.

"It means you knowingly went against the governing body and put the entire…Arcadia at risk because of it."

"Ahh, of course," Hank nodded as he took in the new information. "Zadkiel had no proof of my subconscious thoughts since he alone was the only one that could access them. Unable to prove his claim, he was held accountable for abandoning his post. He was sentenced to be cast out unless Haziel could prove his claims were true. Since she was the only one who had such a strong bond with Zadkiel, she was the only one that could truthfully speak on his behalf. Her word was a good as law in Arcadia, if she said Zadkiel was telling the truth I would have been banished instead."

"But she didn't…" Aaron prodded.

"That is correct sir. For as long as I draw breath I will never be able to understand why she didn't back Zadkiel's claims. As his true love, she had every reason to agree with his allegations against me. Alas, she chose to remain silent, resulting in Zadkiel's banishment from Acadia."

"Jesus."

"As I already informed, Jesus had nothing to do with it sir."

"No. Jesus is just an expression we use when we are at a lost of words," Aaron tried to explain to a confounded Hank.

"A short time afterward, centuries to you, Haziel took her own life. The collective hurt for a long time after that, unable to fathom why she had done such a thing. While she shared a close bond with Zadkiel, she was able to wipe that section of her life away upon his banishment. In Acadia, you are not supposed to feel discomfort or sorrow. For whatever reason, Haziel chose not to forget Zadkiel, instead choosing to hold onto his memory for as long as she could before it was too much to bear."

"Why didn't she just choose to forget?"

"The same reason you choose to remember your father. It is better to have and lost that to never have had at all."

Aaron nodded in agreement. As bad as it was to loose his father, it would have been even worse to have had him wiped from his memory all together. Even at such a young age, there were enough good memories of him that he would hold onto for the rest of his life.

"As the collective struggled to come to terms with what happened, it dug into her conscious in a feeble attempt to find answers for her actions. Suicide did not happen in Arcadia, it was thought impossible by many until Haziel took her own life. After thoroughly digging through her conscious, the collective was able to concede she'd died of a broken heart, unable to come to terms with her involvement in casting Zadkiel out."

"How does that land you down here though?"

"In their findings, they also found what Haziel had chosen not to disclose. She had Zadkiel's conscious still intact, everything up to the point where he heard my subconscious yearning me to take action."

"So Zadkiel had been telling the truth all along?"

"It appears so. Unbeknownst to even myself, I was fighting a battle within to do something other than stand and watch as chaos erupted beneath me. For this, I was swiftly banished. Once cast out of Arcadia, I became a pawn for Zadkiel to play with. He never lost his rage, unable to see that it was his own wife that betrayed him and not me, so he's kept me in a never-ending loop of despair. I am now forced to join a new group, or individual if Zadkiel see's fit, and watch their feeble attempts to survive this place. No one ever does, no one ever goes longer than a few hours down here before they perish."

"Except me."

"Except you sir," Hank agreed. "You are the fist, and only person, that had managed to defeat the obstacle in your path."

"Lucky me," Aaron said sarcastically.

"I believe luck has nothing to do with it sir. I believe you are...different."

Hank stopped short of explaining what he meant by that, choosing to swallow the rest of his words instead. Aaron couldn't help but be intrigued.

What is he not telling me?

"I believe you have a chance, the best opportunity I've seen since being down here, at finding your friends. For that, I have chosen to intervene, to listen to my subconscious once and for all. I was cast out of Arcadia for my inner-desire to help, I may as well fulfill my destiny at least once before I succumb."

"Hey," Aaron said somewhat sheepishly, never great with apologies, "Sorry for threatening to kill you earlier."

"No apology necessary sir," Hank responded, tipping his fedora and he turned toward the cafeteria exit.

XXVI

They made their way towards the Principle's office in silence.

Hank didn't feel much like talking after baring his sole to Aaron, it had taken everything he had to revive his experience in Arcadia. He'd lost his brother forever, even though he was very much still alive and kicking down here, Aaron had come to realize, due to a call-to-action his heart was begging him to take all along. He couldn't help but blame himself for what had happened, choosing to live his condemnation in isolation as a self-issued punishment for letting the one closest to him in Arcadia fall.

Aaron wasn't the most social person so he was ok with the silence, it was easier to try and wrap his head around what he'd just heard in silence than with background noise of awkward conversation to fill dead air.

So there is no God.

Huh.

He wasn't a child; he'd long given up on the belief that Santa Claus or the Easter Bunn were real just like every other adult that walked the Earth. It was part of the transition from childhood to adulthood; taking on the burdens of the real world until it crushed your sole like it did everyone else's. Life may have been so much sweeter had everyone been able to keep the charade up, but it wasn't plausible so people just learned to lose the magic they once had, replacing with an acrimonious dosage of reality to fill the void. For a short period of time, it was a rush to find out such a secret. Aaron remembered having the conversation with his mother and grandpa, to learn that they were the ones putting presents under the tree all along, and he remembered the utter thrill of feeling like a grown-up afterward. He was finally in on the whole thing, he was mature enough to be trusted with such an important secret, a sense that he'd earned his stripes by showing he could handle such intelligence. It became an honor to walk the halls of school the following day, knowing that some of his classmates had no idea and were not important or mature enough to know the truth.

Now, he just felt alone.

No one would ever mistake Aaron as religious, he only went to church for funerals and weddings like a growing number of millennials he found himself hanging around back at the Rusty Knuckle. Aaron had a cold relationship with whomever was calling the shots upstairs, that asshole had allowed his father to be taken from him and, whomever it was, didn't deserve his prayers or time as far as Aaron was concerned. He detested the idea of hoping someone else would come to his rescue, in a world were such horrible things could happen on any given day it seemed preposterous that any adult, would honestly believe someone was watching over them and could actually help them in their time of need. Aaron's grandpa had been in World War II; there was enough proof from his stories alone that there wasn't someone looking out for them.

Turns out, someone WAS watching over them.

That someone just shattered Aaron's mind with how the afterlife worked, making it harder than ever to ignore all the heresy and just look forward to a comfortable spot in the ground where no one would bother him when he died.

Then he went and got himself, and the rest of the group, trapped down here and was secretly hoping more than ever that there was in fact a God that would be able to swoop down and pluck them out of this shit-show. To have a faint hope, a barley audible whisper, in the back of his head that if everything he had seen and experienced could happen, there HAD to be a good version of the asshole on the intercom that could save them from all of this.

Someone that could snap his or her finger, make things right.

Nope.

Surprise pal, you're just as fucked as you were when you were topside!

All Aaron could do was focus on the task at hand.

Find Ashley.

Find the group.

Stay Alive.

Escape.

There was one bright spot to all of this. With the sudden influx of information swirling around his head, Aaron's forearm had become less of a burden than it had been. It still stung like a sonofabitch, but the intense, throbbing pain from the searing of his skin didn't take up as much of his focus as it had earlier.

Aaron hadn't mentioned it to Hank, partially because he didn't want any push back if Hank didn't agree with the plan and partially because Hank was in no mood to discuss strategy with at the moment, but he wasn't heading directly towards the Principle's office to recuse Jack, Debbie and the rest of the group.

He was headed for the gymnasium to rescue Ashley.

Once they'd left the cafeteria, Aaron made the decision that Jack could hold down the fort just a little longer while he went to rescue Ashley. She was all alone and scared, Jack had Debbie and the rest of the group to surround himself with. He'd had enough of this bullshit about not being able to go to the gymnasium till the schedule allowed it, this was Hell after all.

Fuck schedules.

From this point on, it was save Ashley or bust.

"Sir," Hank broke his silence, somehow finding his way to Aaron's side without him even noticing. "May I ask but one question?"

"Shoot," Aaron said without breaking stride.

"Are you from Arcadia as well?"

"What?" Aaron asked, actually stopping and turning his head to look at him. "You go radio silence on me and the first thing you manage to say to me is a question of whether or not I'm a fallen angel like you?"

"Forgive me sir, I don't mean to harass you. I've been contemplating this since we left that room earlier and it's the only logical solution that makes any sense."

"Look around you Hank," Aaron raised his arms and he slowly spun around in the middle of the dark hallway. "Does ANY of this shit seem logical to you? A goddam demon over the speaker made Ashley vanish into thin air before making more than one of my old classmates BURST INTO FLAMES for no goddamn reason. I just fucking HARPOONED a demon. THAT was all logical to you?"

"That is precisely what has caught my attention sir, your impaling of that demon earlier. How did YOU do it?" Hank asked, somewhat accusingly.

It was just around the next corner, at the end of the hallway. He was so close to finding her and rescuing her.

Unless this was all just another twist, a ruse to lead him right into another trap like the good mouse stuck in a maze that he was.

Rescue may have been the wrong word. It was hard to say you were rescuing someone when all you were really doing was freeing her from one nightmare until the next one, inevitably, reared its ugly head.

"I will be happy to grant you your solace as requested sir, but I must insist you answer the question," Hank said, grabbing Aaron's good arm to stop him from walking any further.

"Seriously?"

Hank nodded eagerly.

"I saw screw it. Saw it in a movie once so I figured what the hell, why not. No one else had a better idea so I went with it and it worked. End of story."

"Incredible," Hank glowed; showing a glimmer of hope. "Absolutely INCREDIBLE!"

"It did the job," Aaron pulled free from Hank's grip and continued walking before his curiosity got the best of him and he turned to look back at Hank.

"Why?"

"Sir?"

"Why is it incredible?"

"Sir, for all intent and purposes, you should no longer exist. You should never have been able to defeat that demon."

"Well thanks for the vote of confidence, real wizard with words aren't you Hank."

Hank unsheathed the blade form his cane and offered it to Aaron. At first Aaron was defensive, sure Hank was about to attack when he drew the blade, but once Hank offered the blade handle first Aaron willingly accepted. Weapons were on short supply, so if Hank was ready and willing to hand over his weapon Aaron wasn't going to turn it down.

"Perhaps I have not made myself clear sir," Hank watched curiously, holding his breath once Aaron took the handle. "You should be dead, no mortal creature should be able to handle that sword without...lethal consequences."

"WHAT! You knew it could kill me by just touching it and you offered it anyway? What the serious fuck Hank?"

It was one thing to find out God wasn't real, now he realized he'd been seconds away from death when he accepted the sword.

Does EVERYTHING have to try and kill be down here?

Aaron had a thought cross his mind that hadn't occurred to him yet, that should have been the first thing he asked himself when they were separated from Jack and the rest of the group.

Is Hank lying?

What if it was all bullshit?

What if Hank was just another fragment of twisted torture for Aaron to experience while he was in Hell? It would stand to reason that Hank could very well be working with the voice from the intercom, using an elaborate story to lure him into a trap. Why wouldn't the Devil make a run at his mind? He'd directly tried to kill him at least twice, more if you counted the never-ending possibility that he could burst in to flames at any moment. Hank's story was just crazy enough that he couldn't fully wrap his head around it to know for sure if he was lying or telling the truth.

Common, there HAS to be a God right?

Aaron's mind raced with how he was going to find out for sure if Hank was telling the truth or if he was walking a dark hallway with the enemy this entire time.

If Hank were evil, why would he make the effort to patch me up when I was out?

So he could keep torturing me, obviously.

"Sir, I can assure you I am not the traitor you think I am," Hank offered.

"GODDAMNIT," Aaron shouted. "You can read my thoughts too?"

"I can sir," Hank admitted bashfully. "I choose to ignore most of the things I hear, but I must admit I can hear it all. I am a fallen angel sir, even in Abaddon I possess the ability the same as I did in Arcadia."

"The hell is Abaddon?" Aaron asked.

"Abaddon is the Realm of the Dead, the place where those that were not worthy of a place in Arcadia exist…a dwelling those in Arcadia have come to fear…a dwelling where one must stay once cast out," Hank acknowledged.

"Wait, you mean Hell?"

"What is Hell sir?" Hank questioned.

"Scary, hot place all the bad people go when they die."

"Fascinating. And this Hell is the opposite of…Heaven was it?"

"Yup," Aaron nodded.

"I suppose it doesn't matter what they are calling it these days sir, the ideal of each place is still the same. One is for the worthy, one is for those whom are…not."

Aaron found himself easily agreeing with Hank. From all he'd been told in the last hour or so, if time actually existed in He…Abaddon, it was naïve to believe Heaven and Hell were universally used everywhere. Even from the little information he'd retained from school, Aaron knew there were multiple names for the afterlife depending on where you were in the world and what religion you chose to follow.

If Hank wanted to use Arcadia and Abaddon, two names he'd never heard or didn't remember from school, so be it.

"So you can read my thoughts," Aaron started. "That means you know I am teetering on the fence on whether or not your are telling me the truth or just another enemy."

"An honest conclusion sir," Hank acknowledged. "May I remind you that if I WERE your opponent, I would have made an effort to thwart your attack earlier would I not?"

"Doesn't sound so far fetched to me Hank. What's stopping you from threading your own story to make me trust you? To lure me into yet another goddamn trap that will be one I can't escape? If you are telling me the truth, you know that there is no way out of here. Just one, big, fucking merry-go-round of torture with no escape. Why should I believe after all this time, after all you've allegedly experienced, you just now decided to take up arms against your brother and fight back?"

"Because you didn't die," Hank offered bluntly.

"That's it. I didn't die when I touched your cane-sword and that sparked a fire inside of you to give the whole rebellion thing a shot? Sounds suspicious to me Hank."

"It is not JUST the sword sir," Hank offered. "You didn't die when a demon had you pinned. You fought back, you protected the one's you care for. You must understand that I have seen many forms of bravery, the reckless soul that barrels into an attack without so much as a single thought to what might happen, finding their end as quickly as they found their courage. I have witnessed those willing to sacrifice themselves for others, a noble gesture in itself, but ultimately detrimental to the cause as once they are consumed those they sacrificed themselves for are unable and unwilling to carry on without them, often times meeting their end shortly afterward. You sir, you are the first one that fought back, but did so without the desire to perish as you are aware that your demise will not benefit those around you."

"Still just words Hank. You can spin a sweet vine I'll give you that. In another life you would be one hell of a motivational speaker, but I am more of an actions speak louder than words kinda guy. If we look at your actions, I see someone that was unwilling to help save Debbie when she was being ganged up on by a horde of semi-demons, but you were more than wiling to hand me a weapon that could have killed me instantly. You did treat my arm, so that's a point in the 'you may not be trying to kill me' column, but that could also just be a way to keep me going longer for more torturous fun on your end."

"You're arm sir! You can rectify yourself!"

"What?"

"You did not perish when you touched the sword sir, that means that you are able to weld this for reasons I am not quite sure of at this precise moment. Either way, if the sword will not kill you…"

"It can heal me?" Aaron finished Hank's sentence.

"That is my belief sir. I must warn you I have no experience of this, I've only ever unsheathed this sword once before, so I cannot guarantee it will work. What I can offer is a chance sir, a chance to ease your pain and prove my alliance is one of honestly and not of malicious intent."

Hank put the thin blade in the palms of his hands and offered it to Aaron, just like he'd done earlier. Aaron was less enthusiastic about taking it this time around, now that he knew this sword could have easily killed him. Despite the growing agony in his forearm, that had taken center stage as his quest to rescue Ashley took a back seat yet again, he was hesitant to take Hank's offering.

What if THIS is a trap? What if the minute I touch that handle I die an agonizing death just like he wanted all along?

Hank's story about witnessing those before him die in vain, leaving those they cared about to fend for themselves rattled around in his head as he contemplated the offer.

"Sir, please," Hank said, genuinely enough to be somewhat convincing that time.

A shot of pain went from his forearm up to his still sore shoulder and made the decision for him. If he was going have any chance at fighting the next obstacle that was likely only just around the corner, he needed to be a full strength. Having only one arm wasn't going to cut it. He was already dealing with a black eye from his scuffle with Ronnie, his shoulder hurt like hell if he moved his arms above his shoulder, and now his forearm was badly burned, rendering his left arm all but useless in a fight.

Fuck it.

Aaron grabbed the sword out of Hank's hands and they both stood in eager silence for a moment, waiting for something to happen.

And another.

And another.

Annnnnd another.

After a minute had passed, Aaron looked over at Hank. They were both equally disappointed that the sword had not worked to heal his arm. Hank had lost an opportunity to prove his loyalty, his trustworthiness, to Aaron. The look on his face told Aaron he knew the opportunity had passed and left only another question mark in its place.

"Maybe it's broken," Aaron offered, though he was just as displeased with the outcome as Hank was, though for different reasons. He was not going to have to do the impossible with only one arm.

Hank didn't respond right away, only his eyes were able to communicate. They grew bigger and bigger, a look of astonishment washing over his face.

Confused, Aaron looked back down at the sword that had stolen Hanks attention entirely.

It was glowing.

XXVII

It burned.

That's not how it started though. Initially, the glow was the only thing that changed from the moment he'd accepted the blade from Hank.

Slowly afterward, the throbbing pain in his forearm was replaced with a simmering heat that Aaron swore made his skin warm to the touch. He'd started sweating around the three-minute mark as the burn continued to strengthen.

As he stood there, holding the blade tightly to ensure he didn't drop it while it did whatever the hell it was doing, Aaron's forearm underneath the gauze began to turn a noticeable shade of pink as the gauze started to peel away from his arm. His entire forearm was now completely covered in a slick sheen of sweat as he grinned and bared it through the growing discomfort.

"What's going on here Hank?" Aaron asked, a hint of alarm in his voice from the growing temperature in his forearm.

"I...I'm not entirely sure sir. The blade is having a reaction to your injury, but as to the particulars of what is actually happening I couldn't answer you honestly without a signification amount of conjecture of my part."

"What?"

"I would only be guessing sir, nothing precise," Hank admitted.

Wonderful.

Aaron made the decision he was going to ride out the ever-increasing discomfort in his forearm in hopes that it was the right decision. He was still breathing so it was a plus since Hank had be adamant he should have died instantaneously upon touching the sword. The burning had to be doing SOMETHING, so he decided to see what that something was and hope for the best.

That's right, hope for the best while you stand smack dab in the middle of Hell...or Abaddon or whatever the fuck this place is supposed to be called.

The gauze, now drenched in his perspiration, began uncoiling slowly around his arm as the athletic tape Hank had used to keep it in place lost its adhesiveness. Quickly, the movement of the gauze over the top of his burn became a sore spot, the slight shift of the rough cut gauze against the burned area as it continued to undo itself was almost worst than the burning sensation from the sword. A rough cut of sandpaper like gauze scraping across his forearm was pure torture. Everyone knew the best, and only way, to remove a bandage was quickly, the only other option being a slow and painful process that only worked to drag out the discomfort the more you attempted to avoid it. Aaron reached over with his right hand and ripped the gauze away from the burn area, creating a moment of breath-stealing pain that quickly dissipated as the burning sensation overtook it.

Aaron's forearm was now a noticeable shade of light red, the light pink stage only a moment ago now a thing of the past.

He was burning himself from the inside out.

His forearm resembled his mother's open stovetop, the coils glowing a brilliant shade of red the hotter they became. The area from his elbow to his wrist now pulsated in rhythmic fashion along with the blade he still gripped tightly.

"Is it working sir, have the discomfort resided?" Hank asked eagerly, having removed his fedora and holding in the tips of his hands across his chest as one would at a funeral.

"DOES IT LOOK LIKE I FEEL BETTER?" Aaron shouted, sweat dripping from his brow. "It just keeps getting HOTTER."

"Look sir!" Hank raised his finger and pointed at Aaron's left arm. "It's spreading!"

"Shit," Aaron said, reaching over with his right hand to lift the sleeve on his left arm, the glowing red underneath the skin had passed his elbow and began flowing upward into his shoulder. His veins acting as the method of transportation, his left arm now a piece of glowing artwork as the glowing red veins continued to spider-web up towards his shoulder.

"Help me with my shirt Hank," Aaron demanded, Hank jumping to attention. "You're gonna have to rip in off, I can't let go of the blade."

Hank seemed to understand, hurriedly walking up to Aaron and grabbing his shirt collar with both hands before ripping it all the way down the front. He'd forgotten that Hank wasn't the old man he appeared to be; Hank likely had more strength than he did on a good day. Aaron quickly pulled his right arm out of the shirt and worked to remove his left arm. As soon as his shirt fell off his shoulder and down towards his forearm, it burst into flames. The moment it made contact with the intense glowing area of his forearm the shirt was toast.

"Jesus," Aaron said, waving his right hand to clear the ash from the now disintegrated shirt.

Aaron now stood shirtless as they both watched the red glow continue to spider-web all the way across his shoulders. Once it reached the end of his right shoulder, Aaron assumed it had finished its migration. He was now covered in sweat; a thick sheen covering his body gave the look he'd just exited the pool. His hair was also soaked, drops of sweat freely dripping from his head.

"Now what?" Hank asked.

"I don't know Hank, this was your idea remember? You tell me what happens next? Does the burning ever regress, cause that would be REALLY nice right about now?"

As hot as his forearm was, and it was HOT, Aaron couldn't help but notice that he was able to withstand it. This was noticeable since he'd quickly struggled to remain conscious when the initial burn had occurred, a pain that admittedly caused more shock than anything, but still an agonizing pain nonetheless. Even now, with the burning sensation spreading through him, he was oddly able to maintain his composure through it all. He didn't want to admit to himself, the sweat pouring of his body begged to tell a different story but in a way, the heat was appreciated.

Relieving.

"It's still going," Hank said, his eyes now moving from Aaron's shoulder to meet his.

"Where?" Aaron asked, looking over his body but unable to see any further spreading. "Where's it spreading to?"

"Your…your face sir," Hank gasped.

Aaron felt it the moment Hank said it, his left eye where Ronnie had cold-cocked him outside the bar last night began to heat up. He looked over at the nearest door, using the glass panel each door had as a crude mirror. Since his body had a glowing red spider-web coursing throughout it, he was able to see a reflection of the parts affected in the glass, vaguely. What he saw startled him.

The entire left side of his face was now covered in glowing red spider webbing. The intense heat that had spread throughout his forearm and shoulder now finding itself a new home in his face. Aaron's heart rate began to increase. Up to this point he'd been able to keep it together, but now that it was covering half of his face, Aaron couldn't help but let a sense of panic slip into his conscious.

Pouring sweat, Aaron contemplated letting go of the blade.

The heat was inviting in a way, the same way a warm bed called to it's owner on an early cold morning, that all changed when it seeped into his head. It was one thing to feel his extremities heat up, immensely, but when his head started to get hot he quickly felt like a Pop-Rock about to explode. The pressure started to build up in his forehead as the internal heat continued to rise, Aaron swore he could feel enough pressure just behind his left eye he became worried it would shoot out of his skull.

Aaron had horrific visions of a final torture. One that involved a warm, calming sense to wash over him in right before it became unbearable and the growing pressure in his head caused it to explode. Too many late night horror movie marathons with Jack back in high school allowed him to be extremely creative in coming up with horrible ways he could be killed.

"My head feels like it's gonna explode!"

"Let go of the sword sir!" Hank implored.

Ready to cut his losses and live to fight another day, Aaron sent the message to his left hand to release its grip on the blade.

His hand did nothing, holding the blade tightly.

Aaron tried again to release his grip, but his fingers would not unfurl from the handle of the blade.

He could not let go.

"I can't!" Aaron shouted, his head only moments away from exploding like a popcorn kernel in the microwave.

"My word," was all Aaron heard Hank say before he fell to his knees, no longer able to stand.

"You have to save Ashley Hank, promise me," Aaron pleaded, grateful to have a constant stream of sweat running down his forehead to mask the tears as they formed. "Don't let her die."

"Sir," Hank started before Aaron cut him off with a primal cry of his own.

"AAAAAAGGGGGGHHHHHHH!"

Everything went white.

∎

Aaron opened his eyes.

Am I still alive?

He was still on his knees, with both hands planted on the warm tile floor in the darkened hallway. There was a small puddle circling him, his own sweat. He was breathing heavily and shaking slightly.

But he was still alive.

Yea me.

As Aaron tried to push himself up off of all fours, to rest his hands on his thighs, he realized he was no longer holding on to the blade. It had fallen to the ground, just outside the moat of sweat that surrounded him. He didn't remember letting go of the blade and wondered how long he'd been out this time.

Real hero you are, you can't even stop blacking out.

"Sir?"

"SIR!" Hank shouted.

"What...what happened? How long was I out for?"

"Out sir?" Hank questioned.

"How long did I lose consciousness?"

"I wasn't aware you'd lost consciousness sir, you simply yelled out before dropping the blade and falling over on to your hands."

"Wait...what? I wasn't unconscious?"

"No sir, not that I recall."

No shit.

"Little help," Aaron requested, raising his right arm from Hank to slip under and help him to his feet. "So...what the hell was that?"

"I must admit sir, I have never seen anything like that before. I could not tell you what happened even if I wanted to, you must believe me," Hank pleaded.

"That could have killed me," Aaron shoved his left hand into Hank's chest in disapproval. "You are still on my shit list until further notice."

"Sir," Hank offered, looking down at his arm.

"Don't try and talk your way out of this one Hank."

"SIR," Hank demanded.

"WHAT!"

"Your arm sir."

Aaron didn't even realize it until he saw it with his own two eyes, he'd stopped feeling the pain but considering that he'd momentarily blacked out it wasn't overly surprising to have a short numbing period before the pain reintroduced itself.

That wouldn't be the case though, not anymore.

Aaron's forearm, once badly burned, was completely healed.

"Holy shit," Aaron mumbled, rubbing his arm with his right hand to make sure it wasn't just a cruel mirage. He entire forearm was back to normal; it wasn't even sore to the touch. The hair on his forearm was present too, creating the appearance that nothing had ever happened in the first place.

"It worked," Aaron said to Hank, shock on his face.

"Your face too sir!"

Aaron reached up and rubbed the left side of his face, the swelling was gone. He gently pushed in the area over his left eye, still expecting it to be tender, but felt nothing. He walked over to the glass panel on the door and stuck his face as close to the glass as he could to see that he no longer had a black eye or any swelling.

Holy SHIT!

He didn't even realize it until a few moments later, still rubbing his face like a moron expecting the pain to come roaring back, that his shoulder didn't hurt anymore either. He did a few windmills with each arm, creating circles in the air to test his shoulder and found no pain in either shoulder.

The blade didn't just heal his arm, it restored everything.

"I can't believe it actually worked," Aaron said, Hank standing sheepishly off to the side while Aaron did his calisthenics.

"I am overwhelmed sir."

"Suppose this means I have to trust you now," Aaron said, Hank's eyes glowing at the news.

"I appreciate that more than you know sir," Hank responded, tipping his fedora towards him as he slid the blade back into its cane holder.

"Now what sir?"

Aaron felt a cool breeze as the wet skin of his abdomen reminded him he had torn his shirt off during the process.

"Now we find something for me to wear."

"Perhaps one of these boxes has something for you to wear," Hank offered, looking over at the lockers that lined the wall.

"Not unless you have a bol-" Aaron started before Hank calmly walked to the first locker and ripped the door off like it was nothing more than tissue paper.

Inside the locker was the typical fare you would find in just about any locker, some books and an empty backpack. A small mirror was stuck to the back of the door, a clear sign this locker belong to a girl since Aaron didn't recall any guy he knew checking himself in a mirror before class.

"Bugger, maybe another one?" Hank offered, calmly ripping the door off the locker next to it.

It took them the entire top row of lockers till they found a locker than had someone's gym clothes stuffed in it. Aaron wasn't thrilled with the idea of wearing someone's sweaty leftovers, but after the standard sniff-test he decided it wasn't as bad as he thought and put the shirt on. The front had the Crest Hill crest on it, this shirt was a standard issue loaner for the kids that forgot to bring clothes for gym class.

"Better sir?" Hank asked as Aaron pulled the somehow perfect fitting shirt over his head and down his torso.

"Much better."

"What now sir?"

"Now we go get Ashley."

■

Aaron and Hank rounded the corner, the gymnasium doors visible at the end of the hallway.

He started walking towards them, Hank by his side, when he first heard it.

Ping.

Aaron was used to being on high alert by now, nothing was what it seemed anymore. All it would take it for him to get sloppy for only a second and it could be the end. The blade, somehow, had healed him, but he wasn't eager to find out if that worked more than once. Aaron needed to be on full alert at all times to keep any chance of rescuing Ashley and the rest of the group.

Ping...Ping.

He knelt down in a crouch, Hank quickly following suit, in the middle of the hallway. Head on a swivel, Aaron checked behind them to see if they were walking into an ambush.

Nothing.

They both remained crouched for a moment, Aaron waiting to hear the noise again while Hank struggled to figure out what was going on. Hank tried to speak, but Aaron quickly silenced him while he listened for the noise.

Ping.

Something about that noise was oddly familiar. He couldn't put his finger on it for the life of him, but Aaron swore he knew that sound. He'd heard it before.

After a few moments of silence, Aaron rose from his crouch and began making his way toward the gymnasium doors. Hank, quietly, followed suit.

Only a few steps away from the doors, the noise returned.

Ping...Ping...Ping.

"What is it sir?" Hank whispered.

Aaron didn't respond, just shook his head to illustrate he wasn't sure and quickly covered the distance between them and the gymnasium doors. He pulled up just to the right of the farthest door, allowing him to peak through the glass panel before he went in guns blazing.

Gun's blazing, if only pal. All we have is four fists, four feet, and a thin blade.

Ping...Ping.

Aaron, back against the wall with Hank right next to him following suit, snuck a peak through the glass to see what that familiar noise was.

"Oh you gotta fucking kidding me," Aaron whispered.

XXVIII

Dodgeball.

The ire of soccer moms and helicopter parents alike.

A game with the sole point of pegging the opponent, nothing above the neck to keep it innocuous, as hard as you could to tag them out. Last one standing won, be if for themselves or the team they fought for. The point was to tag people out, but the game always quickly dissolved into a vicious manhunt to eliminate aggression.

Not a single living person played Dodgeball kindheartedly, each person letting go of that rubber ball like they were throwing the last out of the World Series. This was the predominant reason it had been removed from every-day school activities, the bullies taking it upon themselves to dish out as much pain and fear as they could before the game ended but while still within the safe confines of the game. The same reason some people just played football so they could hit people without getting in trouble with the police, people sought the game of Dodgeball to vent whatever it was they were working through at the moment.

As Aaron stood looking through the thin glass panel on the gymnasium door, he saw that Dodgeball wasn't just for the living anymore.

Monsters, full on tail-wagging, horn sprouting monsters, held ground on the far side of the court. These creatures were hideous, straight out of a serial killer's nightmares kinda terrifying. Aaron had thought, naïvely, that after seeing Mrs. Livingston transform into a demon, he'd seen the worst of it. He found comfort in telling himself that Band-Aid of emotions had been ripped clean off and surprise wasn't going to set him back any further than he already was. The entire experience having been as bad as it could have possible been, the only upside being that he'd seen the worst and could take whatever else came his way.

He was wrong.

Dead wrong.

These monsters, canvasing the court for their prey, were one hundred percent pure nightmare fuel.

No two monsters looked the same; everywhere Aaron looked there was another one. The biggest one, thought only by a few feet, stood out over the rest of the court at no less than nine feet tall. It had spindly wings that dripped a thick, nauseating yellow-hued goo every time it moved. Its head was covered, all the way down to where it's neck likely started from what Aaron could tell from monster anatomy, with pulsating zit-like horns than spewed minute amounts of a vile green liquid all over the court. Each horn seemed to throb, acting a barometer for what the monster was thinking. Each time it prepared to attack, its horns began to pulsate quicker; Aaron considered the possibility that these horns were its version of a heart. The monster didn't even have eyes on its head; those were relegated to its hands where dozens of blinking eyeballs lined its fingers. The tail on the monster was a gigantic club, swaying back and forth just obliterating anything that it came into contact with, friend and foe alike. The liquid that perspired from it's wings and horns caused some of the other monsters around it to slip and fall, to great enjoyment of the massive monster along with the utter terror of their opponent.

If that wasn't bad enough, the monster was holding a ball that looked to be lined like a porcupine, with razor thin blades sticking out of it. Aaron wasn't sure he was seeing things correctly until the ball found its target. It hit the victim square in the chest, the razor thin blades puncturing the chest a hundred times over before the victim collapsed in agony and died, screaming. Unlike anyone, or anything, that Aaron had seen perish so far, these people didn't turn to ash and blow away. Their bodies remained on the court, likely to slow down those that had managed to stay alive longer for the monsters to easily hit with their attacks. The bodies were acting as morbid speed bumps, slowing everyone else down to a crawl to make them sitting ducks in an already impossible game.

Fucking Dodgeball.

The victim was a scraggly bearded old man that wasn't much more than skin and bone. Aaron swore he could hear the man's ribs breaking even through the thick gymnasium door he was unwillingly glued to at the moment as he watched the train wreck unfold in front of him. From what he could tell through the thin panel of glass and narrow field of vision, the other side of the court was littered with normal, everyday people, all running for their lives. Everyone was either too scared to throw a ball back or didn't want to entice the already terrifying monsters any more than they clearly already were. The monsters didn't seem like they'd be satiated, instead always on the prowl and looking for the next score or piece of entertainment.

The entire lot of humans, running haphazardly in a feeble attempt to prolong their lives and delay the inevitable, didn't look overly evil; there were both men and women peppered all over the court. Aaron had to wonder if they were in the same situation as he was. He also wondered if there were no children because children couldn't be forced to this kind of Hell or if they had already met a terrible fate before hand.

Did you guys also get sucked into Hell because an asshole died and just happened to be in the same vicinity when Death came for him?

Please tell me you guys are alone, that none of you had children before this. Please.

"Sir, what is it?" Hank asked, nudging him lightly to get his attention. Aaron realized he'd probably been asking for a while and Aaron hadn't even noticed. He'd been glued to the window panel and unable to comprehend anything else going on around him, which was as stupid a thing to let happen as possible, here of all places.

Way to go jackass, could have been barbequed while you gawked through a goddamn window panel on a door.

"Dodgeball Hank, it's fucking Dodgeball," Aaron pulled away from the glass and back to the wall next to Hank.

"I am unfamiliar with Dodgeball sir," Hank looked at him with burgeoning curiosity.

"It's a game kids play. The point is to hit the other opponent with the ball before they hit you. First one to hit everyone while avoiding being hit wins."

"Ahh, I was under such an impression that game was called Baseball no?"

Aaron laughed. Even though after what he just saw all he wanted to do was hurl, Hank's unintentional connection caught him off-guard. An idea of baseball making outs only by pegging the runner with a body shot made the snore-inducing one hundred and sixty-two game season actually sound interesting.

"Close Hank, but two different sports."

"Understood sir," Hank nodded in acknowledgement. "Would I be able to see this Dodgeball perhaps? Are they still having a match inside?"

"Suit yourself," Aaron said, sliding out of the way to clear a path for Hank to the glass panel on the gymnasium door. "I don't think it's gonna go much longer, so you'd better look now or miss all the action from courtside."

Hank eagerly slid closer to the door, looking back at Aaron once more for final approval before he looked through the glass and receiving a nod from Aaron. He took a deep breath and poked his head up to see what was happening on the other side of the door.

Hanks already pale skin turned white as a ghost, his face aligned in abstract terror. Aaron had a pretty good idea what had drawn his attention, a nine foot tall monster with eye's on its hands and a club for a tail would do the trick. Hank's legs started to shake before they gave out on him and he slid down the door into a pile on the ground.

Aaron saw the tears before he heard the sobs.

Hank was a wreck, Aaron feared what he'd seen had finally broken him once and for all.

"My word," Hank muttered over and over as he continued to quietly sob. "My word, sir."

"Yeah, it's not pretty," Aaron worked to console Hank, having had plenty of experience with people loosing their cool when working at the Rusty Knuckle. It wasn't a party until someone snapped and lost control of their emotions at the bar. Most of the time it was over a bad test score or relationship squabbles, either way it usually ended up with incoherent babbling that looked bad for business so he and Glen had become makeshift therapists to clear the area and get the party back on track. No one wants to drink when there is someone having an emotional breakdown right next to them on the floor.

"What do you say we let them finish whatever the fuck is going on in there while we get Jack and the group. We can come back for Ashley once we have them and...THAT is over with," Aaron tilted his head towards the gymnasium door as he spoke.

Hank quickly agreed, eager to put as much distance between them and whatever it was occupying the gym at the moment.

"Very good sir, brilliant strategy."

Aaron was less enthusiastic, he'd had no intention of leaving Ashley behind again no matter how reckless it would have been to barge in there with what was going on right now. Add to it that he no longer had Hank as a sidekick; the man had become a bag of wrinkled mush just at the sight of those monsters. Was a fair bet to say he wasn't going to do much of anything if Aaron went head first into the gymnasium to look for Ashley.

He'd find Jack, they'd better be where that asshole said they were, and then he'd let Debbie and the rest of the group babysit Hank while he and Jack when in to find Ashley.

Strength in numbers pal, don't be stupid about this.

Aaron helped Hank to his feet and they were about to head down the hallway back the way they came toward the Principle's office when Aaron stole one last look through the final glass panel in the row of gymnasium doors at the horror that was happening just on the other side of the door.

His blood went cold.

Somehow Aaron had missed it, though a nine-foot monster acted as one hell of a distraction.

This wasn't just any-old Dodgeball game, this was an event.

There were others in there besides the ones being hunted by the monsters for sport. Aaron's eyes darted back and forth to fully grasp that the bleachers had been pulled out to accommodate all the spectators. In the narrow view he had looking through the glass panel on the door, Aaron could see what appeared to be a cheering section for the monsters. Dozens of demons like the one's he'd killed were jumping up and down ecstatically, practically knocking themselves over to cheer on the hideous monsters on the court. Some even seemed to be engaged in a fight, paying no attention the what was happing on the court as they scratched and clawed at each other like feral cats fighting over a bowl of milk.

That wasn't what caught Aaron's attention though.

Standing courtside, just off to the back and barely within eyesight through the glass panel on the door, was a line of improvised cheerleaders for the monsters. Men and women, bound together in shackles around their ankles, stood in sheer terror at what they were witnessing. There was a smaller demon standing next to them, prodding them to cheer when a monster had taken down yet another human. The entire situation may have been more appalling than the actually game itself, to force people to cheer for each horrific death like it was the game winning bucket stirred an anger inside Aaron that he wasn't sure he was going to be able to keep inside.

Aaron's heart started pounding, he wasn't completely sure until she turned around and he saw her face. All he'd been able to see, what had grabbed his attention in the glass as he'd been ready to walk away, was her amber-red hair tussling back and forth as she jumped on queue to meet her captor's demands.

Ashley.

She was standing in the middle of the shackled cheer line, tears streaming down her face.

"Oh FUCK this," Aaron said, kicking open the door to the gymnasium.

XXIX

"Sir!"

Hank was helpless to stop Aaron as he barraged into the gymnasium, his frail call-out nothing more than a careless whisper in the hastily fading backdrop of the hallway behind him as he steadily marched towards Ashley.

Ashley.

Aaron had no desire to brawl with the monsters that still held court to his immediate left, he was fully aware that to clash with them was to court Death itself, but the moment he'd laid eyes on Ashley all rational and logic went out the window. His life, his safety, didn't mean jack shit if it meant staying in hiding another minute while the ONE thing that had been keeping him going was now standing directly in front of him.

Consequences be damned.

She's with me.

"AARON!"

Ashley caught sight of him and lost it, letting out a blood-curdling scream of his name loud enough for everyone, and everything, to hear her.

The perverse version of Dodgeball that had continued to play out as he'd made his way towards her stopped on a dime, the entire crowd of spectators along with it, as Aaron became the center of attention. He may as well have a spotlight following him as all eyes landed directly on him. The few remaining survivors on the court took the moment as an opportunity to flee, though Aaron was sure they wouldn't get far before they would meet an equally horrible fate as those on the court had.

This place didn't have survivors, no on gets out clean.

"AARON!"

He heard his name again, but this time it wasn't coming from Ashley. Her mouth hadn't moved since she shouted his name, now forming a quivering line across her face as she fought back tears at seeing him in person. Aaron had to wonder what kind of mind games she'd been embattled with in isolation. Wasn't hard to imagine Zadkiel had messed with her, he did dress up a demon as Mrs. Livingston after all.

"AARON, up here!"

THAT came from the bleachers.

Aaron shot a glance towards where the sound was originating, not as easy as one would think in an echo-heavy gymnasium. A basketball dribbling up the court sounded like a Civil War rifle in here, someone screaming from higher up would only succeed in creating an audible vortex that bounced around the gymnasium before it landed with it's intended target. Aaron put his head on a swivel as he tried to pinpoint the exact location of the voice. During his time at Crest Hill he'd never realized how massive the gymnasium really was.

"Up here, to your left…your OTHER left dude, Jesus," the voice chided him.

Jack.

His mind raced at the possibility that Jack was in the gymnasium too. He was supposed to be locked away in the Principle's office with Debbie and the rest of the group, but it stood to reason that what Zadkiel had told him was complete and total bullshit.

Or it was a trap.

"That you Jack? Where are you at man?" Aaron called back, still keeping most of his focus on Ashley only a few steps away from him now.

"Dude, I'm up here waving my hands like a lunatic. How the hell can't you see me?"

Aaron spotted him before the sentence was over, Jack's arms frantically gestating back and forth like he was the inflatable tube-man that car lots used to draw attention to themselves. It was in stark contrast to the still frozen in place crowd around him, making it easy to pinpoint in no time.

"You alright man?"

"I mean, I'm chained to a row of bleachers and being forced to watch these sick bastards kill people right in front of me while sitting amongst these fuzzy-turds, but other than that I'm living the dream dude. You?"

"Same," Aaron replied, ecstatic to hear Jack hadn't lost his marbles like he had earlier, that he was still the same old Jack.

Can't do this alone pal.

"Debbie says hi…she said to tell you that you look hot in your new shir…DAMMIT DEBBIE, this is NOT the time for that shit."

"Is everyone else ok?"

"Yep, the whole gang is here and ready to be rescued. No pressure."

"Yeah, working on it," Aaron shouted back.

Aaron took stock of what was going on around him. Even in the heat of the moment, he had to admit how crazy this all was. They were having a full-scale reunion, shouting back and forth at each other, while the rest of the gymnasium was chalk full of demons and monsters alike, all just staring at them completely dumfounded. Aaron had to imagine that something like this didn't happen down here, humans didn't just barge into a room full of nightmarish creatures and catch up like nothing had happened. He half expected to be impaled at any moment, either a monster or demon tired of the banter and eager for the game to resume.

Nothing happened, everything and everyone remained frozen in place. No one knew what to do next. Aaron remembered Hank telling him that Abaddon was just like Arcadia, one conscious mind linking them all together. Hard to image what was going through all their minds right now.

He noticed that Ashley had stopped crying, seemingly overjoyed to hear Jack's voice and realize that she was around friends again. Aaron wouldn't let that happen again, Ashley wasn't going to be taken away from him or any of them again.

Ever.

"So…you, uh, got any bright ideas?" Jack hollered.

"OH FOR FUCKSAKE," Zadkiel's voice boomed overhead. **"YOU POON FAIRIES REALLY KNOW HOW TO RUIN EVERYTHING DON'T YOU."**

"Let her go," Aaron demanded, knowing deep down it would never be that easy.

Ya never know till you ask.

236

"I HAVE A BETTER IDEA."

Loud music began to play as the lights over the court went out, smothering the gymnasium into darkness.

■

The lights slowly came back to life as the aggressively loud music faded away

The court was empty.

What had been a massacre only a few moments ago, with bodies spread across the court in every area imaginable, had been completely cleared. The hardwood floor had also been polished, the lights dancing across the reflective floor as they came back to full strength.

Aaron took the opportunity to rush over to Ashley, somehow still standing right in front of him even after the lights had gone out and cleared away everything else, embracing her in his arms. Her body trembled against his, unable to wrap he arms around him and instead allowing him to wrap his arms around her completely. He could sense she took comfort in the feeling of protection, however little he could actually offer at the moment, after being forced to fend for herself earlier.

"I'm here, I've got you," Aaron whispered in her ear.

"I'LL ADMIT IT," Zadkiel's voice washed over the gymnasium. **"I DID NOT SEE THIS COMING. I HAD YOU PEGGED FOR AS GOOD AS DEAD LAST TIME WE SPOKE. SET THE HEATER TO DEEP FRY AND SENT YOUR CRISPY ASS RUNNING FOR THE HILLS ALONG WITH 'OLE SHRIVELED UP FATHER TIME TO ROT IN A CORNER LIKE GOOD PETS. INSTEAD, HERE YOU ARE, WITH NO APPARENT SETBACKS IN YOUR QUEST TO GET LAID. YOU JUST REFUSE TO FUCKING DIE DON'T YOU?"**

Aaron didn't let go of Ashley; he wasn't inclined to do so until his arms gave out or he was dead. Instead, he started walking towards the gymnasium doors with her. He would deal with whatever Zadkiel wanted to throw his way in time, right now his sole focus was getting Ashley outside those doors and to Hank. The monsters were gone, Aaron hoped like hell that meant Hank had recovered and could at least help protect Ashley. The thought occurred to him that he might have it backwards, that Ashley may have to keep an eye on Hank.

Either way, Ashley wouldn't be alone.

Never again.

"ARE YOU SHITTING ME?" Zadkiel rang out overheard, the lights flickering at his outburst. **"YOU REALLY THOUGHT I WAS JUST GOING TO LET YOU WALK OUT THE FUCKING DOOR LIKE YOU JUST WON THE GAME AND SAVED THE PRINCESS? YOU'RE NOT GOING ANYWHERE SHIT STICK, NOT UNLESS I SAY SO. SERIOUSLY, HOW CAN YOU BE SO FUCKING RESILENT AND YET THIS FUCKING DUMB ALL AT THE SAME TIME? IT'S LIKE PICKING ON SOMEONE FRESH OFF THE SHORTBUS, WHICH DON'T GET ME WRONG, IS A THRILL, BUT STILL THAT SHIT GETS ON MY NERVES AFTER AWHILE. A FELLA CAN ONLY TAKE SO MUCH YA KNOW."**

"She leaves," Aaron demanded. "You can do whatever you want to me," he said, setting his own terms.

"NOOOOOPE," Zadkiel corrected, the gymnasium doors flying open as forces unseen in the darkened hallway threw Hank inside. Before he landed on the hardwood floor with a dull thud that made Aaron's bones hurt just hearing it, the doors were closed and covered in electric barbwire, the wire actually sparking it was primed with so much electricity coursing through it.

They weren't going anywhere.

"TELL YOU WHAT, SINCE YOU WENT AND GOT ME ALL HALF-MAST WITH YOUR FALSE BRAVADO, I'M GOING TO MAKE YOU AN OFFER YOU CAN'T REFUSE."

"Pass."

"YOU...YOU CAN'T PASS YOU LITTLE SHIT. NO ONE PASSES ON MY OFFERS," Zadkiel raged, the lights flickering in and out with the sudden outburst.

"Pass," Aaron repeated, holding his ground.

In a flash, Jack and the rest of the group appeared in the first row of bleachers just behind where Aaron stood. Ashley was ripped away from his arms and placed on the bleachers with the rest of them. The were all shackled to the bleachers, both hands and feet after Jack has waved his arms to get his attention, and looking back at him with sad looks on each of there faces. Hank was still in a pile on the floor behind him, Aaron assumed that meant Zadkiel felt no threat from him and decided to let him roam free. Made sense, up to this point Hank had done nothing but go along with the events as planned. Aaron wondered if Hank's actions were somehow cloaked so Zadkiel couldn't see them.

"Hey dude," Jack offered somberly.

"Is anyone hurt?" Aaron asked, though he could see nothing to show they were, he had to ask since this was Hell and pain came in more ways than one down here.

"Nope, still good," Jack nodded, looking down the row to anyone that wanted to argue otherwise. No one did. "Ya know, minus the obvious being shackled to a row of bleachers while we watch what is likely to be your painful death. Hey, we DID just get upgraded to courtside though, things might be looking up," Jack cracked a smile, Aaron unwilling following suit.

"SINCE YOU INTERRUPED A PERFECTLY GOOD GAME, YOU GET TO FILL IN. I HAVE FANS TO THAT EXPECT A GOOD, HARD FOUGHT GAME, NOT A TWEEN DRAMA."

On queue, the windows above the gymnasium crashed inward as hordes of demons carelessly flew through them. As shattered glass fell to the floor, enough demons flew in to temporarily block out the overhead lights in the gymnasium. For a moment, they were enshrouded in darkness once again. The herd began to thin out quickly though, the lights making their way back down to the shimmering hardwood below, as Aaron noticed the gymnasium was now packed to the hilt with demons. Each one was on their feet and ready to watch another game of Dodgeball after they were so rudely interrupted. Unlike last time, there were demons lining the court as well, the gymnasium was packed to standing room only this time.

"YOU ARE GONNA PLAY AGAINST MY BEST TEAM. YOU WIN, YOU AND THE SCOOBY GANG GET TO REUNITE AND SOLVE MYSTERIES OR JERK EACH OTHER OFF OR WHATEVER YOU WANT TO DO TOGETHER BEFORE I SKIN EACH OF YOU ALIVE. BUT, AND THIS IS THE BEST PART, WHEN MY TEAM WINS, ASHLEY CUTS YOUR HEAD OFF WITH HANKTARD'S BLADE."

"What about the others?" Aaron asked, seeing the look on Jack and Debbie's faces of unease.

"THEY DIE, DUH."

Shit.

"TAKE A MOMENT TO STRECH YOUR NUTS AND KISS YOUR ASS GOODBYE, GAME STARTS IN TEN MINUTES. Z OUT!"

"Who said I agreed to anything yet?" Aaron asked, holding what little ground he thought he had.

"YOUR PLAYING, YOU JUST DON'T KNOW IT YET. YOU HOLD OUT AND PISS ME OFF FURTHER AND I'LL MAKE YOU WEAR SHORT SHORTS AND HIGH HEELS WHILE YOU DO IT."

Shit.

∎

Aaron stood on the far side of the court; he was assigned this side so Ashley and the rest of the group could see the look on his face when he met his end. He wouldn't even get the chance to die with a little dignity, the last thing they would see was the look of terror as he went down for good.

Fuck me.

"Permission to join the team sir," Hank said, startling Aaron.

"Why the hell would you want to do that?"

"I told you I would fight by your side, that is an oath I intend to keep sir," Hank offered proudly.

"Your funeral," Aaron shook his head. "You still have the blade?"

"Of course sir, though I must ask what you intend to do with it? This game does not require weapons unless I have further confused it with yet another sport sir."

"Just incase," Aaron said. "Never know when I might need to get stabby or whatnot."

240

Hank's mouth curled into a wry smile.

They both took the time to stretch, though in jeans and a three-piece suit the stretching was minimal. Aaron rotated his arms in a windmill form, happy that he'd taken the risk with the blade earlier, his shoulder now completely healed.

The time they had to stretch let Aaron's mind wander more than anything, he relived all that had happened so far in disturbing detail. He'd had it with this goddamn day, he was sick and tired of getting his ass handed to him. The LAST thing he was going to do was just lie down and die, but there was only so much a person could take. Hank had made that clear, but he'd also shown that a person could shoulder more than they think if they have the right motivation.

Ashley.

Aaron wasn't the most athletic kid growing up; he was never confident enough to try out for sports and didn't like the pressure of performing on a big stage with the possibility of letting everyone down. He'd had the same dreams as every other kid, of hitting the game winning homerun or scoring the Hail Mary touchdown, but they were just dreams. In reality, he was more than happy to just be a spectator in front of the TV. Aaron didn't mature into an athletic adult either, letting go of the dream to play professional sports right around the same time he did of being a super hero or astronaut/special agent.

That being said, Aaron could throw a rubber ball as good as anyone. The game of Dodgeball required less skill than it did luck and timing. Sure, one must avoid being hit to stay in the game, but was more about tactically stalking one's prey until the moment arrived when they were vulnerable to attack. Dodgeball was all about offense, but good defense kept you in the game long enough to strike.

That was, unless you were playing against nine foot tall monsters.

Fuck me.

"OK, LETS GET THIS SHIT ON THE ROAD SHALL WE." Zadkiel came back over the speakers. **"I WAS GOING TO SURPRISE EVERYONE BY HOLDING MICHAEL BUFFER'S NUTS TO A FIRE WHILE HE ANNOUNCED FOR US, BUT IT TURNS OUT THAT SONOFABITCH ISN'T DEAD YET. WHO KNOW RIGHT? SOMETIMES YOU JUST CAN'T CATCH A FUCKING BREAK DOWN HERE, IT'S JUST ONE FLAMING TURD MUFFIN AFTER THE OTHER AM I RIGHT? IT'S LIKE, WHY ARE WE SO FUCKING UNLUCKY THAT EVERYTHING**

WE DO IS JUST ANOTHER ROUNDHOUSE TO THE NARDS? IT REALLY MAKES YOU WON-"

The crowd, to Aaron's astonishment, began to boo.

Zadkiel was loosing them.

Holy shit.

"Remember sir, this is a collective conscious not unlike that in Arcadia," Hank reminded him as the crowd continued to boo. "Zadkiel is not ahead of them in anyway, only allowed to run the show as it keeps the rest entertained. They won't hesitate to turn on a dime if he loses them."

Good to know Hank, good to know.

"OH SHUT UP YOU ONERY ASSHOLES. YOU'RE ALL THINKING IT, I JUST SAID IT."

The crowd continued to jeer Zadkiel, Aaron holding back a smile when he saw Jack getting in on the jeering.

"FINE! YOU WANT TO CUT TO THE CHASE? BY ALL MEANS, LETS JUST SWEEP OUR EMOTIONS UNDER THE RUG LIKE ALWAYS," Zadkiel surrendered. **"LET'S JUST ACT LIKE EVERYTHING IS FINE AND WATCH SOME ASSHOLES GET RIPPED APART AT THE SEEMS SHALL WE!"**

The crowd started cheering again, everyone appeared to be back on the same page.

That page being Aaron and Hank's death.

The electric barbwire came down and the doors to the gymnasium burst open.

Both he and Hank were expecting the horrendous monsters they'd witnessed earlier to come bursting through those doors, to make an entrance that was bound to send Hank back into the puddle of mush he'd been outside in the hallway.

Instead, a normal looking man walked through the doorway.

And another.

And another.

And another.

Aaron tried to keep count, but lost track around the twenty-eighth person that walked through the door. They were still coming in, the newest members of the team falling behind those that entered first to form a row the military would be proud of. Aaron couldn't even see the last few people that came in, only knowing they had all made it inside the gymnasium when the doors slammed shut and the electric barbwire was back in place.

"My word," Aaron heard Hank say.

"Relax Hank, they're just people," Aaron observed. "That means this might be easier than we anticipated after all. We just have to beat numbers, not monsters."

"ON THIS SIDE OF THE COURT, WE HAVE THE ONE, THE ONLY, DONKEY SHOW DOUCHEBAGS!" Zadkiel announced, the crowd hitting them with the jeers they'd sent towards Zadkiel earlier.

"AND ON THIS SIDE..." Zadkiel started, the lights dimming and dramatic music began to play and spotlights danced around the nearly forty men. *"FROM RIGHT HERE THEY GREW TO BECOME THE POWERHOUSE YOU KNOW AND LOVE TODAY. THEY ARE THE BEST, THE ONLY, UNDEFEATED CHAMPIONS OF CREST HILL HIGH..."*

Aaron's throat went dry when he put it together.

Standing across from him, finally raising his head so Aaron could see his face, was the one person Aaron didn't expect to ever see again.

The one person Aaron hated more than anything growing up.

"I GIVE YOU...THE CREST HILL STATE CHAMPION FOOTBALL TEAM!!!"

Devin Porter sneered back at him.

XXX

Aaron fought it.

Devin Porter, along with the rest of the Crest Hill State Championship football team, glared back at him.

The last Aaron heard, Devin Porter was doing hard time in Queens after he'd been pulled over with a loaded, unregistered handgun in the glove box of a stolen Kia. His original sentence, according to the humanoid version of Wikipedia Jack became as they ran their errands around Silverton, had only been a couple of years. Devin would have been out for good behavior and overcrowding in just over a year, all he had to do was keep his head down and follow the rules.

But that's not Devin Porter, not by a long shot.

The former QB and team captain, not to mention Homecoming King three years in a row, fundamentally failed to understand the concept of laying low. Anything and everything could and would set him off, reason or consequence be damned. Devin cut his ties with Silverton after Ashley found out he was cheating on her a few years after they graduated. By then, Devin's opportunities had dried up considerably. No Division I school wanted anything to do with him, his grades and attitude a clear indication that Devin was not willing to put in the work to become a team player worth a vaunted scholarship that every teenager in the country was after. Too proud to admit his dream of playing college ball, on his way to professional sports and then superstardom, was dead, Devin withdrew into himself. Ronnie, Silverton's resident antagonist, thought he was a deadbeat, which spoke volumes around town and for Aaron. Unable to hold a full-time job, or even a part-time one for that matter, Devin found himself with ample free time to be promiscuous.

Ashley caught wind after trying to mute the rumors that swirled around Silverton that Devin was going to be a father, cutting ties with him once and for all once she met face to face with the soon-to-be mother of his child. Devin responded by trashing her apartment and leaving town all in the same night, he'd even set a small fire in her living room with the unpaid bills that he'd been ignoring that required the volunteer fighter fighters of Silverton to be called in.

Jack had kept in touch with a few friends that updated him over time about what old classmates were up to via social media, he was always voyeuristically interested in hearing how Crest Hill's finest had made out in the real world. The last he'd heard about Devin was that he'd been driving drunk when he was pulled over for swerving in and out of lanes. Devin blew a .10, well over the legal limit in New York, and proceed to argue with the officer resulting in him being handcuffed while they searched the vehicle to find a loaded revolver in the glove box. Jack had smiled from ear to ear in describing the police dash-cam video that was available online, anyone having the ability to watch Devin's pretty face get pushed into the hood of the car as he dispensed empty threats to the officer. Devin quickly lost his courage when the other officer returns with the loaded handgun and reads him his rights.

He was booked and sentenced to a couple of years, a good chance at early parole if he was well behaved.

Devin responded to the judge's offer by throwing scalding hot water from a Top-Ramen noodle cup he'd acquired from the commissary all over his cellmate after he'd lost the top-bunk in a checker's game on his very first day in prison. His cellmate received third-degree burns on over a third of his upper body, his cellmate he been shirtless after just receiving new ink from a fellow prison gang as part of his initiation into the gang. Devin received another ten years, seven for the burning and three for assaulting an officer afterward while trying to be restrained.

Now, Devin was standing right in front of him, shit-eating grin and all.

Aaron fought against it, with everything he had.

Devin, clearly just another demon in disguise as far as Aaron was concerned, though if anyone were in Hell as the genuine article it would have been him, smirked at Aaron before turning his head to look back at Ashley on the bleachers behind him.

"You miss me babe?"

Ashley responded by flipping him off, Debbie joining in with a forearm-jerk of her own to send a similar message.

Jack threw in a cold stare for good measure.

"You know I like it when you talk dirty babe," Devin responded.

Devin turned back to face Aaron, arrogance plastered on his face.

"Good news Aaron, you and Ashley are about to have one more thing in common," Devin prodded, Aaron not willing to take the bait.

"And just what might that be, you...you hooligan" Hank stepped in, displaying his allegiance to Aaron in the worst possible moment.

"They are both gonna know what it feels like to have my balls against their face," Devin beamed as the rest of the football team laughed behind him.

"My word! You... you arrogant litt-," Hank began, shaking while reaching for his blade before Aaron stepped in and stopped him.

"Not worth it pal, just ignore him," Aaron offered so only Hank could hear.

"You two pretty ladies want a little more cuddle time or should be get this show on the road? Been looking forward to letting the fellas unleash hell for quite some time, nothing quite like the glory days of pummeling a weaker opponent am I right men?" Devin shouted with his arms raised, to a rousing response by the rest of the Crest Hill football team behind him.

Aaron had been fighting it; his emotions pulling at him in ways he didn't think were possible. From the moment he'd locked eyes with Devin, through the snide comments and flashback to Jack's recap of a life wasted, Aaron couldn't help but find pleasure in knowing that even if this was where he died, he would get a shot at THE Devin Porter.

The Devin Porter that ruined any chance he may have had at dating Ashley back in High School. At a life in which he'd had the courage to talk to her even once without fear of being chastised by a superior member of the high school hierarchy in front of everyone.

The Devin Porter that threw away some of Ashley's best years by being an utter douchebag and treating her like garbage.

Aaron couldn't fight it anymore.

A smile formed on his face as the buzzer rang out over the gymnasium for the game to begin.

.

Every game of Dodgeball started the same way, with a row of balls lined up at midcourt and either team, or opponent, lined up on the far baseline of their respective sides. At the buzzer, each member hauled ass to get to mid-court and secure a ball to launch at the opponent. Those that were just a touch too slow wound up being the first victims in the game, easy targets for those that managed to acquire the invaluable balls lining mid-court.

At the very last minute, and an over-eagerness to wipe that smile off Devin's face, Aaron decided on an attack-first approach and charged towards mid-court to secure a ball. The plan went off without a hitch, he was able to acquire not one, but two balls before shuffling backwards to pick out his targets.

Right off the bat, Aaron should have realized something was wrong.

Of the twenty-eight members on the other side of the vaunted meridian that divided each team, only two had made an effort to snatch a ball when the game began. As Aaron stood and surveyed the battlefield, he noticed that most of the balls were still sitting at mid-court waiting to be picked up.

No one on the Crest Hill football team seemed interested in playing offense, not even Devin, whom stood with his arms folded across his chest in annoyed anticipation of Aaron's first strike.

"Sir, they are not playing!"

"Works for me," Aaron said, slinging his first ball with everything he had right at Devin's chest.

Whether or not the demonized Dream Team that stood across from them choose to play along or scoff at the challenge only two men presented was irrelevant to Aaron. As far as he was concerned, the way you won Dodgeball was by pinning those on the opposing side. If the Crest Hill football team wanted to act like twenty-eight iterations of James Dean and his entire nonchalant persona, so be it. Aaron would systematically take each one of them down, starting with the head asshole.

Devin.

The ball, leaving Aaron's fingertips like a fastball thrown by Randy Johnson himself, connected with Devin's chest. The sound the rubber ball made, a dull ping as it made contact, hushed the crowd.

Devin acted like nothing happened as the ball, harmlessly, stuck to him like it had been previously dipped in glue.

A smile formed on his face.

Shit.

"He's…he's not going down sir!" Hank narrated the play-by-play though Aaron could clearly see Devin still standing in front of him.

Smiling.

"You dumbass, you really thought it would be that easy to beat me?" Devin chided, smile still plastered on his face.

"Thought had crossed my mind," Aaron shot back.

"All you did was make this worse on yourself, dumbass," Devin advised.

Aaron didn't have to wait long to find out what Devin meant, the result of his perfectly aimed throw began taking effect right away.

The ball, once attached to Devin's chest like an overgrown sore, slowly began to disappear.

The goddamn ball sunk right into Devin's chest.

One moment the ball had been stuck to his chest, the next it was gone, absorbed into Devin's body.

Then the shit really hit the fan.

Devin began to grow.

Standing at a similar height with Aaron, Devin's entire body began to transform until he was now standing a good foot or more over the rest of the bodies on the court. His legs and arms had gained a considerable amount of muscular definition, along with his chest that now strained against the once loose football jersey he wore.

It was still Devin standing across from him; Aaron didn't see any of the typical demonizing features that the other demons had possessed. His eyes were not blood red and he didn't sprout wings or shed his skin, Devin simply grew to become a bigger version of the asshole that Aaron once knew.

"That's more like it!" Devin laughed, looking over his own body and the recent upgrades.

Well fuck me.

The sole point of Dodgeball was to tag the opponent to render them out. Now that Aaron knew tagging anyone would only make them bigger and stronger made the game unwinnable. It had been a trap, a guaranteed death sentence the moment he'd walked into the gymnasium.

Aaron could, and would, fight. He wasn't about to just lay down and die, not in front of Ashley and the rest of the group. The odds of him making it past more than a few of the normal sized opponents was slim, he figured he would be quickly wiped out by Devin in a matter of moments once Devin realized Aaron had gone for broke and abandoned the game entirely.

The idea of dying, of losing his life in front of his best friend and the girl he still had tremendous feelings for after all these years, was sickening. Aaron tried not to hurl on the court, to keep his composure before it all ended. At the very least, he wanted Ashley and Jack to remember him as the guy that went out fighting.

Visions of his mother, his father, and grandpa flashed inside his head. Aaron felt the sting of regret for the things he'd done wrong and wished he could have done differently. Missing his grandpa's funeral, leaving his mother to mourn alone with only W to console her, and never telling Ashley how he really felt burned away at him until the feeling suddenly vanished in an array of white light that sent him back to the moment at hand.

Aaron was now standing across from his impending death as it practically foamed at the mouth for him to make his next, and final, move.

Fuck it.

Aaron looked over at Hank, giving him the knowing nod of appreciation for standing by his side and of the inevitable end they both were about to face.

Hank's reaction was to scream at the top of his lungs as he charged toward mid-court to collect a ball in each hand. Before Aaron could stop him, Hank had unleashed both balls at the closest opponents, both finding pay dirt as they hit and slowly sunk into the body just like they had with Devin.

Soon, two more massive human beings joined Devin by his side. They all chuckled at Hank's horrendous mistake.

"What the fuck Hank? Why would you do that? You know it just makes them stronger?"

"You gave me the look sir? I thought this is what you wanted, to attack?"

"That was a, 'it was nice knowing you but now it's time to die' look!"

"Time to die sir? You cannot give up. I...I forbid it!"

"Forbid it?" Aaron scoffed. "In case you haven't noticed, there are over two dozen men with the sole intention of killing us on the other side of this court. NOW, there are three that are full-on MONSTERS. I figure we attack, we maybe get a few of them and increase the slight odds that Ashley and the rest of the group have of making it out of this fucking gymnasium once we fall."

"Sir, we MUST try. To forfeit would be inconceivable!" Hank responded.

It hit Aaron like a dump truck that lost its brakes on the highway.

Inconceivable.

The entire time they had been trapped, the only thing that was consistent was the inconceivable. From Ashley being taken away in a cloud of smoke, to a man bursting into flames, a former teacher transforming into a demon, fire shooting from lockers, and Hank and his blade with mysterious healing abilities, they all shared a common thread.

Nothing had been even remotely conceivable.

The only time Aaron had been able to get a leg up on the situation was when he'd abandoned all logic and simply acted on instinct. It was the sole reason he'd been able to spear a demon and believe a tiny blade could heal him.

Inconceivable.

"You two are boring the living shit out of me," Devin cut through the silence in the gymnasium. "Either throw some more balls and make the rest of my team big and strong or cross this white line so I can punch a hole in your chest and take your beating heart as a memento to remember you by."

Aaron smiled. Devin had just sparked an idea that was too absurd to ever possibly think it could work.

"Hank," Aaron said, as he started walking towards mid-court to collect another ball. "I need you to trust me on this pal, I need you to do exactly what I tell you alright?"

Hank nodded hesitantly.

Aaron picked up one of the balls still sitting on mid-court and rolled it gently back towards Hank.

"Hit me with this."

XXXI

I hope this works.

Aaron second-guessed himself right up to the moment Hank let fly with the ball as directed. Hank, either nervous or unable to properly throw a ball, let go of the ball a tad early and sent the ball right towards

Aaron's face instead of his torso as planned. Unsure how it would affect him to take a direct shot to the head, in Dodgeball that meant the person throwing the ball was immediately ruled out and Aaron didn't rule out Hank bursting into flames as punishment in this version of the game, Aaron jumped with everything he had so the ball made contact just below his right shoulder.

The gymnasium went silent, again.

Realizing he'd had his eyes closed the whole time, somehow that made the prospect of a horrifically painful death easier to stomach as long as it wasn't able to SEE anything, Aaron slowly opened his eyes to survey the damage.

The entire gymnasium, Devin and the rest of his goons included, stared back at him in awe.

The ball was stuck to his shoulder.

Slowly, it began working its way inside of him just like it had Devin and the others.

"You can't...he can't...He can't do that can he?" Devin asked his teammates worriedly.

None of them had an answer; only able to offer the blank stare and occasional shoulder shrug as a response. Just like back in high school, they were all lap dogs to Devin's alpha male status. Not a single one of them possessed the backbone necessary to speak up or talk back, instead choosing to blend in with the rest of the team and relish their position as right hand to Devin rather than in his path.

"HE CAN'T DO THAT CAN HE?" Devin called out to a stunned gymnasium.

"OH QUIT YOUR BITCHING," Zadkiel answered through the speakers. *"LOOK AROUND ASSHOLE, THERE ARE NO REFS. THAT'S BECAUSE I DON'T GIVE ONE HOT FUCK ABOUT RULES OR SCORES. I JUST LIKE A GOOD OLD FASHIONED ASS WHUPPIN NO MATTER HOW IT'S SERVED UP TO ME. NOW UNTUCK WHAT'S LEFT OF YOUR SHRIVELED UP MANHOOD AND END THIS BEFORE I GET BORED AND LOSE MY PATIENCE."*

While Zadkiel lambasted Devin, Aaron watched the entire ball absorb into his upper chest until it had completely disappeared from sight.

Then he grew.

It was unlike anything he'd ever felt before. Every muscle, joint, and bone in his body throbbed uncontrollably as it fought for more space inside his body. Aaron would have burst wide open if he's body hadn't nurtured the growth by making the necessary room for everything to grow. One moment he was standing eye-to-eye with Hank, the next he was looking down at him from a good three feet above. He looked down at his hands and smiled as he saw massive palms to match his overall growth, his torso and legs having grown proportionately in the process. All those years of Jack rambling on and on about how the Hulk managed to destroy every shirt he ever wore but keep his pants on without fail made Aaron quickly look down to ensure he wasn't standing naked in front of everyone, and thing, in the gymnasium. Thankfully, just like the Hulk, Aaron had managed to keep his pants on. In fact, he was still fully clothed. Somehow he'd grown to a monster's size but only managed to stretch his clothing out considerably without ripping anything but his shoes, which now lay in a pile of shredded canvas and rubber around his massive feet.

"Ohhh…HELL YEAH," Jack shouted from the bleachers, a slow clap starting then quickly fading out in a matter of moments as Debbie shut him down.

"KICK HIS ASS!" Jack shouted before Debbie muzzled him with her hand over his mouth.

Good idea.

Aaron shaped his newly monster-sized hand into a fist and stepped forward to deliver a crushing right hook to the side of Devin's oversized head. Caught off guard by an attack he never thought Aaron would have the courage to stage, Devin took the full force of the blow and hit the hardwood floor like a sack of potatoes as everyone else on his team winced at the hit and cleared a space around he and Aaron. The initial contact sent a concussive blast that blew away some of the demons in the nearest row of in the bleachers, muffled barks and rustling wings filled the quite stadium as they fought to regain their coveted seats.

"YEEEEEEEAAAAHHHHHHHHH!" Ashley screamed, jumping up so suddenly she nearly pulled Becky off the bleachers with her since they were all still chained together. Aaron glanced over at the sound of her voice and tried not to smile, he was living every kids dream of knocking out the guy that was an asshole to the girl they liked, her raucous cheer only cementing the moment for him.

Focus.

As fulfilling as the moment was, to stand over Devin's inert body after knocking him out, Aaron wasn't fooled. No one was that easy to defeat no matter how big and strong he was. He knew Devin was only momentarily incapacitated; soon he'd pick himself up off the hardwood floor and be ready to unleash everything he had in retaliation.

Devin began to writhe around on the hardwood floor as if he heard Aaron's thoughts and responded in kind, regaining conscious and struggling to make it back to his feet on his own accord. No one dared try to help him up for fear of being the first one to make contact with him after getting his lights knocked out for what Aaron had to assume was the first time, especially in front of the his loyal followers that worshiped and feared his every movement.

"That's…that's gonna cost you," Devin promised as he knelt for a moment before returning to a standing position in front of Aaron. Tilting his head from side to side, a sickening crack vibrating off the gymnasium walls had he reset his neck. He's eyes burned with fury, but they were still HIS eyes. Devin was not a demon, just the stone cold, super-sized asshole Aaron had known since grade school. In a way, his rage infused glare was worse than the blood red eyes the demon's possessed. It was easier to stare at a set of red eyes for whatever reason, never knowing for sure if Aaron was what it was looking at without pupils to confirm made it less personal in a way. Devin, burning a hole through him with his glare, made it very clear that Aaron was his one and only target.

"My turn," Devin snarled, spittle flying from his mouth in every direction like a rabid dog.

"Oh shit," Aaron heard Jack shriek in the background.

Devin faked going high, which Aaron bit on by bringing both of his arms up to protect his head, only to go low at the last second. Devin's fist connected with Aaron's ribs, creating a sonic boom on impact as another sizeable cluster of demons were sent flying from their seats. All the air in Aaron's lungs evaporated as he crumpled and fell to his knees gasping for air through the sensational pain. It didn't take a medical expert to realize he'd broken more than a few ribs with the shot, each agonizing attempt for air a reminder of the damage done, yet somehow he managed to push the pain aside and struggle back to his feet.

Devin's face indicated a mixed cocktail of astonishment and excitement as they locked eyes once again. Aaron imaged most people stayed down after Devin laid into them; this was likely a whole new experience for him.

Devin lined up his next attack.

Aaron didn't give him the chance, instead rolling into a perfectly timed somersaulting as Devin went for his finishing move, a headshot of his own, and exploded up just behind him. Confused to be punching air, Devin turned around just in time to see Aaron's fist slam right into his face with a haymaker. Aaron saw the lights go out in Devin's eyes as a ripple of force from his fist spread across his face; he crumpled back to the floor unconscious. An entire section of the gymnasium bleachers next to Aaron had been cleared, most demons still lying on the floor in a daze not unlike the one Devin was in himself.

Ashley and the rest of the group began cheering wildly, positive they were about to be freed after Devin's collapsed at Aaron's feet for the second time.

Aaron wasn't fooled; he knew Devin would get back up sooner rather than later.

The only way to end a fight in Hell meant someone had to die.

"THAT WAS WORTH THE PRICE OF ADMISSSION ALONE FOLKS, YOU DON'T SEE THAT KIND OF BEATING EVERY...WELL...ACTUALLY YOU DO DON'T YOU. KINDA DILUTES THE MOMENT NOW THAT I THINK ABOUT IT, A REAL TITTY TWISTER OF EMOTIONS GOING ON RIGHT NOW FOR ME. I JUST HOPE THE FINALE DOESN'T LEAVE ME FUSSY. WHEN I GET FUSSY, SOMEONE IS GOING TO SUFFER TO CHEER ME UP."

The two of them could trade blows until they were blue in the face, it wouldn't get either of them any closer to winning. The Dodgeball game a thing of the past, Aaron had to figure out a way to put Devin down once and for all, and quickly. Devin wasn't the kind to slow down; he was a lunatic that would only come back harder and harder each time around until he was too much for Aaron even in his current super-sized form.

Aaron had to cut the head off the snake while he still had the chance, a prospect easier said than done. Killing a demon was one thing; Aaron likened it to hunting a wild animal that was trying to kill him, since it wasn't actually human. Anyone could kill a monster if he had to, there was no moral infringement on survival when it came to the things that go bump in the night.

Devin was a low-life, piece of shit that deserved the prison cell he currently called home. There was nothing good about him and he was beyond saving as far as Aaron, and just about anyone else by the way Jack spoke, was concerned. Even so, Devin was still a person, or at least

256

he looked like one. Aaron had been able to kill the first demon, who also started out masked as someone he once knew, only once it shed its façade and revealed its true form. Devin had not done so, remaining the same, hardheaded Devin they all remembered back in high school.

Why couldn't you just be that ugly, eyeball hands creature from earlier?

When Devin awoke from his forced nap, Aaron got what he was hoping for.

Devin shook his head and raised to his feet to resume battle once more, only this time, his eyes were blood red.

He was a demon, literally.

"Sir!" Hank shouted from below.

He was waving his cane back and forth.

OF COURSE cut the head off the snake.

Hank tossed his cane, with the blade inside, towards Aaron. It landed like a small pebble close to his massive feet. The only reason Aaron had been able to keep track of the tiny object was due to the glimmer the perfectly polished silver cane reflected from the overhead lights, forming a makeshift beacon to keep track of. With Devin still a little foggy, Aaron took the opportunity to step back and kneel to pick up the blade.

Problem was, he physically couldn't do it.

The blade, still of normal human size, was nothing more than a flat toothpick on the hardwood floor that Aaron couldn't get his enlarged fingers to get a hold of. He tried using his index finger and thumb to gently pick it up, but there was no way he could get to such a small item in his current form. Aaron quickly tried to brush the blade into his palm with the other hand to no avail, the blade was simply too small to handle.

You have GOT to be shitting me, SERIOUSLY?

"Hank," Aaron's voice roared, startling even him at first. "It's too small, I can't use it!"

Aaron saw Hank's eyes dart back and forth as he worked to solve the issue.

You'd better think quick pal.

Devin stood behind him, now almost back to fighting shape as he cracked his knuckles.

"Fun time's over, time to for you to take a permanent dirt nap," Devin threatened as he sneered at Aaron.

Now or never pal.

Hank's eyes grew wide, a look of uncertain determination replacing the look of abject confusion on his face. He ran over to where the blade had landed and scooped it off the floor before heading back to mid-court to grab a ball off the line. Hank then ran back to where he'd been standing, set his feet, and hurdled the blade as hard as he could into the air towards Aaron.

We already tried this.

Aaron almost ignored the effort, a pointless gesture that he knew would only result in him having a shiny sliver in his hand IF he even managed to catch the damn thing, and started to turn his attention back toward Devin.

"SIR!" Hank shouted to regain Aaron's attention.

Aaron looked back just in time to see Hank let loose with the ball that was in his hand, directly at him.

"What in the hell are you-," Aaron started

The ball hit the cane in mid-air, attaching itself to the cane like it had with Devin and Aaron.

You clever sonofabitch.

The cane, and ball, landed on the hardwood floor next to him as the ball appeared to melt into the cane. The cane rattled on the floor like a popcorn kernel about to explode, steam rising from the cane as it began to rattle faster.

Then it stopped.

The cane just sat on the hardwood floor, not growing an inch. Devin laughed out loud and proceeded to cross the mid-court line and grab Aaron by his hair and put him in a chokehold, the air slowly fading from his lungs as he gasped for breath that would not come to him.

"Bedtime," Devin whispered into his ear and Aaron began to loose consciousness.

Aaron saw Hank, frustrated his idea hadn't worked, scurry over and scream at the blade, as it lay motionless on the hardwood floor. Hank hurdle obscenities at the blade, using words Aaron didn't think an angel, even one that had fallen, would use, before kicking the blade with everything he had in a white-hot rage.

The blade took flight.

It landed seconds before it exploded, sending a pulse through the entire gymnasium that blew out the remaining windows and all the lights as the place descended into darkness.

Aaron wondered if it was really as dark as it seemed or if he was just loosing consciousness. Aaron reached out with his right arm, tapping the floor around him hoping to find the blade and grab hold of it. Instead, all he felt was the cool hardwood floor beneath his fingertips.

Then the blade began to glow, emitting a blue hue that formed a perfect outline of its shape only a few inches outside Aaron's reach.

"Not gonna happen asshole. You die, right here, right now," Devin promised as Aaron fought to gain even an inch for the blade.

Feeling it all slipping away, Aaron was surprised when he felt a cool; rubber ball hit him in the forehead.

"Forgive me sir."

XXXII

Aaron grew.

His head felt like it was going to explode from the pressure, Hank having hit him squarely on the forehead in his desperate hurl in the dark.

It was working, he could feel his body expanding again.

Of the three options that could have happened, this was by far the best one.

Hank could have thrown the ball errantly, hitting Devin instead and only making a shitty situation worse as his adversary grew bigger and his chokehold grew tighter until Aaron ceased to exist.

Hank could have done exactly what he did, chuck the ball and made contact with Aaron's head, only to see it bounce harmlessly off him as Hank burst into flames for the illegal headshot.

Instead, it had sunk into his forehead and began to do it's magic just as the first one had.

Aaron didn't realize it at first, but he was easily able to breath again. He's neck had grown big enough that Devin was no longer able to wrap his arms around it to keep his chokehold in place. Aaron shrugged his gigantic shoulders to make sure Devin wasn't hanging on anymore.

With everything he had, which turned out to be quite a bit in his new found strength and size, Aaron rocketed his head backwards. He connected with Devin's chin, feeling Devin's jaw shatter before he heard it. The blow caused Devin to stagger backwards, giving Aaron the space he needed to get back on his own two feet and obtain the still glowing blade laying next to him.

"YOUUH AHH EEEHD!" Devin yelled out, trying to form words with his jaw broken and hanging from his face. "I GUUUNA MUHAH YU!!"

Not if I kill you first.

Devin charged, connecting with Aaron's now enormous mid-section and drove him into the wall behind, cracking on impact and spider-webbing outward around them as debris fell from the ceiling.

Devin continued on his rampage, delivering body shot after body shot to Aaron's torso, each landing with a massive BOOM that shook the gymnasium's foundation. It should have hurt, bad, but Aaron could barely feel it. It was the equivalent of a toddler punching an adult, the effort was there but there was no way the toddler could actually do any damage on the adult.

Aaron looked past the fury beating away at his torso and saw Jack, Ashley, and the rest of the group still chained to the front row of bleachers on the other side of the gymnasium. What little satisfaction he took was quickly wiped away when a large piece of debris fell from the ceiling only a few feet away from where they were sitting, unable to run since they were still chained to the bleachers.

This place was coming down around them, piece by piece.

He needed to finish this.

Now.

Aaron refocused on Devin, still wailing away at him with no sign of stopping or slowing down.

Enough of this shit.

Aaron palmed Devin's head; fitting nicely in his oversized hand, and pushed him all the way out till his arm was fully extended. Devin continued to swing viciously, each attempt landing nothing but a fistful of air. Aaron reached down and grabbed the blade, still emitting a blue glow, holding it tightly in his hand.

Suddenly, Aaron could feel himself starting to shrink.

The blade was healing him again, which this time meant bringing him back to his average size.

Oh goddammit.

Realizing he only had a few moments left with the size advantage, Aaron brought the sword above his head and released Devin from his grip to grab the handle with both hands. Devin charged again, but didn't make it more than a step before Aaron brought the hilt of the blade down with everything he had, a crushing blow that immobilized Devin instantly in his tracks. Devin collapsed to the ground and didn't move, Aaron was sure he'd crushed his skull, killing him on impact.

By now, Aaron had shrunk back to his original growth spurt, matching Devin's size as he stood over him. He looked over and saw that Jack and Ashley were still chained to the bleachers.

Aaron looked down at his feet and saw, against all odds, Devin squirming as he tried to get back up. His lower body was completely functional, but his head was severely damaged and unable to send the message to his legs to get up.

Impossible, he should be dead.

Aaron raised the blade to sever the head and finish this once and for all, freeing the group and living to fight another day.

Devin stopped him in his tracks when he looked up at him.

The red eyes no longer there, it was Devin once again.

Sonofabitch.

"Please man...please..." Devin begged. "Don't do this man...He MADE me fight you, he MADE me. Please...please don't do it man."

It shouldn't have worked, Aaron should have been able to see right through the charade and finish the job, but Aaron wasn't a murderer.

"Do it Aaron, you have to do it," Ashley said from the bleachers.

"Yeah, kill that motherfucker," Jack added before getting an elbow from Debbie.

"It's not him Aaron, it's not Devin," Ashley continued. "You have to do it, he's just a monster. He's just a wolf in sheep's clothing. Please, you have to do it."

Aaron's hesitation was enough for Devin to spin around and kick his legs out from underneath him, sending Aaron crashing to the floor.

"You are such a PUSSY you know that," Devin laughed. "You're gonna die, even after you had every chance to win this thing, because you are such as pussy."

Aaron raised the blade, still in his hand after the fall, and in one swoop cleanly cut off the head of the monster before him. The body, no longer burdened with a head, fell to the hardwood floor and burst into a spectacular flame before turning to ash like all the others had.

"OH COME ON! WHO THE FUCK IS THIS GUY!"

XXXIII

"Uh dude, I can see your balls."

Aaron panicked and looked down to see he was still fully dressed, he jeans now slightly baggy after the transformation back to his normal size.

"Just messing with you," Jack smiled back, holding a left over Dodgeball he'd been hiding behind his back.

"Still an asshole I see, good to see nothing changed while I was gone," Aaron shook his head.

"Hey! You guys think I would get big if I hit myself with this thing?" Jack asked, holding the ball out at arm's length to throw it at his chest.

"NO!" everyone shouted in unison.

"Alright! Jeez," Jack relented and tossed the ball harmlessly away from them.

The gymnasium was empty, they were alone.

Not sure what he'd been expecting, Aaron did not think for a minute that Zadkiel would hold up his end of the bet and actually release them if he'd won. Aaron was baffled by it, making note to press Hank for more info about Zadkiel and why he'd held up his end now after lying every time prior.

Who cares, Ashley is free.

She was standing next to him, or over him since he was still sitting on the ground after his fight with Devin had ended. She was still wearing the dress, the one that took his breath away the first time he'd seen her in it, and even though it had seen better days she still looked stunning to him. Everything that he'd been through, every dark hallway and demon he'd faced, was worth it for this moment. The one person that made him keep fighting against the odds was finally standing next to him. He'd panicked, more than he'd hoped he'd let on to the others, when she'd disappeared in that cloud of smoke. Aaron didn't know it at the time, but as the events began to unfold he wasn't entirely sure he would ever see her again.

Aaron reached out and poked her arm as he pulled himself off the hardwood floor, just to make sure she wasn't an illusion. His finger found purchase and she smacked him on the chest in retaliation.

"What was that for?" Ashley asked, pissed.

"Just had to make sure it was actually you and not a beautiful demon twin trying to trick me."

Ashley blushed.

"Are you two going to kiss already? It's getting weird for the rest of us," Debbie said, the rest of the group agreeing. Even Hank nodded in approval.

There might have been nothing more Aaron wanted in his entire life than to kiss Ashley Meyers.

So why aren't you?

Not now.

Aaron knew that nothing was guaranteed anymore, that the next minute could very well be their last. To withhold on a kiss was madness.

You ARE a pussy, Devin was right.

That's the thing though, this wasn't just any kiss.

It was Ashley Meyers.

Aaron had loved her since the first time he saw her he knew deep down she was the ONE. It sounded creepy to say out loud so he never did; though Jack picked up on his affection for her in lighting speed it was so obvious. As asinine as it sounded, to kiss her now, when they were still screwed, felt like a bad omen. The moment had to be special, had to be the perfect moment. Aaron felt like an idiot as he stood there, right in front of her and the rest of the group, mulling it over in his head. His dream girl was standing right in front of him after he'd just risked his life to rescue her.

So why didn't he just kiss her?

He'd EARNED a kiss.

Aaron had spent the last ten years of his life searching for who he was and what he really wanted. Numerous odd jobs and constantly moving had left him still searching. Now, as he stood in a pile of a demon's ashes, Aaron found himself. It had taken an impromptu trip to Hell and coming within an inch of his life multiple times, but he'd figured out what he wanted after all these years. Aaron could die, probably would, but he wouldn't die lost.

The ideas that were racing through his mind must have been similarly racing through Ashley's as well; she seemed just a timid about the kiss as he did. Aaron caught himself wondering what Ashley's story was, he'd missed ten years that Jack could only fill in to an extent of hearsay. It hit Aaron that he didn't know all that much about Ashley, just what he remembered from high school.

It didn't matter, in the end it was still Ashley no matter what trials and tribulations she'd had since he'd bolted town ten years ago.

Aaron could tell they both wanted to kiss, it was obvious enough that the rest of the group called them out on it, it was palpable at this point. Hank had been by his side since the beginning, had heard him mention her name enough times that when he finally put a face to a name he simply smiled in understanding.

Still, neither really wanted their first kiss to be in Hell.

Not the way to start...whatever this is.

In an almost physic agreement, they grabbed each other's hands and squeezed. She smiled and he returned in kind.

To be continued.

■

"So…not to agree with the Devil, but seriously though, Who ARE you dude?" Jack asked as they left the gymnasium and started down the hallway.

Aaron had no idea where they were headed, but he figured the Principle's office was as good a place as any to find Zadkiel and get out of this place.

"He's name is Zadkiel," Aaron corrected Jack.

"Say what now?"

"The voice over the intercom, his name is Zadkiel and he's just a fallen angel that has it out for Hank…and now us I guess."

Jack stopped walking, causing the rest of the group to stop as well since no one was willing to split the group up.

"Hold up, this guy has been torturing us this entire time and it's HIS fault?" Jack said, pointing over to Hank. "Why is he still here, we need to drop the dead weight and make a run for it while Zachariah is distracted."

"Zadkiel," Hank corrected Jack.

"I don't give shit what his name is, what the hell difference does it make what we call him?"

"Cause he's Hank's brother," Aaron responded, Ashley's grip tightening around his hand at the reveal.

"WHAT?" Jack shouted.

"It's a long story Jack, I'll fill you in on all the details later when we are not sitting ducks in a dark hallway. We need to move."

"Tell me," Jack said, not budging.

"What?"

"Tell me. Give me the bullet points or I'm not going anywhere with HIM," Jack said, looking at Hank.

"Fine," Aaron relented. "Hank's from Arcadia, the good place. We call it Heaven. Hank calls it Arcadia. Long time ago he and Zadkiel used to be brothers that were tasked with watching over the world below to witness who was worthy of a place in Arcadia when they died. Zadkiel met a girl and, long story short, the two of them had a bit of a falling out that lead to Zadkiel being banished here and his wife killing herself. Hank was found guilty of treason and banished as well, so now Zadkiel tortures Hank with a version of his own personal Hell for all eternity for his own enjoyment."

Jack, along with the rest of the group, stood in silence.

"Well…OK….any…anything ELSE you want to share?" Jack stuttered.

"Hank has a blade that apparently had healing powers for those that touch it," Aaron started as Hank gave him a grave look. "OH, but that's only if the blade doesn't kill you the second you touch it."

"Jesus…" Jack muttered out loud.

"Oh yeah, he's not real either. Jesus, God, the whole thing is just a myth. More of a community than one guy running the show like we thought."

Aaron could hear a pin drop as they all stared back at him in silence.

"So…but…the Book…WHAT?" Jack stumbled over himself.

"It's a lot man, trust me. I didn't believe it myself, still don't fully in a way, but so far everything Hank has said to me has turned out to be true. He's risked his own life for me, wasn't for him back there we'd all be dead, so I have no reason to doubt him at this point. I get it Jack, it's a lot, but Hank comes with us and that's final."

Jack didn't argue, he was still stunned from what Aaron had told him to offer anything but a head nod and a quick glance over at Hank as he tried to wrap his head around it. Aaron could only imagine how Jack was struggling, Jack worked in a library and had read just about every book he could get his hands on since he'd known him. The information he had in that head had to be vast beyond compare, only to be shattered by Aaron with a few sentences.

Buck up pal, we're going to need that brain of yours working at full capacity if we're ever getting out of here.

"So…so where are we going? What's the plan?" Jack finally asked, the look on his face told Aaron that he'd processed the new information the best he could and would be running through everything in his head for quite some time. Jack had Debbie; Aaron saw them holding hands the same way he and Ashley were and realized Jack was fighting for the same things he was.

"I've been trying to draw Zadkiel out since we were separated, but so far he's not interested in the one-on-one type of encounter. Way I see it, we move to Plan B."

"What's Plan B?" Ashley asked.

"If he won't come to us, we go to him."

"THAT'S Plan B?" Jack rolled his eyes. "What pray tell do you plan on doing when we get there, IF we get there. Do you even know where THERE is?"

Aaron did not.

268

His best guess was the Principle's office; it made the most sense that the guy pulling the strings would be holed up in the big guy's office. Nothing Zadkiel had said or done made Aaron think he wouldn't take residence in that office, Zadkiel was a blowhard and it would be the perfect place for such an egotistical douchbag to think he was the most important player in the game. The microphone was just outside the Principle's door too, which meant he had to be close by every time he'd come on the intercom to hurl insults and make threats.

Aaron just hoped he could be convincing enough to make Jack and the rest of the group buy his half-baked theory.

"Yeah…the Principle's office." Aaron responded.

"He has no idea where to go," Jack said, instantly calling his bluff.

Goddammit.

"You have a better idea I'm all ears."

"You're nuts dude, why the fuck would you WANT to face him head on?"

"Because so far, the only way we have been able to move forward is by killing the demon or monster or whatever the fuck he throws at us!" Aaron shouted back, angry he was fighting with his own best friend instead of fighting the enemy. "I find him, I kill him, we go home."

Jack was about to respond when Becky cut them both off.

"GUYS! Do you hear that?"

Everyone fell silent and listened.

Nothing.

"I don't hear anything?" Jack said.

"SHHH," Becky said, pointing down the hallway towards the Principle's office. "It's coming from over there."

They all listened again.

Nothing.

"Becky, I don-," Aaron started before he heard it.

Squealing.

Very lite and sporadic, but it was there. I sounded like a dog's chew toy beging squeezed, with a long squeal then silence before it started up again. The sound was barely audible, but it was there as Becky had said it was. Aaron looked around the group, but no one knew what the sound was, all offering blank stares and shoulder shrugs each time they heard it.

The sound was growing louder and more frequent now. Whatever it was, it was coming their way.

Sqquuuuuueeeee.

Louder.

SQQUUUUUUEEEEE.

"Does that sound?" Jack started, but paused to listen again. "That sound like a pig to anyone else?"

SQQUUUUUUEEEEE.

"My word!" Hank gasped.

"What is it Hank, what's coming?"

"Entelodont's," Hank muttered.

"What the hell did you just say? What that hell is that?" Aaron asked, the sound growing louder as the walls began to shake. Each locker vibrated loudly as the doors began to pop open on each side of them all the way down the hall.

"Hell Pigs," Jack translated. "He said Hell Pigs."

XXXIV

Hell Pigs.

OF COURSE there would be such thing as a Hell Pig.

OF COURSE they would be angry, violent creatures that destroyed humans and animals alike.

OF COURSE they would be rushing down the hallway toward them this very moment.

Aaron and the rest of the group did what they could to brace for impact as these vicious beasts tore down the hallway towards them. They were massive, on all fours the two beasts had to have been no less than six feet tall, and were moving at an impossible speed. Their hooves tore at the tile in the hallway, sending crushed pieces flying in every direction as they closed the gap between them. Locker doors started flying off as the beast's elongated horns, covered in what Aaron thought looked like dried blood, dragged against the locker-lined walls and tore at each flapping door until it mercifully ripped off its hinges and sailed toward Aaron and the group like ballistic missiles.

"Where sitting ducks like this, we have to move NOW!" Aaron shouted.

There were only two Hell Pigs, which Aaron took as a win over an entire herd, but those two were more than enough and outmatched them easily. They charged down the hallway side-by-side, taking up the width of the hallway between them and leaving no place for the group to duck for cover or hide until the passed. If they were going to survive, they were either going to have to turn tail and haul ass as fast as they could the other direction and hope to lose them further down another hallway or they were going to have to stand and fight them head on.

The only weapon they had between them was Hank's blade.

Run it is then.

The Hell Pigs charged forward, only a hundred yards away now and not slowing down for anything. They absolutely eviscerated anything in their path.

Aaron turned to run the opposite direction when he glanced the locker room entry out of the corner of his eye. The entry to the locker rooms was the best option on the table, Aaron understanding that they could only outrun the beasts for so long and would eventually have to turn and fight or split up. Their best option was to cut into that locker room before the Hell Pigs blew past them. The lockers room entry was also perfect for one key reason.

No door.

Crest Hill had designed the entry to the locker rooms as short tunnel that opened up into the locker room at the end, just like a bathroom in an airport. There were no doors so there was no way for them to be locked out and the tunnel was small enough that the Hell Pigs wouldn't be able to cram inside it without the foundation collapsing around them and burying them in royal blue painted brick.

"LOCKER ROOMS!" Aaron shouted and sprinted across the hallway to the tunnel entrance, making sure Ashley, Debbie and Becky got in first. The rest of the group fell in and Aaron bolted down the tunnel just as the Hell Pigs exploded past them.

"Holy SHIT?" Jack shouted.

There was good news, aside from them still being alive after almost being trampled by two of the most vicious beasts Aaron had ever seen, the Hell Pigs were not hunting them. At least that was the general consensus when the Hell Pigs continued to charge down the hallway not paying any attention to them as they blew past them. There was a chance they had managed to hide before the Hell Pigs managed to target them, but Aaron and the rest of the group had been standing in that hallway when those two beasts came around the corner, only jumping out of the way at the last second. Those Hell Pigs saw them, it was impossible for them not to, they just didn't give a damn and had kept running.

Becky let out a bloodcurdling scream as Aaron put his hand over her mouth to muffle the sound and avoid drawing attention to them for the Hell Pigs to reverse course and come back.

"Becky, they could hea-," Aaron started before Jack put his hand on his shoulder.

Aaron let go of Becky and she collapsed into Ashley and Debbie's arms and they tried to comfort here.

"I'm sorry, I didn't-," Aaron began to apologize.

"Aaron," Jack said, nudging towards the hallway where he and Hank were looking.

Oh no.

Aaron saw what they were looking at, what Becky saw that made her scream, and his stomach sank.

Tony was lying in the middle of the hallway.

He didn't make it.

Aaron had been sure he'd had everyone in front of him when he's pushed them down the tunnel before he sprinted in at the last second. In the moment he apparently had missed that Tony wasn't in front of him.

Now Tony was lying face down, a small puddle of blood had formed around him where the Hell Pigs had trampled him. They probably didn't even notice him as they flew by; he wasn't their target just in the wrong place at the wrong time.

"Dammit," Aaron said, punching the brick wall. Becky continued to sob as Debbie and Ashley tired to console her. Aaron remembered that Becky had taken a liking towards Tony back in the first room, they had found each other hiding under a table. He wanted to say something, to help her in some way, but whatever he said wasn't going to do a damn thing to help her after seeing Tony lying in the middle of the hallway.

"Help me out guys, we can't just leave him there," Aaron said, walking out into the hallway that was covered in brick dust, crushed tile, and locker doors as far as they could see. The lights overheard flickered, the Hell Pig's horns big enough to scrape against the ceiling and tear out some of the lights as they'd charged down the hall.

Aaron knelt, feeling for a pulse and hoping against hope that he'd find one even if it was weak, but instead felt the cold silence of a lost soul under his fingertips. Ashley and Debbie had moved to block Becky's view, she didn't need to see then move Tony, and Aaron was thankful they were all on the same page. Becky was fragile, finding strength in Tony; this would break even the best of them. The three of them began to pick up Tony, Aaron wasn't sure where he was going to lay Tony to rest but anything was better than leaving him in the dark hallway, when Tony's body turned into a bright blue light. The three of them had to cover their eyes it was so bright, until the light receded and it was a dark hallway again.

Where Tony had been lying only moments ago, there was a nothing. The hallway was empty, not even a trace of ash like the other's had left.

"Where'd he go?" Jack asked, Aaron wondering the same thing.

"He has left us sir," Hank offered.

"Left us where?" Jack grilled him.

"He went to Arcadia," Aaron answered for Hank, Hank nodding in agreement.

"He's not stuck down here?"

"Apparently not," Aaron said, looking toward Hank to fill in the blanks.

"Your friend was a good man, a decent and kind soul. He did not belong down here and cannot be kept down here once he has passed. As much as this place may act like an inescapable fortress, it cannot keep the virtuous in once their time has come."

"Are you telling me that if we die down here, we aren't stuck down here?" Jack asked.

"That is correct Jack. Arcadia is for only those worthy; it does not matter where their lives cease. I will admit it is rare, I myself have only seen but a few that ascended to Arcadia in my time, but there is no escaping judgment once your time is up."

Jack nodded, finding a sliver of hope in Hank's explanation. Aaron recalled Jack telling him that if you died in Hell, you didn't get a get out of jail free card, it was case closed and you were stuck down there forever. Now it seemed that wasn't the case, that if you were a good person, you still had a chance in the end.

"One last question," Jack started. "Why do you call him sir and not me?"

"Seriously?" Aaron said, shaking his head and glaring at him.

Not the best time.

"What? I just wanna know what makes you so special in his eyes. Ya know, aside from the whole warrior thing with the sword and demon killing you got going on."

Hank didn't respond, leaving the two of them to go check on Becky and offer his condolences.

"Tony just died and you want a different title, come on Jack," Aaron said, grabbing Jack's shirt and pulling him close. "Knock it off, this is not the time and you fucking know it. Show some goddamn respect."

Jack didn't say a word, the look on his face telling Aaron he got the message.

"So…" Ashley said, coming up behind them without Aaron even noticing. "Becky's in bad shape Aaron, I'm not sure she's going to be able to keep going. She's pretty upset after…" Ashley trailed off, unable to say it out loud.

"We can't just stay here dude, we are sitting ducks if those things come back," Jack countered.

Aaron knew they were both right.

Staying put was to court death, those beasts would be back, it was only a matter of time. They were sitting ducks anywhere they went, but this was worse somehow. Everyone was shaken by what had happened to Tony, even though he was a shy guy they all remembered him from high school and knew he didn't deserve what had happened to him. Tony had frozen in place, unable to move from the fear and paid the ultimate price. Becky wasn't the only one that would have a hard time getting over what happened to such an innocent person for no good reason.

Ashley was also correct, they weren't going anywhere with Becky in her condition. Aaron knew they were stronger together, but to ask Becky to shake off what had just happened was impossible. She needed time to process what had just happened and she wasn't going to do that if they followed Aaron's original plan to bring the fight to Zadkiel.

Becky needed time, time that Aaron knew they didn't have.

"So… what do we do?" Ashley asked again.

Aaron knew the answer, and it tore him apart cause it was the absolute LAST thing he wanted to do.

"We split up."

"But we jus-," Ashley started to argue.

"Right now it's the last thing any of us wants," Aaron acknowledged. "But I can't ask Becky to keep going after this. Right now, the only play we still have is to take the fight to Zadkiel, to confront him while he's still on his toes after what happened in the gymnasium. You guys need to stay with Becky, help her as best you can. If you go towards the back of the locker rooms you should be safe from the Hell Pigs if they come back. Hank and I will go to the Principle's Office and confront Zadkiel once and for all."

"I'm coming with you," Jack argued.

"I need you to stay here Jack, to do EVERYTHING you can to protect everyone and hold off the Hell Pigs for as long as you can if they come back."

"No. Fuck that. Hank can stay and I'll go with you."

"Zadkiel is Hank's brother, I need him with me incase he has anymore bright ideas like he did with the sword back in the gymnasium."

"You don't think I can fight do you," Jack shook his head.

"Jack, I am asking you to stay and protect the people that mean the most to us," Aaron said as he looked at Ashley. "If I didn't think you were capable of doing that I wouldn't have asked in the first place. Hank doesn't know us, he doesn't know what we mean to each other. He will fight, no question, but you will die for them. I need YOU, not Hank, to keep everyone safe."

"And what happens if you fail, if Zadkiel gets the better of you two?"

"If we die, you use that encyclopedia of a brain and come up with a way to get them out of here that was better than my idea."

Jack nodded in agreement, unable to speak as tears welled up in his eyes at the possibility of this being the last time they spoke. Aaron did his best to quell his own emotions as Jack headed back to Debbie and Becky to give him a minute with Ashley.

"I…" he started before she cut him off.

"No. Whatever you are going to say, save it for when you come back."

"I'm not sure I will come back Ashley," Aaron admitted.

"Aaron, I'll be the first to admit that all I remembered about you from high school was being Jack's best friend and never bothering to talk to me for four years when you really should have."

"So you noticed that huh?"

"That and Jack spilled the beans on your crush years ago."

"Remind me to punch him if I make it back."

"WHEN you make it back."

"Ashley…"

"I've heard a lot about you Aaron, your mother is happy to share anything when it comes to you. She really is your biggest fan. For ten years I've heard about this strong-willed guy that was hell bent on figuring out what he wanted in life and wouldn't stop till he did. When you walked into Jasper's the other night, I saw exactly what your mother sees in you. You're not lost Aaron, you just lost track of what you wanted, you were always willing to fight for it," Ashley interlocked her hands in his. "When I was…abducted…I was scared. Terrified. I didn't know what happened and where I was. I thought I was going to die until I heard your voice, I heard you promise me that you were going to find me. I knew you would, I could hear in in your voice that you wouldn't stop till you did. That's when you changed Aaron, when you went from the guy that sped out of town after high school to the man that figured out what he wanted and what he was willing to do for it. That was when you turned into the man that I've been slowly falling in love with for the last decade listening to your mother's stories."

"Ashley, I…"

"Go. Finish this and when you're done I'll be here waiting for you."

■

Aaron and Hank headed down the wrecked hallway toward the Principle's Office. Hank had given Aaron his blade, Aaron holding it firmly in his right hand as they neared the end of the hallway. Just to their left was the Principle's Office.

Zadkiel.

Before they could even round the corner, Zadkiel came over the intercom.

"YOU KNOW WHAT'S FUNNY? HOW EACH ONE OF YOU ASSHOLES ARE SO MUCH ALIKE. EACH AND

EVERYONE ONE OF YOU ARE DOWN HERE BECAUSE YOU FOUND IT EASIER TO TAKE THE EASY ROAD IN LIFE, NEVER BOTHERING TO LIFT A FINGER. NO, YOU ASSHOLES ARE ALL CONTENT WITH BITCHING ABOUT HOW THE WORLD HAS TURNED AGAINST YOU, THAT YOU WERE DEALT AN UNFAIR HAND IN LIFE AND IT'S JUST NOT YOUR FAULT HOW EVERYTHING BAD HAPPENED TO POOR OLD YOU. THEN, THEN THERE ARE THE WORST KIND OF PEOPLE. THE PEOPLE THAT GET IT IN THEIR HEADS THEY ARE SPECIAL, THAT THEY ARE SOME KIND OF FUCKING UNICORN THAT IS MEANT FOR GREAT THINGS, WHEN THEY KNOW DEEP DOWN THEY ARE JUST AS USELESS AS EVERYONE ELSE THEY BITCH ABOUT BEHIND THEIR BACKS. ALL THEY EVER ACCOMPLISH IS GETTING THEIR FIFTEEN SECONDS OF FAME FROM THEIR DESIRE TO BE MORE IMPORTANT THAN THEY REALLY ARE. THAT'S YOU ISN'T IT? YOU DON'T MATTER, YOU WERE BARELY A BLIP ON MY RADAR. WELL, CONGRATULATIONS ASSHOLE. YOU HAVE MY ATTENITION NOW. YOU'VE HAD YOUR FIFTEEN SECONDS OF FAME, NOW IT'S MY TURN TO REMIND YOU WHY YOU SHOULD HAVE KEPT YOUR HEAD DOWN. I'M GOING TO PERSONALLY TEACH YOU WHY YOU ARE STUCK DOWN HERE WITH ME, AND WHY YOU ARE GOING TO WISH YOU DIED A HUNDRED TIMES OVER BY THE TIME I'M FINISHED WITH YOU."

Aaron smiled.

"You've been telling me that since I've been down here and I've been letting it slide, but I think it's important to clear this up for you," Aaron started, tightening his gripe on the blade.

"I'm not trapped down here with you. You're trapped down here with me."

XXXV

Careful what you wish for.

The thought had barely had time to cross his mind before Aaron was standing directly in front of Zadkiel.

Zadkiel emerged from the Principle's Office, exactly where Aaron had suspected he'd been hiding out this entire time though being correct brought him no pleasure. It was like correctly picking the most dreadful nightmare to come true, there was no prize other than your worst fear being realized.

His body barely fit through the doorway as he cracked the doorframe squeezing out in an effort Aaron had to assume he didn't want them to witness by the way he angrily thrust his left shoulder through the wall to free himself after a moment of writing back and forth in the tight space. His efforts left the doorframe in pieces behind him as he strolled into the darkened hallway.

Standing just over ten feet tall, Zadkiel loomed over them. He had a human body, one of monstrous proportions, his skin hotrod red. He'd been expecting much worse from the one that had been pulling the strings this entire time; the game of masking themselves as people from his past played out, Aaron figured Zadkiel would burst out of the Principle's Office in full demon mode. Instead, he saw the universal personification that everyone thought of when they visualized the Devil.

Massive frame.

Red skin.

Horns.

Hooved feet.

The whole nine yards, a pointed tail to boot.

"YOU LOOK DISSAPOINTED," Zadkiel noticed. **"WHERE YOU EXPECTING SOMETHING MORE LIKE THIS?"**

In a flash, the comic book Devil that was standing in front of Aaron turned into an enormous serpent, the circumference of a tractor tire filling the hallway. It's body winded all the way down the hall to where Aaron couldn't see any more in the darkness. Enormous fangs slide out of its mouth as beady eyes bore down into his soul. Aaron hated snakes, something Zadkiel likely knew when he'd chosen to transform into one for greater effect. The sound of a rattler at the end of the hallway sent shivers up and down Aaron's spine.

"SSSSSSSSAMATTER SSSSSISSSSSSY," Zadkiel hissed at him. **"YOU'RE NOT SSSSSCARED ARE YOU?"**

Aaron was terrified; he could feel the perspiration forming between his palm and the blade handle. He calmed his nerves by picturing Ashley, just down the hallway waiting for him. Zadkiel knew he hated snakes, it did Aaron no good to try and hide it, he had to embrace his fear.

"Take any form you want. This one just makes it easier you cut your head off."

"SSSSSOOO BRAVE," Zadkiel hissed. **"SSSSSSEEE WHY SSSSSSSHE LIKESSSSSSSS YOU SSSSSSSO MUCH."**

The snake slithered towards Aaron, wrapping around him, the only part of his body still visible was from the neck up. The serpent opened its mouth to reveal the horrific split tongue that rippled as the rattle down the hall continued. The colossal fangs the protruded from its mouth coming within millimeters of Aaron's face, venom forming at the tips just before he pulled back and laughed.

"YOU'RE TOO MUCH FUN YOU KNOW THAT? SO EASILY...RATTLED...ITS LIKE TAKING CANDY FROM A BABY, WHICH IS EXHILARATING LET ME TELL YOU."

Zadkiel morphed back into his first form, red skin and all.

"SO WHAT'S THE PLAN?" Zadkiel asked, picking his elongated nails in indifference as he leaned against a locker. *"YOU GONNA STAB ME WITH BRO'S TOOTHPICK AND WALK OUT THE FRONT DOOR TO THE SOUND OF A CLASSIC ROCK BALLAD WITH YOUR LADY FRIEND IN YOUR ARMS?"*

"Tell you the truth I hadn't given it much thought after the stabbing you part, but that sounds pretty good to me."

"LOOK AT YOU! THIS COWARDLY LION FOUND HIS COURAGE DIDN'T HE! THAT PIECE OF ASS YOU GOT IS GONNA HAVE TO GET IN LINE, CAUSE NOW I WANNA FUCK YOU. NOT EVERYDAY ONE OF YOU BRINGS THE FIGHT TO ME, YOU GOT ME ALL RILED UP JUST THINKING ABOUT IT."

"You talk a big game, but Hank told me your story. You're not in charge around here, no one is. You're just another one of those cowards you ostensibly loath so much, too weak to do something yourself so you chose to send others to do it for you. Now you are stuck down here after your wife chose DEATH over you. You ask me, your situation is a lot shittier than mine."

Zadkiel's face churned at the mention of his wife, the rage inside him fought to explode out. His entire head began to pulsate a bright red underneath the skin, a glowing rage that was building up right in front of them, just waiting to explode at any second. One moment the three of them were standing in a darkened hallway, the next it was pitch black as Zadkiel roared. Aaron couldn't see six inches in front of his face it was so dark.

"YOU DARE INSULT ME, BRING UP MY WIFE!" the walls shook as he spoke, the metal lockers squealing as they began to twist and bend. *"YOU WILL SUFFER FOR THIS, YOU AND YOUR FRIENDS. I WILL MAKE SURE YOU ARE THE LAST TO GO SO YOU CAN SEE THEM ALL FALL AT MY FEET. THEN YOU TOO WILL KNOW WHAT IT'S LIKE TO LOOSE EVERYTHING AT THE HANDS OF ANOTHER."*

Out of the pitch black Aaron saw Zadkiel's eyes, their red glow breaking through the darkness like headlights.

"You think you're the only one that's ever lost something? Get in line asshole. Only difference is we are standing here trying to make the best of things while you stand over there looking to vent your self-prescribed grief on others to avoid looking in a goddamn mirror for once in your miserable existence."

The emergency lights slowly came to life, the pitch-black hallway now awash in the soft red glow of the overhead emergency lights.

Zadkiel was a full on demon now.

His wings brushed against the walls, his red skin replaced by the same leathery skin all the other demons shared. Zadkiel legs were now covered in hair all the way down to his hooves. His eyes glowed as he stared them down, smoke pouring out around them as they burned, his chest moving up and down as he breathed heavily.

Sicut superius, et inferius;
Et cessabit Moab tuum praesidium palam.
Tenebrae Responsories tua grata nisi voluntatem;
Lucem splendescere qui spem non insinuet

"No…..NO!" Hank shouted as Zadkiel recited his chant.

"What? What is he saying?" Aaron shouted over to Hank as he backed away.

Sicut superius, et inferius;
Et cessabit Moab tuum praesidium palam.
Tenebrae Responsories tua grata nisi voluntatem;
Lucem splendescere qui spem non insinuet

Before Aaron could get his answer, a half a dozen demons swarmed down the hallway towards Hank. Fighting against them, Hank thrashed about violently. Throwing each demon around like a ragdoll as he fought back. For every demon Hank quickly disposed of, another one flew down the hallway to replace it. There was no end to the amount of reinforcements Zadkiel could send at Hank it seemed as Aaron watched on in horror.

Aaron was ready to charge, fight them off beside him, when he felt the blade crumbled to pieces. Zadkiel's was chanting had destroyed the only weapon they had and left him defenseless against a swarm of demons.

"YOU CANNOT DO THIS ZADKIEL!" Hank shouted underneath two demons that jumped on top of him to pin him while a third grabbed a locker clean off the wall to crush him. "You dishonor her memory, prove she was spot-on in letting you fall. You become her worse fear."

"SILENCE!" Zadkiel shouted, sending the demons scurrying away.

Hank was in bad shape, there was a large gash on his forehead and his suit had been torn apart and swathed in enough blood that it couldn't all be demon blood. Both of his arms appeared to be broken, hanging lifelessly at his side as he struggled to stay upright. Hank staggered for a moment, Aaron rushing over just in time to catch him before he hit the ground.

"Apologies sir," Hank muttered.

"Hang in their pal, you're gonna be fine. Just a scratch," Aaron lied, blood covering his hands as it soaked through Hank's clothes.

"Perhaps its time to chop down the tree sir," Hank murmured before losing consciousness.

"HANK!" Aaron begged as Hank's body went still.

Hank remained lifeless in his arms.

Aaron checked for a pulse but couldn't find one, he attempted CPR but Hank didn't respond. He pounded on his chest to wake him up, to shock him back to life, but it was of no use.

Hank was gone.

Aaron laid Hank back on the tile gently.

Aaron's sadness turned to rage.

Zadkiel had murdered his own brother in cold blood. Hank had been a kind man, asking nothing from anyone and serving his sentence in isolated silence as he watched innumerable people meet a grisly fate. He'd found the will to fight, to listen to his inner-voice and try to make a difference no matter what the odds were stacked against them. Hank had offered to put himself in harms way with him, if it meant they might be victorious. They both knew they were going against insurmountable odds, but they both had something to fight for and held on to it when it seemed impossible to take another step.

Now he was gone.

Hank's body did not turn into a blue light as Tony's had, Aaron had to accept that Hank was not welcome back at Arcadia after being cast out.

Fuck Arcadia, you assholes don't know what you lost.

"I'm going to kill you,"

"HAHAHAHAHAHA. YOU AND WHAT ARMY YOU PISSANT."

Aaron locked eyes with Zadkiel.

"I'm going to kill you."

Aaron smashed the box hanging on the wall next to him, the words BREAK INCASE OF EMERGENCY etched on glass falling to pieces on the ground, and clutched the axe that had been hanging behind it. It felt heavy in his hands, much heavier than the blade had been, with its steel head and wooden handle.

He looked down at the axe for a moment before pulling the fire alarm next to the box holding the axe.

You better be right about this Hank.

The smoke from Zadkiel's eyes had formed a thick cloud above them, once the fire alarm was pulled the sprinklers burst to life, spraying the entire hallway with ice-cold water, each drop ripping through the smoke effortlessly until it was gone completely.

As the ice-cold water rained down on them, dripping off the steel head of the axe, Zadkiel cackled.

"THIS IS YOUR PLAN? TO KILL ME WITH...WATER?"

Aaron hurled the axe with everything he had.

"YOU FOOL, YOU KNOW A MORTAL WEAPON CAN'T KI-" Zadkiel started before the axe found purchase on his right leg.

It cut clean through, separating Zadkiel from his right leg just above the knee.

Zadkiel roared out in agony as he collapsed.

"THIS IS...IMPOSSIBLE!" he shouted from the floor, writing in agony.

XXXVI

As they'd headed towards the Principle's Office, Hank had offered a warning that stuck with Aaron.

"You must be prepared to lose sir," Hank offered ominously. "You must be willing to quiet every thought coursing through your mind right now and be willing to accept that this will not end without consequences."

"What does that mean Hank? Am I supposed to back away now, just give up without even trying?"

"On the contrary sir, you must fight smarter if you wish to have any chance against Zadkiel. He will take everything away from us, he will strip us of everything but our will and even that will be questioned. Zadkiel is not inclined to fight fairly sir, he will do anything to make sure he holds the upper hand."

"Great pep talk, thanks."

"I implore you to consider any and all options available to you. This is not your world sir, things are different down here. Reality can and will bend to your will in you want it badly enough. You can do it, I have seen you accomplish the impossible before."

"Wait, seriously?"

"Sir, do you truly believe this undertaking will be as easy as confronting Zadkiel and stabbing him like the demon's before? If you do, we have already lost and your friends are doomed to share my fate for eternity."

"So think outside the box," Aaron nodded.

"Precisely sir," Hank agreed. "You must be ready and willing to use the environment as a weapon in this fight, he will be ready and willing to do the same. Just because Zadkiel has taken permanent residency in Abaddon does not mean he is the only one capable of bending it to his will. Those that arrive here are never capable of realizing they have just as much say in what happens as anyone, there is a collective conscious I must remind you. Fear cripples them from understanding they could be, and are, equals to those that torture them."

"So why didn't you fight back earlier, bring Zadkiel down a peg instead of subjecting yourself to this for so long?"

"My burden is my own sir. I believed my place in Abaddon was deserved for the thoughts I had. It took you fighting back to understand my punishment was of my own accord, that everyone has a choice to make on whether or not to take that first step toward redemption."

"Fair enough."

■

Aaron stood in the pouring rain, still ice-cold as it fell down from the sprinklers above, as he surveyed the situation.

That actually worked!

It was uncommon to still have an axe behind glass, they had been phased out for reasons that likely stemmed from a lawsuit, but Crest Hill was an old school and didn't make many changes over the years to accommodate such a small town. Aaron had no idea what the fire code was, but he remembered the axe on the wall when he was in school and they never got shut down so it had to be acceptable, though nowadays the idea of an axe just hanging in a school would cause mass chaos with parents. Whatever the reason was, Crest Hill never got rid of the axe behind the glass and Aaron couldn't have been more thankful at the moment.

He moved to smash the glass and help Hank when Zadkiel shouted and sent the hoard of demons away, leaving a badly beaten Hank to cling to life for only a few moments. As he lay in Aaron's arms, his life slowly coming to an end, Hank mentioned chopping down and tree. Aaron had no idea what he was talking about at first, but somehow Hank knew he'd eyed the axe and urged him to use it.

When Aaron broke the glass and grabbed the axe, he saw the fire alarm next to the axe and it hit him.

Bend to your will.

Aaron said a quick prayer and pulled the fire alarm, triggering the sprinklers above to shower both he and Zadkiel with ice-cold water. He let the water soak them both before he threw the axe.

■

Zadkiel lay on the ground, holding what was left of his right leg as he writhed in pain; Aaron went to collect his axe.

The water had stopped, the smoke having cleared rendering the sprinklers no longer necessary. The hallway had been partially flooded; two inches of standing water swallowed Aaron's shoes and soaked the socks inside them. He sloshed just past Zadkiel and grabbed the axe from the water, pulling it up as the water dripped off its steel head. Any sign of blood or ash had been long since rinsed in the water, the axe looking as good as new even with the added weight of a soaked wooden handle.

"YOU!" Zadkiel thundered.

"Yep, it's me alright," Aaron answered, coming back to Zadkiel but keeping a safe distance to avoid a sneak attack. "Didn't see that coming did you."

"WHAT DID YOU DO TO ME?"

"That?" Aaron pointed at Zadkiel's missing leg with his axe. "Oh that was just a parting gift from Hank. All I did was deliver it."

"THAT AXE IS A MORTAL WEAPON, IT HAS NO DOMAIN OVER ME!"

"Sure looks like it does from where I'm standing."

"WHAT DID YOU DO TO ME?" Zadkiel demanded, the emergency light flickering at his outburst.

"I just returned some of that agony you enjoyed handing out to me and my friends. You see, you don't get to just die, that would be too easy. What was it you keep prattling on about each time we talk? Oh that's right...Torture," Aaron said with a grin forming on his face.

"YOUR WEAPON CAN'T MORTALLY WOUND ME, FOOL. A LUCKY STRIKE, ONE THAT YOU WILL PAY GRAVELY FOR I ASSURE YOU."

"You feel that water you're lying in right now?" Aaron asked, bringing the axe down by his side so just the steel head set in the water. "You see, that's not just any old regular cold water. No, that was the gift Hank left you that I mentioned earlier."

Zadkiel's eyes widened as Aaron brought the axe up from the water and over his shoulder.

"That's Holy water asshole, and I'm just getting started."

XXXVII

Aaron brought the axe down and took Zadkiel's right wing clean off.

Zadkiel roared in pain, grasping with his arms to rip Aaron apart.

"Ohhh, that looks like it hurt. It did didn't it?" Aaron mocked

There was a part of him that was thoroughly enjoying this. It was dark to think that he would get pleasure in torture, but after what he and his friends had been through, it was all Aaron could do to keep from smiling as he did it.

That was for Hank.

"I WILL CRUSH YOU!"

"You have one leg and one wing, the only thing in your future is a whole lotta hopping and flying in a circle."

Aaron kept telling himself to just finish it, to behead Zadkiel and get the hell out of there with Ashley and the rest of the group. Cutting him apart piece by piece wasn't going to prove anything in the end, just made him feel more like a serial killer with each blow he made. The smart play was to just end it and get out while he could.

IF he could get out

There was no guarantee that killing Zadkiel would release them. They were stuck down here and the best guess he could come up with was that Zadkiel was guarding the gate out, he'd seen as much when Zadkiel showed him the front doors of the school and all the people gathering outside it. Once Zadkiel was out of the picture, they would be able to get out. All the other monsters and demon's down here seemed to be more than happy to bend to Zadkiel's will for whatever reason, killing him surely would be enough to make them stand down and allow them to leave.

Or it would enrage the collective conscious they shared and trigged a death even worse than whatever Zadkiel had planned for them.

Only one way to find out.

Aaron brought the axe up once more, this time he would finish it once and for all, when Zadkiel stopped writing in agony and began to laugh.

"YOU ARE JUST AS DUMB AS YOU LOOK YOU KNOW THAT?"

"Quiet now, it will all be over soon," Aaron promised.

"YOU ACTUALLY THINK THIS IS PERMANENT DON'T YOU? THESE WOUNDS ARE NOTHING MORE THAN JUST TEMPORARY SETBACKS BEFORE I CRUSH YOUR SKULL. YOU FUCKING IDIOT."

"Says the guy with one leg and one wing."

"SAYS THE GUY THAT HAS BEEN LETTING YOU WEAR YOURSELF OUT WHILE RELAXING IN A SHALLOW POOL PLANNIG YOUR DEATH."

Aaron's heart rate picked up rapidly. He hadn't realized it at the moment, but he was tired. Swinging the axe had taken more out of him than he'd thought; he was sweating and breathing hard. He'd been too amped up to realize it, but he had been putting himself through the ringer and Zadkiel didn't even have to lift a finger the entire time. He just lay there and played possum while Aaron wore himself out enacting his own revenge.

Zadkiel brought his palms together in a loud clap, creating a wave in both directions as the water washed away and left him lying on a dry tile floor. Aaron stepped back as Zadkiel's eyes once again glowed bright red, smoke seeping out around them as a smile formed on his face.

"WANNA SEE A MAGIC TRICK?" He cackled.

Zadkiel flapped his remaining wing once and lifted himself off the ground.

Hanging in place as the single wing fluttered relentlessly to keep him in the air, he brought his hand together again, thought this time slowly. As his palms connected, Zadkiel's hands began to glow underneath the skin.

Aaron watch as the veins below his hands began to glow a bright red, spreading through his forearm and up toward his shoulder. Once it reached his shoulder, Aaron saw the red glow come out of the hole he'd left when he chopped the wing and create a new one. It started out as a thin red line that created an outline of a new wing, quickly forming into a full fledged wing that began flapping simultaneously with the other until Zadkiel hung in the air effortlessly.

"OH. YOU DIDN'T THINK YOU WERE THE ONLY ONE THAT COULD HEAL THEMSELVES DID YOU?" Zadkiel mocked. *"I CAN DO IT TOO, WITHOUT THE HELP OF A PATHETIC SWORD."*

Before he knew it, Zadkiel's leg was fully regenerated too.

Zadkiel was completely healed; all the damage Aaron had accomplished vanished.

"NOW IT'S MY TURN."

.

It happened in a blur.

Once second Zadkiel was hovering in the air in front of him, the next thing Aaron remembered was waking up on the ground.

Unable to move his legs.

"YOU LEFT US THERE FOR A SECOND, THOUGHT I DID TOO MUCH TOO QUICK AND HAVE BEEN BEATING MYSELF UP FOR NOT TAKING MY TIME. BUT GOOD NEWS, YOU'RE NOT DEAD! YET."

Everything was hazy; Aaron's vision was blurred as he tried to drag himself across the hardwood floor, his legs unresponsive.

"YOU ARE PROBABLY WONDERING IF YOU'RE PARALYZED RIGHT NOW SO LET ME HELP YOU OUT. YES, YOU ARE PARALYZED. I SNAPPED YOUR SPINE ON ACCIDENT WHEN I BROUGHT YOU HERE, YOUR BODY HIT THE DOOR FRAME REAL HARD."

Aaron tried to speak, but he was able to form words.

"NOW YOU'RE PROBABLY TRYING TO SAY SOMETHING, PROBABLY SOMETHING SMARTASSED ABOUT KILLING ME, BUT YOU MAY FIND THAT DIFFICULT SINCE I MAY OR MAY NOT HAVE TAKEN YOU TONGUE WHEN YOU WERE OUT. SPOILER, I TOTALLY TOOK YOUR TONGUE."

He hadn't realized it, but Aaron didn't have a tongue. His mouth was empty, just a sharp pain anytime he tried to flex the muscle that moved his tongue trying to speak.

Not good.

"I TOOK YOUR TONGUE SO YOU COULDN'T KEEP WAILING LIKE A BABY AND BEGG FOR YOUR LIFE. YOU UNDERSTAND RIGHT?"

"Uhhhhh," Aaron managed to get out through the pain as he tried to speak.

"COOL, YOU TOTALLY UNDERSTAND. NOW, WITHOUT FURTHER ADUE, I AM GOING TO STARTING KILLING YOUR FRIENDS ONE BY ONE. YOU PROBABLY HAVE A PRETTY NASY CONCUSSION FROM ME DRIBBLING YOUR HEAD AGAINST THE FLOOR LIKE A BASKETBALL WHILE I WORKED SOME PERSONAL SHIT OUT, SO YOU'LL JUST HAVE TO LISTEN AS THEY SCREAM OUT TO GUESS WHO I'M KILLING. IT'LL BE LIKE A GAME!"

"UUUUUHHHHH!" Aaron tried again, the pain almost unbearable.

"DO I HAVE A REQUEST FROM THE AUDIENCE? YEP, I THINK THAT SOUNDS LIKE YOU SAID KILL MY BEST FRIEND FIRST PLEASE. WELL, IF YOU INSIST."

"UUUUUHHHH!"

"OK. SO I SPOILED THE SURPRISE OF WHO IS GONNA DIE FIRST, THAT'S ON ME. NEW GAME. YOU GUESS HOW I AM KILLING THEM!"

Aaron continued to fight, pulling himself toward the sound of Zadkiel's voice and emitting a throaty noise in place of words, but it was of no use. The pain had made it impossible to think, to move, to fight. It was all he had to keep from passing out, again apparently.

You failed.

They would all die because he'd been too focused on causing as much pain as possible for what Zadkiel had done, to Ashley in particular. He'd lost sight of the goal and fallen into Zadkiel's trap just like he'd wanted him to. Now Aaron would have to listen to those closest to him be torn apart as one final act of torture before he met his own demise.

"OK, HERE WE GO!"

"Enough!" a voice boomed out overhead, causing Zadkiel to stop speaking mid sentence.

If they said anything else, Aaron didn't hear it before he passed out.

XXXVIII

When Aaron came too, he was sitting in a small chair in the middle of an impossibly small office. The walls felt like they were closing in on him as his vision slowly returned to him, each time he blinked they slowly moved to crush him.

Once his eyesight was fully restored, Aaron realized the walls were not closing in on him, he was just in an office that was the equivalent of a janitor's closet. Between the chair he awoke sitting in and the desk that was large enough to reach either side of the office walls, Aaron was packed in as tight as possible. There was a door on either side of him; one directly in front of him while the other was directly behind him when he turned around to survey his surroundings.

So…am I dead?

Is…everyone dead?

The question popped into his head as he sat in the tiny office, he knees pressed hard against the low rising desk as he shifted back and forth in his chair to find a comfortable position. No matter how much he shifted his body around, he couldn't find a spot that was even remotely pleasant, as if the chair was meant to make the person uncomfortable. Aaron took this as a sign that whether he was alive or dead, he was still in Hell if the chair told him anything. He tried to remember how he'd arrived here, in this tiny office, but was drawing a complete blank after suffering what was likely multiple concussions in a very short period of time.

The last thing he remembered was the blistering pain he'd felt after awaking in gymnasium as Zadkiel started to kill everyone he cared about one by one.

Was I in the gymnasium?

It FELT like I was on hardwood floors, but to be fair I couldn't tell the difference from hardwood and tile at the time anyway.

"Where the hell am I now?" Aaron asked himself out loud.

I can talk!

Aaron wiggled his tongue back and forth in his mouth to ensure he wasn't dreaming, he even bit down on it enough to send a shock of pain through his head as a result.

Worth it.

Aaron was about to stand and survey the rest of his body when the door in front of him opened and a thin lady walked in. She didn't bother looking up at him as she sauntered in, her head buried in a file as she poured over its contents. The lady stepped to the opposite side of the desk and pulled a small chair out to sit on before scooting the chair forward to continue pouring over the contents in her file. Her mannerisms spoke of a woman that was tired of doing whatever it was she was doing, a curved spine and pale skin told Aaron she likely sat at an office desk most of her life and developed poor posture along with distancing herself from any natural light whatsoever.

She wore a grey dress, an oversized belt buckle around her waist was her only accessory as her ears, neck and wrists were all bare. Even her hair lacked color, stark white as it fell to her shoulders.

Not once did the lady even acknowledge Aaron was in the room, no small task considering Aaron took up over half of the real estate as he sat in his chair, his knees still pushing hard against her desk.

The lady looked familiar, but Aaron was terrible with names and couldn't remember how he knew her. He wanted to say she had worked at the school, since everyone else they'd run into was connected to the school in some way it made the most sense, but the more he thought about it the more he became convinced she was never a member of the school staff.

Who are you?

"Am I…dead?" Aaron broke the awkward silence that only he seemed to even notice as she continued to pour of the paperwork on her desk. He may as well have been a poster on her wall, nothing more than backdrop while she worked.

Aaron needed to know if he'd died, it was the only thing he could really think about since coming too, but he also had to clear the dead air and make sure he wasn't a ghost. He'd seen the Sixth Sense; he knew what what was up. The last thing he wanted was to think he was anything more than a spirit that no one could even see. The more he thought about it, the more worried he became that Zadkiel had turned him into a ghost somehow, doomed to always watch and never interact.

Aaron would be forced to take over the mantle for Hank as the one who could see all and do nothing.

"AM I DEAD?" Aaron asked again, this time loud enough that she had to hear him. If not, his knees banging against the desk and moving it slightly would have to be enough

At least you're not a goddamn ghost. Ghosts can move desks.

Wait? Can they?

Shit. Did I move that with my mind and just THINK I moved it with my knees?

Crap, I'm a ghost aren't I?

"I suppose that all depends on your definition of what living is."

As soon as she spoke Aaron knew exactly who she was, he couldn't believe he'd already forgotten her after just seeing her earlier this morning.

"Mrs. Holtzman?"

The thin lady behind the desk looked up at him; if she was surprised he knew who she was she did an excellent job of hiding it. Her face read like someone that heard their name called out in a crowd, she was neither intrigued or bothered by it, just looked back at him with dull eyes that said she didn't care one iota whether or not he knew who she was. Aaron would have never guessed it was her, she was considerably thinner than the woman he'd met at the liquor store.

The woman that was Ronnie's biological mother.

This woman sitting across from his looked like Nicole Holtzman, but only after she'd had the life force extracted out of her, leaving nothing more than skin and bone, along with stark white hair, afterward. Aaron couldn't figure out why he was seeing such a dire version of Nicole Holtzman, all the other figures in his life had looked exactly the way he'd remembered last time he saw them. This was a drastic reversal, the long face and tired aura of this lady felt like a woman on her last leg.

"So, I'm not dead?" Aaron had to clarify, Nicole's answer still hanging in the air.

She didn't exactly say no did she?

"No, your are not dead-"

OHTHANKGOD...or whomever.

"-But my initial question still remains unanswered. What exactly do you define as living Mr....Schutz?"

It had been nearly a decade since Aaron had heard someone use his last name. Living on the road and working odd jobs across the country, most people didn't get to know you enough to get past first names. Aaron couldn't remember a boss or coworker that called him anything other than Aaron. There were a few that thought his name was "Hey Asshole," but for the most part he was just Aaron to everyone he met. All the jobs he worked paid cash and he paid cash for any hotel he could afford so names and information were never exchanged.

The only person that ever came close was Glen when he started at the Rusty Knuckle. Aaron had to provide his ID to prove that he was of legal age to bartend, though by then the road had done enough to age him that no one was going to mistake him for anything under thirty, and that was being generous. He remembered Glen glancing over the ID, nodding, and flipping it back to him as he told him the ID had expired three years ago. Aaron had no idea ID's expired, and Glen obviously didn't care when he hired him on the spot.

"Wait, you're last name is Schutz? Your legal name is Aaron Schutz?" the gaunt version of Nicole Holtzman asked, her interested suddenly peaked.

"Yeah, that's me. How do you know my name? What's in that file your reading?"

"You're last name is Schutz?" she asked again, ignoring his questions completely. "You're last name is, literally, the German word for Protector? Damn. I mean, I heard the rumors and they said you were a priority and all, but...Damn. That's a little heavy handed, even for me."

"Who said I was a priority?"

"What?" the thin lady asked, a look of concern on her face. She'd said too much and she hadn't even realized it.

"You just said 'they' told you I was a priority. WHO said I was a priority?"

"I did? Are you sure? Never mind what I said, just water cooler gossip. Here's the deal Mr. Schutz."

"Aaron."

"Ok. Aaron," she nodded, grateful he wasn't pressing further.

"Bottom line, Aaron, is you're not supposed to be…here," she started, tapping her fingers on the desk to visualize where *here* was. "While I was in town on business to collect, you and your friends apparently got caught in a Burn Zone that allowed you all to walk right through the door."

"Wait, WHAT?" Aaron stopped her. "Who are you? How do I know you're not just another demon that Zadkiel sent to kill me? All I know is I woke up in this closet for an office with one HELL of a headache and the best you have to offer is that you're a businesswoman that somehow opened the gates of Hell for us? Are you kidding me lady? What the hell does that even mean? You were in town collecting what?"

"Ronnie," she answered somberly.

"Of fuck this. You come into this office looking just like Ronnie's mom and tell me that somehow this was all just a big misunderstanding. Nice try, I'm not buying it for one second," Aaron said, looking up towards the ceiling for a speaker that Zadkiel would be listening in on them with. "This is just another sick form of torture isn't it? You just dress up as Ronnie's mom and try to break me with some story like I'm gonna believe a word you tell me? I may not be as smart as Jack, but a few things did stick, and the ONLY one that is doing any collecting is-"

"Death," she said, finishing his sentence for him.

"I am Death Aaron, and I'm here to tell you it's not your time."

XXXIX

Aaron didn't believe her.

This…whatever she was, was sitting in front of him like she was grading his test and acting like it was perfectly normal that she'd just told him she was Death.

He was just supposed to accept that Death was sitting across from him.

Accept that Death was here to…help him?

"Prove it." Aaron demanded.

"Prove what?"

"You say you are Death. Prove it. Prove to me that you are not just another wolf dressed in sheep's clothing."

"I don't have to prove anything to you Aaron. I am not your puppet and I certainly don't care if you believe me or not."

"If you are Death, you will prove it. Every minute you stall only solidifies my accusation that you are not who you say you are."

"And what exactly are you asking me to do? Am I supposed to produce a black cloak and scythe to make you feel better? As I said Mr. Schutz, I am not here to appease you. I am here to fix an error that should never have happened in the first place. What you think or how you feel about it is irrelevant and beyond my concern."

"Liar," Aaron retorted.

"Then perhaps you can answer one of my questions Mr. Schutz. If I am not who I say I am, who else would be able to bring you here? Who would be able to pull you back from the brink of your own certain demise, which is exactly where you were when I found you by the way."

"I passed out. You could just as easily be one of Zadkiel's minions that brought me here to prolong my torture," Aaron scoffed.

"Then why give you back your tongue? Fix your ribs? If I was this…monster you claim me to be, wouldn't I just leave you in such abysmal circumstance to only further your pain?"

"Well.." Aaron tried to rebuke, but did see her point.

"And who else but Death would know the exact situation that brought you here in the first place. Did this…Zadkiel ever say he knew what brought you within his grasp?"

"I mean…" Aaron began to lose steam.

"Tell me Mr. Schutz, if I am not Death, why do I have this?"

The lady pulled an old fashioned clock out from one of the drawers on her side of the desk and set in on the desk between them. She made sure to not expose the face to Aaron, only showing him the clock as a whole while its rhythmic ticking filled the quite room instantly.

"What is that?"

"This, Mr. Schutz, is you. It is the clock that tells me when I need to come get you. The alarm goes off, you're dead."

Aaron froze.

He still wasn't sure she was telling him the truth, but if she was lying she was putting on one hell of an act to sell it. By this time, all the other demons had given up on their act and when full demon mode on him with red eyes. Aaron looked down at the clock between them, firmly under her hand to avoid Aaron getting any ideas of grabbing it to see what the alarm was set to on it. He couldn't be sure, but Aaron swore his heartbeat was in perfect sync with the ticking of the second hand on the clock.

"Now tell me Mr. Schultz. Do you hear an alarm right now?"

"Um, no."

"And what do you think no alarm sound means Mr. Schutz?"

"I'm...not dead." Aaron answered.

"That is correct. You are not dead. Do you know how I know this?"

"Because of the clo-"

"BECAUSE I AM DEATH!" she shouted, the walls quickly losing their glow as a result of her yelling.

■

"Why her?"

"Excuse me?" she said, again raising her head from the folder on her desk.

"Why Nicole Holtzman?"

"I'm not sure I follow Mr. Schutz, what are you trying to ask me?"

"You are sitting across from me telling me you are Death, but you really are Nicole Holtzman. Why?"

The lady nodded slowly in understanding, Aaron wondered if she got this question a lot or just how many time she actually got questions period.

How many people talk to Death? Is this where you go when you die?

"It was the most practical option to collect Ronnie," she explained, removing her glasses as she spoke. "Aside from what you may think from movies and books, I don't walk around in an oversized black cloak making my collections. That is propaganda on a level similar to what you have done to pirates over the years. It's easier to imagine things as they should be rather than accept them for how they really are Mr. Schultz."

"It's Aaron, call my Aaron."

"As you wish Aaron," she conceded. "My task is to collect souls after they pass, unseen. The easiest way to do that is to become a close family member or friend of the deceased. A mother spending one last moment with her child, a husband saying goodbye to his wife, my presence is never felt or questioned. Ronnie didn't have many, if any, friends, but it wouldn't have raised an eyebrow if his mother had showed up to say goodbye. That, Aaron, is why I appear to you as Nicole Holtzman."

Aaron couldn't formulate a response; he was too busy thinking about another funeral instead.

"Did...did you... did you collect my dad?"

"That is not your concern Aaron," she told him. "I do not divulge on my past."

"The hell it isn't lady," Aaron shouted, slamming his fist onto the desk hard enough to leave a mark. "I just went through Hell because of your mistake. You OWE me."

She seemed to take this into consideration as she gently rocked her glasses between her forefinger and thumb, staring back at him. Aaron could tell she was annoyed and didn't care; she likely didn't get many questions about her job and didn't look like the kind of individual that enjoyed talking about much of anything. Even appearing to him as Nicole Holtzman, Aaron could tell the real persona underneath was more than happy to ignore this entire conversation and get back to her work instead.

Finally, she nodded slowly.

"I was."

Aaron had so many questions, he had to bite his tongue to keep from flooding her all at once, something that would undoubtedly shut her down completely and leave him with nothing in return.

He had to take a deep breath.

"Was he in pain?" Aaron asked solemnly.

"I answered your question Aaron, that is as far as I will allow this to proceed."

"Will you at least tell me where you sent him?"

"I will not and that is final Aaron. If you insist on pursuing this further, you will need to find someone well over my status to divulge that information."

"You don't know do you?"

She sighed, Aaron unsure if it was a sigh of exhaustion or if she was hiding something, setting her glasses on the desk next to the open folder. She massaged the bridge of her nose with her thumb and index finger.

"What I do know is that whatever I tell you won't make you feel any better, so I see no point in proceeding with said conversation. Your father is in a place where they do not allow visitors of the living variety. You are on a different path."

"A different path?"

"As I said earlier Aaron, you are very much alive. With that being said, it is up to you to decide what that actually means to you."

Aaron was growing more impatient by the second; this lady kept telling him he was alive only in the sense that he had a pulse. He would admit his life hadn't turned out like he'd thought it would, but who was she, to critique him on how he lived his life? She was Death, the end of all things. What would she know about living?

"You seem upset at my assessment?"

"Oh goddammit, you can hear my thoughts too?"

"Why would I want to listen to your thoughts?" she asked sardonically. "I have your entire life in this folder. I know everything there is to know about Aaron Schutz. Your thoughts are simply unwanted noise to me, they are your own personal soundtrack to your life that I can see on paper just fine."

"There is more to a person than what shows up on a couple pieces of paper," Aaron said defensively.

"That is just the problem Aaron, You are nearing thirty years old and THIS is all there is to know about you," she said, closing and shaking an almost empty folder for emphasis. "The most complete piece of paper in here is your employment history. Aaron, I do not judge, it is not my task and I don't much care to weigh in on the matter most of the time, but you are the definition of a lost soul. This folder tells me you have no job, no place to live, no friends, and nothing to your name but an old car that was passed down to you. The list goes on if you would like me to continue, but I expect you understand my perspective. You asked me if you were alive Aaron, but to look at your file I'd argue that you died a long time ago."

She was right. There wasn't much on record in his life that was worth keeping track of. He was a drifter with a nice car he could never afford had it not been left to him by his father. Aaron didn't want to dwell on the decisions and mistakes that lead him down the path he was on, he didn't think it was necessary since he'd found what he was looking for all this time. He'd found Ashley, the girl that had captured his heart ten years ago and immediately recaptured it when he saw her in Jaspers the other night. Jack and he had been reunited and Aaron had realized that he'd spent most of his adult life running from the most important part of his life, the part that was right where he'd left it ten years ago when he split. It was obvious that she didn't have the most updated story on her desk, she was only reading through the prologue of his life without knowing what he did and making her assumptions based on the information provided. Aaron couldn't blame her; she wasn't doing so maliciously, she just didn't have all the information to know how much he'd changed.

"So tell me Aaron, what are you living for? Any other collection I made would be processed without further ado, but your folder hits my desk and I have everyone screaming at me to make sure you get back to where you should be. What exactly is it you are going back to? It's not my decision, which was made for the both of us before I ever set foot into this office, but I do find my self suddenly curious why such a loner has drawn the attention of everyone around here. It is my professional opinion that you would be better suited moving on from what I see in this file."

"Moving on?"

"Letting go Aaron."

"Listen lady, I get that my file isn't all that great. Trust me, I lived what you read on those pages so I know first hand that so far it's been tough sledding as part of my own doing. The thing is, you don't have the full story. Those pages don't tell you what happened to me while I was down there. What I was able to find in the midst of the worst possible nightmares and circumstances."

"You are referring to your group," she said, flipping over pages in the folder to find the one she was looking for. "Ashley, Jack, and Debbie correct?"

"And Hank."

"I don't show Hank's name on this list? These records are supposed to be impeccable, why is he not on this list?" she demanded, tapping the folder as she spoke.

"Hank fell from Arcadia, he helped me down there. He gave his life for mine, he was a good friend till the end."

Aaron decided it was best to leave out the part about Hank being related to their tormentor. The lady was reacting badly just to hearing his name; he didn't want to set her off further with the whole story, which she somehow didn't know anything about.

"But why is he not on this list?" she asked again, agitated.

Good question, why aren't you in that folder Hank?

"I have no idea lady, you tell me. I didn't make the list and don't care what it does or doesn't say. Hank was real and he is the reason I am sitting here with you right now, that's all YOU need to know."

She seemed flustered; a woman that was greatly concerned had replaced her usual, disinterested aura. Aaron didn't know why a missing name on the list was such a big deal, or why she said he had nothing to live for if she knew about the Jack, Ashley, and Debbie. Maybe she only knew them from the reunion they were preparing, maybe this lady had no idea what was really going on and Hank's name spooked her.

"I need to go back because that lost soul you read about in your notes doesn't exist anymore. I changed down there. It took awhile for me to figure it out myself, but I did and now there is nothing that is going to keep me from getting back to her."

"As you wish Aaron," she nodded, paying less attention to him as she rifled through her notes again. "I will just need you to sign a few forms and you'll be on your way."

Appearing on the desk in front of him was a large stack of legal documents, with bright yellow signature tabs marked throughout. A pen appeared on the top of the stack for him to sign.

"What is this?"

"Does it matter? Once you sign your free to go, that's what you want isn't it?"

It was.

Aaron blew through the stack, only glancing at pages sporadically as he signed them. He knew deep down he should read them, but he didn't care what they said or what it meant for him if he got to go back once he was finished. Ashley's face was burned into his mind; he would do anything to get back to her.

"Done," he stated proudly, dropping the pen on the top of the now messy stack. "What about everyone else?"

"Your friends were automatically processed before you came through. They are already back, but they won't remember a thing that happened."

"So why did I just have to sign these forms?" Aaron asked, looking down to realize the stack of papers was no longer on the desk in front of him.

"Precaution," she answered.

"Precaution? Precaution for what?"

"It's nothing, just…precaution."

"I don't like the way you keep saying precaution, sounds like your hiding something."

"As soon as you leave this office, you won't remember a thing. Not our conversation, your time below, any of it."

"Can I?"

"Can you what Aaron?"

"Can I remember it? Keep my memoires?"

"Why in the world would you want to remember? You were as good as dead when I found you, you can't forget something like that. Ever."

Aaron knew this was an unfortunate side effect to keeping his memories, but he also knew that he'd figured out what he wanted in life and how Ashley really felt while he was fighting to keep himself and everyone else alive. To wipe that all away, to start back at the beginning without ever knowing how she felt meant it was possible his old self would fail to find out how she really felt and drive away after the reunion like he'd originally planned.

He couldn't risk losing here, he wouldn't.

"I need to keep them, please."

"I for one think this is a terrible idea," she started. "But your file says it's your call so someone thinks you are smarter than you really are."

"Thank you." Aaron said while wondering who that someone was.

"Don't thank me. This was your decision; whatever happens because of it, whatever you do or do not do will be squarely on your shoulders from this point on. I will have no part of this…whatever this is," she said, closing the file and getting up to leave the office.

Aaron stood up as well, not sure if he was supposed to go over the desk to follow her or use the door directly behind him.

"You go that way," she pointed to the door behind him.

"Thanks. Anything else I need to know?"

She paused at her door, giving it thought before responding. Her body language spoke to a woman that knew she should just leave and not even acknowledge him, her task had been completed, but she paused long enough that Aaron was curious what she was fighting with internally to telling him.

"It's probably nothing," she hesitated. "It's probably nothing, but you should be aware that he has your scent now."

"What? Who has my…scent?"

"Zadkiel. He has your scent now. You are safe since he cannot break the barrier between your world and his," she sighed. "But mistakes have been known to happen."

XL

He was back.

Aaron didn't wake up as much as he came back from an intense daydream; he was standing in the middle of the high school gymnasium looking over at Ashley in her stunning red dress.

"You look amazing," Aaron told her, not losing the chance to tell her like he had the first time around when he'd just stood there blushing like a teenager.

"You don't look to shabby yourself," Debbie cut in, eyeing him up and down alluringly. "Remind me to tip Mitchell next time I see him, cause DAMN."

"Bad news dude, looks like I'm going to have to murder you if I want Debbie to even notice me tonight. You understand right?"

Aaron turned around to see Jack standing behind him and smiled.

You're all here.

"Don't worry pal, between you and me, she likes you way more than she'd letting on. Just be you and she'll melt into your arms by the end of the night."

"Oh yeah?"

"Trust me, you two were made for each other. Plus," Aaron looked over at Ashley, "I'm taken."

"Holy shit dude. You've been back in town for all of one day and you've managed to knock out the town drunk AND get the girl. You're like Conan dude, wouldn't surprise me at all if you killed a bear with your bare hands by the end of the week."

"You think I'm sticking around that long?"

"Well," Jack said, looking down at his feet as he spoke. "I just figured you'd maybe want to stick around awhile, unless you need to get back. I totally get it dude, you gotta do what you gotta do right?"

"Relax pal," Aaron wrapped his arm around Jack's shoulder. "I think I may have found a few reasons to stick around for awhile."

"YES!" Jack said, louder than he should have as he drew everyone's attention.

"Jack said I could drive the Shelby!" Jack lied to cover his outburst.

"We'll see," Aaron smiled.

"Wait, seriously? You wouldn't even let me sit in the front seat last night."

"I said we'd see didn't I?"

"You do realize I will hold you to that till you crack and give me the keys right?" Jack grinned.

"I'm counting on it."

"Everyone should be showing up any minute. I'll go see if they are here yet," Ashley cut in.

"I'll walk you to the door," Aaron offered.

His heartbeat picked up considerably when they closed in on the gymnasium doors. Aaron leaned into the door while pressing down on the lever, giving it a little extra from previous experience, and the door opened easily. He breathed a sigh of relief as Ashley walked through behind him as he held the door open for her.

She was beautiful; he wasn't just saying that because it was the nice thing to say. Ashley took his breath away.

Walking next to her down the hallway, Aaron couldn't think of what to say. The Ashley he knew was one that had opened up to him, not the one a foot away from him. Anything he could think to say sounded either dumb or extremely creepy without context.

Hey, you ever hear the one about the girl that fell in love with a guy through his mom's stories?

What about the one where we were about to kiss but decided to hold off till we escaped Hell?

Aaron knew it would take time, that he would have to rebuild their relationship to a point where they were back to where they had been down there. He wasn't going anywhere, he would stay as long as it took, Ashley was the One.

They walked in awkward silence, two people that knew deep down they were connected but neither had any idea what to say now that they were finally alone. Jack may have been in the way before, but now Aaron wished he was there to break the ice and be his wingman. Even thought he knew how she felt, he still didn't know what to say to her.

When they got to the front doors, Aaron's hands began to sweat. Thankfully, Ashley didn't notice; she was too busy looking out through the glass panels to see if anyone had arrived. Aaron slowed down, instinctively preparing for the worst as Ashley went to open the doors.

You were the one that wanted to keep you memoires remember, even when she said it was a bad idea you insisted.

Ashley pushed the lever on the door and the door opened without a hitch. The cool breeze from outside as the sun began to set swooped in and hit Aaron. He had never been so happy to see a door come open, to feel a cool breeze on his forehead. The door coming open let Aaron know this wasn't a trick, that he'd really made it back somehow.

"Beautiful night," he said.

"I guess," Ashley shrugged as she walked towards the parking lot.

■

Aaron was busy meeting people with Ashley as they made there way towards the doors. They were tasked with introducing them to the reunion and, in most cases, breaking the news about Ronnie and letting everyone know about the memorial that would be held later. Many of their former classmates had come from out of town, they had no idea what had become of Ronnie and were shocked to here he'd passed. Each one wanted to know what happened, gossip was still going strong even ten years after high school, and that bled into their own backstory and what they were up to.

The crowd began to thin out and Ashley looked cold, so Aaron suggested they head inside and start the reunion. She happily agreed and Aaron jogged toward the parking lot to grab the suits that were hanging in the back of the Shelby. He knew Debbie would be upset that he and Jack weren't ready, but he knew she'd get over it. Debbie's bark was a lot worse than her bite.

He was just about halfway to the parking lot when he saw it.

Someone was trying to break into the Shelby.

You have got to be kidding me? SERIOUSLY?

"HEY!" Aaron yelled to get the guy's attention, hoping to scare him off once he knew he'd been caught.

All that did was make the guy work faster at getting the door open, while startling Ashley enough for her to start walking towards him to see what was going on.

"What is it?" Ashley called out to him.

"Some asshole is trying to steal my car," Aaron told her. "Get inside, call the police."

Aaron knew the police wouldn't make it in time; he didn't need them if he was being completely honest. He just told her to call the police to make sure she was out of harms way and didn't see him beat the ever-living shit out of this guy.

Best she doesn't see me go rage mode before we ever have the chance to talk.

As Aaron got closer, he noticed something was off about this situation. The man wasn't even really trying to get the door open. He didn't have any tools or a lock picking set to get the door open, he was just standing next to the door pulling half-heartedly at the door. Aaron got closer before he realized it was just a ploy to draw him in.

The man turned around to face him and smiled.

His eyes were blood red.

"Mutual friend of ours wanted me to let you know he misses you," he sneered. "Will be seeing you REAL soon."

The man proceed to rip the door clean of its hinges, as if the solid metal door was nothing more than a plastic prop to him, and threw it down before getting in the driver's seat and putting both hands on the steering wheel. Aaron watched has his hands began to lite up, a dull glow turning into a red hot light as the steering wheel began to melt in his hands.

"Consider this a reminder," the man smiled as the red-hot glow engulfed his entire body.

The Shelby exploded, blowing Aaron back off his feet to land hard on the pavement behind him. He looked on in horror as the once prized possession now sat in a flaming pile of metal and rubber in front of him.

Ashley came running up behind him, ignoring his request to call the police, and helped him back on his feet.

They'd found him, just like the lady had warned him. Aaron knew now why she'd hesitated in telling him in the first place. It wasn't a warning she'd offered; it was advice on how to stay alive. She knew Zadkiel could make contact, after what had happened to them all bets were off on what could and could not happen anymore.

Not even an hour had passed since he'd been brought back and they'd already found him and made it clear they were not interested in hiding. They wanted him to know they were coming, to be afraid.

He had to figure out what to do next, or he wasn't going to last long.

"OH MY GOD AARON!" Ashley shouted. "You're car!"

"It's just a car," Aaron said right before kissing her.

Epilogue

He woke up in a panic.

It was another nightmare, this one worse than the last. For awhile now he'd been having the same dream, but it seemed like each time he fell asleep it would get worse and worse somehow. The ending never the same, the fear and anxiety always present, the reminder of the torture coming back to him in spades.

This nightmare had easily been the worst one yet; he'd stayed in it longer than ever before, failing to come out of it like he usually did. Most nightmares ended with a shock or something similar to jolt him back to reality, but this time he was just a visitor that wasn't allowed to leave his own torment. The details were always blurry, but the outline was always the same, enough to recall the main point.

He was stuck in Abaddon and being picked apart, piece-by-piece, as his friends looked on in disinterest at his agony. They were supposed to be the ones he could trust, the ones he knew had his back no matter what, but now they couldn't care less. They were talking amongst themselves and only bothered to share a passing glance as he hollered at the top of his lungs in pain.

He pushed himself off the bed, the mattress soaked in an almost perfect outline of his body as he'd sweat profusely during the ordeal. The pillows were sitting on the opposite side of the room, he was unsure if they were kicked or thrown, but it didn't matter. To the side of the bed, in a messy pile, laid his sheets.

The windows were cracked open; a cool breeze drifting in made the sweat on his body instantly chill enough to make him put a shirt on. He walked to the window and pulled it shut, the trees rustling just outside as the soft breeze danced through them.

He had to make these nightmares stop.

How?

He had these memories for a reason, he was supposed to be able to deal with this or he would have been wiped clear.

He was supposed to remember.

As bad as they were, he knew that the nightmares were in his head because he was being hunted. There was no amount of therapy or counseling that would help him, no one he could talk to about being tortured in Abaddon night after night without earing himself a first class ticket to the mental institute closest to him.

That wasn't an option. He had to fight through it, he had to get control on these nightmares or he wouldn't be able to help his friends. They didn't know they were being hunted just like he was, he'd been unable to tell them anything and didn't even know how he'd start the conversation.

He walked gingerly to the bathroom in the pitch-black room; the darkness had become normal to him after what he'd been through. It was easy enough to flip a switch and have the room lit up, but for whatever reason he was fine with the darkness. In a way, he felt more alert, the light only provided a fake sense of safety he had trouble trusting even though he knew he wasn't in Abaddon any more.

He was safe.

So why didn't he feel safe?

He'd witnessed what Zadkiel was capable of, what he would do if he got the chance. It shouldn't have been possible to make contact already.

It wasn't possible.

Yet here he was, slowing around every corner, avoiding people as much as possible, looking over his shoulder constantly.

Standing in front of the mirror, he turned on the faucet and collected cold water in his cupped hands. He splashed it on his face to a jolt that would have brought back the dead, and let the cool droplets of water fall harmlessly back into the sink as he exhaled heavily.

He had to find a way to stop this, to help his friends.

They were strong, even if they didn't remember. They would need to be for what was coming next.

"My word," Hank sighed.

www.ingramcontent.com/pod-product-compliance
Lightning Source LLC
Chambersburg PA
CBHW030244030726
47493CB00023B/585